Wiliam Owen Roberts was born in 1960. He was educated at the University of Wales, Aberystwyth. After leaving university he worked in the theatre and then as a script editor at H.T.V. Since becoming a full time writer in 1989 he has written 6 original series for television and 2 films – *Provence* (1998) and *Cymru Fach* (2008). His latest tv series, *35 Diwrnod* (co-written with Siwan Jones), was broadcast on S4C in 2014.

His first novel, *Bingo!* was published in 1985, followed by *Y Pla* (1987). *Y Pla* won the Welsh Arts Council Prize for Literature in 1988, and appeared in English in 1991 as *Pestilence*. It has since been translated into 10 languages. A volume of short stories, *Hunangofiant*, was published in 1990. *Paradwys* (2001) was shortlisted for the Wales Book of the Year Award 2002. *Petrograd* (2008) won the Wales Book of the Year Award 2009 (Welsh Language category) as well as the ITV Readers Choice Award 2009. His latest novel, a sequel to *Petrograd*, called *Paris*, was published in 2013 and was shortlisted for the Wales Book of the Year Award 2014 (Welsh Language category). The third novel in the trilogy will be published in 2017.

PETROGRAD

For Elen

The tram-routes remained unchanged but no one knew the route of history.

Ilya Ehrenburg

PETROGRAD

Wiliam Owen Roberts

Translated by

Elisabeth Roberts

Parthian, Cardigan SA43 1ED
www.parthianbooks.com
Originally published as Petrograd, in 2008

ISBN 9781909844568

Cover by www.theundercard.co.uk
Typeset by Elaine Sharples
Printed and bound by Gomer Press, Llandysul, Wales
The author wishes to acknowledge the award of a Writer's Bursary from Literature Wales for the purpose of completing this collection.
Published with the financial support of the Welsh Books Council.
British Library Cataloguing in Publication Data
A cataloguing record for this book is available from the British Library.

SUMMER 1916

1

At the beginning of August, Fyodor Mikhailovich Alexandrov drove his wife Inessa, their two sons and his two nieces, to catch the train for the Crimea. The family chauffeur brought all their trunks, cases and other luggage in a second motor-car to Nicholevski station, where the porters bustled around the platform stacking, sorting and loading it all. Two maids and a cook were also dispatched to look after the family's needs, as well as the wet nurse for Georgik, who was only six months old.

Included also in the party was the young governess from Angoulême, who had been with the family for a little over a year.

'The four of you will share a couchette,' Alyosha's mother told him.

'Four?'

'Mademoiselle Babin, your two cousins, and you.'

Alyosha quietly glowed. He was thirteen, and Mademoiselle Babin only eight years older. In the couchette, there were two pairs of comfortable bunk beds opposite each other. Larissa insisted on an upper bunk, above her governess, while Alyosha bagged the other upper bunk, with Margarita below him.

As the train raced through the vast forests of Russia that night, the three children prepared for bed. Margarita read for a little while, but was quickly asleep, so Larissa and Alyosha amused themselves watching her twitch in her sleep as they tickled her with a feather under her nose.

'I've been looking forward to our holiday for weeks,' whispered Larissa.

'Me too.'

'It's a shame Mama wouldn't agree to come with us. We thought we'd persuaded her, you know. But she said no in the end…'

'Shame.' Alyosha climbed up into his bed and pulled up the blanket to his neck.

'But I don't suppose she would have been in a frame of mind to enjoy a holiday. Not with Papa away in the war. She finds it difficult to enjoy herself at all…'

Larissa soon fell quiet, her breathing becoming even and heavy. Alyosha lay there listening to the noises from without, mainly voices coming and going, with an occasional outburst of laughter, and doors opening or banging shut. Some time later, as he was just dozing off, a shaft of light from the corridor flooded over his face for a brief second, before the darkness returned.

Mademoiselle Babin turned in the narrow space between the bunks, the hem of her dress rustling. He heard an oily click in the keyhole and then the lamp under the lower bunk began giving out a dim glow. In an instant, he could smell the cognac and mint his governess had been sipping earlier and he peeped at her as she began to undress with calm efficiency, and the only glimpse of flesh he managed was the rise and fall of her shoulders. She removed her underclothes from beneath her nightgown, stepped neatly sideways and put them away in her brown leather bag under the bed. She pulled the comb from her hair and shook her head to loosen the pins. Her hair tumbled down over her shoulders, and humming softly to herself she sat down to brush it. Finally she knelt at the side of the bed to say her prayers, her nightgown billowing out.

Alyosha couldn't settle back to sleep. *L'Heure Bleue* filled the compartment and he began to imagine Mademoiselle Babin kissing him, and him kissing her back. He imagined the taste of her skin, as he bit her chin (bit her chin and her smile…) down to her neck (the taste of her neck...) and in his passion (the taste of her sweat...), over her breasts, down to her stomach, lower and lower. Between finger and thumb he squeezed the tip of his erection between two fingernails until he was in agony.

He'd only ever touched Mademoiselle Babin once, and that was when his father had first introduced her to him and his cousins, Margarita and Larissa, a little over a year ago.

The three of them had been standing in the centre of the study when his father ushered her in, erect and confident. He remembered how his new stiff collar had rubbed coarsely against his throat, making his skin burn. With one hand buried deep in his shantung jacket, Fyodor Miklhailovich presented them to her in turn.

'My brother Kozma's younger daughter, Larissa Kozmyevna Alexandrov, who is eleven years old.'

A curtsey.

'And her elder sister, Margarita Kozmyevna Alexandrov, who is fourteen.'

Another curtsey.

'And my son, Alexei Fyodorovitch, who is twelve.'

Alyosha shook her hand formally and her fingers were warm and soft. He was overcome with bashfulness, and couldn't look her in the eye, but there was no shyness on Mademoiselle Babin's part, as she gazed at him fearlessly. His father went on to explain how the three cousins had been close from their infancy.

'More like a brother and two sisters?' suggested Mademoiselle Babin with a smile.

'Exactly... there you have it... just like a brother and two sisters.'

Fyodor Mikhailovich bared his teeth and smiled at her. From birth, he told her, the three had shared the same wet nurse, the same nursery, the same holidays. He recalled fondly a particular summer the two families had spent in the Crimea. The little scamps would only go to sleep if their beloved Daria, a red-faced rustic girl who looked after them at the time, chased them up the stairs, growling on all fours like a bear, reducing them to hysterical laughter as they scampered ahead of her to their beds. Later, when it became time to start their education, they had shared the same private tutors and music teacher.

Through his feather pillow Alyosha listened to the thrum of the train as it clickety-clacked its way through the night. He moved his fingers slowly over his stomach, through the fine hair of his groin, and squeezed the base of his cock, which seemed unusually hot. He listened intently to the sound of breathing, tossing and turning from the opposite bed and then, as quietly as ever he could, trying to bring to mind that feeling as he shook hands over a year earlier, he began to masturbate. But hard as he tried, his penis turned to cotton wool. He continued his pumping, this time trying to imagine the taste of Mademoiselle Babin's breasts, her flesh, her thighs… His breathing came in small gasps, and try though he might, it was hard to stifle his grunts.

Her voice pierced the gloom: 'Alexei?' She sighed softly under her breath before asking wistfully, 'Can't you sleep either?'

'No.'

'Nor me.'

His neck damp with sweat, Alyosha swallowed nervously before venturing, 'It's stuffy in here…'

The young Frenchwoman turned onto her back, her arms lying limply on the bed.

'I'm suffocating… would you mind opening the window just a little…?'

Alyosha slipped down from his bunk as softly as he could.

'You don't think it will wake the girls?'

The cold night air rushed onto his face.

'Can I sleep with you, Mademoiselle?'

'Can you what?'

He climbed back up to his bed.

'I'm sorry, I didn't catch that… Can you what?'

He pretended he was already falling asleep.

2

Two days of travelling brought them from Petrograd to Southern Russia, and by noon of the third day they had reached Simferopol. The sun, high in a bright blue sky, had become hotter hour by hour until it fairly blazed with unremitting heat.

They had thought about breaking their journey here for longer, but after an afternoon spent irritably roaming the torpid streets, with Georgik's constant wailing doing nothing to improve anybody's mood, Inessa decided they would continue on their way in the morning.

'This heat is quite intolerable for little Gosha,' she said, and instructed his wet nurse Dunia yet again to be sure to keep him in the shade.

'I adore the heat,' said Larissa, turning her face to the sun, her eyes shut.

'You be careful you don't sit out in it too long,' Margarita warned her sagely. 'Do you remember after that day at the seaside in Sestrovetsk when you had sunstroke, how you lay shaking and shivering under the sheets, with such a high temperature the doctor had to be called?'

Larissa hated to be reminded of that occasion.

'Do you have to be Little Miss Sensible *all* of the time?'

'I just don't want you to suffer that again, that's all,' answered her sister, rearranging her hat with both hands so that it sat just so on her head.

'You're my sister – not my mother.'

Larissa skipped over to Alyosha and nimbly snatched his

sailor's hat, prompting him, in spite of the heat, to rush after her, swiping wildly as she danced around him, holding it tantalisingly just out of his reach.

The next morning, as soon as their luggage and servants had been loaded into the three hired motor-cars, they drove along the winding narrow roads through the Tartar villages, past the white villas with their tall palm trees, the lilac and the linden trees, past the low houses set amongst magnolia bushes within pale yellow walled gardens, until three hours later they reached their destination, Yalta, eyes and hair itchy with dust from the journey.

Once they'd reached the dacha, everybody's mood lightened. Even Georgik cheered up, sucking energetically at Dunia's breast as she crooned her lullabies to him. Oxana quickly organised the maids so that the luggage was unpacked and the dacha made ready in no time. All the windows were thrown wide open to air the place, and from the lane at the far side of the orchard the familiar sounds of ponies' clip-clopping hooves and the jingle of harnesses from passing carts floated in.

Larissa and Margarita changed into their lightest dresses and when Mademoiselle Babin stepped onto the veranda before dinner that evening, Alyosha noticed the only thing that covered her upper body was one thin blouse. This observation quite put him off his food, and he further embarrassed himself by spilling his glass of *kvas* over the sparkling white damask tablecloth. To cap it all he was horribly aware of the damp patches of sweat at his armpits that grew ever larger as the meal progressed.

Over the following days they quickly established their familiar holiday routine. Inessa spent her days reclining in the shade, reading a little sometimes, and every now again, after supper, she would open up the piano for some music and the cousins would watch her fingers fly over the keys of the old Bechstein which had inhabited that corner of the dacha for as long as they all could remember, always a little out of tune.

Margarita was the only early riser amongst them and had often walked down to the town and back before the breakfast table had been set.

'What on earth is there to see?' asked her younger sister grumpily when Margarita woke her up at crack of dawn one day as she dressed herself.

'All sorts of things.'

'Like what?'

'The day awakening. Look…'

She flung open the shutters, and Larissa groaned.

'Everything smells so fresh. The maids wiping the dew from the cafe tables. The men brushing the leaves from the paths that lead to the beach and the sand still cool and damp…'

'What, that's it? That's all there is?'

'You're too young to understand.'

What Larissa enjoyed was swimming in the sea or hiring a little rowing boat, picnics and ice-creams under the shade of the pines, but most of all – what gave her the most pleasure – was when her Aunt Inessa occasionally consented to take them out to dine under the stars, on the casino veranda, from where Larissa would gaze across into the dining room within at the ladies resplendent in their silks and jewels, and the men so sophisticated and elegant in their evening jackets. Listening to the animated hubbub of these exalted beings made her feel so much older than her years.

'Best not mention these little outings to your mother when you return to Petrograd, dear,' her aunt warned her.

Aunt Inessa had the ability to make Larissa feel that she was somebody special.

Meanwhile Alyosha did exactly as he chose, though his father had lectured him before he left not to neglect his studies. A whole trunk had been packed with books for the children and though Mademoiselle Babin did try to encourage them to read a little every day, it was only Margarita who took any heed. More often than not, Alyosha was to be found in his hammock under the leaves of the cypress tree at the far end of the garden, feeling time dissolving around him.

He usually accompanied his mother and cousins, along with Dunia and the baby and one or other of the maids, on their daily trip to the beach, or, when the weather was baking, on a picnic outing in the shade of Livadia Gardens. They liked Ghurzuv Bay too, especially Georgik, who crowed with pleasure as he watched the great waves crash against the rocks. But Alyosha was bored with his cousins and his mother. He longed for the company of boys his own age. Most of the time he didn't know what to do with himself, he felt so awkward in his own skin. He was in a state of perpetual arousal and masturbated mercilessly until his head seemed about to explode, the blood boiling behind his eyes, his heart hammering like a piston, and his balls left barren and shrivelled.

Everywhere he went, everywhere he looked, flesh was on display: as he played a set of tennis, sat on a café terrace, or loitered aimlessly among the stalls of the daily market. He could even be watching the sailors at their work over in the harbour and some young woman would be bound to walk into view. He could idle away hours at the quayside, gazing at the ladies in their summer dresses and the young girls, brown legs contrasting with their fresh white frocks, their laughter light upon the air as they passed by.

One day he came across Andrei Petrovich Vengerov, Managing Director of Azor-Don Merchant Bank, his father's banker, dressed in a short-sleeved blue shirt, shorts and white sandals. He was out for a stroll with his wife and only daughter, licking their ice-creams as they went. He told Alyosha that they had only just arrived from Petrograd and were staying in the Hotel Billo, above the harbour.

'How is your father?' asked Andrei Petrovich. 'Does he intend taking a well-earned holiday from that factory of his this summer?'

'Oh yes, sir, he intends joining us towards the middle of the month.'

'Glad to hear it. Fyodor Mikhailovich isn't one to put his feet up, is he?'

'No…'

'Do send him my regards won't you, Alexei Fyodorovitch?'

Andrei Petrovich took his leave, arm-in-arm with his wife, who wore a dazzlingly white linen suit. She was a tall, elegant, woman, a little taller than her husband. (Why did this always strike Alyosha as odd?) He remembered something he overheard his mother say not so long ago, that she was having an affair with the poet Bessonov, to the knowledge and amusement of pretty much everybody in their circle apart from her husband Andrei Petrovich. He watched them walk off, with their daughter, a great lump of a girl, following behind them. She half-turned to look at Alyosha, smiling at him from beneath her parasol, but her mother spoke to her sharply.

'Galina, come along and stop dawdling.'

3

The maid Oxana's last task for the night was to go around the dacha extinguishing all the paraffin lamps and bolting all the shutters and doors after everybody had gone to bed. Only then did Alyosha slip out through his bedroom window (the wooden frame still warm under his thighs from the heat of the day), and creep barefoot along the shadow of the building until he reached Mademoiselle Babin's room.

There, underneath her window, he would lurk, the resinous smell of the pine trees strong on the night breeze. He'd peep at her through the window, taking in every detail of her snub nose and her rosebud mouth and her thick blonde hair. In her white nightdress she would sit at her mirror, plucking her eyebrows into two thin bows, gazing deeply into her own eyes, her round dark eyes – just like fish eyes. Or sometimes she would click her lighter open and shut, gazing at the little flame bouncing up and down in front of her with a look of discontentment on her face, a little frown creasing her forehead. (What could she be thinking about, Alyosha wondered.) She never smoked in front of the family, only when she was in the privacy of her room…

Sometimes he'd find her sitting at her table, labouring over a letter, looking contemplative and distant, every now and again sighing deeply; other times she'd be lying on her bed with a book, and more than once he'd watch her fall asleep with the open book on her breast. After nights of desperately hoping to catch her undressing, or better yet naked, Alyosha was beginning to become a little bored. That night was no exception, as he watched her yet again scribble and then scrunch up several attempts at a letter, a wistful look on her face.

As he made his way back to bed, disgruntled, a seashell shattered loudly under his foot, right under the window of Georgik's wet nurse. The shutters were slightly ajar and he saw Dunia, who was sitting in the far corner of the room in a rocking chair, slowly raise her eyes with deep dark circles beneath them.

There was no trace of fear in her voice when she spoke.

'I've seen your shadow slip by every night.

'Not much point hiding now,' she went on calmly. 'Why don't you come in?'

Would she go running to his mother? Then he'd be in trouble. He thought he'd best go in and try to persuade her to hold her tongue, so he clambered in and stood there, looking a little foolish, as Dunia continued to sit, quite unperturbed, rocking the baby gently in her arms. She was twenty-five years old, plump, with smooth, healthy skin. Alyosha knew she was still in mourning after her own baby had died of a fever some weeks previously.

'Come a little closer, then.' She patted the bed. 'Sit here.'

Alyosha gazed at his little brother, feeding greedily at her breast.

'Might as well get to know each other a bit better.'

He started to relax once Dunia told him she had no intention of telling tales to his mother. She began to tell him of her husband, who had enlisted in the army when the war between Germany and Russia had broken out two years previously,

'The last thing I wanted was to see him go, but he said it was the right thing to do, and that he should do his bit like all good Russian men.'

He'd fought in the battle of Tannenburg, and around the Masurian Lakes after that. It was a miracle he was still alive.

'I miss him so badly…'

Alyosha thought of his Aunt Ella, Margarita and Larissa's mother. He could well imagine how at that very moment she too was worrying herself sick about the fate of his Uncle Kozma, who had been fighting on the front since the beginning of the war.

'Sometimes I'm almost beside myself with worrying about him.' Taking hold of his fingers, she asked him earnestly, 'You're not too young to be able to understand that, are you?'

'No.'

'That's why I'm so devout. Twice, sometimes three times a day, I say my prayers and hope they'll keep Vadim safe and bring him back to me.'

She put the baby on her shoulder and, moving as silent as a nun, rose and went to fetch something from a drawer. She came back to Alyosha, and handed him a letter.

'Somebody wrote this for Vadim, and somebody else read it to me in Petrograd… You know Oleg, Oxana's brother?'

'I've seen him, yes.'

'He's a good sort, one of the best I'd say. Oleg taught himself to read and write when he was away at sea, but Vadim and me never got much in the way of education.'

The dacha was utterly silent, and Alyosha could hear Georgik's shallow breathing as he slept. He felt that Dunia had been glad to be able to confide in someone. She hadn't been with them long, so he supposed she didn't know Oxana and the other servants that well yet. He couldn't imagine his mother taking much notice of her, apart from issuing instructions on how she was to care for the baby.

Alyosha asked whether she would like to hear Vadim's letter again.

'Would you?'

She thanked him shyly, then sat there very still, listening intently. When Alyosha had finished reading, she rose and put the baby down in his cot, but before fastening her blouse, she said, 'If you want.'

Alyosha's mouth went dry and his tongue thick.

'For reading the letter so well? Would you like it? For a little while there, I felt as though Vadim was here with me.'

Dunia lifted his hands slowly and placed them on her breasts. They were warm, but what surprised Alyosha most was how hard they were.

4

He was sleeping so deeply he thought he was still dreaming when the noise of a car's horn woke him. Then he heard it again, closer this time, and the noise of the engine spluttering and coughing as it approached the house. He squinted over and saw Oxana and another maid running out of the dacha, having already taken off their aprons, to greet their master. The motor-car came to a stop, as the brake was pulled up stoutly.

Alyosha swung his feet over the hammock, stood up and brushed himself down. He was wearing a light cotton suit, a wide-brimmed straw hat and his new smart white shoes that were always made for him every year, especially for the holidays. He made his way over to the wrought iron gate, and saw through the bars that Ivan Kirilich, the chauffeur, had put his hat on for the occasion. Fyodor Mikhailovich stepped out into the sun in his braces and bowler hat, his dark jacket over one arm and two newspapers, the *Ryetch* and the *Novoye Vremya* under the other.

Alyosha felt a little ashamed of his father. His whole appearance seemed so awkward and inappropriate in such fierce heat. He used to be a handsome man with a thick head of hair and a luxuriant black moustache, but he had begun to put on weight and become jowly, and he puffed and panted a lot more than he used to when he took any exercise. His eyes too were always red-rimmed these days, and were a little painful to look at.

His father nodded at him.

''Lyosha, how are you? Where's your mother?'

She called his name, and Fyodor Mikhailovich turned to see her standing on the steps. He beat his hat lightly against the balustrade to rid it of some of the dust of the journey, then stepped towards her. Still two steps above him, Inessa bent from the waist and offered her cheek to her husband's parched lips.

'How are things?'

'As well as expected.'

Inessa insisted on wearing a wide-brimmed hat at all times to protect her skin from the sun, so she was still snowy-white. As everybody else had caught the sun, this made her look as though she came from a strange tribe. Fyodor blew his lips and smoothed down his moustache with his finger and thumb.

'It's been hotter,' she informed him.

'How are the mosquitoes this year?'

'Not too troublesome.'

'Do you have difficulty sleeping?'

'Not at all.'

'Let's hope I don't either.'

They seemed to have run out of things to say; there was a moment of silence.

'So everything's going well then?'

'So far.'

He bared his teeth and smiled at her. Inessa turned and entered the dacha and Fyodor followed in her footsteps, like some local tradesman come to deliver the weekly order. Alyosha dawdled some distance behind them.

His mother accompanied his father to his bedroom, the clatter of their shoes on the parquet drowning out their voices.

Alyosha could never remember a time when they had slept together. Their bedrooms were separate worlds, their own private domains. So it was back in Petrograd; so it was also on holiday in the Crimea.

He never saw his mother enter his father's bedroom, though

on many occasions he heard his father shuffling over to his mother's room: a shadow moving soundlessly across the strip of light under his door as he passed; a light rap and a whispered 'Inessa?'. Sometimes the shadow would move back and forth for a little while before he heard the door open. Other times there would be silence…

The next day Fyodor Alexandrov went with his family to the beach. Ivan Kirilich the chauffeur drove them all there. Alyosha was happy to go too as he had made a new friend, Dimitri, a lanky, sallow boy he had met a couple of days earlier. He'd been meandering along the beach with Margarita and Larissa; they'd been collecting shells, following their noses, until they reached the woody peninsula at the far side and walked along it to the next beach. They came upon Dimitri engaged in the same task, sorting through a fistful of shiny black shells that had been swept up with the tide and left on the ebb of the Black Sea. Dimitri was rather shy, with not much to say for himself, but Alyosha saw his chance to make a friend.

'Who?' asked Inessa.

'Dimitri,' answered her son.

'Yes, of course he may join us for lunch at the Pavilion.' She shaded her eyes with her hand. 'You'll be very welcome, Dimitri.'

'Thank you,' he answered shyly.

As usual, Inessa sheltered from the sun under a wide parasol, while Mademoiselle Babin had already put on her bathing suit, so that all she had to do on reaching the beach was to take off her dress and she was ready to sunbathe all afternoon.

Fyodor Mikhailovich invited Margarita, Larissa, Alyosha and Dimitri to join him for a bathe, but when he reached the water's edge, for some reason his appearance became sombre, and he abruptly turned on his heel back up the beach. The children plunged headfirst into the waves regardless. Larissa was a strong swimmer and she swam far out, challenging Dimitri to a race over her shoulder. Alyosha swam after them, with Margarita bringing up the rear. Then, breathless, they all lay on their backs in the sea, gazing up at the sky. After a while, Alyosha looked back to the shore, where his father stood watching as two men carried a young man who had lost his legs up the beach towards his wheelchair.

The Pavilion stood on sturdy wooden pillars above the sea. From lunchtime until late in the afternoon the place would be overflowing with people who climbed the wooden steps from the beach to escape the blazing heat over a cooling lemonade. There was always a welcome breeze up there, making the edges of the tablecloths dance a little.

The round tables varied in size, the biggest grouped in the centre of the floor, the smaller ones around the edges.

'We'll sit there,' Inessa informed the waiter imperiously.

Hardly had they sat down (and Fyodor was somewhat dismayed to see the young man who had lost his legs sitting at a nearby table) when a little wave of excitement rippled through the room. Inessa, who had her back to the entrance, was the last to see the famous actress Nina Charodeyeva making her way past the tables, wearing a diaphanous green dress and a flamboyant hat. She was a very slender woman, clearly no stranger to starving herself.

Larissa was thrilled.

'Look who just came in, Aunt Inessa.'

Inessa turned her head to look as a whole table of people rose to their feet to greet Nina Charodeyeva. A bald, middle-aged man bent low to kiss her hand. Alyosha saw that the scene had riveted his mother's attention. The next in line to pay his tributes to the actress – which had her smiling broadly – was the famous actor Alexei Dashkov.

'Nina, my darling,' he said with a mischievous insincerity, as he raised her bony hand to his lips.

'Why is everybody staring at them?' asked Fyodor loudly.

'Sshh!' hissed Inessa irritably, without moving her gaze from the actor.

'You look more beautiful than ever.' Alexei Dashkov had grasped Nina Charodeyeva's two hands and held her at arm's length, the better to admire her body – which was just skin and bone under her dress.

'Oh, you love to talk such nonsense …'

The rest of the table had resumed their seats but the actor and actress considerately remained on their feet, so that everyone could see them.

'Not a bit of it, it's simply the truth…'

'Oh really? You mean every word?'

'Every last syllable…'

Between finger and thumb, she pinched his cheek hard enough to leave a mark on his sun-bronzed skin.

'You're a very bad boy, Alexei Alexeivich, and I should be very cross with you after those rude things you said about me in the restaurant last night…'

'I think we should order, don't you?' asked Fyodor, who was very thirsty.

'Hush, can't you?'

Inessa didn't want to miss a word.

'*Me* saying rude things behind your back? Oh Nina, sweetie, how could you believe such a thing? Who's been trying to stir things up again between us?'

'Do you think I was born yesterday?' asked the actress playfully.

'I'll order a beer,' said Fyodor, and motioned at the waiter.

Inessa frowned as the waiter came over. Their drinks were quickly served but Alyosha saw that his mother left hers untouched, her attention riveted by the actor, try though she might not to make it too obvious. Alexei Dashkov stood with one hand on his hip, a cigarette in the other, which every now and again he would bring to his lips, followed by a sip of black coffee from a tiny cup on the table, no bigger than an egg cup. Inessa was in ecstasy. Here in the flesh before her was the man whose picture she had so carefully cut out of her magazines when she was a girl of fourteen, and pinned on the wall beside her bed. Every night, the last thing she would do before falling asleep was kiss his face.

She had even named her son after him – Alexei. Gazing in wonder at the actor now, she thought he looked so much younger than his age. He was strong-boned and his skin looked fresh and smooth. There was something a little sleepy about his grey eyes – like a lizard in the sun – and a look on his handsome face that reminded her of a particularly famous photograph where he was leaning his elbow on a piano, newly-exhaled curls of blue-grey smoke wreathing his face, and gazing languorously into the eyes of his leading lady.

He seemed possessed of an indolent stillness. But it was a stillness, as everybody knew, which hid a tumultuous, almost animalistic lust that had made him a sexual idol in the eyes of thousands upon thousands of women. His first wife had died in mysterious circumstances, which gave rise to all manner of rumour and supposition, and had kept the telegram wires clicking frantically between Moscow, Petrograd and his native Odessa.

He had given his public fresh reason to talk when he ran away with the wife of the Artistic Director of the Moscow Opera to the Hôtel de Paris in Monte Carlo. She deserted her husband and children without a backward glance, giving rise to a scandal that filled the pages of both Russian and French magazines for months. At the time many were convinced it would be the killer blow to Alexei Dashlov's career, but it proved quite otherwise, and apart from the Church, who had censured him severely from the start, and continued to do so, everybody thought he was a god.

Presently Fyodor Alexandrov said, 'Does every conversation have to come to a stop?'

Inessa turned to face her husband.

'Do you have a pencil?'

'I'm never without a pencil.'

She clicked her fingers, tore a piece of paper from her diary and thrust it at her son.

'Go over and ask him to autograph this...'

'I don't want to...'

'Alyosha, don't be tiresome...'

'He doesn't have to if he doesn't want to,' Fyodor said rather shortly.

'I'll go,' Larissa said, already on her feet, and took the pencil and paper from her aunt.

Inessa watched her go over, her hand clutching her throat. She felt quite weak, and positively faint when Alexei Dashkov looked over, flashing his famous smile at her.

She turned to her husband.

'Did you just see that? Did you? He smiled at me! Me out of everybody!'

Perhaps, had somebody else not claimed his attention, Alexei Dashkov might have crossed over to their table. Larissa came back alone however, and placed the piece of paper into her aunt's two open palms. It was as much as she could do not to raise it to her lips and kiss it.

5

Fyodor spent most of his time in the dacha, reading a book on Russian history by Karamisin or a volume of his favourite poetry by Catullus. More often than not, Mademoiselle Babin stayed behind too, complaining that she had rather overdone the sun and that the heat was too much for her. Inessa carried on with her daily routine as before, making sure to visit the Pavilion every day, until one of the waiters informed her that Alexei Dashkov had returned to Moscow. After that, Inessa began to get up later, often missing breakfast altogether, and would lie about the dacha until the afternoon, when she would take her outing to the beach, returning by the evening to bathe and change, take supper on the veranda, and then stay up late playing cards until they were soft and moist with so much handling.

She would often berate Alyosha for being such bad company, telling him it was just as well she had Margarita and Larissa to talk to. The girls liked nothing more than listening to their aunt's worldly conversation, so different from their own mother. Alyosha wondered darkly to himself why his mother sought out his company on holiday when he was but a shadow to her the rest of the year.

Alyosha's favourite spot was still the hammock in the garden. From here he could hear Ivan Kirilich whistling as he washed and polished the hired motor-car, just as he did back in Moscow. Ivan had the mouth of a toad, the lower lip jutting out, and when he smiled a crooked row of little teeth appeared. It was a twisted, rather cruel smile and sometimes Alyosha fancied he would like to cause him some harm if he could. This was only a feeling, as the chauffeur had never said a cross word to him, but somehow, he always had the impression that the smile on his face hid some poisonous intent.

One morning Ivan marched over in his shirtsleeves to where Alyosha lay swinging idly beneath the sweet-smelling flowers of the linden tree, and sat down against the trunk. He had a brown bottle of beer in his hand, and looked hot, sweaty and bad-tempered. He took a long swig and spent a few minutes without saying anything.

The motor-car was the problem. There was something wrong with the engine, and he'd spent the last couple of hours with his head under the bonnet, trying to fix it. He explained how a wire had worn away until it snapped, which had meant a long and sweaty journey on the bike to Yalta to fetch a new one, and an equally laborious journey back.

'There's nothing worse when you're used to driving…'

He took another long pull of his beer.

'My father always wanted me to become a chauffeur, from when he was working as a labourer on the railway between Petrovsk and Belsan, when it was being built in the last century.'

Ivan Kirilich loved his work.

'Have I told you about it?'

'You have.'

'Have I?'

'More than once.'

'Are you sure? I can't remember telling you…'

Another swig.

'Well, it's worth telling again. Now that was backbreaking work for you. Just imagine, out there in all weathers with pick and shovel, from break of dawn until dark, and it was dangerous too, with all the dynamite they had to use to blast a way through the rocks for the track. That's why my father was so determined that I wouldn't be following in his footsteps.'

Alyosha was practically dozing in the heat.

'One afternoon, who should visit but the Chairman of the Railway Company, along with one or two other bigwigs, to inspect the work and see what progress had been made, and when my father saw how smart and polished their driver looked – some straight-backed young man with black gloves and a smart uniform and a peaked cap, all spanking clean and shiny – he decided there and then, that was the job for his son when he grew up. And just look at me today. Driving a motor-car, not a bike like some beggar.'

'A bike suits me fine…'

'Suits you, maybe…'

The fine blonde hairs on the back of his hand shining in the sun, Ivan Kirilich wiped his lips with his wrist.

''Cause you don't know any better…'

He belched.

'It would do you the world of good to get to know the inside of an engine like that…'

'What for?' Alyosha asked lazily.

'So that you'd get to understand the workings of it, of course… You're bound to want to drive a motor-car yourself one day… What if you break down in the middle of nowhere? Or in the middle of the night far from town?'

'Pfff. Shouldn't think so…'

'It's a handy thing to know, the mechanics of an engine… Come on. Get up. Let me show you…'

'I don't have the patience right now…'

'You just don't know what might be around the…'

Alyosha looked up when the chauffeur trailed off mid-sentence. Walking along the garden path towards them, her sandals crunching on the gravel, was Mademoiselle Babin. He noticed that her hair was damp and her cheeks rosy, and her breasts, unrestricted by a corset, jumped about inside her blouse like two little squirrels. He struggled to a sitting position as she approached and Ivan was already on his feet, holding the bottle discreetly behind his back.

'I'd like to post this…'

She held out a letter.

The chauffeur smiled.

'I can do that for you, miss.'

'I'd prefer you to drive me into town. If it's not too much bother.'

She flirted with her eyes.

'Not at all. As long as the engine fires, that is. It's been playing up…'

Ivan opened his toad's mouth in a smile, revealing the uneven row of small teeth. Mademoiselle Babin held the letter close to her body and Alyosha could only see the reverse of the yellow envelope. He hauled himself to his feet.

'I'll come as well,' he said.

'You stay where you are,' said Ivan, rolling the bottle into the rose bushes behind him.

'We won't be two winks…'

'I want to come…'

'What *for*?'

'If the boy wants to come with us, Ivan Kirilich, then let him. It'll do him more good than lying here doing nothing all day…'

The chauffeur puffed out a cheek and blew out from the side of his mouth. Mademoiselle Babin deftly stepped to one side to avoid a wasp which had been bothering her for a while.

'Come along then you two, I don't want to miss the post.'

The young Frenchwoman led the way to the car. Ivan grabbed Alyosha's arm to prevent him from following.

'Know who her lover is?' he murmured.

Alyosha shook his head.

'You don't?' Ivan provoked him. 'Someone who's a very close relative of yours.'

'Who?'

He tapped the tip of his nose.

'Nothing gets past me. I get to hear it all in the end.'

'Well, are you going to tell me or not?'

'Are you coming?' asked Mademoiselle Babin a little impatiently by the gate.

'Just coming,' answered the chauffeur, before whispering, 'Larissa and Margarita's father.'

A blush slowly warmed Alyosha's cheek; his eyes burned.

'*Uncle Kozma? Never!*'

Ivan winked at him then strode off briskly after the governess.

6

The best place to eat by far in Yalta was the terrace restaurant of the Hotel Billo, overlooking the sea. It was head and shoulders above the rest and during the summer months, at the height of the tourist season, everybody who was anybody wanted a table there. As Andrei Petrovich Vengerov was a guest there, he had a certain advantage, and a generous tip to the head waiter from Tiflis would always ensure his party a table in the best corner. As Fyodor Mikhailovich was a most valued customer of the Azor-Don Merchant Bank, he made sure to invite the whole family to join him and his wife and daughter for dinner. So it was, one evening, that Fyodor, Alyosha, Margarita and Larissa squashed into the motor-car to be driven to the hotel.

'There's no need to wait…'

Fyodor was interrupted by Inessa.

'No, Ivan, better that you do…'

'Surely if we say midnight…'

'If you think I'll be able to tolerate the conversation until then…'

Fyodor gave in and ordered the chauffeur to wait for them.

Important and influential though he was in Petrograd's banking circles, Andrei Petrovich was nevertheless a modest and rather kind individual, always concerned with other people's welfare before his own, especially the family of such an important client as Fyodor Mikhailovich Alexandrov. So he was at pains to make sure everybody was supplied with menus and drinks, and that they were all quite comfortable.

The conversation was a little desultory to begin with. Andrei Petrovich admitted that, even on vacation, he found it hard to break his usual habit of rising with the sun, just as though he had to get to the bank. But at least he had the pleasure of walking along the quayside watching the seagulls squawking over the night's leftovers. He confessed rather bashfully that he was something of a poet, and every morning he'd sit down to write a little poem, or a verse or two. The smell of fresh seaweed seemed to give him inspiration.

Inevitably, the men's talk turned to business, and they were soon deep in a conversation involving interest rates and share prices, excluding their wives completely.

Alyosha had found himself next to Galina – the big lump of a daughter, with his cousins on her other side. She didn't seem to want to talk to any of them. Inessa stared moodily out at the neverending sea, as the waiter hurried over to light her cigarette. She felt a gentle breeze stir through her hair, and noticed three little rows of flickering lights from a ship in the far distance until they were sucked silently into the night.

Irritably, she stubbed out her cigarette before it was even half-smoked, crushing it with unnecessary force. She was so bored she felt like screaming, and as she'd had a glass of champagne before leaving the dacha, and considerably more at the table, she was feeling rather woozy and light-headed. She gazed at the surrounding tables – everybody seemed to be having far more fun than she was. All of a sudden she felt furious with Fyodor as she remembered his boorish behaviour that afternoon in the Pavilion when they'd seen Alexei Alexeivich Dashkov.

At times like this, she wouldn't have given a fig if her husband fell down dead before her. Often an image popped into her head, an image of her standing at the edge of his grave in a widow's veil, a wreath in her hand and tears rolling down her pale cheeks. She was almost overwhelmed by an urge to just get up and leave, and might have done so had all the lights not suddenly been extinguished. Apart from the little candles flickering in the seashells on the tables, which threw up flickering yellow light onto the expectant faces, turning the restaurant into a graveyard of goblins, the terrace was plunged into darkness.

A shadow leapt from the shadows, strumming the strings of a guitar dramatically, and some of the men at the farthest tables whistled feebly. Fyodor and Andrei's conversation trailed to nothing as a spotlight suddenly blazed down onto the round stage in the middle of the balcony. A gypsy whirled into its glare, her tightly-fitting silk dress cut low on the bodice to expose her voluptuous shoulders and breasts. All eyes were nailed to her. The gypsy stared challengingly through slanted eyes at some meaty-faced general before opening her mouth to sing a mesmerising lament to a lover who had spurned her, full of hate and blood revenge.

Still singing, she stepped from the stage, moving proudly with her shoulders held well back, breasts thrust forward, and looked sidelong from her black eyes at her audience, all cruel splendour, with something between a smile and a grimace upon her painted lips. She snaked her way sinuously amongst the tables, the gaping men risking a quarrel with their wives later to drink her in as she tempted and provoked, her varnished fingernails caressing a shoulder here, barely brushing a thigh there. As she spun from one table to the next she seemed to leave a sigh behind her.

She came to Alyosha and stared into his eyes, a spray of her spit like fine dew on his face as she sang the chorus. Inessa suddenly got to her feet and took the gypsy's hand, spinning her around like a top. The audience roared its approval as one, several of the men getting to their feet to applaud. Andrei looked at Fyodor in astonishment, and was about to protest, but thought better of it, not wishing to offend, and sat there in silence, though his eyebrows were knitted in confusion and embarrassment.

The meaty-faced general offered Inessa a white rose, which she held between her teeth as she danced, clapping her hands together above her head and stamping her feet. Transfixed by his mother's performance, Alyosha didn't notice his father calling for the chauffeur, but the next thing he knew, Ivan was there, and he was ordered to return to the dacha with Margarita and Larissa, his protests in vain. As his cousins climbed into the car, he realised that he had left his sailor's hat behind at the table, and ran back through the hotel to the terrace. The place was in uproar. Wherever he looked, people were on their feet, clapping and howling in a frenzy of desire and longing.

The gypsy was singing as if possessed, the guitarist attacking his instrument as if it was a wild beast to be tamed, and as Alyosha squeezed past the crowd to reach the table, he saw his father, looking wan and anxious, holding onto his mother's wrists as he spoke to her, plucking her towards him every now and again when she seemed to resist, the tears streaming down her cheeks as she laughed in his face.

WINTER 1916

1

The cousins, who had always been educated together at Fyodor and Inessa's house, were introduced to their new tutor in early October. Herr Professor Karl Krieger was possessed of a head of crinkly red hair and a strutting, rather pompous manner.

'I was born and brought up on the lower slopes of Grotenburg mountain,' was one of the first things he announced as he stood before them, 'which means I hail from Detmold. Whose town of birth was that?'

The three cousins looked at him blankly.

'Why, the Princess Pauline zur Lippe née zu Anhalt-Bernburg, niece to Catherine the Great of Russia.'

Herr Professor K.K. (as he became known to his pupils) had not come to them directly from Detmold, but from Minsk, where he had lost his post with another family due to anti-German sentiment. He would not have joined Fyodor Alexandrov's household had he received a better – or indeed any other – offer, for he was secretly appalled that he was expected to share the tutoring with a Frenchwoman. As any patriotic German would, he felt nothing but contempt for France and all things French.

When he placed his spectacles on his nose he looked like a country priest, and as the weeks passed, Alyosha, Margarita and Larissa noticed that he only possessed two suits – one dark blue, of some thin cloth, and a heavier black one – both too tight across the shoulder and the sleeves an inch or so too short above his wrists.

'The trivial external aspect of life is the last thing to interest me,' pronounced Herr Professor K.K. 'Why is that, you may ask?'

His three pupils looked at him unenquiringly.

'I take so much more sustenance from the internal life of the soul than what passes for so-called real life. Apart from the odd game of billiards in the back room of the Francis Albert on the Nevskii, of course. Who is your favourite writer, Alexei?'

'Pushkin,' he replied without much thought.

'Larissa?'

'Tolstoy.'

'Margarita?'

'Anton Chekhov.'

'Indeed. My own favourites are Goethe, Schiller and Heine, and to a lesser extent, Milton and Shakespeare, in the definitive translations of Schlegel-Tieck; and when you three begin to flag, when your heads start to droop in a half-doze over your work, then I will ask you to put away your exercise books and take out your copies of *Faust* and you will sit there memorising some of that sublime poetry. Do we begin to understand each other?'

Mornings were given over to grammar, German literature, Mathematics and Ancient History. Margarita had a natural flair for literature, while Larissa's favourite subjects were Geography and French. Alyosha didn't care for any of it, though he was bright enough, so it was he who bore the brunt of Herr Professor K.K.'s wrath.

'I'm never afraid to punish,' he said on many an occasion.

At the side of his desk he kept a black leather case, which housed four canes that he had brought with him all the way from Westphalia to Russia.

The clock always crawled towards midday. Mademoiselle Babin had an altogether more emollient teaching method, so after lunch they could look forward to the lighter atmosphere of the afternoon, when she taught them French, English and Geography.

Autumn sank into winter. A blue twilight crept through the

streets and the yellow lamps lit up, row by row, along the canals, their soft light turning the water to velvety darkness, and throwing long shadows under the arches of the bridge. Then the days became even shorter, the city plunging swiftly from day into night. It turned bitterly cold and they were allowed to have their classes in the salon, where a cosy fire blazed. Sometimes Mademoiselle Babin took them for a stroll, testing them on the French and English words in turn for the things around them.

To the shops on the Nevskii Prospekt the four might go, stopping to salivate over the produce in Yeliseyev's window: the fresh sturgeon, the caviar on ice, the exotic, out-of-season fruits from the Crimea, and the beautifully decorated French patisserie and gateaux. The girls liked to linger before the various windows displaying the latest fashions from abroad, mainly Paris.

'Look at that…'

Mademoiselle Babin enjoyed nothing more than testing them on the names of the sparkling gems at Fabergé, Cartier and Bulgari. The young Frenchwoman's eyes sparkled in imitation as she admired the jewellery, longing to wear the brooch by Bolin on her breast.

Alyosha had of course pestered Ivan Kirilich several times to elaborate on what he had told him in Yalta.

'Were you serious about Mademoiselle Babin and Uncle Kozma?'

'Am I the type of fellow to lie about such a thing?'

Alyosha wasn't sure. He'd seen how much the chauffeur enjoyed goading the other servants in the kitchen. He was full of sly tricks, never happier than when he had managed to provoke a quarrel or a fight. But then something happened that made Alyosha forget his concerns on this subject entirely.

It was late afternoon, and the four of them were on their way home after drinking hot chocolate in the Hôtel de l'Europe Astoria. Above their heads, heavy grey snow clouds were gathering around the spire of Saint Isaac Cathedral, darkening the sky. They waited for a tram to pass before crossing the street but there was a motor-car behind it – a black Dellanay-Belleville – and the driver, one hand carelessly on the wheel, the other arm draped around his companion's shoulder, had turned to say something laughingly to her. Inessa.

His mother.

Mademoiselle Babin, who had already crossed the road with Margarita and Larissa, called out to Alyosha, standing there on the other side as if turned to stone.

'Come along, what's keeping you?'

Alyosha appeared not to have heard so she called to him again. He didn't stir. Tutting under her breath, Mademoiselle turned to Margarita and Larissa.

'What on earth has possessed him? Girls, you stay here please.'

Mademoiselle Babin crossed back to Alyosha, where he still stood, staring at something further down the street. Dusk had already begun to fall, and besides, Mademoiselle Babin had always been rather short-sighted – vanity alone keeping her from wearing spectacles – so she was none the wiser to what had him so riveted.

'Lyosha?'

There was an irritated edge to her voice:

'Is anything the matter?'

After that afternoon, Alyosha kept an eye out, but never saw the driver of the Dellanay-Belleville amongst the visitors who came to the house. He found it hard to believe that he was the only one to have noticed his mother in the passenger seat; after all, the motor-car had raced past literally under their noses. Perhaps his cousins had seen her but chosen to keep quiet so as not to embarrass him? He might have asked Margarita but he was never alone with her and Larissa was all ears and not to be trusted. So he kept it all to himself; but that image of the man with his arm around his mother's shoulder came to torment him every night.

Eventually, consumed by curiosity, he began to creep into his mother's bedroom when he knew she was out, to see what he could find, furtively going through her things. One afternoon he took up a great armful of her stockings and garters and buried his nose in them. The silk and the satin…

It didn't take him long to come across a small silver key on a red ribbon, and when a further search unearthed a battered vanity case in the bottom of her mahogany wardrobe, it took a matter of moments to turn the key in the lock and open it.

The temptation to read his mother's diaries was overwhelming, but to avoid discovery, he read them little by little, when he knew he was safe. Turning the pages of the oxblood leather volumes, Alyosha felt he was beginning to truly know his mother for the first time in his life.

Inessa's life outside the house was clearly very different from her life with his father. The world she described in her diaries seemed to him a strange and exotic one: a world of fashion, of artists and actors, musicians and singers. There was a long entry describing the evening at the Pavilion in Yalta when Alexei Alexevich Dashkov – the most famous actor of the Russian silver screen – had given her his autograph. This had been carefully preserved, along with some photos she had cut out from various magazines.

He read of her love of concerts and any kind of performance – opera, ballet, theatre – and equally her love of clothes. That was no great secret, as she was always beautifully dressed and immaculately made-up. No detail was too small: when wearing a peep-toed shoe she would always varnish her toenails a daring dark green, to match her eyes.

Finally he came across one bald statement – so brief he almost skimmed over it – where his mother simply noted that she loved

Mita Petlyura Golitzin with all her heart. Was this the stranger in the motor-car? It must be, but he could find no further clues in her diaries. He began to fantasise about following his mother through the streets of traffic, past the trams and carts and the luxurious coaches pulled by horses whose coats had been groomed to a burnished brilliance, the purple and gold livery of the servants of the Court a bright blur as they thundered past. In his mind's eye he watched as his mother walked past the row of motor-cars waiting outside the Hôtel de l'Europe Astoria and into the hotel, the doorman opening the door for her, to keep her tryst... with Mita Petlyura Golitzin.

Alyosha felt a slow resentment grow inside him towards him mother. She had never acknowledged his existence, not really. She did not treat him as other mothers treated their sons. He couldn't claim that she was ever cruel to him, nor did she lose her temper or belittle him, but neither was she ever loving. Her attitude towards him seemed entirely neutral – or at best she seemed sometimes to feel a little sorry for him for some inexplicable reason, looking at him with an expression of awkwardness almost, and a tone of regret when she spoke to him. But most of the time Alyosha felt she really wouldn't mind very much whether she saw him at all.

He wondered what the reason might be for this indifference. Did the blame lie with him? Had he done something unforgivable when he was younger and so lost her approval forever? Something he was not even conscious of having done? His mother loved his little brother Georgik far more than she loved him, of that he was sure. Inessa doted on his younger brother and had done from the day he came into the world. Had she ever doted on him like that? He doubted it.

2

Alyosha might never have noticed Aisha if it hadn't been for the parrot. The old bird had been in the family for years and had been a familiar sight in the kitchen for as long as he could remember. Twice a year Roza insisted on having it deloused. The cook was a skinny, sallow, buck-toothed old woman, who never ventured into the rest of the house, but who reigned supreme in the kitchen. She stomped around in men's slippers (her brother's cast-offs), terrorising the younger maids, and wasn't much liked by anybody else because of her constant carping and her tendency to tell tales on them.

As far as delousing the parrot went, it was easier said than done. It had a vicious temper at the best of times, and an absolute loathing of any kind of water: above all a bowl of warm water with a hefty slug of cheap vodka added to it.

Such a vile and thankless task always fell to the youngest maid. That was the time-honoured tradition, and the most recent addition to the staff was a young girl called Aisha, who had only joined the household since the family's return from Yalta.

Since he was tiny Alyosha had always been allowed to join in the fun. It fell to Oleg, Oxana's brother – a great big bear of a man, not much less wide than he was tall, with a slightly Armenian nose – to catch the bird. He often popped in to see his sister from the naval garrison at Kronstadt, where he was stationed, coming into the kitchen through the back to fill his stomach and have a gossip with whoever was there. He suffered from dropsy, which gave his face a swollen appearance, and his skin always had an unhealthy sheen to it, his upper lip perpetually shiny with sweat.

The minute Oleg put his great paw into the parrot's cage, the bird was wily enough to know something was afoot and did everything possible to avoid being caught. The sailor managed to grab it by the neck in the end and carry it over to the tub of warm water, where a nervous Aisha stood waiting in her petticoat.

The bird, becoming ever more agitated, squawked and flapped its wings in protest, sending out little puffs of dust and lice, its big black curved beak opening and closing as if it was about to suffocate. A daft smile on his face, his yellow teeth much in evidence, Oleg held on to the bird like a leech; but the minute the less-experienced Aisha took it from him the parrot attempted another frantic bid for freedom, screeching in a most anguished way.

'Hold it tight!'

'Stinks!'

'Hang on to it now! Or it'll get away!'

'It stinks! Pooh!'

Everybody else kept well clear, laughing fit to burst in their various corners at the sight of the young girl, half-naked and soaked to the skin, running frantically around the kitchen table in hot pursuit of a squawking parrot.

After that afternoon, Alyosha dreamt only of her. He became distracted and inattentive to everybody else. If he saw her, he blushed like a girl. Aisha was everything.

'What you looking at?'

'You.'

He went out of his way to bump into her. She was always rushing back and forth from the kitchen, summoned to fetch and carry by the ring of the bell.

'Got work to do. Or I'll catch it from Oxana.' She smiled. 'Why are you looking at me like that?'

'Your eyes.'

'Last time I looked I had two, same as everybody else. What's so special about that?'

He thought her eyes were wonderful, round and light green, with only a suggestion of eyebrows, so that she looked like a girl living in perpetual astonishment. She was very good-looking, in an original sort of a way – there was no wonder that so many men gave her the eye.

'How old are you?' asked Alyosha.

'I'm not too sure.'

'Why?'

'Do you have to ask so many questions?'

She had a temper too.

'I think we must be around the same age.'

He managed to glean, after some persistence on his part, that Aisha was an orphan, taken in by the nuns of the Pokrovskii Convent. That's why she knew so many of the psalms by heart, though her singing voice was dreadful. The sisters had given her a little education, albeit very elementary, so that although she couldn't write, she knew her letters and could read a little, if the words were short and the sentences simple.

'If you like... I could give you lessons.'

'Oh, yes? What sort of lessons?'

'To read and write.'

'Read and write?' she laughed.

He frowned. Why was that such a funny suggestion?

'And what good would reading and writing be to someone like me?'

'Everybody wants to better themselves. Experience new things...'

'Do they?'

'Of course they do.'

She eyed him carefully, biting her lower lip.

'How about it?'

'How about what?'

'I'll teach you how to read and write.'

'Not me.'

'I'd love to. I'd really love to. You'd be really good at it. I'm sure of it.'

That's when they kissed for the very first time.

3

Alyosha was late coming down to breakfast that morning and his father had long since left for his munitions factory. As he took his seat he noticed with a start that Aisha was waiting on them for the first time. Oxana was supervising with a gimlet eye, occasionally giving her a quiet instruction or a little nod to indicate approval, so Alyosha didn't dare even acknowledge her presence, though he longed to touch her hand when she served him.

His mother was questioning Dunia, who stood before her with Gosha in her arms, about the baby's eating habits and sleeping pattern. Dunia answered patiently, smiling down at the baby and stroking his cheek with the back of her little finger. Finally Inessa pronounced herself pleased at how much Gosha had grown and told Dunia that she was very happy with her care, dismissing the girl with a smile.

Herr Professor K.K. was already eating, sitting very straight in his chair, his napkin tucked in under his collar, but Mademoiselle Babin was even later than Alyosha, and slipped into her chair with a murmured apology as the Professor was clearing his throat and announcing that he had received some very good news indeed.

'Believe it or not, I have received a telegram from Berlin informing me there's a contract in the post from Stralau Verlag to publish the book I'm currently writing.'

'Very good,' Inessa answered dryly.

'It's a book about paternalism. I worship the idea.'

He bit into his piece of toast, beaming. Alyosha knew only too well by now of the Herr Professor's undying love for the aristocracy. He talked about it almost as much as he did about Goethe.

'In my humble opinion, in Western Europe at least, the Catholic Church and the great aristocratic families are the absolute cornerstones of every successful and enduring monarchy there ever was, and the family is the sacred breakwater that stands between us and the rampant liberal individualism which has come into being through enthroning and lauding democracy above all other political systems. One of my original reasons for deciding to come to Russia was so that I could learn more of the lineage of the Tzar and his family, the ways of the Court, and of the ancient traditions and customs of the Holy Church, which of course is the main subject of my book.'

'Very good,' Inessa repeated tonelessly, hoping that the man wrote better than he spoke.

All that week the children had very merry lessons. They had never seen their tutor in such high spirits, with a spring in his step and something approaching a twinkle in his eye. One morning, the minute he had left the room after the morning's lessons were done, Margarita and Larissa had a fit of the giggles. Alyosha had been aware of their whispering together for most of the morning, obviously nursing some secret.

'Will you tell me what's so funny?'

'Why do you think the Professor has bought a new suit and oiled his hair so carefully?' Larissa asked him archly.

'I don't know,' Alyosha answered impatiently, 'maybe he's already spent the advance he's had from his publishers in Berlin.'

'No, that's not it at all. He's trying to impress her, isn't he?'

'Who?'

'Who d'you think?'

Alyosha felt a small stab of jealousy.

'Not Mademoiselle Babin?'

Margarita shook her head.

'Who then?'

'Take another guess…'

His curiosity piqued now, Alyosha told his cousin impatiently he had no idea. When she told him he was incredulous. He stared at Larissa.

'Valeriya Markovna? Our piano teacher? I don't believe it.'

She held out her hand to him.

'I bet you!'

'You girls – you're just making something out of nothing.'

'Margarita, tell him what we heard.'

But even then, Alyosha had his doubts. That sour-faced woman? He couldn't remember ever seeing her pinched expression break into a smile. The most enthusiasm she ever displayed was for rapping his knuckles with her little ivory stick when he hit a wrong note. It couldn't possibly be true. His cousins were pulling his leg.

Later on Alyosha asked Aisha about it.

'What? You've only just heard about it?'

They were huddled together inside the large linen closet on the first floor.

'They're mad about each other…'

How had he not noticed?

'Why else would a piano teacher start rinsing her hair with camomile to make it lighter then?'

What on earth did the two of them see in each other? Alyosha wondered. He shuddered at the sudden unwelcome picture of them that popped into his head. But then an even more unwelcome and graphic image replaced it, that of his mother Inessa, in a heated embrace with her lover, her Mita Petlyura Golitzin. He saw his hand on her back, moving to open her blouse, fondling her breasts, his head bending lower to bite her flesh, and lifting her skirt higher and higher…

Aisha felt his erection wither in her fist and redoubled her efforts until it stiffened once more. He squeezed her breast tighter and kneaded it with his fingers, breathing heavily as he nuzzled her neck, her hair tickling his nose and the sweat on her skin smelling like mouldy flour.

Then: 'Stop it! That hurts…'

'Don't, Aisha…'

'Your nails…'

'Don't stop, please don't stop….'

'Aw!'

'Keep going, keep going, keep going…'

Suddenly, the doors of the closet were flung open and the light flooded in. Standing before them, with his legs straddled wide, was Ivan Kirilich the chauffeur. While Alyosha struggled to close the buttons of his trousers he yanked a shrieking Aisha out of the closet by her earlobe, pincered firmly between his thumb and forefinger. Alyosha hurried after them towards the staircase as Ivan berated the young maid loudly: 'You dirty little bitch.'

Alyosha caught up with them and grabbed Ivan's arm.

'It's not her fault, let her go…'

Ivan let her go, only to give her a clout across the head.

'Don't hurt her!'

Aisha, released, fled. In spite of always wearing shoes with a built-up insole to give him a couple of extra inches, Ivan Kirilich was a very short man and Alyosha could already look him in the eye. He did not fear the chauffeur and now told him coolly that if he had any ideas about running to his parents to tell tales, he in turn would do everything within his power to bring about his dismissal.

Ivan gave him a long, baleful look and then said quietly, 'You've got a lot to learn yet, haven't you?'

'I'm not looking for any lessons from your kind, thank you very much.'

'Maybe not.'

Ivan laughed, though his eyes were calculating.

'But someone like me could teach you a hell of a lot more than those two clowns who get paid to do it.'

His toad-like mouth grimaced into a parody of a smile, exposing the crooked row of tiny teeth.

'Just you be careful. This is how scandals start.'

He tapped Alyosha's shoulder twice.

'And then all kinds of trouble follow.'

His smile vanished.

'Such as?' Alyosha asked.

'Blackmail.'

4

Alyosha was eating his breakfast while he listened to his mother and father squabbling. With Kozma Mikhailovich Alexandrov back from the front for Christmas, Fyodor thought it only right to host a supper to welcome his brother home, but Inessa pouted at the idea.

'Just thinking about having to spend a whole evening in the company of that crashing bore Ella is more than I can bear,' she complained.

From the moment the two women had met, Inessa had decided that her brother-in-law's wife was a hypocrite, pretending to be modest and unassuming, but in fact an arch snob who found fault with everyone and everything apart from her own blessed family, and who looked down her nose at Inessa, always putting her down or making catty little comments.

Inessa had formed this opinion on the basis of one conversation she had overheard during their very first meeting, where she wrongly assumed that the person Ella was discussing in less than favourable terms was herself. This led to her taking implacable offence, though Fyodor had often tried to reason with his young wife, telling her that his sister-in-law was a shy woman who would never have been so malicious, and that Inessa had surely misunderstood. If she could only give her a second chance, she was sure to see her many virtues and become fond of her. All his pleading left Inessa quite unmoved – her mind was made up.

There was a little more than ten years' difference in age between the two women, and when Inessa married Fyodor, Ella was already mother to Margarita, and had just lost her second child – the boy that Kozma had been longing for. This loss shook her deeply, though she took strength and comfort from her faith, which had always been important to her. Later Larissa came along, but that was not the same as the birth of a son.

Fyodor sighed and said, 'It's a miracle that he's with us at all when so many others have lost their lives… What if this turns out to be the last time we see him?' He rubbed his eye with his thumb. 'It's perfectly possible isn't it? More than possible… It goes against the grain, having to think of such things in the first place, but that's how it is…' He blinked, his eye bloodshot. 'How would a person feel then? I'd never forgive myself.'

'Seeing that woman once a year is more than enough for me…'

'You can be so unfair…'

'Unfair…?'

'And so unreasonable as well. We've barely seen Kozma this year… and after all, since our mother died last year, I'm the only close family that he has.'

'Fyodor, now look here…'

'No, you look here, Inessa…' He mustered as much authority as he could. 'Just you look here for once…'

'Oh, this is ridiculous… Alyosha, would you leave us?'

Alyosha rose and left the room and Inessa and Fyodor resumed their squabbling; but by the time Fyodor returned from his factory that evening Inessa, after spending the whole day brooding, seemed to have had a change of heart. Her husband gazed at her in some astonishment as she told him what she had in mind.

'But this morning…' He hesitated, anxious not to offend. 'I understood you to say quite the opposite…'

'Yes, yes, I know… that was because the thought of spending the whole night in Ella's company was insufferable. You know as well as I how many dire evenings we've had with her over the years. But this way, do you see, if we make it a more lavish occasion with plenty of other guests, I can easily keep her at arm's length.'

As he gazed at his wife's sparkling eyes, Fyodor, though he couldn't begin to understand this unexpected capitulation, nevertheless felt obscurely that she had turned the matter to her own advantage.

Seeing his seeming hesitation, she rebuked him:

'Don't look so glum, it will be a wonderful evening, you'll see.'

Inessa squeezed his middle playfully, just as she used to do, and added, with a little laugh, 'I'll make sure of it.'

He bared his teeth in mute agreement.

5

The girls were in high spirits since the return of their father, and Larissa was full of gossip about the latest developments in the romance between Valeriya Markovna and their Wesphalian tutor, claiming not only to have *personally* seen them walking out of Yeliseyev's delicatessen arm-in-arm, but to have also been told by Mademoiselle Babin that Valeriya Markovna was typing up Herr Professor K.K.'s manuscript on *The History of the Russian Orthodox Church* with her own fair hands.

Alyosha had romantic troubles of his own, so was not much interested. Though he was still seeing Aisha, something had changed; he didn't understand why, but she seemed far more reluctant than before. Every time he tried to guide her hand to his crotch she'd pull away.

'Stop it.'

If he tried to touch her breast, she'd rear away from him.

'Gerroff.'

When he tried to kiss her she'd pull a little face and once, when he'd succeeded, he saw her wipe her lips with the back of her hand. Alyosha didn't know what was wrong, or why she kept refusing him.

'Are you carrying on with someone else?'

'No.'

'I believe you are.'

'You believe what you want.'

Every conversation became a verbal battering, with each giving as good as they got. Not having the least idea why she was behaving like this, Alyosha felt frustrated and angry in turn, and although he didn't want to feel like that towards her, sometimes he thought he hated her.

He certainly didn't intend giving her up without a fight – especially as she still slaked his desire, when the mood took her. Even if the mood didn't take her as often as he would have wished, it was certainly better than nothing. But at the same time he was desperate to take things further. He wanted to go all the way. The thought of it consumed him, night and day.

'How many times do I have to say 'stop it'?'

'Aisha…'

'What are you, deaf, or just not listening?'

Lying on his back in his own bed, Alyosha gazed at her miserably as she buttoned up her blouse. Seeing his expression, she softened a little, and said, 'If I let you, you'd soon get tired of me and then you'd be off. You're all the same.'

'I'm not.'

''Course you are – I wasn't born yesterday. I hate the way that ugly bastard Ivan Kirilich keeps looking at me too. What if he tries to have his way with me when there's nobody around in the kitchen? Who's going to keep him off me? You?'

Finding the situation quite unendurable, the next day, after lunch, Alyosha went to the park where he knew he'd find Dunia pushing Georgik in his pram. Since the summer holidays he had written several more letters to her husband for her, and had read to her the replies Vadim had got somebody to write on his behalf. This had cemented Dunia and Alyosha's friendship and she now spoke her mind quite freely.

'There's something cruel in that Aisha's nature.' She paused reflectively. 'You know, some girls are like that…'

A bit piqued, Alyosha asked, 'Are like what?'

'Oh, you know, they enjoy playing games with their men… I'd keep clear of her if I were you. Heavens, I'm surprised somebody hasn't already spilled the beans to your father. Ivan's told everybody downstairs and Oxana's threatened to go to your parents more than once. It would be much better if you found a nice girl from your own set, instead of wasting time on that one.'

6

Kozma Mikhailovich Alexandrov arrived at his brother's house on the evening of the soirée clad in full military dress, his sword at his hip and his silver spurs clinking against the marble floor of the entrance hall. Ella was on his arm and Margarita and Larissa trotted behind. Fyodor and Inessa came up to greet them. The two brothers embraced and then kissed the hands of their sisters-in-law. Ella's gown was simple and unadorned, and Margarita and Larissa were demurely dressed in their Sunday muslins, though they had pink ribbons in their hair.

Before long a host of people had arrived, amongst them several officials of the French embassy, army officers, and several of Inessa's theatrical and musical friends. Fyodor did his duty as a host and made sure people were introduced to each other.

'Andrei Petrovich.' He steered the Managing Director of the Azor-Don Merchant Bank by his elbow. 'Come and meet the Marquis Villasinda.'

After doing the honours he left them to it. Inessa was similarly employed, as well as keeping an eye on the servants to make sure the champagne was flowing. The last few stragglers had arrived. The well-known poet and critic Chiva was one, in a blue suit, his hair rather wild and his beard in need of a trim. Velyaminov, from the University, was another, his soft collar all wrinkled, absent-mindedly brushing a little cigarette ash from his sleeve. They gave each other a wide berth, as they had written spiteful reviews of each other's recently published volumes of poetry.

Mademoiselle Babin was sitting quietly by herself on one of

the chaises longues. She wore a black and yellow striped dress, with a colourful Turkish stole across her shoulders. Her hair was arranged in two great coils over her ears, and her only jewellery was a little brooch. The girls came to sit next to her.

'I'm so glad Mother relented and let us come tonight,' said Larissa, entranced by it all. 'Alyosha!' she called out to her cousin as he went by, and when he turned his head, stuck out her tongue at him and laughed.

She admired her handsome father, standing nearby, talking to Louis de Robien and Etienne de Beaumont from the French Embassy. She eavesdropped on their conversation for a while, but it was very dull. They were discussing the military situation, and whether there was any hope at all of pushing the Kaiser's armies out of the Carpathians and Galicia. But her father's attention seemed to wander, and he kept looking over to their chaise longue.

'We've managed to hold out at Verdun,' Etienne de Beaumont was saying in his monotonous voice, 'and we're intent on kicking the Turks out of Asia Minor...'

'Excuse me gentlemen,' said Kozma Mikhailovich, coming over to where they were sitting. He bowed to Mademoiselle Babin and said, '*Bonsoir*, Mademoiselle, I hope you're having a pleasant evening. Tell me, how are these two getting on with their lessons?'

'Very well indeed; I have no complaints.'

'I'm very glad to hear it.'

'In our composition lessons, we've been practising the art of writing an elegant letter.' Mademoiselle looked at him directly for the first time. 'Everybody likes to receive a well-written letter.'

Ella came over to join her husband, a strange smell, a little like sour milk or old sawdust, wafting from her. She was about to say something to her daughters but their attention was caught by Louis de Robien's raised voice.

'The Balkans are the appendix of Europe. Always have been.'

'Supper is served,' Oxana whispered in Inessa's ear.

As they ate, Kozma entertained them all with tales of army life, and described in some detail the beauty of the Polish countryside. He was always a man to revel in nature, unlike his brother, who was an urbanite through and through.

'I don't suppose you were able to see Karsavina dance while you were in Warsaw?' asked Inessa, when there was a pause in the conversation.

'I did, as a matter of fact. She put on a performance especially for the officers.'

'And how was it?'

Kozma caught Mademoiselle Babin's eye through the flowers across the table.

'Magnificent. Beauty and grace personified.'

'That's one advantage of going to war,' declared Inessa. 'Having the opportunity to see a true artist at work.'

Kozma went on to describe the *esprit de corps* that existed amongst the officers, the loyalty and companionship, and the surprise visit made by the Tzar himself to the regiment.

'What was he like to speak with?' asked Andrei Petrovich with great curiosity. 'I can't imagine being in the same room as him.'

'Rather a cautious man.'

'Cautious in what way?'

'Like all truly wise men, he thinks before he speaks.'

'As he decides what happens in this war, it's rather a good job that he does,' said the Marquis Villansinda, taking a sip of his premier cru. His face was ruddy, and his nose fleshy, though he had a straggly little beard, and an even sparser moustache.

'Yes, indeed,' said Fyodor, emotion in his voice.

Kozma seemed to have a limitless store of amusing and informative anecdotes about army life and the course of the war, and talked like a man who had not a care in the world; but when Fyodor gazed at his brother's square, handsome face, he fancied that behind those clear eyes that seemed to survey the world with a calm, far-seeing gaze, there lurked a sensibility which had lost all capacity for being shocked by anything, having witnessed every imaginable horror on the battlefield. Yet he had not lost that habit of his of looking a little beyond people, rather than directly at them, and he could still be a little arrogant and opinionated at times.

As the meal drew to a close, Fyodor got to his feet and raised his glass in a toast.

'To the Tzar and his family!'

'The Tzar and his family!'

'And to the armies of Russia.'

'The armies of Russia!'

'To a speedy victory against the Kaiser.'

'A speedy victory.'

'To the fall of Berlin.'

'The fall of Berlin.'

There was no mention of the spilled blood and the butchery, the latest catastrophic losses in the trenches, or the disastrous advances against the well-armed German armies. Fyodor knew of these things. That afternoon his brother had visited him at his munitions factory and they had lunched together at the Imperial Yacht Club, where Kozma had told him of the sheer madness of the fighting and the chaos at the heart of the Russian army.

'I saw Prince Dolgorukov with a fat cigar in his mouth, whipping his poor horse like a demented buffoon, straight into the path of the bullets. Even above the enemy's artillery you could hear him cursing in French. Before they reached the first line of barbed wire over half his men had fallen…'

Fyodor noticed he hardly touched his food.

'When it comes to warfare, a clueless idiot like that belongs to the last century. Or even the century before that. They can't adapt.'

'What about their men? How do they feel?'

'We ask them to sacrifice their lives with unquestioning obedience, Fyodor. And that's what they've been prepared to do, without complaint, up until now at any rate. The truth of it is, the Kaiser's armies have plenty of everything but we're sorely under-equipped. We need twenty more factories for every one like yours. We lack arms, we lack ammunition, we lack bayonets. We lack everything apart from men. But how long will even that last?'

'You're painting a very bleak picture.'

'Believe me, the truth is even bleaker. But not a word of all this tonight, of course. Ella worries quite enough as it is.'

'Good heavens no, I wouldn't dream of it.'

Inessa was in her element that evening and was all animation and charm. Her brow and neck glowed palely like marble, her hair shone, and her gown from Madame Duchet on Morskaya Street was stunning. It was in the Parisian style, cut low at the front, and with a narrower skirt than most of the other women were wearing, showing off her slender figure to perfection. She flitted here and there, like a delicate butterfly, talking fifteen to the dozen, her voice warm and flirtatious whether she was speaking to man, woman or child. She was all lightness and laughter, as if the secret Inessa had emerged from her chrysalis for the evening's festivities.

Inessa fancied that Ella was looking at her with disapproval, but for once she cared not a jot. She was in full flood, telling somebody about a wonderful new restaurant called Cubat, which was quite divine. Having become rather alarmed at his wife's heightened mood and incessant chatter over the course of the evening, Fyodor approached and asked whether she would be willing to give them a song. Several of the guests within earshot of his request started to clap in anticipation, as she had a beautiful singing voice. Inessa went with alacrity to the grand piano and, smoothing her gown neatly under her, ran her hands across the keys so that the little hammers bounced against the strings, and then began to sing, her rich contralto voice enchanting her guests, who now gathered around her.

She had just finished her second song, an aria from *Eugene Onegin*, when the door opened.

They all turned as one to see a tall, slender officer of the Army's Medical Corps standing there. He wore a monocle in his left eye and under his nose a small, square moustache.

'Mita Petlyura Golitzin,' he said, clicking his heels and bowing, 'My apologies.'

He explained he'd been delayed by a bad accident involving a tram and two coaches on the Elagin Bridge which had brought the traffic to a complete standstill.

Fyodor Mikhailovich walked over and welcomed him.

'Thank you.'

He joined the rest of the guests, placing himself next to the Marquis Villasinda's wife.

'My wife was in the middle of entertaining us.'

Mita Petlyura Golitzin bowed an acknowledgment.

'Inessa?'

She seemed to freeze for an instant, and then began a popular ballad. Everyone joined in the chorus – everyone but Fyodor, who seemed to be quietly absorbed by thoughts of his own.

Alyosha watched Mita Petlyura Golitzin remove his monocle and polish it on his sleeve, before corkscrewing it back. He had deep-set, black-brown eyes in a pale narrow face. There was something a little reedy about his speaking voice.

Alyosha turned to look at his mother and her pose at the piano reminded him of the two photos of her that had fallen out of one of her diaries, from the year she got married. She would have been seventeen years old, and about to be married to his father, who was then forty-two. The difference in age seemed enormous to him. Was it even possible for two people to bridge such a huge gap?

In the first picture his mother was sitting on a piano stool, her hair in two long plaits down her back. The instrument was open in front of her, the ivory and black keys awaiting the dance of her fingers. In the second picture she was actually playing the piano, or pretending to, as the photographer had posed her so that her head was turned as she looked over her shoulder into the lens.

Tonight, when she threw a glance over her shoulder at her audience, it was as if the past and the present had merged. Alyosha gazed at her. She was breathtakingly beautiful, and he realised that she had not changed very much over the years. She was still only thirty-one years old – not so very old he supposed – and her expression still had that quality: of searching out that someone who would finally appreciate her beauty fully, as it deserved to be appreciated.

Inessa finished her song, stood up, and made a playful little curtsey in acknowledgment of the wild applause of her guests.

By and by the dancing began in the grand salon, couples taking to the floor underneath the twinkling chandeliers, and the little group of musicians slowly becoming redder and redder as the temperature rose. Between the twirling skirts of the women and the huge, vivid bunches of flowers, the room was transformed into one great, colourful carousel.

Larissa insisted on dancing with a reluctant Alyosha.

'What's the matter?'

'What d'you mean, what's the matter?'

'You're so quiet. Aren't you enjoying yourself? I've never had so much fun in all my life. Why can't we do this every night? Wouldn't that be glorious? Though I suppose you'd be awfully tired in the morning…'

Alyosha's mind was in turmoil. He knew something nobody else knew. The tall, slim officer. In the dress uniform of the Army

Medical Corps. Mita Petlyura Golitzin. With his monocle in his left eye. And his square little moustache…

'Why do you keep staring at that man?' asked sharp-eyed Larissa.

'What man?'

'Aw! Careful, you clod! You stepped on my toes again!'

When the dance came to an end, Alyosha was allowed a respite and they went to sit next to Margarita. He watched Golitzin cross the floor to where his mother stood talking to Louis de Robien's young wife. Inessa raised her eyes to his and the next instant he had offered her his arm and they were walking together to join the other couples in a cotillion. Although they were not the most graceful couple there – his mother seemed to hold herself a little stiffly – Mita Petlyura Golitzin looked at her with an expression that Alyosha had never seen on his father's face.

'Where's your father, Margarita?'

Alyosha hadn't noticed Aunt Ella approach.

'I'm tired. We should be going… It's very late…'

'Must we? Couldn't we stay just a little longer?' her younger daughter said plaintively.

'No indeed, enough is enough…'

'Oh, Mama, please!'

'Larissa! Don't try my patience, child!'

Alyosha politely got to his feet. 'I'll go and find Uncle Kozma, shall I?'

He looked all around the grand salon and then the other reception rooms, but there was no sign of his uncle. He passed Oxana, who disappeared downstairs to the kitchen, laden with serving dishes. He padded down the corridor towards his father's study, the music from the orchestra fading, but as he was about to knock on the door, it opened and his uncle stepped out into the corridor, closing the door carefully behind him. They gazed at each other for a moment.

'Where are you going?' Kozma asked him eventually, looking a little beyond him.

When Alyosha explained, he said, 'Very well. Tell your Aunt Ella we'll be leaving shortly.'

His uncle returned to the study and Alyosha made his way back down the corridor to the grand salon, but the click of the study door made him turn his head in time to see Mademoiselle Babin slip away in the other direction.

The last of the guests didn't leave until the early hours of the morning, and by the time Fyodor was finally allowed to go to bed he felt exhausted and old. Undressing slowly, he remembered meeting his wife for the first time ever, how eager Inessa had been to impress him, always doing her very best to please him, because as she told him, her happiness depended on his happiness. What were his hopes for their marriage back then? Love. Respect. Contentment. Security too, and a ballast against loneliness. And of course the desire for an heir. He remembered his own father telling him a man wasn't a man until he had fathered a son. He had two… or at least, he was quite certain he had fathered Alyosha. As for Gosha, he had sometimes entertained doubts as to his paternity.

He still loved Inessa; loved her without reservation in spite of all. He was convinced that she had loved him once, in the early days of their marriage, but equally he knew that her love had quickly faded, perhaps within a year or two; he couldn't remember now. But he remembered clearly enough the sickening realisation, not long after Alyosha was born, that his wife was having an affair, with some *soi-disant* bohemian artist. In the circles in which they turned in Petrograd, everybody knew everybody else's business. Fyodor was told soon enough of his wife's indiscretion, but tortured himself with more details than he needed to know by putting a private detective onto her. So he came to know all about her lover, Mili Samoilovich Petreuko: his tall, slightly stooped figure, his luxuriant moustache and cherubic lips, his wide, furrowed brow (creative angst), his deep-brimmed hat worn at an angle, the silk cravats. He wore mascara, and his lover's underwear, and arranged orgies in various apartments. He'd even seen the inside of Sedletz prison's high red walls on one occasion, for scribbling obscene graffiti on the doors of the Danskoi monastery.

Every other day the detective would come to his office at the factory to make his report. Fyodor sometimes had the impression that he was experiencing some voyeuristic glee as he turned the pages of his little notebook, reading out in a monotone, 'And then she asked him, "Why? Are you ashamed of me?" And then Mili Samoilovich, raising his voice a little, answered, "No of course not." And then she said, "I love you," and he answered, "I love you too"... and then I didn't quite catch the next bit because somebody came to sit between my table and theirs, but the next thing I heard after that was that she couldn't bear the thought of life without him. Then he said...'

That might have been the first time, but it was by no means the last, that Fyodor Mikhailovich employed a private detective to report on his wife's affairs with various men. He was no fool after all, even if he chose not to tell his wife that he knew of her infidelities. But this time, with this Mita Petlyura Golitzin, it felt different, and he had resolved to get rid of him one way or another. Without causing a scandal of course, that was all-important. The question was, how?

7

Alyosha had another uncle, Inessa's younger brother. His name was Artyom but everybody called him the Parisian, as most of his time was spent in that city. He possessed the rare gift of being able to raise everybody's spirits in no time. No matter what the occasion, he was always brimming with mischief and fun, and he was so witty and charming that he was universally adored.

He had a roving eye too, which made the mother of every pretty daughter fearful and jealous in equal measure. Artyom much preferred the company of women – and not just the young ones either – women to 'stir the loins' as he told Alyosha once, when he was far too young to understand.

Artyom was the dandy of the family. For years before the war broke out, he'd think nothing of throwing a few things into a valise and driving all the way from Paris to Petrograd on a whim. And each time he visited it would be in a spanking new, gleaming motor-car which was proof enough that he was flourishing in France as an arms sales agent to his brother-in-law.

Margarita and Larissa were as fond of Artyom as Alyosha was, and had unilaterally adopted him as an honorary uncle. Whenever he visited he came laden with presents for everybody, for his generosity was legendary. He always brought the latest things from Paris: novelties for the children, beautiful clothes for his sister from the fashion houses, and he could even charm Fyodor with his imaginative and thoughtful gifts, though he was always rebuked by his brother-in-law for his extravagance. Artyom just laughed.

He liked a joke too. In 1913, the last Christmas before the war broke out the following summer, he produced a canvas and presented it to his brother-in-law. With a sly wink at his sister, Artyom said casually, 'I've no idea if it's any good or not. I picked it up in the back of La Rotonde in Montparnasse. But people in the know say he's getting quite a name for himself. The fellow – Picasso's his name – is a Spaniard, but he spends a lot of his time in Paris.'

Fyodor thanked him gravely, but in his life he had never seen anything quite so tasteless. Of course Artyom knew exactly what his brother-in-law's opinion was, and how he would struggle to find a place to hang it, which would neither insult the donor – nor force the recipient to look at it more than he had to. Inessa, of course, adored it and it was really for his sister that he had bought it. She had read plenty of articles about Picasso in her various quarterly magazines and began to explain rather patronisingly to her husband what made him such a talented artist.

This year again, war or no, Artyom made the journey from Paris. He did not keep his own apartment in Petrograd so he always stayed with his parents, in his old bedroom from when he was a boy. The journey took longer than usual because of a few necessary detours, but he arrived at their door two days before Christmas.

Old Til the porter limped across the hall to greet him, and told him his father, Vasillii Karlovich Riuminskii, was taking his post-prandial nap as always; but as soon as his mother was told of his arrival she rushed out to hug and kiss him as though he were still a little boy.

'So lovely to see you my darling…'

She was wearing her pearl collar as always.

'And you too, Mother. You're looking very well.'

Anna Timurovna pinched his cheeks affectionately and said, 'Am I indeed?'

'You haven't aged a day since I last saw you.'

'Oh, you've always been a kind boy.'

'Mother really, it's nothing less than the truth: you're looking wonderful.'

'And so are you, Tyoma, as handsome as ever.'

She clasped him to her again and Artyom felt the little watch she always wore, on a ribbon, pressing into his chest.

'I'm so glad you're home safe and sound.'

She ordered Til to wake her husband, and before long they were sitting in front of the fire in the salon exchanging news of family and friends. In no time Artyom felt he had never been away. But soon his parents turned to reminiscing, and Artyom found himself pretending to be interested in anecdotes he had heard a dozen times already, concerning individuals he had never known and who had been in their graves for years. He joined them for dinner of course (and found the soufflé rather dry) but after that he put on his overcoat and muffler and stepped out, with a sigh of relief, into the bitter winter night.

He went directly to see his friend Yevgeny Ivanych, or Orlov as he was known, but the maid (she'd always been a sturdy girl but now, he noticed, she'd really started to spread around the waist and hips) told him her master wasn't at home.

'You don't happen to know where he went?'

'The master's business is the master's business. He never says a word to me about where he's going.'

'So I don't suppose you can tell me when you're expecting him back either?'

'Like I said, Sir…'

'Yes, yes. Well, give him my card, won't you?'

Artyom walked down the street to hail a *droskii-cab*, and instructed the driver to take him to the Plikin. They drove along the unfathomable Neva, the river in darkness, its blue bridges ribboned with lamplight, throwing shadows onto the façades and pillars of the palaces along its banks. Artyom lit a cigarette as they crossed the bridge over to Vasilyevski Island, and watched the dancing silhouettes of the little boats in the water beneath, and the solid, still barges, come from far-off forests, carrying their cargo of damp logs.

As they trotted along, the cabman half-turned and told him, 'You'll find the Plikin's not called that anymore.'

'Oh? What's the new name?'

'This craze of changing everything all the time is getting ridiculous if you ask me. Why aren't people satisfied with things as they are?'

Artyom repeated his question a little louder.

'It's now the Solovyov restaurant-bar, if you please. On leave are you, Sir?'

For the rest of their journey to the Vladimirski Prospekt the cabman tried to find out what he could, but as ever with strangers, the Parisian disclosed very little. Everybody in Petrograd knew that most of the city's cabmen also had a lucrative sideline as the ears and eyes of the Tzar's secret police – the Okranha.

Artyom rather expected to see the Plikin transformed, but when he stepped through the heavy curtains he saw that it was exactly the same as before. The same girl took his hat and coat at the cloakroom, and the same waltz was being played as he made his way downstairs and entered the smoky, densely packed room beneath; and, as always, he found himself momentarily blinded by the dazzle of the three huge chandeliers.

He didn't remember the tables being so close together, though. He had to step sideways between the chair-backs to reach the bar, passing the laughing dark-suited men and bare-shouldered women. It seemed the fashion was for sipping champagne through little silver straws. Artyom saw his reflection in the great mirror behind the bar, and then he heard someone calling him.

'Artyom!'

It took him a while to spot his friend Perarskii, who had got to his feet and was waving at him from one of the tables. Kukushkin was there too, one arm draped languidly over a chair. The three embraced warmly, with much back-slapping and ribbing about who had put on the most weight and lost the most hair, and the waiter brought a fresh bottle of champagne to their table before they had even sat down.

'So how's Paris treating you, my friend?'

'Like a king.'

'Are you still working for Fyodor Mikhailovich?'

'For my sins.'

'You don't feel like doing something else?'

'Such as?'

'We're a bit hurt that you seem to manage so well without us. Don't you miss us?'

'I do, I do, every waking moment, which is why I have to drown my sorrows with that good French wine and try and find some momentary solace with some little mam'selle.'

'Oh, it's like that is it?'

Kukushkin pursed his heart-shaped mouth in mock disapproval.

'I seem to remember that the last time we met, you had two on the go at the same time. I trust that has been rectified, and you now have at least half a dozen.'

Artyom puffed contentedly on his cigar and commented that some things in Russia were just the same as ever.

'Now that so many husbands and lovers are away fighting, there are rich pickings to be had amongst the poor lovelorn women of Petrograd, let me tell you,' Kukushkin remarked.

'Well, I hope you're doing all that you can to comfort them.'

'I feel it's my contribution towards the war effort. It's important to keep morale strong after all.'

Perarskii winked at Artyom, who suppressed a smile. Kukushkin was always inclined to exaggerate his success with women.

'So why isn't Gruzin with you tonight?' asked Artyom, taking a sip of champagne.

'Home in bed.'

Perarskii re-lit his cigar.

'Laid low with a cold.'

'And Orlov?'

Kukushin tapped his finger against his nose knowingly and Perarskii laughed.

Artyom looked from one to the other expectantly, but they kept him dangling with lots of heavy hints and double entendres and sniggers. Really, they were such a pair of overgrown schoolboys sometimes, Artyom thought to himself. He let them be, and by the time they'd reached the casino, they could resist no more and told all.

'So who is she?'

'Some hysteric.'

'Would I know her?'

'I'd have thought so. Zinaida.'

'Zinaida Ernestovna…'

'She's a hysteric,' Kukushin repeated, deliberating where to place his chips.

'Oh but he can't live without her!' said Perarskii histrionically. 'She is his life, the very beat of his heart!'

'And the minor detail of whether she wears a ring on her finger?'

'She does indeed.'

The croupier looked as arrogant as a Polish aristocrat as he reminded the table that this was the last chance to place their bets.

'Nobody knows much about the husband. A businessman.'

The wheel spun.

'Must be doing all right, though, as they live in one of those huge houses on the Znamenskaya…'

Artyom lost heavily at the tables that night, but as ever, it seemed not to bother him in the slightest.

'After all,' he remarked carelessly, 'there's plenty more where that came from.'

8

At three in the morning they were waiting impatiently for Kukushkin to open his front door for them. When he finally managed to turn the key in the lock, they entered a cold and unwelcoming apartment, and though everything was neat and tidy (almost painfully so) it was a real bachelor's abode, without any of the home comforts a woman would have provided. The grumpy maid was summoned and told to fetch them some vodka, which she did with bad grace, but Artyom was tired of alcohol and once she had shuffled back to her room he brought out a little leather pouch from his waistcoat pocket.

'All the way from Marseille, gentlemen.'

'Marseille…' Perarskii repeated in a dreamy voice.

'Pure as the driven snow, I assure you.'

'Wonderful stuff.'

'A little souvenir for you from la Belle France…'

'So what took you to the South? Business?' Kukushkin asked.

Artyom, busy cutting the cocaine into three neat lines, gave him a bland reply and changed the subject back to Orlov's new mistress.

Kukushkin, his eyes nearly closed and his speech slurred, mumbled, 'Half a chance, and I'd give her one.'

Artyom didn't respond, already a little tired of his friend's bluster.

'I'd have her on her back and give her a good seeing-to. She'd be begging me for it, and after a night with me she wouldn't want to know about Orlov, I'm telling you… one night with me…'

With that his head fell forward and Kukushkin began to snore gently, though every now and again he'd wake with a start and look wildly around the room before falling straight back to sleep.

Artyom and Perarskii, stimulated and enlivened by their friend's share of the cocaine as well as their own, spent the rest of the night talking, and Perarskii told Artyom that Zinadia Ernestovna had actually left her husband a week or so ago to go and live with Orlov.

'I'm not sure how much say he had in the matter, to be frank…'

'How so?'

'From what he said she simply turned up at his door, bag and baggage. I mean, what's a man to do?'

'What, with no notice, no discussion? She just presented him with a fait accompli?'

'Precisely.'

Artyom shook his head in disbelief.

'I'm surprised that Orlov of everyone – sly old dog that he is – even let her over the threshold.'

'So is everybody else.'

They laughed.

'But that's just how it was. She came straight out with it: she'd come to stay and it wasn't a flying visit; she was there for good. Well, he knew he was playing with fire, becoming involved with someone like that. She's a wild woman, I'm telling you Artyom. I daresay that was part of her appeal. But I think he got more than he bargained for.'

Artyom chuckled as he imagined his friend's discomfiture.

'So he's met his match at last, has he, old Orlov.'

'Let's say she knows her own mind. I think she has his measure. After all, he's always been such a bachelor about town; his reputation must have preceded him. I'm sure she realised if she wanted to keep her man she'd have to hold on to him for dear life. Perhaps she felt the easiest way of doing that was to have him where she could see him, right under her nose.'

'Wouldn't you have loved to be a fly on the wall when she arrived with all her luggage.'

'Absolutely. But you know, it doesn't do to be too cynical. She's told me herself that she worships the floor that he walks on and – well, I may be wrong of course – but I really do think Orlov loves her too, in his own way.'

'Ah, but does he love her enough to give up his independence, that's the question?'

'That remains to be seen. But the damage has been done now, hasn't it? Zinadia Ernestovna can never go back to her husband.'

'No, of course not. She's thrown herself on Orlov's mercy hasn't she? I suppose he'd be a bit of a cad to kick her out. Poor Orlov.'

'Don't feel too sorry for him. I think he's having the honeymoon without the expense of the wedding at the moment. How long that's going to last is anybody's guess, of course.'

9

On the seventh of January, on Christmas Day, every last church bell in the city rang out. Artyom accompanied his parents to the service at Kazan Cathedral, and then drove them to Inessa and Fyodor's house to spend the rest of the day there.

Under his thick woollen overcoat, the Parisian was wearing a light grey suit of the most perfect cut, and he was shod in a pair of fine leather boots from the most fashionable shoemaker in Paris, to be found in a surprisingly small workshop behind the Avenue de l'Hippome.

Artyom entered the house laden with so many presents that he was only just visible, peering out from behind them. It took Ivan and Oxana a good few minutes to divest him of them and to carry them through to the salon. Vasillii and Anna followed their son, and Fyodor and Inessa came to greet them. Fyodor kissed Anna's proffered cheek and said, 'Welcome to our home, and season's greetings to you.'

Inessa and Fyodor helped them take off their many layers, as Ivan and Oxana were still busy arranging the presents. Vasillii was wearing his loose Turkish trousers, a small silk cap upon his head, and his tartar slippers on his feet. He thought it most appropriate for an old man like him to dress traditionally on Christmas Day, and besides, the trousers were very comfortable after a large meal.

After exchanging greetings, his first question to his son-in-law was the same as always: 'So, have you managed to get out on the river recently?'

'Sadly not – things are so busy at the factory at the moment. But I did manage a bit of duck shooting at Lake Lagoda a fortnight or so ago.'

Hunting and fishing had always been Vasillii Karlovich's passions. For years he'd been a prominent member of the Karelian Hunters' Union, and had been its president for three consecutive terms; but his chest had been so tight this winter, he hadn't managed to get out half as much as he would have liked.

Anna was complaining to Inessa that her hands were quite frozen, in spite of her gloves, and Inessa ushered her through to the salon.

'Come along, Mother. The fire's blazing; we'll soon have you warm again.'

Not long after, Kozma, Ella, Margarita and Larissa arrived too. Kozma looked a little monk-like in his long, loose coat, which reached to his ankles. Alyosha noticed the melancholy expression on his uncle's face, though he greeted his nephew warmly enough. He didn't look very well either: his eyes were pink and watery, and his nose was streaming; his aunt told them that he'd been in two minds whether he should come at all, as he really wasn't himself. As usual, Ella was dressed plainly in a dark dress, but her daughters had worn their best muslins and their pink ribbons, which exactly matched the colour of their noses and cheeks when they first entered the house.

When they were all settled in front of the fire in the salon, Artyom produced one of his special surprises for the family to wonder at. It was the very latest camera, brought from Paris. He carefully took out the equipment from its wooden box, lined with purple velvet, and proceeded to erect the tripod and place the camera on it. Another box was full of little bottles of various chemicals, different lenses, and a couple of flashes.

'So you understand what you're doing with that?' asked his father.

'I do indeed, Papa. I've even been for a few lessons.'

'Who exactly gave you these lessons?' asked his mother a little doubtfully, having seen many of her son's sudden enthusiasms come and go over the years.

'The man himself, the best photographer in Paris… Monsieur Hugo Monges. I was lucky that he agreed to take me on. After all, no point buying all this equipment if I can't get some decent photographs from it.'

He started to arrange the family in a pose, with the children in the front. He had to chivvy his mother a little, who was very comfortable where she was and had no inclination for moving, but he persuaded her in the end. Finally satisfied with his arrangement, Artyom disappeared under the black cloth and with a blinding flash took his photograph. The family relaxed their poses, but Artyom wanted to be sure of a good image so told them not to budge until he had taken a second.

'And don't move a muscle until I tell you!'

Complaining happily, the family resumed their poses.

'It won't take long I promise. Alyosha, I know your face is ugly as sin but don't try and hide it behind Margarita's shoulder…'

Laughter.

'Now stop laughing, you have to stand still. Are we ready? Lala, smile!'

'I *am* smiling!'

'Mademoiselle, move a little away from Kozma Alexandrov, to the right if you please. There, excellent. I think we have it.'

But still not satisfied, he went bounding around the house looking for 'better light', and, once he had found it, in one of the upstairs bedrooms, insisted on their all moving up there, ordering Ivan to help him bring his equipment. Finally he was satisfied and told them he thought he had captured an image that was really 'avant-garde', not that anyone but his sister was much impressed by this. Luckily they were saved from further experimentation by the announcement that luncheon was served. They all trooped thankfully down to the dining room, where the table had been laid with the best china, and decorated with candles and flowers. As always, it fell to Vasillii Karlovich to say grace, giving thanks for all the blessings of the previous year.

'Christ is born!' announced the old man.

'Glorify him,' responded the family and servants as one.

After they had all been seated, Anna Timurovna went around the table to draw a cross of honey on each of their foreheads.

'In the name of the Father and the Son and the Holy Ghost,' she intoned, 'may you enjoy all the sweet things of life in the year ahead…'

A little bead of honey trickled down between Artyom's eyes and onto the tip of his nose. He poked his tongue out and licked it off, with loud slurping noises, which set Larissa off into uncontrollable giggles, much to her mother's disapproval.

'Behave,' she hissed.

They all took a piece of bread, and Larissa managed to control herself as she chewed her piece.

The traditional Christmas meal duly followed, all twelve courses of it. Afterwards, so stuffed they could barely move, they returned to the salon for the opening of the presents, and soon the carpet had disappeared under a mounting pile of gaily coloured paper and ribbon. There were gifts to be admired, gifts to be amazed by, gifts to be immediately played with; and they all squealed or cooed or murmured gruff appreciation, according to their age and sex. Nobody was forgotten.

'Here you are.'

Larissa handed a gift to Mademoiselle Babin.

'From Margarita and me.'

'Thank you, girls.'

She unwrapped the little package and nestling in its box was a very pretty necklace. The Frenchwoman raised her eyes to find

Kozma gazing intently at her. She lifted the necklace out of the box and held it in front of her.

'Well?' asked Larissa excitedly, 'Do you like it?'

'It's quite lovely.'

'Won't you wear it now? Here, let me fasten it for you.'

Alyosha was lolling on the sofa next to his grandmother, wishing he hadn't taken quite so much pudding. She was warning Vasillii under her breath, 'Don't you dare start asking Kozma about the war. Today is a day to forget all wars.'

'I'll ask him what I like, woman. It's not as though you can believe what you read in the newspapers any more.'

'No need to bother him with all that.'

'Just a load of propaganda. I'd rather get to the heart of the matter, never mind how terrible… What do you think, Alyosha?'

'I agree with you, Grandfather.'

'Good lad. Hear that, Anna? The boy agrees with me.'

Everybody was in high spirits, and Alyosha noticed his mother and father behaving quite affectionately towards each other. Even his grandparents couldn't bicker for long, though his grandfather, who seemed to be getting a little muddled, repeated several times, 'I don't know where I'd be without my family.'

Life, he told them, was a blessing and an honour.

'Never mind who – every single person has a contribution to make. To live a good life a man must be like a blind man who sees nothing and desires nothing apart from what he wants to see and desire. Do you understand what I'm saying here, Alyosha? It's important. Because it's the nearest a man will get to knowing true happiness. Then again, children are a great comfort. Through his children, a man is given a second chance to make amends for his own failings. I'm so glad, Inessa, that you made a good marriage, and you, Artyom, are doing so well in Paris, working on behalf of your brother-in-law's interests. I'd hate to think that my children had inherited my weaknesses…'

'What are you weaknesses, Grandfather?' asked Alyosha.

His grandfather chose a reddish cigar from the proffered humidor.

'Let me see…'

He snapped the box shut.

'What are my weaknesses?'

He considered the question carefully as he cut the end of his cigar and then lit it. After a few languid puffs he said, 'Nothing would disappoint me more than seeing a son of mine gamble, as I used to. I know he never will because he's a wiser man than his father. I couldn't conquer myself, and until a man can do that, he'll not make much of himself in this life.'

He leaned over and squeezed his grandson's knee affectionately.

'Alyosha, promise me you'll never be a gambler.'

Alyosha promised.

His eyes a little moist, the old man continued.

'Your father is a good man, a very good man, and he's been very good to an old beggar like me. I'm so ashamed of some of the things I've done.'

He glanced at his wife.

'Things I can never undo… things…'

He found his handkerchief and blew his nose.

'You be like your father – be a good boy. And work. Don't be a layabout. Work hard in all your endeavours. Do you promise?'

'I promise.'

'Sooner or later, one way or another, a man is sure to show his true colours. Every one of us is the visible fruit grown from those invisible roots in our heart. The way a man lives his life is bound to influence his own nature, and his family and fellow man – for better or worse. Just remember, the earthly acts of man follow him to the Judgment Day. Just you remember that. We are all held to account in the end.'

'Papa, why don't you have your nap now, so that you're rested before we go to Mass?' suggested Inessa, and with a little chivvying from Anna, the old man shuffled off.

Fyodor, Inessa, Anna, Kozma, Professor K.K. and Mademoiselle Babin started a game of *durak*. Anna was surprised that Alyosha wouldn't join them, reminding him fondly how she had taught him to play when he was just a little boy. But he had other plans.

The previous night Aisha and Alyosha had gone all the way, to his intense surprise. He'd been sleeping soundly when a noise woke him, like a hedgehog moving around in a pile of shrivelled leaves. Must be mice, he thought sleepily but then he opened his eyes properly and saw her creeping towards him on tiptoe. Before he could say a word she'd pressed her hand over his mouth and had slipped into bed next to him. It was all over in a minute, before he had time to think. Aisha, who hadn't even taken her dress off, rose from the bed but as she left, whispered that she'd be back the next day – the best Christmas present he would ever get. It was only after she left the room that he realised she smelled of drink.

Just as he was about to slip away to look for Aisha, he was waylaid by his uncle, who with a wink said, 'Follow me…'

He led the way to Fyodor's study and once there, motioned for Alyosha to shut the door.

With a lift of an eyebrow, he pulled a little grey package from the inside pocket of his waistcoat.

'From a little place I know of. A special gift from your old Uncle all the way from Montmartre.'

He held it out but as Alyosha made to take it he playfully swiped it out of reach and slapped his hand away.

'Oh no, no, no. Not so fast. First you have to swear that you won't say a word about this to anyone. This is between you and me, man to man, and if by some mishap these should happen to get into the wrong hands, you make up whatever cock-and-bull story you want – as long as it doesn't involve me. Deal?'

'Deal.'

Artyom grinned, ruffled his nephew's hair like he used to do when he was little, and tossed the package in front of him on the desk.

'Have fun,' he said, and left him alone.

As soon as the door closed behind him, Alyosha quickly unwrapped the package, wondering what on earth it could be that he'd had to swear not to tell anybody. A few seconds later he understood. As he looked at one image after another he felt a sort of shiver run through him, a combination of intense excitement and revulsion. He stood quite still as he slowly went from one postcard to another, with their various combinations: a man with a woman, two women and a man, a man and three women, two women, and, most grotesque of all, a woman and a Great Dane.

Every pose, whether lying, standing, straddling, crouching, kneeling, left nothing to the imagination. They were doing things to each other which Alyosha had never in his life even imagined possible. He felt the stirring of an erection growing. Who were these men and women? In one image, a man with skinny legs, wearing a helmet and a snake's tattoo on his arm, was grabbing a woman by her legs as she stood on her hands, exactly as though he were pushing a wheelbarrow, except that the base of his penis showed clearly that he had planted himself in her.

When Alyosha rejoined his family, after running upstairs to hide the postcards under his mattress, Artyom winked at him and said, 'Everything alright, Alyosha? You're looking very flushed.'

In the meantime it had started to snow, falling heavily for a while and then stopping abruptly. The brilliance from the dazzling white outside poured into the room. Alyosha opened a window an inch or two and a smell like a split, ripe melon filled his nostrils. He gazed out at the stillness of the city, as above his head a steam-filled pipe from under the floorboards of one of the bedrooms hissed softly.

The light soon faded, the weak sunlight softening the furniture's edges, until Oxana came in to light the lamps.

Later that evening, when Inessa was at the piano and the whole household had gathered round to sing, there was a loud crash. They rushed to the door to see what had happened but found it completely jammed. The Christmas tree, which stood in the hall, must have collapsed and fallen against the other side of the door. After some effort they succeeded in opening the door just wide enough for Ivan to squeeze through, and, with much grunting and a few oaths, he eventually managed to move the huge tree.

Larissa and Alyosha found the whole thing hilarious, especially the sight of Ivan Kirilich squeezing his belly through the rather small gap in the door. Margarita tried to hush their helpless giggles, but she didn't have much authority, as Inessa and Artyom were also laughing loudly, having had far too much cognac to worry about hurting the chauffeur's feelings.

Only then did someone notice Ella. She was kneeling on the carpet, her eyes fast shut and her hands clasped in prayer. With a dolorous intensity she said, 'This is a terrible omen of the tragedy about to befall us.'

Her husband offered her his hand but she stayed on her knees, gazing blankly at the wall. There could be no worse luck in the world than to have a Christmas tree fall, she told them. Everybody followed in the furrow of her thoughts. Would this be Kozma Mikhailovich's last Christmas here on earth? Would he return home safely from the front ever again? That's when Mademoiselle Babin started to sob – sobbed like a woman in absolute torment – so much so that she had to leave the room to try and collect herself.

That night, when the family had gone to bed after returning from midnight Mass, Alyosha, his whole body on fire, crept out of his bedroom. He climbed the stairs as quietly as possible, to the top floor of the house where Aisha slept under the rafters.

He'd had another look at the postcards from Montmartre before stuffing them under his mattress. They weren't quite as shocking the second time around: in fact he found three of them in particular very arousing, and he was tempted to masturbate, but the thought of Aisha in her bed made him hold back.

As he approached her door through the gloom, he thought he heard a low murmur then a little gust of laughter, quickly suppressed. He held his breath and listened, afraid to move in case a floorboard creaked; but all was quiet once more, so he wondered if he'd imagined it.

He opened the door to her room.

Apart from the dim glow from the incense-burner in front of the little red icon, the room was pitch black. Gingerly inching towards the bed he was assailed by a sickly stench of sweat and drink. As his eyes gradually became accustomed to the darkness he caught a glimpse of a muscled nape and shoulder, and beneath, Aisha's head on the pillow, at an angle, her eyes closed but her jaw moving as she ground her teeth savagely against each other.

The bed creaked in tandem with a muffled grunting, until a tapping of fingers, ever more frantic, pat-pat-pat on damp flesh, brought the creaking to an abrupt stop, apart from the heavy panting of the man as he tried to catch his breath.

'Uh?'

Aisha murmured something, and a great growl of a voice seemed to ask a question as he turned his head to glare at Alyosha. Then, in a wink, he'd whipped the blankets away and leapt out of bed, instinctively, like an animal about to be savaged. It was Oleg, Oxana's brother, squaring up belligerently as though waiting for the boy to make the first move.

Alyosha just stood there for a few moments, too overwhelmed to act. He stared at the surly face of the naked lover, the broad, becalmed sailor. The smell of the incense assailed him, and the dim little light seemed to enter his head like a white-hot poker, searing his brain and frying his reason. Suddenly released from his paralysis, he thrashed out wildly at Oleg, fists flying, feet kicking.

'Oy! Behave!'

He hit out frantically, but it was the work of moments for Oleg to spin him around and grab him around his chest, pinning his arms so that he was as trussed-up as a chicken waiting for the pot.

'Right, behave, d'you hear me?'

Alyosha bucked and kicked blindly but to no avail; Oleg merely tightened his hold.

'Calm down, lad. I don't want any trouble here, not if I can help it,' he said in an attempt to placate the boy.

In response, with as much force as he could muster, Alyosha butted the sailor in his face with the back of his head.

'You deserve that, you oaf!'

Oleg groaned as he staggered back towards the foot of the bed. Emboldened, Alyosha spat, 'And there's another one where that came from,' and was about to lunge when Aisha grabbed at his hair.

'Stop it!' she screamed.

She had two fistfuls.

'You leave him alone!'

She yanked him with so much force that she sent him flying, and he banged his elbow with an agonising crack against the wooden chest of drawers.

Alyosha staggered to his feet against the wall, shaking and shivering.

With his hands still held over his mouth and nose Oleg's voice was muffled and thick.

'Look...'

His elbow throbbing unbearably, and a searing pain in his temple, Alyosha blundered towards the door.

'Look at all this blood…'

He couldn't walk straight, his head still spun and his limbs felt clumsy and heavy.

'Fetch me a cloth, girl!'

Aisha hissed something but Alyosha failed to catch it.

'What?'

The last thing he did hear, as he finally staggered out of the room was Oleg saying, 'You've broken my fucking nose, you little bastard.'

SPRING 1917

1

Inessa continued to write a daily letter to Mita Golitzin, but after a while he stopped answering. When news from the front reached them of further losses, Inessa ordered all the newspapers to be sent to her daily. How was it that 15 million uniformed Russians were not succeeding in beating the Germans? Why hadn't Russia marched on Berlin by now, and vanquished the Kaiser? Where had the triumphant spirit of 1914 gone? How had hope disappeared? It wasn't helpful that her father insisted on repeating, 'They only have to blow on Russia today, for her to be in danger of turning to dust.'

For the first time in her life, Inessa began to follow the twists and turns of the Russian army's battles against the German and Austrian armies, with a consuming interest. She measured her days by the morning and evening papers. She devoured every detail of the latest campaign in the Carpathian Mountains. The Russian army were fighting hard and holding their position, according to the *Novoye Vremya*. Battling courageously and resolutely according to the *Ryetch*. If there was such high morale, why then were soldiers throwing their guns away, and slinking home from the trenches of the front at dead of night? Why was that happening?

There was a call for more arms, for more bullets and shells, so that Fyodor was busier than ever. He'd leave the house for his factory very early, and was rarely home until late at night. But he was worried about his wife. Ever since Christmas, Inessa had been suffering from painful headaches, so much so that the doctor had to be called more than once.

'Do you feel any better today?' he'd ask her.

'No better than yesterday.'

She spent hours enclosed in her darkened room, the heavy curtains tightly shut, a damp cloth pressed to her forehead, trying in spite of the pain to write to her lover. Inessa tried to shut the present out of her mind, and live in the future, longing for the balmy days of victory. She yearned to see peace reign once more.

'What if he's been killed? What if he's dead?' she'd wail.

Oxana did all that she could for her mistress.

'Why don't you try and eat something?'

'I don't have an appetite.'

'I'm sure you'd feel better if you could manage to eat just a little.'

'The only thing I need is to be left in peace.'

For hours, Oxana sat quietly at the foot of her bed, her masculine face creasing in anxiety when she looked up from her knitting (baby clothes for Gosha mainly) to check on her listless mistress.

Oxana was illiterate, like her grandmother and mother before her. Her mother had died eighteen years previously. Her brother Oleg was stationed at the garrison port of Kronstadt, on an island at the head of the Gulf of Finland, to the west of Petrograd. She also had a younger brother, Artur. Artur had been one of the first to enlist in 1914. She could remember watching him march with his regiment down Morskaya Street to Isakievski Square, led by Prince Belski – splendid in his uniform, on his horse, whose black mane shone in the sun.

'Left, right, left, right!' the officer in the green tunic had shouted, his spanking new leather straps squeaking as they strained across his chest.

'Left, right, left, right!'

Oxana remembered the thousands of well-wishers who had turned out to wave the soldiers off. She remembered standing next to Inessa, who was on her feet in the back of the motor-car, waving her silk handkerchief.

It all felt so long ago. By now, the iron hand of war had Russia by the throat and was slowly squeezing the life out of her. It was a daily ritual to listen to the knell of the church bells announcing yet another memorial service. Everybody's clothes turned to black. Tears of mourning were on everyone's cheeks. Even the tram cables seemed to give out a low keening over the city streets. Oxana sometimes longed to return to the country.

After Inessa suffered a particularly bad run of sleepless nights, Oxana insisted that Ivan drive out to fetch her grandmother from the tiny village where she lived, to the south-east of Petrograd. Now at a great age, she still eked out an existence as the village healer and was held in high esteem for her natural ability to treat children and adults for many ailments, like colic and corns.

'Where?'

'Tichwin.'

'Tichwin?'

'Why are you repeating what I've just said? You heard me the first time.'

'I don't suppose this Tichwin is likely to appear on a map?' the chauffeur asked sarcastically.

The old crone eventually arrived towards evening, a wicker basket filled with herbs and remedies over her arm. She smelled of flour, and field mice in straw.

'Where is the patient?' she asked and, giving instructions to Roza and Oxana, prepared her medicine, so that the kitchen smelled like a barn. Though it gave off an oddly sweet smell, it tasted bitter and Inessa grimaced as she took the first sip. She crinkled her nose and narrowed her eyes, but Oxana insisted that she had to finish the whole cup if she wanted to feel the benefit. Inessa sank back onto her pillows once she had managed to gulp the whole lot down, shut her eyes and fell asleep; but the next day she was on her feet, her headache quite disappeared. Ivan drove the old lady home with money in her pocket.

Inessa, though still pale and a little weak, seemed to have recovered from her sickness, and thanked Oxana for bringing her grandmother to see her, admitting that the bitter medicine had done the trick where the doctors had failed. Her appetite improved and she joined the family for dinner once more, though with Fyodor so busy, she usually just had Alyosha and his tutors, Herr Professor K.K. and Mademoiselle Babin, for company. As she had usually brought the conversation around to the war and the latest casualties before the soup had been cleared, Alyosha tended to let his thoughts wander; he spent most of the meal staring miserably at Aisha if she was serving them. They had managed to avoid each other since Christmas, but it was impossible not to see her at meal times.

For the first time in his life, Alyosha experienced violent pangs of jealousy. He felt such hate, he could have murdered the sailor. He spotted him now and again about the place; occasionally in his uniform, shirt and bell-bottomed blue trousers, but more often than not in a big overcoat, which he wore over an old, frayed shirt, unbuttoned no matter what the weather, to show his great hairy chest to everybody. Alyosha often lay awake at night thinking of various ways to injure him – badly. He'd had the show-down with Aisha of course, but it hadn't gone well. He had grabbed her wrist one day as she tried to hurry past him.

'What does Oleg have that I don't?' he hissed.

She'd tried to wrench herself free from his grasp.

'Answer me!'

'Let go of mc first!'

Aisha rubbed her wrist.

'Well? There must be something.'

'Dunno. Not really.'

'You're such a liar!'

'There's no reason, I said.' She smiled slyly at him and added, It's just that I'd rather mix with my own kind, that's all...'

'What do you mean?'

'People that aren't like *you*.'

2

It was towards the end of January, when the weather had turned bitter, that Herr Professor K.K. completely lost his temper with Alyosha. Since his lessons had resumed after the holiday he had been constantly inattentive, his mind on Aisha instead of the book in front of him. He rarely concentrated on his schoolwork, and gave his teacher little or no attention, which had led to many reproofs and even a complaint to his father – all to no avail.

Herr Professor K.K.'s patience had finally run out. He asked Margarita and Larissa to leave the room, and they quietly did so, throwing sympathetic and worried glances at their cousin. But as the Professor was about to raise his cane to administer the first stroke, a scream reached them from somewhere. The teacher hurried to the door, thinking it might be one of the girls, but the noise came from the bowels of the house.

Alyosha recognised the screamer and rushed past his teacher to the kitchen. When he reached the bottom of the stairs, he saw Dunia sitting in a chair against the wall, beating her breast and wailing.

'There is no heaven, there is no hell! It's all a lie!'

She cried out, through her tears, that God did not exist. Ivan Kirilich stood limply by, holding a yellow piece of paper between his fingers. It was a letter, in official type, informing Dunia that she was a widow. Vadim had been killed in action.

That was not the last of it. Before February was out, Oleg and Oxana heard of the death of their younger brother Artur. The sister made the journey to Tichwin to break the news to her grandmother. The old lady was so overcome that she collapsed, but she came to herself by and by, thanks to her boundless faith in the Tzar.

'He will look after us and all will be well.'

Oxana was not so sure. Since Artur's death she had sunk into a black slough of despair, and could barely drag herself out of bed in the morning to dress herself. She moved around the house tending to her duties like a woman with all the life emptied out of her. It seemed that every day somebody somewhere was losing a loved one, and the shadow of the war had fallen over Petrograd and the Russian empire beyond.

Inessa's headaches returned and her appetite diminished, and although she drank the bitter medicine, this time it did nothing to allay the pain.

Margarita confided in Alyosha how worried her mother was too – Kozma's regiment was involved in the worst of the fighting, not far from Warsaw. As if that wasn't enough, more than five thousand soldiers had died of typhus and dysentery before even reaching the front. The family hadn't heard from him in over a month.

Alyosha made a half-hearted attempt to concentrate on his lessons, just enough to give his tutor no reason to punish him. But as it happened, a gradual change had come over Herr Professor K.K. since the beginning of the month, which seemed quite unaccountable to Alyosha. He was far less prickly, and not half so keen to find fault and threaten the cane. Margarita was convinced that it must have something to do with the piano teacher, Valeriya Markovna, but it was Alyosha who worked out the true reason. Russia was losing the war and as a result, anti-German feelings were spreading like cholera, nowhere more so than Petrograd. Because the Tzarina was of German stock, it was widely held that she must be undermining every military campaign by revealing Russian strategy to Berlin's spies, using

Rasputin as an intermediary. Thanks to various inflammatory articles and editorials in the press, feelings were running high, and one Tuesday afternoon they flared into savage violence on the Nevskii Prospekt, when mobs went on the rampage, smashing the windows of any shops bearing foreign names. The rioting became ugly and dozens were injured. Several pianos were hurled through the third-floor window of one shop, the wood shattering with discordant fury on the street. A policeman who tried to put a stop to rioting in a storeroom was kicked to death.

No German was safe: every one of them was in danger of being denounced as a spy at any moment. As he watched his tutor discuss Goethe, Alyosha mused to himself what a fickle and random thing power was, and how a situation could be turned on its head in less than a day, less than an hour, less than a minute. He realised that Herr Professor K.K. was in mortal fear and dread that someone – anyone, including Alyosha – could report him on a whim; because of this he could trust no one, and so he had to be pleasant to all.

So who, wondered Alyosha, was the strongest now? And who the weakest?

Ella meanwhile decreed that it was no longer safe for Margarita and Larissa to walk over to their cousin's house unchaperoned as before.

'But why not?' complained Larissa.

'Because the streets are too dangerous for you two to be out alone.'

'We're not little children.'

'Lala, just listen to what Mamma says for once,' scolded Margarita.

To begin with, Ella would accompany the girls herself. Then there was an incident when a beggar – an ex-soldier who had lost both his legs – clutched Larissa by her ankles as they were walking home after their lessons, and spat at her that he wouldn't let her go until she had emptied her purse. She tried to tell him she didn't have a purse, and that he was hurting her: but the more she and her sister begged him to release her, the more he grabbed on to her, and if anything squeezed her even more furiously, until there was something quite mad and desperate in his unyielding grip.

After that, their manservant was ordered to accompany them as well.

3

Aisha asked to see Fyodor Alexandrov very early one morning, before he had left for his factory. She told him she was giving her notice.

'Where will you be working?' he asked.

'A rubber factory in the Viborg area.'

'When do they want you to start?'

'As soon as I can.'

Meeting her green-eyed gaze, he smiled and said tenderly, 'If that's what you wish,' before adding, 'It's a pity though.'

Fyodor knew they would miss her, especially as another of the maids had already left at the beginning of the year for factory work. But Aisha had been a loyal servant, so he gave her a generous tip, and wished her well, telling her he understood her reasons.

She gave him a little curtsey and thanked him.

This war was creating an insatiable demand for more and more workers, to replace the men who were being drafted into the army, sent to the front to die in their thousands. At the end of the last week of the month, Aisha bundled up her few belongings and left.

Flicking through the latest edition of her fashion magazine, *Zhurnal dlia zhenshchin*, Inessa told her husband airily that it would be easy enough to replace her.

'I wouldn't be so sure,' Fyodor answered, using the silver tongs to drop another lump of sugar into his cup.

'With all the young girls coming to the city from their villages in search of work? Of course it will be tedious to have to train her up, but I'm sure we'll find someone in no time... Goodness, how many have come knocking on our door looking for a place over the years?'

Inessa soon changed her tune.

One afternoon after lunch Dunia came to her, still dressed in black from head to toe, to inform her that she too wished to leave. Inessa refused point blank to accept her notice, and even telephoned her husband at his work to tell him that he had to instruct the wet nurse where her duty lay.

'Who else is there to feed my poor little Gosha?'

By the time Fyodor arrived at the house his wife was practically hysterical.

'She cannot, she *shall not* leave.'

'There's nothing we can do to prevent her...'

'No! You tell her that she *must* stay.'

'*Inessa...*'

'Don't Inessa me... don't start lecturing me about being *rational*... in that long-suffering voice of yours...'

Her lips made a straight, hard line.

'I know where she's come from, I *know* that she's clean. Who's to say her replacement wouldn't be dripping with syphilis? What would become of my little baby then? Are you happy to take such a risk?'

Dunia agreed to stay after some persuasion from Fyodor, who appealed to her sense of loyalty and her duty towards the family, who had employed her when she was at a low ebb and kept her in their service all this time.

'I know this is difficult,' he told her, 'but, Dunia, it's important that you face up to your situation honestly.'

The wet nurse kept her eyes lowered as he went on. 'You're a widow now, that's the truth of it. You don't have a husband to support you any longer. What you need more than anything at a time like this is the strong and constant support of this family, to give you time to get over Vadim's death, and to come to yourself after such a terrible loss.'

By the time Fyodor had finished, Dunia's emotions were in such turmoil she felt she had gravely wronged her mistress. Before leaving his study, Dunia looked up at him, stricken, and asked,

'How could I have been so ungrateful when Inessa Vasilievna and yourself have shown me such kindness?'

'We only want what's best for you.'

'I can see that now, after what you have said. What came over me, to make me think I wanted to leave your service in the first place?'

'I hope that you are happy in your work here.'

'I am indeed. I'm very happy.'

When she went back to the kitchen, she put the baby to her breast and started to hum softly under her breath. But in no time she felt as heavy-hearted as ever, with the depression that had enveloped her like a thick fog since she had heard of Vadim's death, sucking every drop of vigour and joy out of her.

4

In his creased cotton shirt with its frayed collar came Oleg, Oxana's brother, rapping on the kitchen door in search of a bit of food to fill his belly. Dunia opened the door to him with a grumble. He had brought one of his fellow sailors with him, a lad by the name of Rodion, who was so short he was practically a dwarf. He bore a surprising resemblance to Napoleon, with the same thinning hair, which seemed to expose more and more of his wide forehead with every month.

They made themselves at home, sitting at the table. Oleg helped himself to the vodka without ceremony, while Rodion rolled himself a cigarette from a pigskin pouch of cheap tobacco – some stinking *makhorka*. He smoked quietly, his feet up on the corner of the table.

The parrot screeched noisily from its cage.

'Fuck off, you cunt,' Rodion snarled.

'Fuck off, you cunt,' the bird replied.

'Fuck off yourself.'

'Fuck off yourself.'

'Fuck off, you cunt.'

'Fuck off,you cunt.'

'Fuck off yourself.'

'Fuck off yourself.'

'Fuck off, you cunt.'

'Rodya, for fuck's sake, shut up!'

This came from Oleg as he wiped the sweat from his upper lip with the back of his hand.

'There's no shutting the little bastard up once he starts.'

Rodion muttered something, rubbing his knee, which was aching with some incipient arthritis, as the back door opened wide. A chilled Aisha came in, bringing a gust of cold evening air in her wake, and stinking of rubber from the factory in Viborg.

'Here she is, my girl.'

Too tired to answer after her long shift, Aisha took off her gloves and warmed her frozen hands at the stove as Oleg wrapped his arms about her waist.

'I was starting to think you'd found someone else. Where were you?'

'Don't…'

He pulled her towards him.

'Get off me, Oleg…'

He had his cheek against the small of her back.

'You're like a block of ice. Let me rub your thighs. Thaw you out a bit. Give me a kiss.'

Everything demanded all at once: Aisha turning to face him and him starting to squirrel into her. It became a sort of skirmish, a squealing – don't, don't – as fingers burrowed and pinched where they weren't meant to, rough nails scratching and hurting, until she stopped giggling, started cursing and finally gave Oleg a ringing slap on the side of his head. Then they both burst out laughing. She cupped his cheeks in her hands, rubbed her damp nose on his forehead and gave him a great smacking kiss. Oleg smiled as he slowly moved his two thighs back and forth between hers.

'Don't call that much of a kiss. Give me another one.'

He'd sucked her lips into his mouth before she could pluck them free.

'Yuck!'

'What's yuck?'

'You taste like a sewer. When did you last scrub your teeth, you dirty bugger?'

With two fingers Oleg hooked the sides of his mouth, stretching his lips out wide so that she could inspect the yellow pegs within. Aisha snorted. Her lover threw Rodion a wink and slowly ran his tongue over his scrawny moustache.

'She's a girl and a half, eh?'

Aisha extricated herself in order to spit heavily into the black coal bucket by the stove.

'Come here.'

Oleg lunged at her.

'Leave me alone, can't you?'

He pulled her back to press her bottom against his erection, but she pulled free from his grasp.

'Don't!' she said irritably. Oleg, rubbing himself rhythmically through the cloth of his trousers, asked her what was making her so peevish.

'I'm just tired.'

He snorted.

'Those factory shifts. On your feet all day.' He took a swig of his vodka. 'I warned you plenty, didn't I? Expect you miss working here now, don't you?'

'Huh!'

Oxana came in from upstairs, a basket of dirty linen under her arm. Her square face was pale and pasty, her mourning dress giving her a sombre air.

'Who gave you the right to plonk your great big dirty shoes down here?'

She put the basket down in front of Rodion, forcing him to move his feet. He scowled at her and was about to say something, but Oxana turned to Aisha.

'And what brings you back here yet again?' she snapped. 'I thought you were meant to have left us?'

'Ask your brother.'

'We're not doing anybody any harm,' answered Oleg, looking at his sister.

Oxana started to sort the clothes, placing them in two piles on the table. Georgik whimpered and Dunia, who had been dozing in her chair, moved him to the other breast. Aisha went over to them and knelt down to stroke the little boy on his downy head, asking Dunia if the rumour was true.

'What rumour?'

'That you've been offered a better place with another family?'

'Who told you that?'

'Who d'you think? Ivan of course.'

'After I told him to keep his mouth shut.'

'Fat chance of that. So it's true then?' persisted Aisha.

Dunia hesitated, then answered slowly, 'Not exactly.'

Oleg turned to look at her.

'Why? What happened? Did you change your mind?'

Without lifting her eyes from the baby, Dunia answered, 'Yes.'

'But you'd been offered a better position?'

'Well, yes.'

Oxana scowled at her brother.

'Now, don't you start stirring the pudding. Personally, I'm very glad you'll be staying, Dunia. I'd be sorry to see you go.'

Ignoring his sister, Oleg said, 'What?' He made an enigmatic little gesture with his hand, as though he was plucking something from the air above his head. 'So this position came with a lot more money, did it?'

Rodion listened quietly, leaning his chin against the edge of the table, which made him look as though someone had cut his head off with an axe. Dunia kissed Gosha's forehead.

'How much more exactly would this new family be paying you then?'

Blushing now, Dunia answered, 'Money isn't everything in this world.'

'Money isn't everything in this world?'

Rodion made a face at the parrot.

'Fucking hell, I've heard it all now,' Oleg declared irritably. 'That's what I call talking through your arse, talking fucking rubbish. Who's been feeding you that line anyway? Inessa Vasillievna upstairs? That spoilt, selfish bitch been talking you out of it has she?'

Dunia didn't answer. Oleg got to his feet and said baldly, 'This isn't *right*.'

'You've had your say.'

There was something in his sister's tone of voice that suggested it was time he minded his own business.

'When she's been offered a better place? Won't somebody else tell her? Why am I the only one saying it?'

'Because you're the one with the biggest gob.'

'Oh, ha, ha. Will one of you please tell her? It's easy enough for her, easy enough for that Inessa woman… Don't you see what I'm trying to tell you? Who has she lost? Nobody. Not her husband, and not a brother like Oxana and me.'

There was a sudden stillness in the kitchen. Even Oleg was quiet for a moment as he remembered his little brother Artur. When he had collected himself he continued, 'That's why you have to think about what's best for yourself now, Dunia. Isn't that right, Rodya?'

The dwarf nodded his head simply.

'Whatever you do, don't let them take advantage of you. What terms have you agreed to stay on in this house, Dunia?'

'The same as before…'

'Did Inessa Vasillievna offer you a raise in your wages?'

'Well, no.'

'Why?'

'I don't suppose she thought of it.'

'Didn't you think of asking?'

'Oh, I wouldn't dare. Not when they've shown me such kindness.'

'So what exactly are your new working conditions?'

'That's enough of all these questions now – I'm tired.'

'Has Fyodor Mikhailovich or Inessa Vasillievna offered you more holidays?'

It became clear that Dunia had not asked for anything. Oleg went on to tell her that she must go back to her master and mistress at the first possible opportunity and insist on getting what was only fair and due to her under the circumstances.

'She's only interested in feathering her own nest, that one.'

His sister piped up in protest, insisting on defending her mistress, but the sailor from Krondstat was having none of it.

'After all, you have to understand that things have started to change, Dunia.'

He wagged his finger at Dunia as if to emphasise his next point.

'You have the upper hand now. Remember that.'

Clutching his ragged sleeve in his fist, he wiped the unhealthy sweat from his face.

'It's important that we all remember that.'

5

At last Ella received a letter from her husband. As always, Kozma described his life at the front with lots of small details of everyday life, and gave a humorous and lively account of the regiment's progress in the war. But this time he could not fool his wife and Ella felt heartsick on his behalf, in spite of the superficial optimism. Between the lines she sensed a bleak hopelessness – and sometimes in a turn of phrase or an unguarded observation, she felt an inexpressible sadness weighing on him, impossible to put into words.

Ella put the letter down and gazed unseeing out of the window, engulfed by a sudden wave of nausea. When she came to herself she went over to the icon, kneeled down, and prayed furiously for the body and soul of Kozma Mikhailovich, and for him to be returned to her fit and well.

Seeing her mother thus when she came into the bedroom, Larissa knew, before saying a word, how her mother would feel about her request to attend the fashion show.

'But *why* can't I go?'

'Larissa, there's no more to be said on the subject.'

'Mother – I beg you!'

'For the very last time – no!'

Although Larissa stood her ground and tried to reason, she was taken aback by her mother's harsh, terse reply.

'You're not going and that's that!'

'Aunt Inessa would take me. And Mademoiselle Babin.'

'How can you have the gall to think about fashion at such a wretched time?'

Larissa tried to find some way of answering her mother, but she felt the ground shift beneath her and although she continued to plead for a few more minutes, she knew she would not be allowed to go this year. Ella then seemed moved to impart some unpleasant truths, previously withheld, and there was an edge to her voice as she spoke to her daughter.

'You might as well know,' she said. 'You're growing up now; you're no longer a child. It's important that you start to understand some things.'

Aunt Inessa was the subject of her bile.

'If your poor Uncle Fyodor knew of even half the things that woman does behind his back, and it's been going on for years too.'

Shyly and carefully, Larissa asked, 'Like what, Mama?'

'I'm not about to discuss her peccadilloes with you,' replied her mother, before adding in a tight, censorious little voice, 'But Fyodor should have got rid of her years ago.'

'Why?'

'He should have simply thrown her out of the house and prevented her from ever seeing Alyosha and Georgik again.'

'Like Anna Karenina?'

Her mother's expression softened a little as she looked at her daughter.

'Little one, life is an awful lot more complicated than anything you will ever read in a book. I said at the time, I remember telling your father that his brother was a silly fool to have his head turned by that worthless woman, and it would only end in tears, but then when –'

Ella stopped short, as though she realised she was in danger of going too far. She grasped her daughter's hand, stroking the young skin that felt as soft as chamois leather.

'I spoke out of turn. Forget what I just said, Lala dear – put it out of your head. It's not important, not really.'

It seemed to Larissa that it was very important, but her mother continued, 'The only thing of true importance is that Russia wins this war and that the Tzar, along with every last general, officer and soldier can return home safely to his family, and life can go on as before.'

6

'Were you keeping my seat nice and warm for me?'

Alyosha had moved along to the next seat in the row so that Zinaida Ernestovna could sit next to his mother, complaining to Inessa about the filthy streets as she did so. He could smell the *Ambre Antique* scent that she wore and feel the warmth of her body as she settled into her seat next to him.

He couldn't help staring at her. He had often heard her name, for she had been at the centre of a great scandal when she left her husband to go and live with Orlov, one of his Uncle Artyom's close friends.

His father didn't have a good word to say about her. Fyodor Alexandrov thought Zinaida Ernestovna was a selfish, shallow woman, concerned only with gratifying her own desires. Worse still, she seemed to positively flaunt herself, lacking the sense of propriety to hide away from society after defying its conventions with such flagrant disregard.

She was also a prize hypocrite. For years, when Zinaida Ernestovna had been a respectable married woman, she wouldn't let her friend, who was conducting a discreet affair, over her threshold. To her mind, an adulteress was beneath contempt. When she began her affair with Orlov, another friend of hers had suggested that perhaps she should not have been quite so quick to judge others in the past, given her present behaviour. But Zinaida had bridled, and said her situation was quite different, and not to be compared. Love was what she and Orlov shared, not some sordid liaison based only on lust, and it was a love that had to be bravely declared to the world, no matter at what personal cost. Her refusal to try and hide her feelings for the sake of convention set her apart, she said, from others in the same boat. Her readiness to face the wrath of society had turned her affair into an honourable and courageous act. She saw herself as some beautiful heroine in a motion-picture, who dared to challenge the values of a hypocritical and shallow society.

Her friend – and many others when this was duly recounted to them – smiled wryly, and pointed out that everyone found different ways of justifying their own bad behaviour to themselves, some being more original than others. Zinaida Ernestovna simply tossed her head in disdain at such a prosaic interpretation. She didn't give a fig for people's good opinion. She was so head over heels in love with Orlov that the real world outside that bubble hardly existed for her. And while many now shunned her, she still had some loyal friends, Inessa amongst them.

The heavy curtains had been pulled across the Palace Theatre's majestic windows, shutting out the day, and as the orchestra played their first notes, three dozen models followed each other in stunning succession down the runway that had been erected in the aisle between the now packed seats. Up above, in the galleries, hundreds of others craned down at the gloriously attired mannequins, amongst them Mademoiselle Babin, her mother-of-pearl opera glasses clutched to her eyes so that she would not miss as much as an embroidered buttonhole of all this splendour.

Inessa, too, marvelled at the clothes, and admired the slender bodies that they covered. Valentina Mironova, the beautiful actress, looked adorable in a chic little velvet *panné* hat, pulled low over that famous brow. (Inessa had a photo of her with Alexei Alexevich Dashkov, from one of the films they had acted in together.) And then there was Natalya Kowanko, who passed within inches of where they sat, in a loose and uncorseted gown of shimmering green. The ballerina Vera Karalli earned a patriotic cheer when she appeared in a military-style coat in homage to the soldiers in the field. And Ekaterina Geltzer caused a stir when she appeared encased in a chinchilla cape, smoking from a long holder as she shimmied down the stage, her famously long hair cropped into an eye-catching shingle which exposed her beautiful neck to perfection. But the star of the show was undoubtedly Tamara Karsavina, who, in a midnight-blue sheath of a silk gown, her only jewellery a heavy cuff of sapphires and diamonds, seemed to not so much walk as glide, her perfect dancer's body shown off by the smooth, fluid lines of the dress.

As Inessa said as they sipped their champagne and picked at their caviar blinis at the reception afterwards, hosted by two of Petrograd's most prestigious fashion houses, it had been a blissful hour and a half of escape from all their cares.

Alyosha, after listening to a couple of songs from Igor Seversky, who was there to entertain the guests, became bored and decided to explore a little. He soon found himself quite lost in the bowels of the theatre behind and below the stage, and ended up in a dingy corridor, walking past several rooms from which emanated much laughter and chatter, and the occasional shriek at the pop of a cork. Some of the doors were left open, just a chink here, fully ajar there, and he caught a glimpse of naked shoulders and backs, a bouquet of roses nestling in an elbow, men and women toasting each other, glasses being drained.

Thinking he should try to make his way back to the reception, he found himself at some sort of an office. He looked through the heavily frosted glass and saw the blurred and shadowy outlines of a couple. The door was a little ajar and, curiosity piqued, Alyosha crept closer for a better look. Sitting on the knee of a bearded, bald man with a turquoise cravat about his neck, was a naked girl, one arm draped across his shoulder and nape. She was leaning towards a silver dish that the man was holding for her, and sucking up into her nose through a little straw something that looked like the good white flour Roza used to tip out onto the kitchen table to make dough.

The bearded man then tossed the dish on the desk in front of him before burying his face in her young breasts. The girl laughed and threw her head back, shutting her eyes as she pulled him to her, gripping his head with her fingers. Alyosha felt his mouth slacken, and it slackened even more when a second naked girl got up from where she must have been kneeling behind the desk.

He eventually found his way back to the reception, and saw his mother laughing with Zinaida Ernestovna and two young men to whom he was briefly introduced, Peraskii and Kukushkin. The room had begun to empty by now, though there was still plenty of champagne and caviar to be toyed with.

He heard, without listening, snippets of conversation:

'… everybody's out to cheat their neighbours…'

'… nobody can understand it…'

'… I don't even understand myself!'

Alyosha bristled when Kukushkin ruffled his hair as though he was a small boy.

'Enjoying yourself?'

His mouth was heart-shaped, and his little square moustache moved with his lips when he spoke. Alyosha ignored him and watched Lazareva Petrovna Vengerov, sister of Andrei Petrovich Vengerov, the Managing Director of the Azor-Don Merchant Bank, who was talking to Zinaida Ernestovna. She was an exceptionally pretty woman, her features framed beautifully by a mane of hair dyed a bright red and a wide-brimmed hat. She had a well-proportioned body, with a small waist, emphasised by a silk sash tied into a bow at the back of her white dress.

Alyosha took in every detail, from her high heels to her painted nails, for there was a quality about her that demanded attention. From the way her fingers lingered on his hand when he lit her cigarette, it seemed as though there might be something between her and Peraskii. Her eyes seemed to glow with a sly flirtatiousness when he smiled at her, and she mouthed something quickly that nobody caught but him. He was the only one to call her Laza.

As they left the theatre his mother said musingly, 'Orlov treats Zinaida Ernestovna rather shabbily.'

'Why? What does he do to her?'

'It's not what he *does* that's the problem, but what he *doesn't* do.' She put her gloves on.

'Zinaida Ernestovna deserves better.'

As Ivan drove them home through the city, they passed ragged groups of wounded soldiers smoking on street corners – some on crutches, some with a limb missing, others blind. Outside several shops were queues of women, empty baskets over their arms.

As the car turned into the Morsakaya there was a loud bang. Alyosha thought it was the car backfiring but then the front window shattered into a thousand pieces. His mother screamed piercingly in his ear and clutched his arm, and Ivan Kirilich pressed down hard on the accelerator so the motor-car lurched forward, heading towards three tall Cossacks on horseback, who galloped narrowly past them in pursuit of some miscreants.

Alyosha felt the sting of the cold on his face as his mother's unremitting screaming assaulted his ears. He noticed for the first time how bald Ivan had become when his hat was whipped from his head. There were spots of blood on Alyosha's white trousers where his mother's nails had broken the skin on his wrist.

The minute they were safely indoors, Inessa rushed to the study to telephone Fyodor, who returned immediately from the factory. He stumbled through the drifts of snow to the motor-car and Ivan showed him the hole in the leather. The bullet was nestled there still, its tip hard like a boil under his finger.

Fyodor spent the rest of the evening placing telephone calls, distracted with worry and brooding about the future.

7

After that, Inessa was reluctant to leave the house. She stopped playing the piano and was almost permanently supine, complaining of her aching head more than ever from the gloom of her bedroom.

When Ella heard of the incident she locked her dry hands together in prayer to thank the Almighty for having guided her so well when she forbade Larissa from attending the fashion show. Providence was on her side, that much was clear – though for how long, she wasn't sure.

Ella decided that she and her daughters should show their support for the war in a more public-spirited and practical way.

'What do you mean by "practical?"' Margarita asked.

From that day on the two sisters no longer shared any more lessons with Alyosha. Instead, every morning they put on their nurses' uniforms and followed their mother to the dark wards of Saint Mary Magdalen Hospital to care for the wounded soldiers. Baroness Wrangel had organised a rota of gentlewomen to help the nurses.

'I hate it,' Margarita complained at the end of their first day. 'I hate the smell of the place, and the blood… I can't bear to see all that blood.'

'Then hate must be your master, because go you will,' her mother told her.

'Mama, I'm begging you – it makes me feel sick.'

Her mother interrupted her.

'What are your inconsequential worries and small discomforts compared with the pain and suffering of those hundreds of brave soldiers lying in the wards?'

Larissa was far quicker to adjust to the new regime: she found the smell of iodoform quite tolerable, and had no objection to caring for the young men in their pyjamas, with their closely shaved heads and deep, dark eyes. She soon became accustomed to the intensity of their gaze. Most of them lay lifeless on their beds; very few were well enough to sit up, though there were always a couple bent over a game of draughts near the window. One solitary patient shuffled up and down the length of the ward in his silent slippers all day long.

'Nurse!' a full-lipped young man called out. 'Can't you turn me onto my other side? I haven't been turned in hours.'

He was too heavy for her to turn him on her own.

'Margarita?'

She knocked on the door of the small office at the top of the ward where her sister spent as much time as she could, hidden away with a book.

'What is it now?'

'I'm not strong enough to turn one of the patients on my own. Will you give me a hand?'

No sooner had they struggled to turn the full-lipped boy than there was another request from the patient in the opposite bed.

'Nurse? I'm burning up with fever. And my mouth is so dry. Could I have some water?'

Larissa fetched him some water and placed a thermometer in his armpit.

'I've been sick again, nurse,' whispered the man in the next bed apologetically. 'They keep telling me I have to eat, but I can't seem to keep anything down. Back it all comes, even water.'

'Don't believe a word of it, nurse – he's as strong as an ox.'

Then another voice from the far corner: 'Ruslan wants to ask you something nurse, only he's too shy.'

Larissa, observed by the other patients now, crossed the ward.

'So what does he want to ask me?'

'Will you marry him?'

'You don't want to listen to him – he's only pulling your leg.'

'Of course I'll marry him.'

'Will you really?'

'Isn't she a darling?'

'Fair play to the little nurse.'

'I'll marry you all!'

Laughter rippled through the ward.

Late that night as they were undressing for bed, Larissa said to Margarita, 'I wouldn't mind being a proper nurse one day.'

Margarita longed only for lessons, and the next day, as they were getting ready to leave for the hospital, she asked her mother when she might return to her books.

'They'll always be there for you…'

'That's not what I mean, Mama.'

'… to accompany you on your journey through life.'

Ella placed her nurse's cap carefully on her head.

'You and your sister have had quite enough formal education already. Tie this ribbon under my chin would you, child?'

'I can't learn on my own.'

'Your father insisted on you joining your cousin for lessons. If I'd had my way… but there you are, I would never go against your father's wishes. A man must be master of his own house, or where would we be?'

Margarita couldn't tie the bow quickly enough, so strongly did her mother's breath smell of garlic.

That afternoon Ella caught her reading in the little office again. She snatched the book away, furious.

'What in the world are you doing lazing in here?' she said. 'It's a disgrace, when there's so much work to be done.'

Margarita wondered if Larissa might have complained to their mother, but her little sister swore she hadn't said a word. As a punishment, Ella arranged that Margarita spend the rest of that day helping in the operating theatre.

The room was small and stuffy, and the window boarded up. Hanging from the wooden beam was a cast-iron chandelier which provided the only light. The first patient to be brought in and placed on the operating table was a young Tartar, who was due to have his right leg amputated. Before the saw had even touched the putrid flesh however, Margarita was sprawled on the floor in a faint.

She began to suffer from dreadful nightmares. She'd wake with a start at the dead of night, her body dripping with sweat, feeling exhausted because she had been running and running and running from ward to ward, and no matter how far she ran there would always be a pool of blood at her heels, growing ever deeper and wider so she had to keep running and running, and whenever she stopped to catch her breath the blood would be following her. So she'd run again, up the stairs this time to try and get away, but the blood would simply rise up, step by step, almost touching her heels, until she locked herself in a room and felt safe for a while until the blood reappeared, pouring in under the door, so she had to stand on a chair, but the blood was quickly rising, so she had no choice but to climb out of the window, but the window was too narrow and, try as she might to squeeze through the opening she couldn't pull herself free and the blood was rising higher and higher…

8

'Arrested? How?'

The piano teacher Valeriya Markovna was in such a state, and so out of breath, that she could hardly manage to string two words together. She stood there, quite unable to speak for a while, pulling at the sleeves of her light grey frock in a desperate effort to collect herself.

She had spluttered Fyodor Mikhailovich's name when she had first rushed over to the house, but as he was not home, Oxana had taken her to Inessa instead.

When she eventually regained her power of speech, Valeriya Markovna recounted how she and Herr Professor K.K. (or Karl, as she shyly referred to him a few times) had arranged to meet for a light lunch in the Français Albert, a restaurant just a stone's throw from the Politzeiski Bridge on the Nevskii. (Inessa had known for months of their little romance, and thought it rather comical that the two clearly thought their affair was a well-kept secret.)

Karl had arrived well before her. In fact, he was so early, he decided to have a game of billiards in the games room, towards the back of the building. She was a little late leaving her last lesson and so annoyed to have her way obstructed by a small crowd listening to a man outside the restaurant. He had climbed up onto a wall and was ranting and raving about the war, punching his fist in the air to emphasise what he was saying. Valeriya Markovna didn't pretend to know much about politics, but she knew enough to realise that he must be a Bolshevik.

Whether the rowdy crowd at his feet were supporting him or attacking him she had no idea, as she squeezed past and hurried into the restaurant without stopping. Unfortunately the tables in the middle of the room were all taken by the time she arrived and so they were shown to a table by the window, facing the crowd, but she and Karl did their best to ignore the rabble and continue their conversation.

Once they'd ordered, Karl began to tell her about his latest researches into the Orthodox Church. But their food had not even arrived when, out on the street, who should come towards them but Aisha, the former maid, arm-in-arm with a broad-chested sailor, and the way the pair of them were stumbling over each other's feet, it was all too clear that they were in a state of inebriation. When the girl spotted them, she yelled,'Oi!'. She came right up to the window and started rapping on it with her knuckles. With a disdainful twitch of his lips that clearly indicated they should ignore her until she went away, Karl raised his fork to his mouth. Aisha only knocked all the more aggressively. Because of the thickness of the glass and the noise from the rabble, it was impossible to make out exactly what the girl was saying; but she turned to say something to her sailor, who then glared threateningly at them, pressing his great nose up against the window.

His hair had been cropped so short it was possible to see the blue veins under his skin. His face was squashed up against the window as he glared at them. The sweat from his upper lip smeared against the glass as he hissed, 'German bastard', while Aisha was by now banging her fists against the window with all her might and shouting that Karl was the Kaiser's spy and calling him by the foulest names Valeriya Markovna had ever heard, and many others that she had not. Blushing deeply, she told Inessa that she distinctly remembered the sailor shouting, 'You and your kind murdered my brother, you miserable Kraut!'

By now he was bellowing. Valeriya Markovna wanted to leave at once but Karl said they shouldn't succumb to such tactics and continued eating his food calmly. After all, he told her, he had done nothing wrong. But by now the couple's drunken howling had attracted some of the crowd, and they too started to beat against the window. The entire restaurant had stopped eating and were looking on askance, and a few of the diners were already making to leave.

'There's a fucking bastard German in there! Oi lads, I'm telling you, there's a Kraut spy eating in there!'

A middle-aged lady in mourning black satin quietly crossed towards them from her table in the far corner. Every eye in the room watched her progress between the tables, like a summer river meandering through a meadow, until she reached theirs.

Karl raised his eyes to hers.

'Madam?'

A second passed.

'Can I help you?'

She slowly lifted the sugar bowl and sedately tipped its contents over his wiry red hair. The mob outside went wild, whistling and cheering and out-doing each other with shouted insults. The Maitre d' hurried towards them and begged them with some urgency to leave his restaurant at once by the back entrance. Two anxious-looking waitresses were already standing at the coat-check with their coats and scarves held ready.

Someone lobbed a saucer, and Herr Professor ducked just in time. The saucer crashed against the window and fell with a clatter at Valeriya Markovna's feet.

'Fucking Berlin bastard!'

'He's a spy!'

'He should be arrested!'

'How can he sit there stuffing himself when my boy is dead in the ground, slaughtered by his countrymen at Tannenburg! It's not right!'

Next to her ear, what must have been fifty men and women were battering the outside of the window with their fists, while within, the whole room seemed to be panting and straining like a bull in a heat-haze.

When Valeriya Markovna finally came to the end of her account, she was completely drained, while Inessa was too stunned to respond for a few seconds, as she tried to digest what she had just been told. Eventually she stood and rang the electric bell, and when Oxana appeared, she told her to telephone her husband and summon him home immediately. By now Valeriya Markovna was sitting with her head in her hands, sobbing uncontrollably but silently. Inessa, never one to dispense sympathy with ease, patted her shoulder awkwardly and murmured, 'Now, now, everything will be alright, you'll see.'

Oxana returned, to say that Fyodor had gone to the Imperial Yacht Club for lunch and nobody knew when he would be back. Hearing this, Valeriya Markovna sobbed afresh and implored Inessa, 'Sombody has to do something to save Karl, before they tear him limb from limb.They'll kill him, I know they will. They will kill him!'

Ivan was duly despatched to the Imperial Yacht Club, with a scribbled note from Inessa telling him what had happened, and on reading it Fyodor immediately excused himself and made a telephone call to an old friend. Michael Maktuyev was fairly high up in the Home Office, and although Fyodor knew him well, he was none too sure whether he would help him on this occasion. On the one hand, he was a highly intelligent and cultured man, but he was also something of a cynic and would always put his own interests first, nevcr being one to raise his head above the parapet. However, in his quiet, distinguished voice, he told Fyodor soothingly that he would certainly look into the matter and telephone him back.

'Would you be kind enough to telephone me at home?'

Michael Maktuyev promised to do so, and a mere quarter of an hour after Fyodor had arrived back at the house, the telephone rang. It was not Michael Maktuyev however, but an apologetic civil servant informing Fyodor that the tutor from Detmold had been formally charged on three counts: 'Undermining public order', 'Passing military secrets to Berlin', and, finally, 'Slandering Tzar Nicholas II'.

Fyodor laughed his dry laugh.

'I regret to inform you, that is the situation… that is the situation unfortunately,' the voice repeated faintly before trailing off with something Fyodor didn't catch.

'Why didn't Michael phone me himself? Why this spinelessness?'

'Prince Maktuyev was called to Tzarskoye Selo to see the Tzarina.'

'Oh, I'm sure he was.'

Suddenly Fyodor recognised the voice on the other end of the line: Kukushkin, his brother-in-law's friend. Of course, he remembered Artyom telling him that he was a civil servant.

Kukushkin, in a clear attempt to bring the call to an end, asked, 'Is there anything else I might assist you with?'

'Yes. Tell Michael I know full well he's sitting next to you now listening to every word. I'm surprised at him, of everyone. You too. What happened to honour?'

He placed the mouthpiece carefully back on its stand. As he gathered his thoughts for a moment, he saw that Alyosha was standing at the door, presumably having heard the whole call. Unwilling to appear weak and ineffectual in front of his own son, he picked up the telephone and asked to be connected to the Ministry once more.

'I insist on speaking directly to the Minister,' he blustered, threatening to submit a formal complaint if he wasn't put through immediately.

After speaking to the Minister for some ten minutes, he was assured that this matter would be given his earliest attention.

9

Mid-morning the following day, Herr Professor K.K. returned to the house with a small bruise on his temple and a swollen lip. He looked a broken man, and could hardly say a word about his ordeal, though everyone treated him with great kindness and sympathy.

'The condition of my release,' he told Fyodor and Inessa, 'is that I have exactly twenty-four hours to leave Russia.'

'And if you don't?'

'I'll be re-arrested, and sent to the prisoner of war camp in Omsk.'

Inessa shivered at the thought of being sent to such a place, hundreds and hundreds of miles away from Petrograd, on the other side of the Urals.

'We mustn't let that happen,' said Fyodor, and assured him he would do everything possible to facilitate the professor's journey. He told Oxana to put herself at the tutor's disposal to help him with his packing. Herr Professor K.K.'s greatest worry was that his exile would make it impossible for him to finish his book on the history of the Orthodox Church. He needed to live in Russia to have access to the sources. He was more distressed about this than anything else.

'All those hours of labour that I spent sweating over it will be for nothing now.'

That night as the family sat down to supper with him for the last time, they were all rather melancholy, even the children. (Inessa had invited Margarita, Larissa and Ella over so they could make their farewells.)

When the meal had been cleared away, Herr Professor K.K. got to his feet, took a sheet of paper from his pocket, and carefully unfolded it. He began by thanking the family for their welcome and for entrusting him with the education of Alyosha, Margarita, and Larissa, which, he said, had been a privilege indeed.

'May I wish you three young people every success in your lives and…'

He paused for a moment to listen to some heavy gunfire, sounding at such a distance like a low, persistent cough. The window panes shivered briefly.

'Let us hope that Petrograd's fate will not be the same as that of the Rome of Marius and Sulla.'

Fyodor felt in very low spirits, and racked his brain for a suitable response to the tutor's speech. Alyosha on the other hand, while looking properly subdued, had realised that, although he felt sorry for his tutor, in his heart he was quite looking forward to seeing the back of him and his wretched cane.

His father roused himself sufficiently to make a graceful speech of thanks for Herr Professor K.K.'s commitment and devotion to his duties, and rued the times in which they lived, when the likes of Aisha and Oleg could destroy the reputation of a good man. That riff-raff, such as they, had deprived his son of the benefit of such a fine educator, was a disgrace and a tragedy,

'For where will I find your equal while this war rages?' he asked.

Fyodor could no longer hold back, and went on to excoriate Rasputin and the Duma's spineless ministers for letting matters degenerate to this sorry state of affairs.

Alyosha was forced to get up the next day to see his tutor off. As dawn broke, Herr Professor K.K. stepped onto the first train bound for Finland. His plan was to break his journey at Helsingsfors, before travelling to Sweden to catch a boat from Stockholm to Hamburg. Unwilling to burden the poor man with more worries, Fyodor Alexandrov said nothing to this, but in his heart, he thought the tutor's sojourn in Stockholm might be considerably longer than planned, as crossing the Baltic Sea was a highly perilous undertaking, and not to be undertaken lightly.

Fyodor and Alyosha were not the only ones making their farewells. Valeriya Markovna stood on the platform too – and Alyosha was quite taken aback at the passion with which Herr Professor K.K. kissed the back of her hand, before snapping upright and clicking his heels in the Prussian manner. The door slammed shut behind him and, although he took a window seat, he didn't look at one of them as the train finally pulled out of the station.

10

Fyodor had an unpleasant experience on the way to his factory, but kept it to himself and warned Ivan to keep quiet too, for he didn't want Inessa to be alarmed any more than she already was.

Outside a bakery on Gogolya Street an untidy queue had formed – women with their small children and babies mostly, though there were a few men too. They were waiting to be served, but the queue was long, and a restless straggle had spilled over into the road, forcing Ivan to slow the motor-car almost to a halt. They were driving with the top down, because Fyodor preferred it that way, even when the weather turned cold, enjoying the chance for some fresh air before he arrived at the factory. It usually had to be raining or snowing or really cold, before he would instruct Ivan to put the top on.

Fyodor had his head buried in a thick wad of paperwork containing rows and rows of figures relating to the previous six months' sales, and projected figures for the next six months, predicated on the raw materials reaching the factory in the first place. The government were demanding an estimate of how many shells and bullets he could supply to meet the unending demand from the front.

As Ivan tried to inch the car forward through the crowd, Fyodor lifted his head and looked around him. Everywhere he looked he saw thin, haggard faces, large eyes staring dully, ragged clothes and woefully inadequately shoes.

Many of the faces had turned towards him. He noticed a tall, sallow man whose eyes had sunk into the swamp of his face gazing evenly ahead out of two hungry eyes. He was barefoot and his hands were clenched under his armpits against the cold. At his side was a woman whose face was so swollen her eyes had been squeezed into narrow slits. She wore what looked like a nightdress, tied tightly with a cord, and a straw hat on her head. Her lips moved continuously, though whether she was talking to herself or to someone else, Fyodor couldn't tell. Hatless and shivering at her shoulder was a short, hairy man with a simian face, deep blue eyes and a purple snub of a nose, banging his red-knuckled fists together rhythmically.

As Fyodor surveyed this miserable spectacle he wondered angrily what was being done to rectify the situation. He felt a cold fury grow as he considered these people's plight. The government was very much to blame, there was no doubt about it. It was unreasonable in the extreme to expect people to queue for hours at a time, every day, half-freezing to death, just for a loaf of bread to fill their empty bellies. It was a disgrace, an absolute disgrace.

And these were the people who were whispering amongst themselves that the Tzarina was in cahoots with the Kaiser. These people had long since lost any respect they might have had for the Tzar himself, and had even less respect for the shopkeepers and merchants who they believed were becoming fat on the back of their misery. The people, in short, were fast reaching the end of their tether, and were leaving the city in their hundreds, returning to their villages where they thought there was a better chance of feeding their families. He knew this from his many discussions with the managers at the factory, who were worried that production would have to be slowed down, or even halted, if the exodus continued, for sheer lack of manpower. But who could blame them for leaving?

He felt his head become suddenly naked. Somebody must have crept up behind him and swiped his bowler hat. He saw it briefly spinning against the sky before being caught by someone nearer the front of the queue. It was flung up again and this time several arms stretched up to try and catch it. People started to enjoy the game and there was much laughter and shouting as the hat was hurled up and caught time and again. Fyodor half-rose in his seat but fell back sharply as Ivan saw his chance and, accelerating smartly, drove swiftly on.

As Fyodor turned to look back over his shoulder, he saw a small boy stamping his hat into the mud.

11

Two policemen knocked on the door.

'What do they want?' asked Fyodor from behind his desk.

'A word with you.'

'You'd better show them in,' he replied. Which Oxana did.

Fyodor stood to greet them.

'What can I do for you?'

'Our apologies for disturbing…'

'Take a seat, won't you?' Fyodor gestured.

'We'd rather stand.'

'As you choose.'

'We won't be long.'

The shorter one seemed to be the spokesman, though the taller one concurred with everything he said, half-mouthing the other's words.

'The streets are getting more dangerous every day.'

'That's true enough.'

'And even worse at night. More murder. More rape. More theft.'

They quickly got to the point and made their request, and Fyodor was equally swift to agree to it.

When Inessa was told however, she turned to her son and asked, 'Has your father finally taken leave of his senses?'

She almost stamped her foot.

'Does he really want to make us an easy target for every deserting soldier with a grudge tramping around the city just looking for trouble?'

Fyodor tried his best to reason with her but in the end Inessa became almost hysterical.

'Do I have to remind you, I already know how it feels to be shot at,' she shouted.

Her husband begged her to calm herself.

'Alyosha and I. This much closer–'

She narrowed the space between her finger and thumb.

' – and he or I would be dead. Dead in the ground. Do you hear me? Dead in the ground!'

'Which seems to me even more of a reason to do our bit to help keep law and order.'

'Not on *this* roof!'

'But don't you think that…?'

'Not on this roof, I said!'

She was immoveable.

'And don't dare say another word, or I shall lose my temper.'

Fyodor didn't dare say another word, but she lost her temper anyway.

'To put a policeman with a gun on the roof tomorrow morning? What if someone started firing at him? What about Gosha? And Alyosha? What about me? Do you have to insist that you always know what's best when it's quite clear that you don't?'

She would brook no further discussion and stormed off, and so Fyodor found himself having to talk to a very irate policeman the next day.

'Well, there you are, if you won't help us, how can you expect us to be able to help you?'

He placed the mouthpiece back on its hook. He noticed that his fingernails were rather long. They needed clipping. How had he neglected to notice? He pushed his finger into his ear and felt the wiry hair sprouting there. That needed a good trim as well.

He rang the bell and ordered a whisky. Before he even heard

Oxana's soft footfall, her light knocking on the study door, he had already imagined himself draining it in one.

He didn't. He merely sipped it.

As he rolled the glass between his hands, he listened to the familiar sounds of the city. But if he strained, he could also hear the crack of distant gunfire: tac-tac, tac-tac, tac-tac.

12

In February 1917, an unexpected visitor returned from the front. Kozma Mikhailovich Alexandrov called on his brother and sister-in-law on his way to see Prince Maktuyev and several other ministers, on the orders of no one less than the Tzar himself, from his military headquarters in Mogilev.

'My orders are to bring to an end, with all possible expedition, the growing civil unrest in Petrograd,' he explained.

His brother noticed that Kozma had lost weight; his cheeks were hollow and his eyes seemed to have sunk deep into his skull.

'While we wage war against the Kaiser what happens? Riff-raff turn to rioting on our streets. Where is the respect for our soldiers' sacrifice? Does nobody have a sense of honour anymore?'

'More wine?' Inessa suggested.

'Not for me, thank you.'

'Quite sure?'

'Yes. I need a clear head for what lies in store.'

Earlier that afternoon Kozma had been driven in a motor-car along the Nevskii where he drowned in a sea of grey: soldiers in their greatcoats, unemployed workers, servants, maids and drunks of all shapes and sizes. He was repulsed by the state of the streets: the shells of spat-out sunflower seeds, the horse dung that nobody had bothered to clear away, the air of dilapidation and neglect. The front wheel of the motor-car went into a crater in the road, which sent him flying against the door, causing him to wince with pain from the wound in his shoulder where he had been shot some two months previously.

'I couldn't believe the rubbish that was being sold. Tobacco, red ribbons, obscene postcards, beer, cakes, biscuits, and, as far as I could see, anything else people were willing to buy.'

'They're like cattle let loose without the farmer and his stick,' said Inessa, 'trampling and soiling wherever they go, without the slightest concern for anything or anybody.'

Wistfully, Kozma asked, 'Where did those sturdy men in their blue shirts go, who used to brush the streets clean every day? And the flower-sellers with their bunches of snowdrops? Do you remember?'

'Of course we remember.'

'I can smell those little girls now. They always used to drown themselves with some cheap *eau de cologne*.'

'And their filthy fingers,' shuddered Inessa. 'I never bought anything from them in my life.'

Fyodor told his brother about the gunfire and the rioting, the looting of the shops and how the slush-filled streets could swell with a clamouring mob from one moment to the next.

'And what of the factory, Fyodor? How long d'you see the strike lasting?'

'As things are now, I'm living from day to day.'

'People with nothing to do are always looking for trouble,' said Inessa.

'The strike has to be broken.'

'That's easier said than done.'

'There has to be a way.'

'How? I can't offer them better wages. Not with the cost of my raw materials spiralling.'

'I have twenty-five thousand soldiers at my disposal here in Petrograd.'

'And you think these twenty-five thousand solders can use brute force to get them back to work? Besides, what if they refuse the order to shoot? Or worse still, actually make common cause with the workers? These are husbands and brothers and sons to women who are starving, after all. You'd do well not to forget that.'

'We're at war! Everybody has to take his share of suffering and sacrifice.'

Kozma scratched his yellow nail against the white tablecloth.

'And without bullets, Fyodor, my soldiers are being slaughtered like sheep.'

'I realise that. But as I say, I know the mood of the workers. I even have some sympathy for them.'

Inessa fumed at her husband's idiocy, over her *pâté de fois gras*.

'I've no wish to disrespect our Tzar,' Kozma Fyodor said. 'Or you, or any of our brave officers who have fought so courageously and tirelessly for Mother Russia. But the people are heartily sick and tired of this war. There is no food. There is no hope. That's why they feel they have nothing more to lose and have taken to the streets.'

'Alyosha and I were very nearly killed by some hothead,' Inessa told her brother-in-law.

'Yes, I know. Ella told me all about it in one of her letters. I've had to put a stop to these hospital visits she and the girls were undertaking. It's far too dangerous.'

'You're quite right,' said Inessa, 'I've had to tell Alyosha he mustn't go near any of the front windows of the house.'

Even if Alyosha couldn't see them, he could hear the people out on the street shouting for bread. Over the days and weeks the gatherings of tens and then hundreds grew to thousands, as more and more workplaces and factories shut their gates. The workers of the Obuhkov Plant came out on strike, followed by the shipbuilders from the Neva shipyards, the French factory and dozens of others. All along the Nevskii Prospekt the words of the *Marseillaise* could be heard on the damp air, sung by the thousands who marched along it under a forest of red banners proclaiming, 'Peace and Bread.'

Kozma sent daily bulletins to the Tzar at his headquarters in Mogilev. The message was the same each time: the situation was deteriorating. Gunfire in the streets was commonplace. Anarchy was on the loose. Discipline amongst the soldiers was fraying and in danger of unravelling completely.

One evening he walked the streets dressed as a worker in order to fully acquaint himself with the extent of the discontent. He found himself in Viborg, and descended some steps into a beer cellar. There he found desperately poor men hunched over their glasses, listening to others who were distributing pamphlets and exhorting them to act, rise up, and revolt. Kozma listened as they told him that the imperialists had flung the world into the crucible of war in 1914. That the entire bourgeoisie had waged a holy crusade for world markets and the victory of capitalism and how the cowardly Social Democrats of Europe had allowed it to happen.

'Why should the sons of the working classes be sacrificed on the altar of money? Why is it always their blood being spilled to keep the rich in luxury?'

Such unworthy, unpatriotic gibberish made Kozma feel sick. Their outlook was so superficial, so simplistically black and white. He left and, finding the nearest church, knelt down and prayed to the Almighty to give him the strength to do his duty by his Tzar and his mother country. Gradually he felt the warmth of that mystic communion seep through him. He felt renewed and replenished with the thrill of supernatural conviction deep inside him – he could almost feel the hand of Jesus upon his shoulder – and he resolved to take up the cudgels once more to try and re-establish law and order in the city of Petrograd.

With the stench of pain and confusion from the streets oozing from his uniform, Kozma Mikhailovich walked into his brother's study late one night at the end of March.

'It's all over.'

'What do you mean, it's all over?' Fyodor asked.

'Exactly what I said.'

'How? Kozma, you're not making any sense.'

'The Tzar is going to abdicate.'

'When?'

'Tomorrow. Tomorrow morning.'

He yawned with exhaustion.

'That's what everybody's saying, anyway.'

Fyodor was incredulous.

'But who would replace him?'

'They're talking about his brother, but they say it's quite likely that Grand Duke Michael will refuse to take on such responsiblity. And who can blame him?'

Fyodor was finding it difficult to digest this information.

'This is not what I would have expected of Tzar Nicholas. Are you sure this will come to pass? What happened to honour, to duty and faith?'

Kozma was slumped in an armchair, his weary legs stretched in front of him and his arms hanging limply over the sides. He didn't respond and Fyodor asked, bewildered, 'The Tzar to abdicate? After over three centuries of Romanov rule?'

On the streets the singing and roaring and wild shooting into the air had begun. The Tauride Palace was overrun by hordes of soldiers and workers. The imperial double-headed eagles were ripped from the façades of official buildings. The festivities continued all day and late into the night.

Every last soldier, with the exception of some half-dozen Tartars from the Petroplavlosk regiment, went over to the people. The news spread that the entire garrison at Tzareko Selo – the regiment responsible for the Imperial family's protection – had refused to shoot at the people, and that the Romanoff family had been arrested and put under lock and key.

Three days later, towards the end of the afternoon when it had begun to darken outside, Fyodor called Inessa and Alyosha to the study to tell them that Russia had a new government and that Prince Lvov was its Prime Minister.

'What *exactly* does that mean?' Inessa asked.

'I've just been offered a position of the highest honour,' her husband answered gravely.

13

Artyom was on business in Lisbon when he heard of the growing unrest in Russia. Sitting outside a café on the Rua de Barros Queirós, he leafed through the newspapers, reading in *Le Monde* of Tzar Nicholas II giving up his throne after three centuries of divine rule. Putting all the reports together, it did not bode well. He sat there, warmed by the sun, worrying about what was happening to his mother country.

Prince Lvov was the new Prime Minister and Prince Sergei Urusov was Home Secretary. The paper named various others who had been conferred with a ministry or promoted to high office, including Alexander Kerenskii. Among them, Artyom was hugely surprised to come across the name of his brother-in-law. Fyodor had accepted the post of adviser to Minister Konovalov, who was in charge of Industry and Commerce.

The *Le Monde* editorial gave a very tepid welcome to Russia's new Provisional Government. Its verdict was that it was simply an undemocratic rehash of the old Duma clique. Who had elected these men? Not the people. *Le Monde's* great fear was that Prince Lvov's government would pull Russia out of the war against Germany, thus liberating the German troops from defending the Eastern front and allowing them to hurl themselves against the weary armies of France and Britain.

Artyom brought his business in the Praca de Don Pedro IV to a speedy resolution and caught the train to Barcelona. There, he made his way to the offices of a company called Impex, where he was welcomed by a man by the name of Pablo whom Artyom had only met once previously. Pablo was Impex's chief accountant. It was he who paid him.

'Everything just as it should be?' he asked as Artyom counted the money.

'Neat as a pin.'

Pablo smiled. Artyom placed the dollars into a specially designed compartment at the bottom of his suitcase (which had been made to his exact specifications by a man he came to know when he began shooting clay pigeons on the Plateau d'Issy). He then checked into the Hotel Motrico for two nights, where he was warmly greeted by the receptionist who remembered his generous tips from his previous stay.

Alondra joined him on the terrace of the Café de l'Opera. He rose to greet her but she gave him a resounding slap across his cheek.

'Why on earth did you do that?'

'Because you deserve it.'

Artyom looked as insouciant as a man can look with a scarlet imprint of a small hand on his face.

'And there was I expecting a kiss.'

Alondra sat down.

'So I take it you haven't forgiven me for not keeping our appointment in Bilbao last year?'

'Forgiven you! When you left me kicking my heels, waiting for you in that hotel by the harbour? How do you think I felt, all on my own? Do you know how much trouble it took me to find an excuse to go to Bilbao in the first place?'

'Things became a little complicated for me.'

'I daresay.'

'I was forced to change my plans at the last minute. But darling, I did send you a telegram.'

'Oh yes, and a telegram is a fine thing to keep a woman warm at night. You're just impossible, Artyom. I don't know why I even bother with you, I really don't.'

'You bother with me, my angel, because I give you something your husband never could.'

Alondra smiled. Her hair and eyes were black as a February night. Artyom leaned towards her.

'How about that kiss?'

Alondra pouted and turned away slightly.

'Do I have to beg?'

Artyom slid his hand up her skirt under the table. Alondra giggled.

'Why don't we go back to the hotel?' he whispered in her ear.

When he got back to Paris, a letter was waiting for him. It was a long account from his sister of all that had taken place at home. He read parts of it out to Jeanette when they were lying in bed. He paused over the paragraph where Inessa told him of the shooting incident on the way home from the fashion show, which had almost killed her.

'Petrograd sounds like an awfully dangerous place to me,' said Jeanette, stretching across Artyom to stub out her cigarette in the ashtray on the bedside table.

'Things are not good.' He was worried.

He got up.

'Where are you going?'

'To piss.'

Artyom was more shaken than he cared to show by his sister's letter, which conveyed the enormity of the March revolution to him in a way no newspaper report had succeeded in doing. Inessa had also mentioned Fyodor's new post in Prince Lvov's Provisional Government, and how he was working harder than ever, with many responsibilites, and how much she worried about the future, for herself and her sons.

'If it wasn't that I have business in Paris that will keep me here until mid-May, I'd go there,' he said to Jeanette when he came back to the bedroom.

'You'd be mad to go.'

'I feel an obligation.'

'To do what?'

'To help my family.'

'Be careful my darling – you're in danger of developing a conscience, and then where would you be?'

Artyom mustered a smile but he didn't like Jeanette making fun of him.

'Anyway, what would be the point? Your brother-in-law is a member of the Government. What could you do that he can't? Are you getting dressed?'

'I have a meeting.'

He made his way to the Brasserie Balzar on the rue des Écoles. He ordered a coffee and sat outside, watching the world go by. A shadow fell across his face, then the sun reappeared as the man sat down opposite him, taking off his soft hat and placing it on the table.

'Francisco.'

'Artyom.'

They shared the briefest of handshakes.

Francisco Farr was an American, or at least that's how he introduced himself when they had first met a year previously.

'I'm from Indiana originally, though I was raised in New Mexico,' he'd said.

They had arranged to meet in the Orangerie in the Place de la Concorde. Degas was exhibiting there at the time.

'I hear you know something of the art world yourself,' said Fransisco.

'I bought a Picasso for my brother-in-law once.'

'He's too modern for me.'

'He's too modern for my brother-in-law.'

After looking at the exhibition that day they took a motor-taxi to La Coupole in Montparnasse. When Farr excused himself to go to the lavatory, Artyom quickly rifled through his jacket pockets. Francisco Farr might be the name on his passport, but the cheque book belonged to one James Long. Well, as far as Artyom was concerned, one name was as good as another. Not much point trying to guess which, if either, was his real name (the truth tended to wash up eventually, like jetsam on the beach). One thing Artyom did know for sure, Francisco Farr worked for the Mannesmann brothers. And they were dangerous people.

'I heard you've been in Portugal?'

'Did you indeed? And where did you hear that?'

Before Farr had to respond, a short man even shorter of breath arrived at their table.

'I'm so sorry I'm late,' he wheezed.

Farr motioned to a chair.

'Sit there in the sun and get your breath back, Albert.'

The man's surname was Bartels.

'So what's the situation in Russia by now?' asked Farr.

Artyom answered that he had received a letter from his sister only that morning, but it had taken a few weeks to reach him.

'At least Lvov has kept the country in the war,' Bartels said, after taking a large puff from his asthma pump. 'He stuck to his word on that.'

'Yes, but for how long?' asked Artyom. 'This man Lenin seems to be promising people all sorts of things. Peace, land and bread for all. He knows how to make the Bolsheviks very popular.'

'Clever,' Farr nodded.

'But there are cleverer men than him in Russia,' said Artyom.

The sun had disappeared behind the clouds, so they decided to leave the terrace and eat inside the brasserie. They finally got down to business over cigars and brandy.

Francisco Farr explained to Albert Bartels that Artyom was the Western European representative for a large armaments factory in Petrograd – one of the largest in Russia.

'And would I be speaking out of turn if I tell our friend here that you're happy to sell to whoever's buying?'

'I have sold to everybody, it's true. Berlin was our biggest market until war broke out in 1914. But since then, all Fyodor Mikhailovich's armaments have gone straight to the Russian army – which is only right. But even if we wanted to sell to the French Government, avoiding the German blockade would be very difficult.'

'If you haven't sold any arms in Europe for Fyodor Mikhailovich since 1914,' asked Albert Bartels, 'how have you made a living, if you don't mind my asking?'

'I've had to adapt. Silly not to. Over the years I've made many connections.'

'So Mr Farr tells me.'

Albert Bartels scrutinised Artyom, wheezing gently.

'Artyom knows who's who and what's what,' added Francisco Farr. 'He knows the worth of a gun. He knows how to make things easy for people to get their hands on the things other people say they can't have.'

'So how exactly can I help you, Monsieur Bartels?' asked Artyom.

Monsieur Bartels had a friend in need. His name was Abd-el-Malek and he lived in Morocco. Albert Bartels had lived in Morocco for some time and had learned Arabic, a beautiful language indeed. The country too.

'Extraordinarily beautiful. Have you been there?'

'Not yet,' Artyom answered.

'But like many of the world's poor countries it is under the yoke of foreigners. In Morocco's case the French and the Spanish have carved it up between them. They haven't done much for the country – more harm than good in fact. My friend Abd-el-Malek, like any patriot worth his salt, would like to remedy this situation and would like to see his country rid of every last Frenchman and Spaniard.'

'What exactly are your friend's needs?' asked Artyom.

'Whatever it's possible to export from southern Spain, from Seville or Cadiz or even Malaga. We could arrange to take shipments either in Tetouan or Melilla. I'm sure that I can rely on your utmost discretion.'

'That goes without saying.'

'The usual terms?' Francisco Farr inquired.

'I'm afraid not,' Artyom answered. 'Given the difficulty of the enterprise, I shall have to ask for an extra five per cent commission on this: fifteen per cent in all.'

'That won't be a problem,' Albert Bartels said, without hesitation. 'How soon can you move on this?'

'The moment I return from Petrograd.'

SUMMER 1917

1

Artyom took the train from Paris to Calais and, in spite of the blockade, sailed to Dover. More trains to London and Newcastle, and then another boat, this time under escort, to Stockholm. From Sweden he crossed the gulf to Finland, on a ferry to Abo, then took a train from Abo to Helsingfors.

Finally, he caught a train from there to Russia, reaching his destination at ten o'clock one morning, the entire journey having taken him two-and-a-half weeks.

It was June when he arrived in Petrograd, and the sun was sparkling on the canals and city gardens, though the grey walls of many buildings were still pockmarked after the fighting of the spring.

After spending the day with his parents, Artyom made his way that night to the Plikin, where he met his friends. Kukushkin was already drinking heavily.

'On the outside things don't look too bad, but on the inside everybody's frightened... frightened of what might happen next,' he said. 'Frightened that the Kaiser might reach Petrograd, because Prince Lvov would rather carry on fighting than risk offending France and Britain. But the soldiers are deserting in their thousands.'

'So I understood.'

'There are two governments in Russia today,' opined Perarskii. 'Since the revolution in March, the Soldiers and Workers' Committees have grown in influence. Soviets they call themselves. There's not a day goes past without them making this demand or that. The way they carry on, you'd swear they were in charge of running the country. But no country can have two governments.'

'So what will happen?'

Kukushkin held up both his hands and then dropped them in a gesture of despair.

'At the moment it's hard to say. That's exactly what creates all this uncertainty. On the one hand Lenin and his lot have plenty of Soviets in the army, the navy and the factories, so they could use them to demand more power for the left, but there are those to the right of Prince Lvov who are just as determined to win. And guess who'll be caught smack in the middle! Poor fools like us.'

'So what does Orlov make of it all?'

'Orlov?' Kukushkin laughed, 'He has more than enough problems at home, without having to worry about Russia as well.'

The next day Artyom dined with his sister and Alyosha. The Parisian smiled at his nephew and pinched his cheek, examining him with his head to one side.

'I do believe you've grown again! Whatever does your mother give you for breakfast? You must be very nearly as tall as your father now, eh?'

'Come and sit down,' Inessa gestured.

'He's growing up fast.'

'Yes, I suppose he is.'

'You'll be a man in no time. Where will you go to college, Alyosha? To Zurich like your father?'

'I don't know yet, Uncle Artyom.'

Inessa sat as her chair was moved closer to the table.

'Thank you, Oxana. There are other things to worry about before that.'

'University is not for everyone of course,' Artyom laughed. 'Just look at me!'

'You could have gone if you'd wanted to. You certainly didn't lack the ability; you had more than enough of that. Mama and Papa always said so.'

'But of what use would Schopenhauer, Kant or Nietzsche have been to me? What have all those dead ideas got to do with real life? Mmmm? I think I've done rather better by not going near the place at all. I don't think I've missed out on anything, anyway. But that's just me, of course.'

Artyom looked at Alyosha and his face became serious for an instant.

'It's difficult to know what you want to do with your life when you're young. It's difficult when you're older, come to that.'

He took a sip of white wine, and was laughing again as he put the glass down.

'Anybody can change, can't they? Change a lot too. How can we be happy? In my opinion, when a man has come to know himself, and knows what he wants out of life… well, that's the closest to happiness you'll be… perhaps. What do you say, Inessa?'

'I say eat your food before it gets cold.'

'So where is Fyodor? Won't he be dining with us tonight?'

Pouring himself some water, Alyosha replied, 'That would be a miracle.'

2

Between his advisory post in the Government and his work in the factory, Fyodor had very little time for anything else. He'd return to the house very late each night, either from the factory or the Ministry for Trade and Industry, accompanied by two young detectives who were assigned to protect him. The pair had quickly become a fixture amongst the family, and the shorter, fatter one flirted shamelessly with Mademoiselle Babin at every opportunity.

Although Inessa had protested furiously at the idea of giving them board and lodging to begin with, she had been forced to accept that her house was as much fortress as home. She even became used to the revolvers in their leather holsters, which the two men were never without. And every day, before they left the house, she got used to seeing them take out their flat Crimean caps from their pockets and shake out the creases, before placing them on their heads, pulling them low over their ears.

Better locks were fitted to the doors and windows. Twenty-four hours a day the front entrance was guarded by two soldiers, loyal to the Provisional Government, who checked every visitor's credentials carefully before allowing them into the house. It was also deemed necessary to arm the chauffeur, so every time Ivan left the house, he would have a gun strapped over his shoulder, and a wide brown cartridge belt around his middle. This made him feel more important than ever and he liked nothing better than keeping the soldiers company, or sharing a glass of vodka with one or other of the detectives at the kitchen table.

Although Artyom didn't show it, he was shocked to see how much weight his sister had lost, and saddened that her eyes and hair had lost all of their sparkle and shine. The house looked unkempt too: there were fine layers of dust everywhere, where previously every surface had been polished to burnished perfection.

He had to wait up until almost two o'clock in the morning to see his brother-in-law. Fyodor looked exhausted, but welcomed Artyom warmly, and agreed at once when he asked if he could have a word with him. Ushering him into his study, he asked his detective to bring glasses, armagnac and coffee from the kitchen.

'I know you have many demands on your time Fyodor, but I'm truly worried about my sister. She's not herself. She's lost so much weight and she tells me she's not sleeping. I think the strain of living like this is beginning to tell on her very badly. She hates even the sight of a gun, you know.'

'I'm afraid there's nothing I can do about the situation.'

'I realise that, of course. But look, I'm going back to Paris before the end of the month. I've got business to attend to there.'

'Well I'm delighted that you're managing to make a living. But remember, as I've said many times, once this war comes to an end, things will be much easier and we'll be able to re-establish our markets in Europe.'

Artyom ignored this.

'I really think perhaps Inessa should come back with me,' he said. 'I've already suggested it to her and she refused. But I thought maybe you could persuade her? So many have left Petrograd already. I think it's a good idea. I'd be willing to take Alyosha and Georgik as well, of course. What do you think?'

Fyodor coughed into his handkerchief but said nothing. The silence grew.

'What is it? Is there something I need to know?'

'Your sister is in mourning.'

Artyom quickly ran through family and friends in his head, but could think of nobody. He racked his brains in case there was somebody who had eluded him, but no name came to mind.

'Forgive me, but who is she mourning?'

'The man who has been killed.'

'A relation?'

'The man she loves.'

Fyodor told him about Mita Golitzin. Artyom gazed at him, nonplussed. It was impossible to fathom his brother-in-law's feelings. In the end he stammered,

'So how, er, how exactly was he killed?'

'By his own soldiers, in the Carpathian Mountains. They'd swallowed the Bolshevik propaganda, were sick and tired of fighting, and were desperate to get home to their families. He tried to stop them deserting. Which was very heroic of him, or very foolish, I leave it to you to decide.'

Fyodor paused, then said, 'There comes a moment in a relationship sometimes, where something dies, doesn't it?'

'Yes.'

'The trouble is, my moments are hours.'

Artyom had no response to this, but before he left he tentatively asked, 'So where does this leave you and Inessa?'

'You could say we've been separated in all but name for some time now.'

'Will you divorce her?'

'Never.'

3

Inessa complained bitterly to her brother about the loss of her maids. Where did nearly every one of them go in the end? Out to protest on the streets, marching and shouting under those silly red banners, making a spectacle of themselves.

'Nobody actually *wants* to work any more, Artyom. That's the plain truth of it. These people have begun to think that they can live like lords without having to lift a finger. You remember that Aisha that used to work here, Alyosha?'

'Yes of course, Mama.'

He blushed in spite of himself.

'Well, there's a perfect example for you of what I mean.'

'You can't be expected to manage without your maids, Inessa; it's just not right,' her brother said. 'Don't bother Fyodor with it. He has quite enough on his plate as it is. You leave it to me – I'll find you someone, don't you worry.'

Artyom was as good as his word. Under all the joshing, Alyosha had come to see that his uncle was a highly practical and effective man, and somebody you would be glad to see on your side in crisis.

The new girl, Lika was a shy and quiet creature, and Inessa insisted that Oxana comb her hair thoroughly in the garden, to check her for headlice, which might be carrying typhus. Oxana combed through every last strand, and assured her mistress there was not a single nit to be found. Inessa still needed convincing, such was her terror that Georgik's health might be imperilled by some disease the girl might be carrying, so in the end she ordered the girl to strip so that she could be thoroughly examined by their doctor for any traces of illness or infection. He declared that apart from being underweight and undernourished, Lika was sound as a bell.

Artyom tried one last time, before he left Petrograd, to persuade his sister to return with him to Paris.

'Why won't you? It would do you so much good.'

She shook her head.

'Just for a while, until things are more settled here. We could even take a little trip to the Riviera if you like. Georgik would love it. Don't you remember Mama and Papa taking us to Nice one summer? Building sandcastles and eating ices?'

'There's no sand in Nice – only pebbles.'

'Cannes, then? We must have been in Cannes. I remember us sailing out in the bay and getting caught in a summer storm. And I started to cry and you told me not to be such a big baby. And when we finally reached terra firma again, Papa confessed that he'd felt like crying too, do you remember?'

He smiled at her.

'You caught the sun, I remember – look, you still have a few freckles on your arms even now. Me too… Inessa, what's the matter?'

'Nothing.'

'I can tell there's something the matter.'

'Oh don't say anymore, Tyoma, I beg you! Not another word. I can't bear it.'

'Inessa, I do sympathise with you… for your loss.'

He squeezed her wrist.

'Thank you, Tyoma.'

They hugged for a long time.

It was July by the time he left. As he gazed out of the window for a last look at Petrograd, Artyom tried to fathom what he had achieved by coming, but he was none the wiser. He had a deep feeling of foreboding, as though he had just said farewell to his family for the last time in his life. But then he gave himself a little shake and told himself not to be so ridiculous.

In the lobby of the Grand Hotel in Stockholm he read the latest news from Russia, in the *Svenska Dagbladet*, and realised he had left Russia on the very day the Bolsheviks had tried to take power. Their attempt had ended in failure: many of them had fled for their lives from Petrograd, while dozens were imprisoned, Trotskii amongst them.

4

Late one afternoon in August 1917, some stinking lump of a miscreant hurled himself at Anna Timurovna Riumininski as she was about to enter her house after visiting with a sickly neighbour nearby. When the old lady felt ragged nails clawing at the nape of her neck, and an arm around her middle wrenching her back violently, lifting her off her feet, she began to scream with all her might.

She inhaled the rancid smell of his hand as he clamped it over her mouth and nose, until she felt she was about to suffocate. Til, their ancient doorman, flung the front door open and shuffled over to his mistress – who was on the ground by now – as fast as his creaky hips would allow, but luckily his shout of terror sent the oaf lumbering off. He helped his mistress to her feet and into the house. Her injuries were mercifully only cuts and bruising to her legs and a sprained wrist from her fall. Her husband insisted on bathing her wounds himself, and then applied arnica to the bruises.

There hadn't been a policeman out on the streets since the last one had been shot in the back of the head in full daylight some three days previously. The attack did nothing to improve the health or the spirits of either of them: they had already been feeling very out of sorts since Artyom had left. Anna Timurovna suffered from arteriosclerosis and Vasillii Karlovich had always had a weak chest, and now his bones were creaking with age and worry. Their days were already lived in mortal fear, and every night they locked every last window and door against intruders.

Now they were truly terrified, and their daughter reluctantly saw they could no longer live on their own. She suggested they come and stay under Fyodor's roof for their own protection, at least until things settled down.

It took no time before her mother was trying Inessa's patience sorely, and though she tried to reassure and comfort her mother, the old lady did nothing but complain and find fault.

'It's all very well for you to talk like that, Inessa…'

'But you feel safe enough now that you're living with us?'

'Feeling safe, indeed…'

'Well, safer than you did in your own home, anyway. Two soldiers always guarding the front door…'

'Everything is so confusing. Why did Prince Lvov resign?'

'According to what Fyodor said, he had very little choice.'

'But why?'

'Why? Why? Why? How should I know?'

'Well, who is this man Kerenskii who's been appointed Prime Minister instead of Prince Lvov? Is he going to be any better? What is he doing in order to bring things back to how they were, I'd like to know.'

'His very best, I'm sure.'

'His very best, indeed.'

'I really don't think this is getting us anywhere.'

'How can I ever feel safe again?'

'Oh Mama, please, that's quite enough! Nobody will touch you here; you're perfectly safe. There are soldiers outside, and two detectives under our roof every night. Really, what more do you want?'

The two women bickered so badly that there was no peace to be had, and in the end it became impossible – as always – for them to live in the same house. Anna and Vasillii returned home, becoming virtual prisoners inside their own four walls as they were too terrified to venture outside.

Vasillii, long since disheartened by recent events, felt in his bones that the times were utterly doomed, and saw daily indications that things were going from bad to worse. As the months had gone by, he had gradually lost all hope that the previous regime might be restored; once his beloved Tzar and his family were taken prisoner he believed there was no going back. From his infancy, Vasillii had been taught to accord the Tzar and Mother Russia the same respect and reverence that he gave to the Good Lord and his son Jesus Christ. It was exactly the same fight for God Almighty and the true faith as it was for the Tzar, his family and the very soul of Russia.

Who had dared imprison the Tzar? To chain him up like a dog? Just thinking about such a thing was a daily torment and outrage for Vasillii.

'How has such a thing come to pass?' he would ask anybody who was willing to listen. 'Who could ever glory in such a vile act but atheists, savages and Jews?'

5

Who could save Russia? One evening at the beginning of August, Kozma called on his brother and invited him to sail down the Neva with him, to Volni Island and back. As Fyodor followed his brother down the stone steps of the quay to the wooden jetty he noticed an unhealthy reddish shine on the skin of his face, and the gooseflesh of his neck. He seemed sombre and morose. He told Fyodor that one hardly had to be a prophet to realise what was happening. The resignation of Prince Lvov and appointment of Alexander Kerenskii in his place had not saved the situation. As the army rank and file had lost all faith in their officers, so had the officers in their turn begun to lose faith in the Prime Minister and his cabinet.

Kozma was the first to admit that things were far from easy for the new Prime Minister, but his great weakness was to try and stay friends with everybody: in his effort not to offend anybody, he succeeded in pleasing nobody.

The days for sitting on the fence were quickly coming to an end. Every time Kozma looked one of his soldiers in the eye the only thing he saw was contempt. Since the March revolution, the authority of the army had been undermined, and consequently that of the government itself. Were the army to disintegrate, it would only be a matter of time before the government disintegrated in its wake. History had taught them that much. Why would Russia's experience be any different from every other country's?

With a tight little smile, Kozma said, 'This is between us, brother to brother?'

He went on to say that while some were still prepared to stay loyal to Kerenskii's government, he and many of his fellow officers wanted to see a radical change.

'Radical?'

'And quickly.'

'How radical?'

'Look, don't misunderstand me, Fyodor. I don't blame you for your loyalty to Kerenskii, Savinkov, Chernov and their ilk. But you have to admit that their supporters are becoming thin on the ground and before long the Prime Minister will be like that little island over there, lonely and utterly isolated.'

'And so…?'

'There are those willing to step forward and do what needs to be done, before it's too late. Kerenskii can stay where he is, just as long as he is prepared to sign up to a new government which can better protect the future interests of Russia.'

Fyodor looked at him closely.

'Here's a question you need to answer honestly: is Kerenskii serious about offering the country a secure leadership? Can he win the war against the Kaiser? Or is he only after power for his own ends? Most importantly, can he put a stop to the constant clamour from the trade unions? The strikes? The never-ending street protests? Dealing with the riff-raff intent on stealing the lands of the great estates for themselves? And what about the communist committees of soldiers and sailors' deputies, who challenge all central authority? And what about stamping out Bolshevik propaganda in the army? What is their sole aim? To see holy Russia die so that some appalling socialist republic can live? If we don't step into the breach now, history will condemn us.'

He gripped his brother's knee.

'I know that very many men in the army think change is long overdue, change for the better. Fyodor, can you in all conscience continue to give your blessing to a feeble government which is damaging Russia's true interests?'

'So are you suggesting that I resign? Is that what you've been trying to tell me tonight?'

Kozma told his brother that General Kornilov intended to attack Petrograd and arrest Alexander Kerenskii and his cabinet. The plans had already been drawn up. But Kornilov was a soldier through and through, with no political skills. Once Kerenskii and his ministers were under lock and key, the next step would be to create a new government, and Kozma was proposing his brother as the country's new Prime Minister.

'I truly believe you are the man to lead Russia today.'

6

Fyodor paid a visit to Andrei Petrovich at his office at the Azor-Don Merchant Bank. His old friend was sorely disappointed when he heard the purpose of his visit. He spoke plainly.

'I won't hold back, Fyodor Mikhailovich. Forgive me, but if one of the highest officials in Kerenskii's Provisional Government lacks faith that his property is absolutely safe in a Russian bank, what possible chance do I have to persuade anybody else?'

'These troubled times make us all more cautious about money. I'm no exception,' Fyodor replied.

'Confidence in a bank is a very sensitive thing,' said Andrei. 'If a life in banking has told me one thing, it's that. The slightest change in the political weather is felt in the financial world almost instantly. It will react quicker than anything, to tell the truth.'

Of course, Andrei had no choice but to accede to Fyodor's request. He gave the order for his money, his bonds and his share certificates to be transferred with all due expedition to a branch of the Crédit Lyonnais in the Nevskii Arcade.

With the business over and done with, cigars were brought out. As the two men smoked, they discussed the fragility and instability of the political situation.

'Russia desperately needs a strong man in charge,' said Andrei Petrovich.

'Nobody with any sense would disagree with that,' answered Fyodor, thinking of his brother's extraordinary offer.

'Ever since March I feel that Russia – the old Russia that you and I and so many others know and love so dearly – is vanishing all around us. My muse has left me. I've barely written a line. With all due respect, Fyodor Mikhailovich, I know you're close to the heart of Mr Kerenskii's government but he seems to be throwing us to the lions: those in Berlin and those closer to home – the Bolsheviks. In all honesty, I'd be hard pressed to say which one is worse, Lenin or the Kaiser. Come to that, there are plenty who are convinced that Lenin is the Kaiser's man in any event. It's the eleventh hour and if somebody doesn't intervene soon, all hell will be upon us.'

Fyodor had yet to give his brother an answer. He was in an agony of indecision and had almost confided in Inessa one evening, but held back. He realised that becoming Prime Minister of Russia would change her world as well as his. Alyosha's and Gosha's too. The whole family would be affected. Could he really see himself as the leader of the country? The idea of it made his head spin.

His brother and his cabal of plotters had no doubts about his suitability: they were practically unanimous according to Kozma. But the weight of such a responsibility, the enormous burden of having to make decisions, and act for the greater good, without thought of personal gain or advantage: that would take sacrifice and courage. He knew his Classics, knew that courageous men could leave their stamp on the world behind them. True courage could transform the lives of men, for better or worse.

Was he man enough for the task?

Kozma was pressing him for an answer. There was no more time for prevarication.

Was he man enough to do what needed to be done, to save Russia?

OCTOBER 1917

1

As Alyosha and Mademoiselle Babin were leaving the schoolroom after the morning's lessons, they saw Fyodor ushering his brother and two other men into his study. Kozma Alexandrov half-turned, and Mademoiselle Babin opened her mouth slightly as if about to say something, but he frowned and raised his finger to silence her.

The study door closed. Mademoiselle Babin hurried off towards her room, but Alyosha stole over and put his ear to the heavy wood. The low murmuring of male voices was too muffled to understand but, intrigued, he decided to run to the dining room and open the second door to the study, which was hidden behind heavy curtains on both sides.

He succeeded in opening the well-oiled door an inch or two without discovery. He could hear his father pouring and then handing round some drinks, and then the conversation resumed. A gentleman by the name of Kornilov did most of the talking. Alyosha listened with astonishment to him declaring that the only answer now was to kill Alexander Kerenskii, along with every other Jew in power.

His father disagreed.

'That would add fuel to the fire.'

But Kornilov was adamant that Kerenskii had to go.

'There's not a man in the army staff with a shred of respect left for him.'

Kozma backed him up.

'The only way to save Russia is to stage a *coup d'état* without further ado.'

Kornilov was to orchestrate it, and Fyodor would be the new head of state.

'I don't want to see any more bloodshed,' Fyodor argued. 'There's been enough of that already. Surely there must be a better way.'

They continued to argue, though to Alyosha's mind they seemed to go round in circles. They were interrupted a couple of times when Ivan brought in some messages that needed Fyodor's immediate attention. Eventually, they agreed that they needed to convince Kerenskii that he only had two viable options: to resign immediately, or to work with General Kornilov, and in due course, with Fyodor Mikhailovich and a cabinet of his choosing. Failure to comply with either of these would lead to a third outcome: his arrest.

There was a long silence. Then Alyosha heard his father say that he would present him with their ultimatum at once.

After making his farewells, Kornilov said, 'Give him twenty-four hours to answer, not a minute more.'

The moment his visitors had left, Fyodor Alexandrov strode across the study, flung open the door, and yanked Alyosha from his hiding-place by the scruff of his neck. He had known he was there the whole time but could do nothing about it. Alyosha had never seen his father so angry.

'What possessed you to do such a thing?'

He had absolutely no right to poke his nose into important matters like this – matters far too complex for him to have any hope of being able to understand. Alyosha, stung by this, replied that he was perfectly able to grasp that his father and his companions were plotting against the government.

'Why would you want to do such a thing, Father?'

There was a long silence and then his father said earnestly, 'On pain of death, Alyosha, you must never breathe a word of what you heard today. Not one word. Do we understand each other?'

As soon as Mademoiselle Babin had Alyosha to herself, she tried to find out what he knew. He was torn between keeping his word to his father, and wanting to show Mademoiselle Babin how well-informed he was. He noticed a little pulsating vein in the Frenchwoman's neck and a certain wildness in her round, dark eyes. He suddenly felt uncomfortable and made an excuse to get away, but she gripped his arm tightly and insisted that he tell her all that he knew.

'I don't dare…'

'I'm so worried about your uncle…'

'I've promised not to say!'

She grasped his hand.

'I really can't!'

She gazed at him and for some reason he felt himself yield to her. The second the words were out of his mouth he regretted it, but before he could even beg her not to breathe a word to anyone, she had rushed out of the house.

With her head in a muddle and her emotions in disarray, the young Frenchwoman paused a moment, realising she didn't know where she was going. Why had he not told her? Didn't he trust her to keep a secret?

She found herself at his door. There was no telling if he was home, but she had no choice, and she knocked furiously.

Ella looked up from her sewing when the maid showed her in. Margarita and Larissa ran in to greet her. They all sat there, talking of this and that. Tea was offered.

Mademoiselle Babin felt that there was a noose around her neck and she had difficulty speaking, stuttering and tripping over her words, so much so that Ella asked her if she felt quite well. She suddenly made her decision, to face Ella honestly.

'Where is Kozma Mikhailovich?'

'Why do you ask?' asked Ella mildly, catching a weak reflection of her own face in the highly polished table.

'I must speak with him. Where might I find him?'

Ella placed her hand flat against her cheek, as though she was suffering from toothache. She closed her eyes and breathed the air deeply into her lungs, lifted her shoulders and then pushed them back, as if trying to stiffen a resolve that had softened and melted inside her.

Mademoiselle Babin's complexion was waxy pale, and her fingers played furiously with a little ribbon on her lap.

Ella opened her eyes in a moment and stared at her with hatred. In that long gaze, the two understood each other perfectly, and there was no more to be said.

Mademoiselle Babin left, closing the door carefully behind her.

2

Inessa had lost a ring: a very valuable diamond ring, and more importantly, one of great sentimental value as it had been her maternal grandmother's. Anna had given it to her daughter one Sunday evening, many years ago, after returning from church, when her daughter's engagement to Fyodor was about to be announced.

After looking through her jewellery box, she rummaged through her drawers, full to bursting with gloves, bits of lace, veils, satin slippers and countless bottles and pots of cosmetics and perfume. Then she went through her clothes, until the room looked as though it had been ransacked, but in vain.

'Lost? What do you mean, lost?'

'Lost means lost.'

Fyodor tutted impatiently.

'You've simply put it somewhere and forgotten where.'

'Are you trying to say I'm losing my mind?'

A search was ordered, from top to bottom, and even their two detectives were enlisted in the hunt. Every room was gone over with a fine tooth comb, turned inside-out and tipped upside-down, but to no avail.

'I can't understand it,' said Inessa hopelessly. 'I simply don't understand.'

'For heaven's sake, just try to calm down and think…'

'I have thought! I've done nothing but rack my brains since it went missing.'

The next day, Ivan appeared, bearing four pairs of silk

stockings, a pair of red leather gloves, two hats... and the diamond ring.

'Sir, look what I found.'

Fyodor called his wife at once.

'Where?'

'Under Lika's bed.'

The mistress looked sour.

'Good, Ivan. Very good.'

Fyodor squeezed his shoulder.

'You are a good and loyal servant.'

'The little thief had them hidden in an old sack. I've had my doubts about that one for some time.'

He smiled, showing his crooked little teeth.

'She didn't take me in with that little Miss Innocent act of hers.'

The chauffeur took the opportunity to boast.

'Sooner or later, I'm a man who gets to the bottom of everything.'

The young maid was called to account, but instead of admitting her crime and begging for forgiveness, Fyodor and Inessa were stunned by her hard-faced impudence and her insolent attitude, which was utterly lacking in shame. She actually started to answer them back, and even dared to curse them for paying her such a pitiful wage.

Had Fyodor's workload not been so heavy, and had he not had dozens more pressing matters to attend to, he would have brought the girl before her betters; but he didn't have the patience. Thinking she hadn't heard him the first time, or that she couldn't believe her luck, he repeated, 'That's all. You can pack your bags and leave.'

Lika simply stood there, staring at them levelly, and then casually took out a cigarette and lit it, blowing the smoke out of her nostrils.

'I'll leave when I'm ready.'

Inessa felt as though she were about to explode, and took a step towards the girl but Fyodor placed his hand upon her arm to restrain her as Lika continued talking.

'And you'd better not try to kick me out, or anybody else either. 'Cause I'll just go straight to my boyfriend, and you can have the pleasure of having it out with *him.*'

With the tip of her shoe, she rubbed the ash from her cigarette into the rug.

'And who is this *boyfriend*, if you'll allow me the liberty of asking?' spat Inessa.

Her girl's eyes sparkled.

'A Bolshevik from Kronstadt.'

Oh dear Lord, thought Fyodor, and so it begins.

The maid leaned her face to one side and looked belligerently at her employer.

'We should all be grateful to them. My friend was one of the thousands who put a stop to that General Kornilov.'

That much was true. Alexander Kerenskii had defied their ultimatum and so Kornilov attacked Petrograd in September 1917. Faced with such a threat, the Prime Minister had released Trotskii from prison and armed the Bolsheviks, who stopped the army in their tracks. The *coup d'état* had failed. Kornilov had been arrested and his officers had fled, Kozma amongst them. As far as Fyodor Mikhailovich was aware, nobody had yet betrayed his part in the plot, but he'd be the last one to underestimate the Bolsheviks. He certainly didn't need any attention from that quarter. Much as it went against the grain, he decided to pretend a magnanimity he was far from feeling and let the girl stay.

Ivan was outraged.

'You're making a big mistake, sir, if you don't mind me saying. Having a Bolshevik in the house is like letting a snake loose in the salon. That one won't rest until she's poisoned all the other maids with all that socialist claptrap.'

'Thank you for your advice, Ivan, but she's staying.'

'Shall I chuck her out for you? You've only to say the word and I will.'

'No. Lika is to stay here. For the time being, anyway.'

'You're quite sure of that, now?'

'Quite sure.'

'Well, then. You know your own business, I suppose. But I think it's a big mistake, myself.'

To add injury to insult as far as Inessa was concerned, Lika was allowed to keep her booty, apart from the diamond ring, which Inessa instructed Oxana to disinfect in a solution of ammonia and water.

'There's no knowing where that little slut has been. Especially if she's been consorting with those dirty Communists from Kronstadt.'

Anna was outraged when she heard what had happened. She thanked the Lord that all her treasures had long since been put under lock and key at the Crédit Lyonnais, safe from light fingers. Vasillii could scarcely credit it, and was profoundly disturbed and worried by such an outcome.

'Anarchy and murder at every turn. What is the world coming to?'

He lifted his glass and took two gulps of vodka, as he always did.

'This hoyden Lika is even worse than that grasping Polya from Anton Chekhov's story,' he scolded. 'She was a little thief too.'

As well as putting rouge on her cheeks, Lika had started painting her eyelids and lips. Every morning she'd persuade one of the other maids to lace her up in the pink corset that her lover from Kronstadt had brought her. The next time he came visiting, he fastened a charm-bracelet about her wrist. He'd probably stolen it from somewhere, but Lika didn't care a jot. She loved to shake her wrist gently so that the little charms chinked against each other on their gold chain.

Oxana observed the difference in her as she went about her work in the kitchen. Her posture was different: she seemed to have grown an inch or two because she didn't hunch her shoulders against the world anymore, and she walked with a spring in her step. She often had a half-smile on her face and hummed happily to herself, making no effort to be silent when she was above stairs.

The only advantage of this to Inessa was she could at least hear Lika approach a while before she appeared, what with the light jangling of her bracelet, and her cheery if tuneless songs.

3

By the end of September 1917 the Bolsheviks had won the majority of the seats on the Petrograd Soviet. Lenin's authority grew as Kerenskii's shrank. Under the slogans and the graffiti those who had hidden in the shadows came out into daylight.

It seemed every street corner had turned into a talking-shop as soldiers, sailors and students stood discussing and arguing amongst themselves.

Like so many giant hedgehogs, motor-lorries full of soldiers rumbled by, and in their wake marched gaunt yellow-faced men from Oranienbaum, pulling guns on small wheels behind them, like dogs on leads.

Feelings ran high, and often the arguments would turn into sudden scuffles, and then everybody would pile in, whacking, kicking and punching until they ran out of steam and slunk off to bathe their cuts or anoint their bruises.

Wherever Alyosha went there'd be a young man or woman thrusting a pamphlet or tract at him, printed on cheap paper with cheap ink, so that often the words were blurred and difficult to read, though there'd always be a reference somewhere to the 'bourgeoisie', usually writ large.

The future was pregnant with possibilities, but the quest for freedom was heady and time-consuming work. People barely had time even to sit down to eat – mealtimes became no more than a hurried re-fuelling before rushing off to the next meeting. Meanwhile, children ran wild in unruly gangs, celebrating the closure of all the schools and finding themselves at liberty to do just as they fancied.

Such was Petrograd by day. By night it was a very different matter.

With the street lamps lit only sporadically, from the darkness came the sounds of gunfire, dogs barking, the odd lorry revving in the distance. Alyosha would lie in his bed listening to the night. But what bothered him more than anything was the stink from the privy, which he could smell even with the door firmly shut. Fyodor thought the waste pipe must be blocked. Alyosha's bedroom was as cold as a cave, sucking all the warmth from his bones. He hardly ever saw his father, and his mother stayed in her room for hours every day.

The familiar ticking from the clock in the hall had long since ceased.

One morning Ivan did not appear.

'He's not in his room,' reported Oxana, who had been sent to look.

'Well, he must be in the house somewhere.'

'I've been looking.'

'Go and look again,' Fyodor said, rather irritably.

A little later she returned.

'Well?'

'The motor-car has vanished as well.'

In the end, only two servants remained: Oxana, from a deep sense of loyalty, and Lika, for reasons of her own.

Late one night, Alyosha heard his door open.

'Who's there?' he asked sleepily but then recognised his father's shadow.

'The Bolsheviks.'

'What about them?'

'They've attacked the Provisional Government.'

Alexander Kerenskii and the cabinet members who had not already been arrested fled the city at once.

The next day at breakfast, Alyosha asked his father, 'What's going to happen now?'

'As far as I'm concerned, I'm not going anywhere.'

'We can't possibly stay. They're sure to come for you,' said Inessa, looking pale and drawn. 'They're *bound* to come for you. How can you doubt it? And then what? What will happen to us? To Alyosha and Gosha? And what about me? We have no choice, Fyodor! We have to go away.'

'But where would we go?'

'I don't know. Somewhere safe. For the time being anyway, until order is restored. We could pack our things right now and just go, somewhere far away from Petrograd. Are you listening to me? What about that region around Ekaterinoslav, where we went on holiday that time? Nobody will find us there. Or we could go to Finland. Yes, let's go to Finland. We'd be safe there.'

He shook his head decisively.

'Why?'

'Nobody is going to chase me out of my own country.'

'But what other choice is there? Fyodor! We must run away or they'll kill us all!'

When the two detectives disappeared, Fyodor shut himself in his study and took up his pen to write to various state officials and politicians. He was quite clear in his mind that his duty lay in trying to do his utmost to vanquish this latest threat to Russian democracy.

Out of the blue, Kozma came to the house, in worker's clothes, with a cap on his head. Inessa opened the door to him.

'Quickly, let me in, before I'm seen.'

She bolted the door behind him.

'Is my brother here?'

'In his study.'

Since the failure of Kornilov's *coup d'état*, Kozma had gone underground, moving frequently and keeping to the shadows. His brother was overwhelmed to see him and embraced him warmly.

'Where are Ella and the girls?' he asked.

'Safe. But what about you? Why are you still here? I'm surprised they haven't come for you yet.'

'That's what I've been trying to tell him, Kozma,' cried Inessa, 'but he won't listen to me.'

'Only cowards run away,' answered her husband. 'Anyway, I'm convinced Lenin and his gibberish won't last long. Who's going to put up with a government which nationalises the banks and the factories? I know from experience that the working class can't run anything themselves.'

'I wouldn't be so sure,' answered Kozma. 'They're arresting and shooting everybody who opposes their new order. Many of the officers from the Tzar's old army are making for southern Russia. They intend to regroup in the Kuban and then they'll fight.'

'Why don't we go to the Kuban as well?' implored Inessa.

'We are not going anywhere,' Fyodor told her grimly.

'What about Mademoiselle Babin? Is she still with you?' asked Kozma.

Oxana was summoned and told to fetch her.

'I heard a rumour a couple of days ago that they were digging up the corpses in the cemeteries of the aristocracy.'

Inessa was aghast.

'But why?'

'In case there was any silver or gold buried with the dead.'

When Mademoiselle Babin entered the study and saw Kozma she couldn't contain herself and flung herself into his arms, holding his head in her hands.

'Where have you been?' she whispered into his ear. 'Where have you been all this time? I thought something awful had happened to you.'

'Why are you still here?' He held her away from himself a little so that he could look at her. 'Didn't you get my letter?'

'What letter?'

'You must leave Petrograd immediately. Go to the French Embassy. I'll take you there.'

'And what about you?'

'I have other plans.'

'I'm not going anywhere without you!'

'Clementine, listen to me.'

'I'm not going anywhere!'

Kozma cut through her remonstrations firmly, and told her to go and pack immediately. Mademoiselle Babin refused.

4

Alyosha slipped out of the house. Posters in the streets announced that all political power had been transferred to the Petrograd Soviet of Soldiers and Workers' Deputies. There'd already been gunfights between the Bolsheviks and those still loyal to the Provisional government. All the previous skirmishes seemed like child's play compared to what now went on daily on city streets and squares.

Alyosha saw a gang turn a yellow tram onto its side and a young girl with small, dark hands dragging barbed wire behind her; others were rolling barrels, stacking boxes, making little nests where they could shelter from the slaughter. Eight windows of a house were blown clean out when the artillery opened fire two streets away.

Screams followed an explosion, small stones ricocheting off the walls. The barricades were woefully inadequate, and the streets were dug up into trenches to provide shelter from the bullets; and when someone shot at the ancient old clock that stood above the Nevskii, time stopped.

Early one cold November evening a petrified Oxana went to her mistress.

'What should I tell them?'

People were thumping on the front door. Inessa went up to her husband's room, Alyosha on her tail. Standing in front of the mirror in his best clothes, Fyodor was slowly combing his hair, gazing deeply into his own eyes. The echo of the furious knocking against the wood filled the empty hall beneath.

Shaking, his wife said questioningly, 'Fyodor?'

He didn't hurry, but finished combing his hair and then adjusted his shirt collar a fraction. When he finally went down to open the door, there among the gang who had come to arrest him were Oleg, Oxana's brother, in his sailor's uniform, and Aisha, wearing a loose fur coat and hat, and carrying a rifle almost as big as herself, slung over her shoulder by a strap, the stock resting against her thigh.

Once Oleg had declared their purpose, and after everybody else who stood behind him had had their say too – all talking in urgent voices across each other – Fyodor courteously invited them to eat at his table. After some debate amongst themselves, they agreed that he should take them to the kitchen were they helped themselves to the best champagne, the bottles that Artyom had brought them from Paris a few years previously.

A cheery-faced young woman, her hair in braids, sat on his lap and threw her arm around his shoulders. She slowly licked his face with her black tongue. This had them all in stiches. She then lifted his hands and placed them on her breasts, telling him to have a good old squeeze, which had them in hysterics. After polishing off the champagne, they went to the cellar and worked through the '88, '91, '94 and '98 vintages, until they could barely stand or speak, though they could still sing, after a fashion, and raise their glasses in constant toasts.

'To the brave sailors of Kronstadt.'

'The brave sailors of Kronstadt.'

'To the revolution!'

'The revolution.'

'To the new Russia!'

'The new Russia.'

The kitchen was reduced to a pigsty. Between the cigarette ash and butts, and the constant spitting and pissing, the floor was filthy. They smashed the glass covering the portrait of the Tzar (which had hung above the mantelpiece longer than anybody could remember), and Oxana couldn't prevent herself from sobbing into her apron when Rodion took great pleasure in slowly burning his eyes into two holes. Through the blue-grey tobacco smoke and the coughing and the shouting, the whistling and the laughing, they held a competition to see who could draw the best caricature of Fyodor on the white walls.

After they'd all had a turn, they made the master of the house draw the funniest cartoon he could of himself, and then Oleg judged that they were all joint first, apart from the parrot, who came second and Fyodor who came third. Then they all staggered upstairs again and arrested Fyodor officially in the hall (they'd forgotten that they'd already done this once) and singing, and firing their guns as they went, the Cheka disappeared down the street, their pockets full of silverware and whatever else they could fit in them, and the parrot on Rodion's shoulder squawking, 'Fuck off, you cunt.'

5

Fyodor didn't come back and they heard nothing. The telephone stopped working. Though Anna and Vasillii sat for hours waiting for some news, they too heard nothing of their son-in-law's fate. The old couple tried their best to comfort their daughter, but Inessa was disconsolate. She could think of nothing but Fyodor, and felt guilty for her previous treatment of him.

A night went by, and then two, without any news. By the evening of the third day Inessa was almost beside herself with worry. Fyodor might be dead for all she knew. And yet she dared not stir outside the house, though even within the four walls she didn't feel much more secure.

To rub salt into the wound, Lika decided to move into Inessa's bedroom, the best in the house. When her mistress found her in there her outrage pulled her out of her misery for a moment.

'Get out!'

'Don't think I will, ta very much.'

'Get out of my room this instant!'

'Why don't *you* get out of *my* room,' and Lika gave her a little push and slammed the door in her face.

Inessa felt she had very little hope of getting rid of her. Every evening before she went out she'd spend an hour or more powdering her face, painting her lips and arranging her hair. She'd choose various gowns from her mistress's wardrobe, throwing the ones she'd rejected on the bed until there was a great heap of frocks and petticoats lying there.

Hours later she'd roll home, howling drunk, sometimes only

as dawn was breaking if it had been a big night. Quite often she'd drag some soldier or sailor with her – once even the portly policeman who used to patrol the street – and then the party would continue, their laughter and carousing filling the house. One night, Alyosha was woken by the sound of a gun being fired, and a chandelier shattering loudly.

Although Anna and Inessa worried that it was too dangerous, Vasillii decided he would try to find out where they had taken Fyodor, and Alyosha said that he would go too (in spite of his mother begging him not to).

They started with the old police stations, or at least those that were still standing, as many had been burned to the ground. But as soon as people understood that the man they were searching for had been taken away by the Cheka, nobody knew a thing, and their curiosity disappeared at once.

Next, Alyosha and his grandfather ventured to those places that were in the Bolsheviks' hands. After a long day spent tramping the streets fruitlessly, they passed by the Imperial Public Library. Between each iconic column that spanned the main entrance stood a guard, holding a brush or a truncheon by way of a weapon. Behind the grilles on the lower windows Alyosha saw frightened eyes peering out.

They wandered on. Plastered on the walls were posters explaining the new order, often with little knots of people reading them. The only shops left open were food shops – but many of the shelves were empty.

Outside the banks some stood listlessly while others banged on the doors, cursing or crying according to their temperament. The doors remained shut. Everywhere they went that afternoon they heard rumours and whispers, but it was impossible to know which held any truth.

Vasillii and Alyosha joined a queue of silent people patiently waiting their turn outside the oak doors of the University anatomy theatre to identify the bodies that had been shot the previous night. They waited there for over two hours, Vasillii talking to himself under his breath for much of that time, his eyes nailed to something on the horizon.

Finally it was their turn to inspect the rows of corpses, with their crusted wounds, their waxy feet, their yellowing stomachs, the hairs clotted with dried blood. They looked carefully at each one but Fyodor Alexandrov was not lying amongst the dead.

They returned home.

'What are we going to do?' asked Inessa. 'How will we ever find him?'

'We'll find him somehow,' answered her father, without having the first idea how.

'Why don't we ask Lika?' suggested Alyosha. 'She's always running around with the Bolsheviks.'

Inessa went to knock on her bedroom door.

'What's it worth if I tell you where he is?' asked Lika, a cigar in her mouth.

'Whatever you want.'

But it was Vasillii who found Fyodor, in the Smolni Convent. The Cheka had turned the cellars into a temporary prison.

He brought the news home with a heavy heart.

'What will happen?' Inessa asked.

'Because Fyodor Mikailovich supported Alexander Kerenskii's Government, he's been sentenced to death,' her father answered sadly.

'They'll shoot him?' asked Mademoiselle Babin in horror.

'So I understood.'

'They'll shoot him?' echoed Alyosha, as stunned as everybody else.

'So they said.'

Her eyes wide with shock, Inessa whispered, 'But… but there must be something we can do to save him… isn't there, Father?'

'Well, I suppose…' Vasillii's voice trailed away to nothing.

'What? What must we do?'

'Are we ready to throw ourselves on Lenin's mercy?'

1918 – 1921

1

After spending eight years in exile from his country, Stanislav Markovich Feldman left for Russia at the end of January 1918 not knowing what to expect, or what lay ahead of him. It was a long and arduous journey from Paris via Calais, London, Aberdeen, Bergen and Stockholm by boat and by train. He was forced to wait a few days in Stockholm until his visa was granted, then it was back on the train for the last leg of his journey. As it thundered northwards, weaving in and out of the many estuaries of the Gulf of Bothnia, Stanislav pondered what to do with the rest of his life. After all these years away, would the new Russia welcome him back and give him a fresh direction?

He reached Petrograd in the snow and ice of February. He jumped up onto the tram, squeezing in amongst a group of soldiers who filled the carriage. He turned his head away from the stink of the one standing next to him. In spite of the fact that he was suffering from a heavy cold, he was still assailed by the smell of sweat and cheap tobacco. Within a few minutes, the snow from their boots started to melt, soaking the wooden floor of the tram until their soles squelched in little puddles. He tried to read a newspaper over someone's shoulder, marvelling at the empty white columns where the censor had been at work. The tram slowed down, then stopped completely. After a few minutes, the soldiers became restless, and a few of them cursed loudly. Stanislav rubbed the condensation on the window with the palm of his hand and saw that there had been a collision between a *droskii-cab* and a motor-car. The motor-car's wheel was warped out of shape and there was a big dent in the fender. He couldn't see either of the drivers.

Eventually the tram jerked back to life and resumed its journey. It juddered past several partially-erected barricades – or were they partially-demolished? He could see evidence of recent fighting everywhere in the pockmarked walls, and noticed that all the banks were shut. Here and there, soldiers in red-peaked caps were checking people's documents. Stanislav felt uneasy, as he did not have a passport or a laissez-passer, and hoped his luck would hold and he wouldn't be questioned.

Even when the war had been at its height in the French trenches, there had always been food of some description for sale in the shops and markets of Paris; it was very different from what he could see through the shop-fronts of Petrograd. Although the city's buildings looked as solid as ever, the people's faces were drawn and pale. The bitter weather was of no help. He had forgotten how savage the winter could be, and regretted not bringing a thicker coat with him from France.

The shape of his future was shrouded in fog.

On the corner of Konno-Gvardeiski Boulevard he stepped down from the tram. He walked past a soldier who had lost an arm; he warming his remaining hand over a brazier while half-listening to a drunken women playing the accordion a yard or two away.

Stanislav disappeared into a dark courtyard, and climbed the stairs, which stank of cat's piss. He was a little breathless and dizzy by the time he reached the third floor. He knocked on the door, more nervous than he'd expected. From one of the higher floors a door opened, and he heard two young voices raised in anger. Then the door slammed shut and the voices faded.

When she opened the door she gasped. She wrapped her arms tightly around him, her head pressed against his chest. He could smell the coarse roots of her hair, earthy as a newly-kicked ants' nest. They held each other for a while, then he followed her into her tiny living room. He took in the back of her head, her nape and shoulders. He was glad to see she stood as straight-backed as ever, but he could tell from the way her woollen shawl hung from her narrow shoulders that she was thinner.

'When did you arrive?'

Katya shut the door behind them.

'Last night.'

She wiped away a tear and asked, 'So where did you stay?'

Stanislav named a mutual friend.

'D'you remember him?'

'Yes. Yes, of course I do. How he is these days?'

'Not bad.'

She hadn't even realised that this friend was back in Russia. Stanislav explained, as he put down his canvas bag and took off his gloves, that it was at the behest of Maxim Gorkii.

'Will tea do you?' She smiled wearily. 'I've no coffee.'

He smiled back.

'Just the thing.'

Katya busied herself with the samovar. Stanislav idly picked up a book that lay open, page down, on the table, but it came apart in his hands. She smiled as she watched him get down on all fours to pick up the loose pages and then try to put them back in the right order. It took him quite a while and by the time he was done he was rather flushed.

He caught her eye and snorted, 'Reading Nietzsche in the middle of the day?'

'I read whenever I get the opportunity. As you know… he doesn't like seeing me read.'

She said this with a quiet bitterness.

'You haven't changed a bit.'

Stanislav was gazing at her as he used to do. Katya placed his cup at his elbow.

Without catching his eye, she murmured, 'Nor have you, Slava.'

2

It had been a full five years since they last saw each other, when Katya had visited Stanislav in his little room on the Rue du Bac one evening to tell him that she had decided to marry someone else. Stanislav had been completely felled by her decision, and deeply hurt. For a long time he felt very bitter towards her. It was no secret that she was lusted after by a good many of Paris's other exiles – but she had chosen him. Everybody asked: what could a woman like Katya Schmit possibly see in some orangutan of a man like him? It made no sense; why, it went against nature. Was she blind (it certainly lent credence to the old saw that love *is* blind). They had made an incongruous pair, it was true: Stanislav Markovich Feldman, an eccentric bohemian, insisted on carrying an umbrella even in fine weather, wore sunglasses in the winter, and always kept his hair long. He never washed, rarely shaved, and always had a disreputable look about him. Then there was Katy, an exceptionally beautiful woman, her blue eyes and blonde hair proclaiming her extraction (her family came originally from a town near Estonia's southern border).

And then she left him, and for a man he had long since detested. In fact, Maxim Bogdanov was one of the few men Stanislav hated almost on sight. Stanislav had been honest enough with himself to recognise that he harboured jealous feelings – he couldn't deny it – for the simple reason that he was poor and Maxim was rich.

Poverty had been a heavy burden in Katya and Stanislav's relationship from the very beginning. It had poisoned their relationship. That, and his selfishness: in other words he wasn't ready to be 'tied down'. They had argued constantly, screaming and swearing at each other, usually in public places like the Café de la Paix, or in that cellar club on the Rue St. Bendodît, at their usual table under the picture of the bald woman with the moustache. Katya possessed a fiery nature, and even the wrong word or glance would, as quickly as the flick of a switch, provoke a furious rage.

They had decided to remain friends for the sake of their daughter, but they had lost touch since Katya returned to Russia with Maxim.

'Is Irina here?'

'No. She left for Nizhny Novgorod with my mother and sister a couple of weeks ago.'

For a second, Katya seemed to shrink a little.

'With things as they are, even getting up in the morning is a strain,' she sighed. 'Nobody can live properly… food is so scarce… you spend half your time queuing for a loaf of bread, and Maxim didn't feel it was safe for her to stay here with us.'

He had been looking forward to seeing his daughter, but it seemed it was not to be if she was hundreds of miles away, so he put her out of his mind. He asked Katya to tell him what had been happening in Petrograd, and learned that Alexanser Kerenskii and many of his cabinet, including Victor Chernov and Boris Savinkov, had managed to flee the city the previous October, and had probably escaped over the border. The rest were rotting in the Cheka's prisons. But only a few days ago, Maxim had been told (by a dependable source, so he said), that the Tzar had managed to escape from Tobol'sk and was busy assembling an army to attack Petrograd (just as General Kornilov had hoped to do), but the Communists were trying to keep this quiet for fear of causing more panic and unrest.

Stanislav told Katya that on the train from Finland he heard a rumour that General Denikin had escaped to South Russia to raise an army to fight both the Germans abroad and the Bolsheviks at home. But another traveller had told him that the leaders of all the other factions had been arrested, and that Moscow and Petrograd were under military rule. It was impossible to know who to believe. *Isvetza* and *Pravda* had been the only newspapers for sale in the railway station in Finland Station. And the only news they gave was about closing the courts, nationalising the great estates, and how all private property was to be put in the hands of tenants' committees.

Katya said she and her neighbours were of the opinion that the French, English, Germans and Americans were all taking advantage of the situation to buy up factories, land and Russian banks for next to nothing. All the Bolshevik rhetoric about putting things in the hands of the people was just one big swindle to strip the country of its wealth, and that in fact Lenin was operating on behalf of the foreign bourgeoisie – though claiming just the opposite. The whole thing was just so damnably devious and warped, and the endgame would be that the Russian Empire would be under the feet of foreign capitalists.

Gazing at the twilight outside as Katya moved around the room, lighting the lamps, Stanislav thought to himself that she hadn't changed a bit. In her heart, she was still a Menshevik.

'How long do you plan on staying in Petrograd?' she asked.

'Not long. After all these years in exile I think I should make for home.'

'What do you hope to do?'

He hesitated a moment then said, 'Find myself again.'

He smiled.

'Or find love.'

A few hours later he was on the train to Moscow.

3

Their troubles, as they struggled across Russia's vast expanses, didn't bring them closer together. On the contrary, it drove them apart, and though Alyosha did his best to be cheerful, he decided his governess was not the ideal travelling companion. She complained constantly: about the packed trains, the dirt, the smells, the lack of good food, the endless delays – in short, everything.

Alyosha agreed with her about the endless stops, at least. Sometimes they would be stranded for days. Worse was in store: more than half their luggage was stolen one night, while their train had stopped in a siding on the outskirts of Krasnodar, several hundred miles to the south of Moscow. Mademoiselle Babin was bereft. She loathed not having all her things about her – her clothes, her cosmetics and perfume, her bits of jewellery.

She began to smoke more and more heavily.

After one particularly uncomfortable night, when Mademoiselle Babin claimed not to have slept a wink, she turned on her young charge and told him viciously that it was all his fault that they were in this vile predicament. She was livid that she had ever been persuaded to leave Petrograd in the first place – that's where she should be, instead of wandering around these endless wastes with a useless young boy on her tail. It was insupportable. She should never have allowed Kozma Mikhailovich to talk her into it.

She finished her diatribe and fell into a reverie as she remembered that night. He had come to her room in Fyodor's house without warning. He hadn't even knocked on her door. She was changing for dinner, and was standing in front of her wardrobe mirror, half-naked, turning this way and that, looking over her shoulder at her bottom, standing on tip-toes to admire the length of her leg and the neatness of her feet in their pink slippers. She was only wearing her stays and her stockings, her shoulders and face un-powdered, though her hair had been carefully piled up and pinned. He entered the room so quietly that she only noticed he was there when she bent slightly to tie a garter on her stocking.

He had kissed her then with such passion. Squeezed her and felt her and stroked her like a man half-starved. He didn't even bother to undress properly, just ripped off his jacket impatiently, undid his flies and took her, his trousers around his ankles. Afterwards, lying on the bed with her, he'd said, 'It's not safe for you to stay in Petrograd.'

'I don't want to leave without you,' she had answered. 'I've made that perfectly clear often enough.'

'Why won't you go south? To the Crimea? Go to the dacha. You'll be safe there.'

'But what about you? Can't you come too?'

There was a pause.

'Will you answer me?'

'I'll follow you there as soon as I can.'

'Do you promise?'

He had kissed her forehead.

'Do you promise you'll join me there? Do you?'

'As soon as I can… but somehow, I must try and get my brother out of the hands of the Cheka first. It won't be easy, but I've been talking to Vasillii and I have an idea which I think might work. Well, we'll see. It's risky, but I live in hope. What else can we do in times like these?'

'Without her?'

She had cut across his train of thought.

'What?'

'Without Ella? When you come to the south after me? Will you come without her? Kozma, do you promise to divorce her and marry me?'

'I promise you that, Clementine. You have my word. That's one thing I'm determined to do. I promise to do that, if it's the last thing I do.'

The long journey from Petrograd to the Crimea was a nightmare. It should have taken three days, but in the end it took almost a month, thanks to the constant delays – especially after leaving Moscow. In a society where equality was the golden rule, there was a rumour that all the trains had to run at exactly the same speed. Every train was crammed with people and their luggage. Escaping from the Bolsheviks to southern Russia were politicians of every persuasion, civil servants, army officers in mufti, businessmen, policemen, aristocrats, landed gentry, poets, actors and actresses. They were all desperate to get away from the chaos of Petrograd. Some were aiming for the Don, others for the Kuban, and many for Terek.

The longest delays were between Tula and Kharkov, the railway stations along the route a packed muddle of humanity. The delays caused endless worry, with all sorts of rumours flying around. But the worst times were in the depths of night, when they were jolted out of an uneasy sleep by the train coming to a juddering stop with a squeal of the axle: the sound of uncertainty and fear. Shadowy figures, illuminated by swinging lamps, looming out of the gloom on the tracks: and then the dull clanking of doors being opened, and gruff voices ordering them to produce their documents. A few people would always be dragged off the train into the darkness – Jews, usually. They rarely returned, and eventually, after a long whistle, the pistons would start moving and they'd lumber onwards.

4

When they finally arrived at the dacha, they had to set to work airing the place and sweeping the cobwebs away. To their disappointment, there were no letters awaiting them from Petrograd. They soon discovered that news of any sort from that city was scarce; they were far likelier to hear about the goings-on in Moscow. Occasionally Mademoiselle Babin or Alyosha might find a copy of *Isvetza* in the village, but it would be invariably at least a week out of date, so the reports were already old news – though a constant theme concerned the efforts of the 'former people' to snatch back political power and restore their former privileges. On the front cover of an old copy of *Pravda*, Alyosha read of the necessity for the workers to fight the bourgeoisie, be they Russian, German, American, English or French. They needed to be defeated, wherever they were in the world.

Their only visitor was the one-legged gardener-cum-caretaker. Usually he'd appear towards late morning, slightly drunk, wobbling on his crutches as though he was about to teach Alyosha how to dance. Mademoiselle Babin found his habit of dribbling tobacco juice down his beard, which was stained yellow as a result, utterly revolting and could hardly bear to look at him as she pointed out all the little jobs that needed doing around the dacha and garden. He invariably promised to see to them but, however often she reminded him, very little was actually done. The pane of glass in the summerhouse remained cracked, the weeds continued to flourish, and the gate stayed off its hinges.

In desperation the young Frenchwoman found someone in the

village who promised to help. Nikolai Milynkov worked in the village bakery in some capacity or other, but his shift seemed to be over by midday, when he'd turn up at the dacha stinking of naphthalene.

He fixed the new pane of glass in no time, but when Mademoiselle Babin gave him a list of other tasks he insisted on Alyosha helping him. Alyosha quickly grew to loathe being in his company because Nikolai Milynkov was never happier that when quizzing him endlessly about Mademoiselle Babin.

The last thing Alyosha wanted to do was discuss his governess. Since leaving Petrograd at the insistence of his mother, his grandparents and his Uncle Kozma, he'd been feeling pretty low about everything. For the whole of the journey he'd been worrying about the family he'd left behind – his father most of all.

5

By the end of March, food was becoming very scarce and Mademoiselle Babin and Alyosha were living a hand-to-mouth existence. Although they had both grown to hate the sight of Nikolai Milynkov, they had to tolerate him because he rarely came to the dacha empty-handed.

He was an unpleasant character, who never did anything for anyone unless he thought he might profit from it. Worse still, he was a drunkard, and became garrulous when he was in his cups. Thanks to him, the whole neighbourhood soon knew that a defenceless young woman was living on her own with only a young boy for company.

Soon all sorts of unsavoury types began to call at the dacha under the flimsiest of pretexts. Mademoiselle Babin remained outwardly courteous, as many of them brought a few vegetables or a loaf or two of bread with them. It was another matter once they had left – usually only after much hinting that it was time for them to head for home – as then she would speak of them to Alyosha with the utmost contempt, before turning on him for good measure, cursing his family for ever persuading her to come to this godforsaken spot.

As the weeks of their exile dragged by, Mademoiselle Babin's fury with Alyosha only increased. They would go through periods of not uttering a word to each other, and it was always hard work then to break the ice. More often than not, Alyosha would be the one to attempt it, starting a conversation about something neutral – a little joke about how Herr Professor K.K.

used to oil his hair, for instance. It depended entirely on her humour how Mademoiselle Babin would react, but quite often she would continue her stony silence, with an expression on her face that could turn milk sour. If she did comment, it was quite often to belittle him and she would often leave him humiliated with her insistence that he was a child who knew nothing of the ways of the world.

Stung by this on one occasion, he blurted out, 'I knew all about the Herr Professor's affair with Valeriya Markovna before anybody else did, anyway.'

He went on to tell her, embellishing slightly, about the early morning scene on the platform at Finland Station, and claimed that his piano teacher and tutor had not only embraced passionately, but that she had tried to prevent him from getting on the train, hanging onto his arm and sobbing. He was taken aback when Mademoiselle Babin simply roared with laughter.

'What's so funny?'

Her teeth were yellow in the candlelight. Alyosha became even more irritated when she laughed again. Mademoiselle Babin leaned towards him, one elbow on the table, a glass of red wine held at an angle between thumb and forefinger. The cleft between her breasts was a dark little valley. For some reason she was whispering.

'The only reason that stupid oaf of a man paid any attention to the goose was to get closer to her brother.'

Her brother, thought Alyosha.

Yes, Valeriya Markovna had a brother, that was perfectly true. He had taught the violin to Larissa for a while until she persuaded her mother to let her stop. And his father had seen him perform at court once, before the Tzar himself. Mademoiselle Babin was staring at him with her black, round eyes. He felt her hand, soft and warm, squeezing his fingertips.

'Shall I tell you a story? A true story?'

'Yes, please.'

'As you know, I was born and raised in Angoulême, but I was never happy there because I longed to live in Paris. After pleading with my parents, I was eventually allowed to go and stay with my aunt, my father's sister. This was four years ago, in the summer of 1914. My aunt was very different from my mother, something of a *bonne vivante*. She and my uncle were considerably better off than my parents. They lived in a three-storey villa on the Avenue des Chalets. They had no children of their own and welcomed me as a daughter. They took me rowing on the lake in the Bois de Boulogne, and I saw horse racing for the first time, at Ateuil. My uncle even taught me how to place a bet. Your grandfather likes to gamble, doesn't he?'

'I think so.'

'One day my aunt took me to the Hôtel Ritz on the Place Vendôme. That was a real treat, I can tell you. We sat at a table for two in the tapestry salon. I can see that room in my mind's eye now. Two things happened that day. The Maitre d' stood and announced that war had been declared between France and Germany. And within the hour, I had been introduced to the man who was to turn my head completely. My first love. René Darduard. I have no shame in telling you, he was the first man I went to bed with. We'd arrange to meet in the afternoons. He had a flat on the Rue Cortot in Montmartre.

She smiled as she reminisced.

'I can see myself now, standing on the balcony one day after we'd made love, Paris before me wrapped in a blue mist, columns of white and grey smoke rising from the buildings. It had been raining too, a sudden shower, and that smell, a rich mixture of all sorts of things, filled my nostrils. René came to join me and wrapped his arms around me. I don't know how long we stood there on that balcony, gazing at the city. Children playing. Men at their work. Women chatting. The same as always, I suppose.'

She sipped her wine slowly and licked her lips. Neither of them said a word for a while until Madmoiselle Babin broke the silence.

'I'm sure you can finish the story for me?'

'René went to war and didn't return?'

'He was killed within a few weeks. The Battle of Marne, in September 1914. That's why I came to Russia two years later. I wanted to put as much distance as I could between me and France. It's dangerous work loving a soldier.'

Her face was piteous, with grey-black shadows under her eyes.

'You'd think I would have learned my lesson, wouldn't you?'

6

Watching Nikolai Milynkov whistling blithely as he meandered up the path under the acacia trees to the dacha, Mademoiselle Babin told Alyosha, 'I'm determined to be rid of him.'

She was equally determined to leave the dacha as soon as possible and return to Petrograd.

'I don't quite know how yet, but I will find my way back one way or another.'

'We mustn't…'

'We mustn't what?'

'Uncle Kozma told us to stay here, come what may. He said we wouldn't be safe if we left…'

'Stay, then – but I'm going back. My mind is made up.'

'But how do you know that he's even in Petrograd? He could be in southern Russia by now. He was talking about going to the Kuban to join the Volunteer Army to fight the Bolsheviks, once he's succeeded in getting my father released from the Cheka.'

She had one of her sudden changes of mood and turned on him furiously.

'I cannot stomach staying here any longer. I'm leaving. Don't look at me like that! I'm not ashamed of everybody knowing how much I love Kozma Mikhailovich.'

Nikolai Milynkov was down on his haunches examining something by the gladioli.

Alyosha said quietly, 'The question is, does my uncle love you as much?'

'Of course he does. How dare you!'

With another lightning change of mood, a mischievous smile appeared, and for a second she looked the radiant young girl she must have been when she met René Darduard.

'Why am I even discussing this with you?'

Her expression darkened.

'If it wasn't for you, I wouldn't be in this predicament.'

'I didn't want to leave Petrograd either,' he protested.

She ignored him.

'Kozma insisted that I go with you. He begged me. Said it would be safer for me in the south. All I wanted was to stay with him, to be with him… to marry him. Why else do you imagine I came to Russia? For the pleasure of teaching you and your cousins? No. The reason I came to Russia was to look for a husband.'

He thought she'd told him she wanted to escape France and her memories. Which version was the truth? At that, Nikolai Milynkov strolled in, with a cursory rap on the door. Before he had uttered a word, Mademoiselle Babin lifted her arm, barring his way.

'Stop! Stay where you are!'

He stopped.

'I want you to understand one thing. You are never to put a foot inside this dacha again. Do I make myself clear?'

She turned on her heel and left the room. Nikolai Milynkov turned to Alyosha with a look of panic in his eyes.

'Does she mean it?' Nikolai asked.

'Yes.'

'What's come over her?'

'We intend locking up and leaving.'

'Leaving for where?'

'Petrograd.'

'Petrograd? You'll never get there, not a chance. Not with things as they are from here to Moscow. It's chaos out there. It's fast turning into civil war between the Whites and the Reds. Don't you read the newspapers? You'll end up murdered if you leave now.'

Mademoiselle Babin reappeared, and told Alyosha they should think about packing. She was intent on leaving.

Until an unexpected development changed her mind.

7

Neither of the letters Stanislav posted, the first from Le Havre and the second from Helsingfors, ever reached Moscow. His mother couldn't care less. He was there in the flesh, standing before her after all those years of living away. She began to cry quietly, a low whimpering. It was so overwhelming to see him that it rendered her speechless for a while.

She had long ago given up any hope of ever setting eyes on him again, so much so that she was reluctant to believe the evidence before her. Was it really him? Was it a ghost? Was he really home? She hugged him to her fiercely, holding him tight, stroking and patting and hugging and stroking, so fierce and tight he would surely be black and blue by the time she'd finished with him.

Word of his arrival spread in no time, and a stream of neighbours and family came knocking furiously on the door to see the return of the prodigal for themselves. There was crying and laughter, drinking and laughing and crying and eating and more drinking all that afternoon and evening.

The shadows lengthened, the lamp was lit, and the welcome continued, cosy and crowded. It became a night to remember, with no shortage of conversation, eager as everybody was to share their experiences and stories of all the upheavals that had taken place on the streets of Moscow in his absence. As more vodka warmed throats and stomachs, the disagreements began. Some supported the revolution; others were violently opposed to it. The worst thing, everybody agreed, was the violence and uncertainty: you never knew where the next blow would come from. Standing at the window Stanislav's Uncle Konstantin lay into the Bolsheviks, swearing they had given every dimwit a licence to do just as he pleased, according to his own idiotic fancy.

'The stupider the idea the more they like it.'

Stanislav took a slow appreciative suck on his pipe before asking, 'Like what exactly?'

'You come along to the hospital tomorrow morning and you'll see for yourself. All I'll say is, be prepared for bedlam.'

From her perch near the stove, one of the neighbours nodded in agreement and said, 'Only about two months ago, a bit less maybe – it was during one of the quarterly meetings we hold anyway – one of the newly qualified doctors, a young lad called Grigory, put in a request to the Registrar. He'd spent last year, or the year before that, I can't remember now, in a hospital in Geneva, where he'd lost his head over some girl – Austrian, from Vienna, I think they said, he showed me her picture, pretty little thing...'

Her husband nudged her and said, 'Get to the point, woman.'

She glared at him but continued, 'Head over heels he was, as I said, but she was a real hothead, and of course he went the same way, swallowed every last word of it, hook, line and sinker. Anyway you're never going to believe the request he put in during our Quarterly Meeting.'

'That the hospital elect a soviet, I expect?'

'Worse. That the lunatics elect one. Did you ever hear such nonsense in your life? Talk about milking democracy until it bleeds. I laughed my head off to start with, because I thought he was pulling our legs. I should sooner have wept – turns out he'd never been so serious about anything in his life. He tried to persuade us until his voice was hoarse. Now the staff are split down the middle over it and we do nothing but argue...'

'Terrible arguments,' echoed somebody, and there was a collective grunt of agreement.

'There's no peace to be had to just get on with your work, and the poor lunatics have been whipped up into a frenzy at the thought of all these new rights that are coming their way. I'm telling you, no good can come of it – if the Bolsheviks insist on carrying on like this, deliberately dismantling and destroying every last bit of the old Russia, then they'll end up destroying the innocent as well.'

The next day, Stanislav slept late. His mother had left a note in her cramped, laborious handwriting, to tell him she wouldn't be home until late afternoon, so if he was going out he shouldn't wait for her. She didn't say where she was going and as he yawned luxuriously he idly tried to guess her whereabouts, but after such a long absence he had no idea by now how or where she spent her days. Though he'd slept long and well, his head still felt foggy and his body was stiff and heavy. He was sorely tempted to go back to bed and as there was nothing to stop him, he did.

He slept soundly for some time, and dreamed of seeing somebody like himself walking in the Bois de Boulogne, amongst the clamour of carriages and horses. The next second he was standing in perfect tranquillity. Before him were verdant meadows stretching as far as the eye could see, cows grazing peacefully, and he felt himself becoming lighter with every step that he took, as he climbed the slopes higher and higher, with Paris beneath him becoming smaller and smaller, until it disappeared completely beneath the clouds. He travelled effortlessly from country to country until he noticed a blackbird flying towards him; but when it came closer he saw it wasn't a blackbird but a bird-woman. He asked her name, but she didn't answer and when he asked again, she opened her beak and a baby slid out, mewling his name…

His mother came back to the flat a very happy woman. As she prepared supper, Stanislav heard all about it. It had been a long and tiring day, but the fruits of her labour made it all worthwhile. She had trailed from office to office before finally hitting upon the right one – that was important, because it would all be for nothing if she made a mistake and applied to the wrong department. By that point her feet were burning and her back was killing her, so she'd been glad enough to sit down when the clerk told her to wait while he went to enquire. Two hours later, he'd come back with the best news possible.

'It's what I've been hoping for more than anything,' she said to her son.

The rumour she had heard was confirmed: the Bolsheviks had passed a law granting amnesty to all the prisoners and exiles who had been convicted, or forced to flee to escape arrest under the Tzar. The long exile of every last one of Russia's *émigrés* had come to an end. He no longer had anything to fear – he was a free man who could live his life in his mother country without having to look over his shoulder constantly.

'Tomorrow, as a sign of thanks, I want us to visit your father's grave.'

8

Four officers of Anton Denikin's army approached the dacha. They did not so much request as inform Mademoiselle Babin and Alyosha – albeit with the utmost courtesy – that they intended billeting with them for a while.

'Until we have our orders to move against the Reds.'

They had very little news to impart but their leader assured their new hosts that Lenin and Trotskii's unlawful government was about to topple.

'Tzar Nicholas II will be back on his throne before the year is out, never fear,' one of the other officers added. 'And Holy Russia, united and invisible once more, will be freed from the claws of the Antichrist and his servants, the Jews and Freemasons.'

Three of the four officers seemed convinced of this (the fourth didn't seem quite so confident) and saw themselves riding triumphantly all the way to Moscow.

Alyosha was in his element. One of the officers was more than willing for him to ride his horse up and down the road. Alyosha thought there wasn't a purer or better sound in the world than the clip-clop of a horse's hooves beneath him. Mademoiselle Babin cheered up as well. Two of the young officers began vying with each other for her attention, and were forever trying to get her to laugh at their witticisms. Her mood lightened by the hour and within a mere couple of days she was quite restored to her old self, her eyes sparkling with mischief. She even made her peace with Alyosha.

'Forgive me for being so unfeeling these last few weeks,' she said to him.

Her hand on his felt hot and soft.

'I don't know what came over me.'

In the evenings, one of the officers would play the piano while the others would take it in turns to dance with Mademoiselle Babin. Only one of the officers was aloof, reading quietly in the corner, or sometimes retiring to his room as soon as they had finished eating.

A sort of heavenly peace seemed to spread though the dacha. For the first time in ages, Alyosha felt something approaching happiness. The only one not pleased by the new arrivals was Nikolai Milynkov. Though Mademoiselle Babin had given him his marching orders he still called with offerings of food and drink from time to time, and with the extra mouths to feed the Frenchwoman tolerated his presence as a necessary exchange. He loathed seeing her flirting and laughing with the officers, and sat there for hours, glowering and glaring at them and muttering under his breath. He looked hunched and miserable, and he winced every time he heard Mademoiselle Babin laugh. His unhappiness seemed to consume him; but he still returned, a sack of potatoes or couple of rabbits slung over his shoulder, to endure more torture.

Late one night matters came to a head when the youngest officer, whose beardless, pink-cheeked face shone like a young priest's, tried to tickle Mademoiselle Babin under her chin during a game of *vint*. Nikolai Milynkov wiped his hands on his trousers, rose to his feet and through gritted teeth challenged him to a duel. There was a moment's silence and then everybody roared with laughter. He stomped off in high dudgeon and they had to persuade the fourth officer, reading as usual in the corner, to finish the game in his place.

Very early the next day, Nikolai Milynkov returned armed with a heavy, old-fashioned pistol from the Crimean War. He burst in to where Mademoiselle Babin lay peacefully sleeping, kneeled by her bed and begged her to get rid of the officers. She was in such a deep sleep, she barely stirred. Nikolai squeezed her hand.

Alyosha was woken by her screaming. He ran into her room, to be confronted by the sight of Nikolai Milynkov aiming his pistol at Mademoiselle Babin, who lay cowering in a ball at the foot of the bed.

'What are you doing?' Alyosha yelled, but by now the screaming had brought the officers running in too, one after the other. Nikolai Milynkov took to his heels, barrelling past Alyosha and sending him flying, and careered out of the dacha, only to stop when he was halfway across the garden, retrace a few steps, then stop again in the middle of a flower bed. He raised the pistol to his head, pressed the barrel to his temple, shut his eyes and pulled the trigger.

Nikolai Milynkov pulled the trigger again.

Nothing happened that time either. The officers, who had naturally given chase, started to laugh.

'Long live the Soviets!' he yelled defiantly.

Then he took to his heels again, and that was the last they ever saw of him.

9

Mademoiselle Babin wanted Alyosha to listen carefully to what she had to say.

'I can't bear to stay in this wretched dacha any longer. What are we meant to be waiting for anyway? And for how long?'

'I'm still young,' she appealed to him in a slightly plaintive, self-pitying tone. 'I've hardly begun to live my life. Try and understand. I have my whole life ahead of me: I can't just wither away here.'

He looked at her blankly.

'There will always be these difficult decisions to make, and we all have to face them when they come our way. You too, Alyosha, someday you'll see. For instance, you might find yourself madly in love with somebody. But perhaps you might meet somebody else and find yourself falling in love with her as well. Can you imagine what it must be like to be in love with two women at the same time? Well, then you'll have to look into your heart and ask yourself, which one do I truly love the most? Which of these two do I love enough to spend the rest of my life with her? You will find it a terrible thing to have to decide, because making such a choice can never be easy.'

Touching his cheek tenderly with the back of her hand, she said, 'You're old for your age – I'm sure you can understand how I feel.'

The White officers were heading off and she was going with them, leaving him behind.

Alyosha started shaking and he thought he might be sick. He

had never in his life had to spend any time on his own. He had never been required to decide anything for himself. There had always been somebody on hand to protect him.

'Why can't I come with you too?'

'Alexei, I've already explained why not…'

'I can't be on my own.'

'You'll be safer here than anywhere else.'

Mademoiselle Babin squeezed his arm and whispered that it was far too dangerous for him to travel to Moscow with Anton Denikin's army. He continued to plead, but this only served to replace her previous sympathy and tenderness with a curt and rather petulant impatience.

'Why on earth should I burden myself with the responsibility of looking after you? It will be hard enough just looking after myself.'

'I promise I won't be any trouble…'

'You're not to come with me and there you are. Let that be an end to it.'

Mademoiselle Babin packed up her things, only to be told by the officers that she had far too much. She had a hard time of it, deciding what to take and what to leave, and had to cull and cull again, as the officers were adamant she must travel light. Alyosha watched her quietly as she made her deliberations, now adding this, now taking that out.

One of the officers seemed to dance attendance on her more than the rest: the pink-cheeked, beardless one. In his company, Mademoiselle Babin simpered and smiled even more than usual.

'I'm not as naïve as you think,' Alyosha told her. 'I know what you're doing. What was all that talk of loving my Uncle Kozma?'

Mademoiselle Babin was fastening the buttons on her squirrel-fur coat.

'What if he comes here for you and sees that you've gone?'

'Tell him whatever you like.'

'How do you think that will make him feel?'

Alyosha realised he was just a nuisance to her now. Whatever pitiful reasons she gave him for why it was better and safer for him to stay in the dacha, he understood her real motivation: nothing was to stand in the way of her happiness. No wonder she'd laughed so much night after night. It was perfectly clear to Alyosha that she had fallen in love with the beardless officer – Yakov, son of no less than Prince Gavril Sergeevich Peshkov.

'I don't think you understand what love is,' Alyosha told her accusingly.

'Oh really? And you do, I suppose?'

'You just want to marry into money.'

'Just like your mother, then.'

This talk of his mother angered Alyosha. He felt oddly protective of her.

'There's no need to drag my mother's name into this.'

Prince Yakov Sergeevich Peshkov appeared at the door in full uniform, his scarlet gloves in his hand and his sword on his hip.

'Do you know, Alyosha, your mother could barely exchange a word with me, other than to enquire about your progress, though I lived under her roof and ate at her table as one of the family. Don't you think that's extraordinary?'

Mademoiselle Babin placed a letter and a hand-drawn map in his hand.

'Keep these safe.'

The letter was addressed to his father, and the map showed the route to Batumi, where she told him he'd be safe from the Reds, as the English army had landed there, apparently.

'Take care of yourself now.'

He trailed after them as they left the dacha, and watched Prince Peshkov place her on her mount as though she was a china doll. Her last words to him, thrown gaily over her shoulder as she set off, were, 'You be a good boy now!'

He stared dully at them as they trotted out of the dacha, their figures becoming smaller and smaller until they disappeared out of sight down the road.

10

Mademoiselle Babin and the Whites did well to leave when they did, because a few days later the Reds took their place. The soldiers arrived at the dacha on horseback one afternoon. As luck would have it, Alyosha had seen them coming in time to climb up the big beech tree in the garden where he could observe them without being discovered.

He had left all the doors unlocked but he heard the sound of glass being shattered and saw a procession of shadows stream past the windows. The looting and smashing carried on until the evening, when the Reds finally made off, loading their horses with as much as they could carry, including, Alyosha noticed from his perch, the ormolu clock that had stood on the mantelpiece in the salon.

By the time the last one of them had left a full, yellow moon hung in the sky.

Too tired and stiff to do more than curl up and sleep that night, the next day Alyosha spent hours trying to restore some sort of order in the dacha, righting the furniture, replacing the remaining pictures back on the walls, and sweeping up the broken glass. As he placed a vase which had somehow remained unscathed back in its niche, he realised he was standing on somebody. He stepped back. His father's eyes stared up at him.

He picked the portrait up from the floor but cut his finger quite badly on a shard of glass. He sucked the blood and wrapped his finger in a bit of rag. He carefully took the picture out of its frame, rolled it up, and placed it in a heavy wooden chest, then did the same with all the other pictures that were undamaged. Finally, he locked the chest and went into the garden, where he hid the key behind a large stone at the bottom of a hedge.

Early next morning Alyosha awoke to a sort of scraping noise. He crept out of bed, thinking perhaps some of the soldiers had returned, moved the chair he had placed under the door handle, unlocked it, opened it as quietly as possible and listened. The noise seemed to be coming from the kitchen. In his stockinged feet he crept downstairs and made his way there, hesitating outside for a moment before slowly opening the door, to see an old man with his back to him, rummaging through the cupboards. He must have heard the door open but he didn't turn around, simply carrying on unperturbed in his hunt for food.

The food thief turned out to be a milky-eyed, gentle soul. Alyosha and he shared a bit of bread and cheese together. In no time, they were talking away like old friends. Leo was clearly a Tartar, but he claimed to be the only son of the second wife of a Greek coffee merchant from Odessa, who used to run a very famous café called Reiter.

'Have you ever been there?'

'Café Reiter or Odessa?'

'Odessa.'

'No.'

'Would you like to go there?'

'If I ever have the chance.'

'You'll have to make your own chance. There's not a better town on the face of this earth.'

He was in his element reminiscing about the place. Especially the food: the pork, the patés, the butter, the cheeses and the wine. His favourite dish was rabbit stew. In his perfect heaven, there would be rabbit stew to eat every day, from now to eternity, with potatoes and carrots and lots of black pepper.

Leo didn't think much of the Reds, though his opinion of the

Whites was no higher. When it came to rape, violence and looting, there was nothing to choose between them: soldiers were soldiers, and the stench of their sweat was just the same no matter what their colours were. No wonder so few men had any appetite to fight in their armies, and those that had been forced to bear arms took the first opportunity to slip away home. He felt there was some malign spirit infecting the very soil of Russia. The devil was at work in this, harvesting according to his whim.

He had measured, thoughtful opinions on all points – when he was sober. But once he'd been drinking – and he started mid-morning – he found it hard to express the incoherent thoughts that flitted through his head in a way that made any sort of sense.

There'd been some falling out between him and his family but Alyosha never got to the bottom of that. Sometimes, by the evening, Leo seemed to drink himself sober and his befuddled mind would clear. That's when he'd start making lengthy speeches. In his opinion, there was no hope of creating a just state without righteous citizens.

'But who's willing to listen to an old tramp like me?'

The Russian people had been rotting away for generations, just like sheep being eaten alive by maggots in the summer heat, wanting only to be allowed to find a cool and shady spot where they could rest in peace. The trouble was, there was more vodka and syphilis in Russia than common sense. That's why it had been so easy for hotheads to mislead the country.

He could see no possible reason or sense in pitting Russian against Russian. The Whites were killing in order to protect the sacred rituals of past centuries, private property, and the living Church in Christ. The Reds were killing in order to forge a new path to an earthly paradise in the dawn of the future, but they were blundering on without a road map. He hated Marxist intellectuals.

He hated them with a passion because they took advantage of the sincere aspirations and hopes of the people in order to win power for themselves. Their credo must be based on lies because God was the only source of true power. Matter was weak, the spirit was strong.

'Religion doesn't weaken natural emotions, Alyosha: rather, our intense need and desire for deliverance strengthens and purifies them.'

Leo was mortified by the state of his own body and soul.

'Why have I been reduced to wearing rags?' he wailed. 'Why is my will so weak? Why is my spirit so feeble?'

Alyosha could only answer truthfully, 'I don't know.'

However, Leo's mood could lighten in an instant.

'A miracle and a wonder, boy. That's what life has always been for me.'

In his own way the tramp was rather devout, and the psalms and verses he recited every night testified to a religious upbringing.

'It's an unfortunate development that modern man demands a scientific explanation for everything in the universe, instead of humbly accepting the existence of mysteries and miracles,' he concluded.

Before turning in every night he'd kneel shakily before the icon of Saint Geraison, touching it tenderly with his thin, yellow fingers. Sometimes, he'd lift it up and place it against his cheek. In that state, he looked like a man who had been damaged by some experience for which there was no cure.

11

'They'll be handing this dacha over to some Communist Commisar before you know it. Him or his brother. Or his brother-in-law. Or whoever he owes a favour to for something or other. The children of the proletariat are just as greedy for their share of the pie as the children of the old bourgeoisie.'

The tramp taught Alyosha how to smoke his cheap Turkish tobacco. Over a clay pipe of the stuff – alternated with scoffing a jar of pimentos that had managed to go undiscovered until then – he warned him one evening, 'As the son of a man who owned an armaments factory in Petrograd, they'll sling you straight in jail if they get their hands on you.'

'I'll make sure they don't. I'll run as far as I can from their clutches.'

'It's hard to run away from the Cheka. They're everywhere.'

'Well, they won't catch me.'

'Brave words, lad, but they don't mean a thing. Listen. I know I talk a lot of rubbish, but you must understand: I'm serious about this. I think you should change your name.'

'Why on earth would I do that?'

'You need to forget who you used to be.'

'Never.'

'You're not thinking straight, boy. Claim that chauffeur you had back in Petrograd as your father. Better yet, claim me!'

Alyosha burst out laughing.

'Yes, yes, very funny. I'm telling you, it's time you got your head screwed on and started taking sound advice when it comes your way. You listening? Or you'll end up in the gutter with a bullet in your head.'

Leo sighed.

'You and your like, you're scum as far as the Reds are concerned. Unless the Whites manage to return and rescue the children of the bourgeoisie – if that happens, you'll be free to be yourself again.'

Leo always slept on the wooden floor as he couldn't abide the softness of a mattress. He was not in good health and Alyosha would sometimes be woken in the early hours by his racking cough. He never took his clothes off either, and Alyosha had never seen him wash. Consequently the stink of him – an unholy mix of horse-piss and a strong blue cheese that had been left in a warm place for too long, so Alyosha decided after some deliberation – was sometimes overwhelming.

Leo was usually up and about before Alyosha, but one morning there was no sign of him. By mid-afternoon Alyosha began to feel uneasy and he went to knock on his door. When there was no answer, Alyosha went in and saw Leo lying on the floor in his usual place, but with his milky eyes wide open and his lips blue. As he approached he almost gagged, so strong was the stench, and had to press his nose into his sleeve to prevent himself from retching.

Leo's hands lay on his chest, clutching the icon, the two little fingers curled around it like two fish hooks. Alyosha tried to lift him onto the bed, but his body was as stiff as a board and as unyielding as a millstone, impossible to shift. The best Alyosha could do was take the sheet from the bed and cover him with it. He had never seen a dead person before. The last glimpse of Leo's mouth before it was obscured by the sheet was particularly unnerving for some reason: round and dark, like a mousehole. He decided almost at once that he couldn't stay under the same roof as a corpse.

'*You need to change your name...*'

He packed a few clothes in a leather bag, tying a second pair of boots around his neck.

'*Forget who you used to be.*'

He closed the door quietly behind him as he left.

12

Stanislav had arrived in Moscow with several scripts in his suitcase, with the intention of knocking at the doors of the city's theatres. The reception he found there was lukewarm to say the least. A few directors promised to read his work but they seemed far more interested in asking him about the latest innovations in European theatres, and what productions he has seen there before leaving, than in his own writing. He was at pains to tell them that one of his own works had actually been staged in Paris, at the Théâtre du Vieux-Colombier, trying to emphasise his avant-garde credentials. In truth his play had received a very mixed reception, but there had been some discussion of the possibility of giving it a more extended run in the autumn repertoire.

There couldn't have been a happier man in the Latin Quarter than him at that time, and he had been inspired to start writing another play. Then the 1914 War broke out, and his plans, like those of so many others, went awry. All talk of a run was at an end, and the lights finally went out at the theatre when it was closed down by court order (Stanislav had been in the building when the police arrived to evict them forcibly and nail the door shut) for staging an anti-militaristic cabaret.

After another fruitless day of distributing copies of his work, Stanislav stopped off for a drink in the café Bon on his way home to his mother's. He sat on one of the red chairs, amongst the actors, musicians and poets who frequented the place, longing to be a part of their world. He eavesdropped on the conversation of the group of young people on the next table. A young woman in a fur coat and a bright green hat that looked as though it had been made of billiard-table baize was saying, 'It's a thousand times easier to smash something up than build something new. And violence only ever leads to more violence.'

'We should boycott the Communists' new order, or at least try to ignore them,' agreed one of her companions; but a couple of the others seemed more hopeful that a better society would soon emerge from the chaos, where artists such as themselves would flourish. There were bound to be teething troubles to begin with after all: you couldn't nationalise every bank, factory, mill, and trade, never mind putting the land in the hands of the people, without upheaval. But then a dissenting voice piped up that seemed to have far less faith in the ability of the Reds to create a new Russia.

'They say they're giving us freedom. But has anybody stopped to ask: what is freedom? It's like happiness, isn't it, more of an ideal than a reality. Freedom's always one of those things that's just out of reach; it's just a dream.'

Stanislav couldn't help himself – he just had to butt in.

'But that's no reason for not trying, trying to *make* it a reality, surely?' he said. 'Doesn't our striving to achieve such a thing give meaning to our lives, whether we succeed or not?'

'The only freedom I need, friend, is freedom from the Communists.'

Throughout their discussion the future hid coyly out of sight. Stanislav asked himself whether his own future lay here in Moscow. Would he ever belong?

That evening after supper, he sat down to try and outline the plot of a short story or play, using his own experiences as the raw material. He cast his mind back to all that had happened to him. Thirteen years previously, in 1905, when he was just a boy of fifteen he'd begun to work underground for the Bolsheviks. Back then he had believed absolutely in the cause: to create a world where all were equal and free under the law. He had seen it not as some local or national upheaval but as a huge undertaking to see communism victorious across all five continents, bringing freedom to every corner of the world.

But the Tzar's police had come for him in the middle of the night, his mother in her nightdress, wailing as she watched them take him away. They kept him in solitary confinement for over six months, six months that felt more like six years. Every now and again they'd question him about printing and distributing leaflets, disseminating socialist propaganda in Bukitov factory and army barracks. Through all those endless months he betrayed nobody, though he came close several times, but it nearly broke him.

Then one day they opened his cell door (to take him for yet another interrogation, he assumed), and said, 'Get out.'

And that was it. He stepped out of the prison gate into the fresh air. Waiting for him was his father, who had finally managed to secure his release after paying a heavy bail. They went home together at once, where his mother already had his suitcase packed. The next day, Stanislav set out on a train for Europe with a fake passport and his parents' blessing.

He stepped off the train at the Gare du Nord, his sense of wonderment that he had managed to reach Paris on his own undimmed by the squalor of station. In his pocket he had a single address, and he left the station, climbed onto a horse-drawn tram, and after asking a few surly Parisians for directions, eventually managed to find the hotel in the Place Denfert-Rochereau.

The next few days were a blur of unfamiliar streets and voices as he tried to find his way around the Latin Quarter. He eventually stumbled upon the library for Russian exiles, in a filthy courtyard off the Avenue des Gobelins. It was through going there every day that Stanislav came to know other *émigrés* and fell in with a crew of Bolsheviks. They used to meet once a week in the upper room of a café on the Avenue d'Orléans. There they'd discuss politics, and exchange news from Russia. One evening at the beginning of May a short, bald man in a dark suit and white shirt came up the stairs with a briefcase under his arm. This was Lenin. Stanislav was introduced to him, and was later invited to his flat in a small street near Montsouris Park. Krupskaya was there too. Over supper Lenin questioned him closely about the political situation in Russia and Stanislav, flattered that Lenin would ask a young man like him for his opinion, did his best to answer intelligently.

He attended many meetings and took to the streets to protest on several occasions. He saw a picture of himself in *Le Parisien* when he marched at the head of a crowd to the Mur des Fédérés to commemorate the martyrs of the Commune of 1871. But little by little his enthusiasm for the cause faltered. There was no direct action in Paris as there had been in Moscow in the wake of 1905, just endless, stultifying discussion, nit-picking over tiny matters of policy, and constant, exhausting infighting and bickering, with factions formed and positions taken. He gradually disengaged from this world, and saw less and less of them. The last time he ever saw Lenin, he was sitting on a bench in Montsouris Park, autumn leaves at his feet, surrounded by mothers with their small children, deep in thought.

He fell in with a different, younger, more bohemian crowd, though they could be just as argumentative at times. They congregated in cafés presided over by bad-tempered waiters, and here he got to know the sad alcoholics, the struggling artists and their limpid-eyed models; in short the demi-monde of the Left Bank. He spent his days idling and reading, he stopped washing and didn't change his clothes for days on end. He grew his hair long and dabbled in all sorts of new experiences. Mysticism. Morphine. Hashish. Cocaine. He took to drinking in the afternoon. But he also started to learn about the arts: painting, sculpture, literature. He wrote a short story which was published by a small, obscure magazine.

His favourite café was Le Rendezvous des Ficares, opposite Montparnasse station, where he was always sure to meet a friend. It was here that he met Katya, when she came in with two friends for breakfast one day, and he had not yet gone to bed. They soon became lovers and he moved in with her after a while. Then she fell pregnant.

The more Stanislav sat, pen in hand, reminiscing, the more the realisation grew that somehow he had got closer to being himself – that it had been easier to discover his true self – in Paris than here in Moscow. Paris, he thought, felt like home, not Moscow. It had been worth spending this time back in Russia for him to learn that.

One morning, he decided to return.

Telling his mother was difficult. Very difficult.

'But when will I see you again?' she asked him piteously, her eyes saying, 'If at all.'

'It won't be so long next time, I promise,' he answered.

'I hope not, son.'

He kissed his mother farewell and caught the train to Kiev, but could go no further. Kiev was in chaos, what with the fighting and the hundreds of refugees arriving there daily from every corner of Russia and beyond. There was an acute shortage of lodgings: hundreds were camping in makeshift tents, and many others, who had nowhere at all to shelter, were sleeping rough. It was certainly no part of Stanislav's plan to stay a minute more than he had to, but with the fierce fighting to the east and south-east of the city there was no way out – it was far too dangerous for the trains to run.

He spent weeks kicking his heels, waiting in vain for the fighting to abate enough for him to risk leaving. But the fighting intensified, and his funds dwindled alarmingly. He tried to ration himself to one meal a day, but some days he wouldn't eat at all. It didn't help that he was paying a ridiculous amount for his cupboard of a room. When he complained the couple who rented it to him said they could have asked twice as much. Though he went looking for work to tide him over, there was very little to be had. He started to rue the day he had ever left Moscow.

Finally, he had a little luck when, after being rejected by every other theatre in Kiev, he was offered some work at the Puppet Theatre. They weren't interested in any of his scripts, as their audience consisted mainly of small children. The priests and nuns in charge of the orphans sometimes brought the children as a treat. But if he could turn his hand to simple storytelling, then they could pay him a small amount for the work. He found the work surprisingly enjoyable, and having a full belly was even more gratifying.

But most important of all, he found Tamara.

13

One night, soldiers forced everybody out of the train and herded them onto the platform. It was en route to Kharkov from Rostov. Little by little, as the soldiers searched the carriages and corridors, all shapes and sizes of children blossomed from the shadows, some so covered in soot and dirt they looked like little devils. Amongst them was Alyosha.

The train hissed impatiently. It stood for hours, the soldiers standing guard to prevent any of the passengers from getting back on. In the depths of the night – without the familiar long whistle of warning – it built up steam, and disappeared into the darkness. The hundreds left on the platform were stranded, tired and irritable but oddly resigned. The men, women, children and animals all stood around aimlessly, or lay down if they could find a corner without being trampled. There were rumours flying around that another train would arrive in the morning, or in the afternoon, or not for days… nobody had any idea why they had been taken off in the first place. The usual excuse was 'fighting further down the line'.

And anyway, that was usually just another rumour. If there was one thing you learned quickly enough, a hopeful guess didn't go a long way to soothe the agony of not knowing. After a few hours, people were beginning to feel thirsty and hungry, and those with small children who were starving had started to beg for some food.

Riding the trains had already taught Alyosha how to steal. It had also found him three new friends. Mishka had been hiding in one of the big coal bins, though this had its risks, as you could suffocate. That's why he always kept a big nail in his pocket, so that he could make little ventilation holes in the side of the bin. Boris preferred to squeeze into any gap he could find in the sides of the trains, though quite often another child would have got there before him. His second favourite place was on the rod above the axle, just inches clear of the track. Once, he managed to squeeze past the pipes and stuff himself inside the engine, crouching there next to a little girl with a grey toad in her hand.

Their sister Masha preferred the boxes where they kept all the stray bits of equipment, in the very last carriage – but it held the highest risk of discovery because the ticket-collecters often checked here for stowaway children. So sometimes she climbed onto the roof instead. It was on the roof of a train between Verkhne-dneprovsk and Poltava that Alyosha and Masha had come face to face for the first time.

14

By now people were beside themselves, and scuffles broke out every now and again. Mishka was whimpering with hunger, and listening to him was almost too much for his sister Masha to bear. When during the second night on the platform a pale, feral-looking man beckoned her to him, she went, and after disappearing with him into the bushes for a while, she returned with a lump of slightly putrid meat. It didn't taste much better than it smelled, but at least filled Mishka's stomach enough to silence his moaning. She let him have most of it.

The rumoured train did not come up the line, and the next day the four decided to head northwards on foot.

Masha, Mishka and Boris were orphans, but their uncle – their mother's brother – lived on a farm on the southern outskirts of Chernigov, a town to the north-west of Kursk. The brothers and sister had been trying to make their way there for months, by any means possible: train, carts or on foot.

Mishka had just turned fifteen, and was tall and sturdily-built, with wide shoulders and two fists that he was always ready to put to good use. His large frame seemed to need more fuel to sustain him than his siblings, and hunger affected him far worse than them, so that he made far more noise and fuss than his small brother Boris, who by now had learned to suffer in silence.

Mishka had lost an eye and wore a black leather patch over the empty socket, but though Alyosha asked Masha several times what had happened, she always refused to tell him.

Masha was thirteen, but a good head taller than Alyosha. Her face was like a cartoon cat's, with her arched brows, her little snub nose, always pink at its tip, and her thin lips. She had blue eyes and two fair plaits, long legs, and was as skinny and flat-chested as a boy who had grown too fast.

Boris was only ten and a half, but crafty and quick, and had learned the tricks necessary for survival before the rest of them.

So Alyosha too had begun his apprenticeship in this new way of life, where one lived from hand to mouth, and on one's wits. He had to unlearn everything that he had been taught; and he changed, as much on the outside as on the inside, into a very different boy.

15

Alyosha did his best to fit in with the other three. He didn't always manage to warp and bend his past into something new, but he tried his very best.

Every morning he woke with his head full of memories of Petrograd. They were so vivid, he was often convinced he was back home in his bed for a moment or two. For the next hour or so, his old self would be rubbing along with his new self, until he managed, through an effort of will, to banish Alyosha so that he could find the strength to deal with the challenges of the new day. Then, with a sort of emptiness mixed with homesickness, he'd feel another slice of himself peel off at his feet.

They slept wherever they found a bit of shelter: a corner of a deserted stable, a Jewish cemetery, huddled under a hedge or against a tree-trunk. Once they climbed into a pigsty, where the sow and her piglets offered an unexpected source of warmth. There'd occasionally be a grand mansion to squat in: already looted and ruined, its master and mistress no doubt murdered by their own tenants, and the building set alight, so only the shell remained. Sometimes, a few things had survived, and just eating from a plate or drinking from a cup would remind Alyosha of his old life.

They stole to live, and lived to steal. Filling their bellies was the constant concern. Alyosha learned how to catch, in one second – with just one swift, sly glance – the essence of a man. Whenever a stranger approached, all four would tense imperceptibly, never knowing whether to expect friend or foe, predator or victim.

Mishka hated gypsies.

'They're dishonest fuckers, every last one of 'em,' he would say.

He didn't believe a word any of them said, not since one of them had tried to rook him once. He thought nothing of pelting them with stones if they crossed his path, shouting at them to 'Fuck off, you fuckers, get the fuck away from us!'

Every so often they'd glean a little news from a band of retreating soldiers, Reds or Whites – though they tended to keep clear of them if they could, from whatever side. They could rarely make much sense of what they heard in any case, more than to confirm their belief that the further they remained from the fighting, the safer they'd be.

They stayed in the countryside as much as possible. If they entered a village, they could never predict what welcome they might get, but any town was dangerous. There were thousands of children like them wandering the length and breadth of the country. Orphans mainly, whose parents had been killed in the fighting, but others like Alyosha, who had become separated from their parents and were desperately trying to find them again. They were all hoping to find shelter or a place of safety somewhere.

The four spent their days tramping the twisting paths of marsh or forest. They trudged through heavy rain, and crossed wild rivers on rickety, slippery bridges, which more often than not lacked any sort of handrail, though where the flooding had been particularly bad the river was often impassable. Sometimes they had to make a long and exhausting detour to avoid an area where they had heard the famine was particularly bad – they knew by now that famine made people desperate, and it was always worth avoiding such places if they heard about it in time.

From week to week, and then month to month, Alyosha's skin darkened and his hair bleached under the sun. He had the beginnings of a straggly beard, and gradually grew to feel more comfortable in the skin of this strange new boy he had created for his own protection.

One evening, after a long day's hike that had brought them to the outskirts of a village, he tried to beg from an old woman.

'Got a kopeck? Just a kopeck, one kopeck, that's all I'm asking.'

The old woman tried to hurry on past him, but he rushed her, grabbing her by the wrist. She tried to free herself by swinging her basket at him, but he'd already pushed the sleeve of her dress up, to expose her forearm.

'Let me go! Let me go you devil!'

He told her he'd bite her to the bone and swore she'd die of syphilis.

'Help! Help me! In the name of Christ Jesus our Saviour somebody help me!'

The old woman was terrified, but clung on to her basket, screaming at the top of her voice – mad, angry screams. Over the infernal noise that she was making, Alyosha could hear people running towards them, and dogs barking. With a last desperate tug he managed to wrest the basket from her, and took to his heels with the militia's bullets hissing past his head.

His hair was so long by now he had to tie it back. His beard started to thicken. His weather-beaten face was usually filthy and his clothes had long since turned to rags. Alyosha looked every inch the young lout that he had become.

16

Soon after the revolution in October 1917, the Petrograd Academy of Performing Arts closed its doors and every last member of staff lost their job. About a month prior to this, two of the final-year students announced their engagement. Their names were Tamara Bobrikov and Yury Kashivin. Of all the student couples, they were deemed by far the best-looking. In spite of the closure of the Academy and the chaos in the city, they decided to remain in Petrograd. Then, late one night, the Cheka came knocking on their door and examined all of their possessions for hours. It became clear that they intended arresting them on one pretext or another. It was also made clear that this outcome could be avoided. To begin with Yury was outraged, and said he'd rather be shot, but Tamara spoke to him quietly and dissuaded him from any further protest. Then she rose and made her way to their tiny bedroom, followed by the biggest of the Cheka. The door closed behind them.

The next morning the couple left for Kiev, where Tamara's parents lived. They settled in that city, though it was hard for two energetic and talented young people like them to be idle. After kicking their heels for a while, they decided to establish a puppet theatre. The idea would never have got off the ground had it not been for Tamara's mother, as it was she who actually created the puppets. Her skill was so great that you could almost swear they were made of flesh and blood. Or so thought Stanislav the first time he saw one of their shows.

Afterwards he compared notes with Yury and Tamara about ending up in Kiev.

'Tamara and I feel pretty bleak about our future here in Russia,' Yury confessed.

'I can understand that only too well. As I told you, I decided to try and get back to Paris. There's nothing much to keep me here. Not as things are, with the country being devoured on all sides.'

'I never thought I'd even contemplate leaving,' said Yury.

'It's not an easy decision,' answered Stanislav.

Yury squeezed his fianceé's wrist.

'What have you got to say, Toma? You've been very quiet.'

She'd been smoking silently, her mind far away.

'You could do worse than go to Paris,' suggested Stanislav. 'Once it's safe to leave the city.'

'How long did you say you were there for?' asked Yury.

'Nearly eight years in all.'

'That's quite some time. So how did you make your living?'

'When I first arrived I was just a lad of fifteen, and my father kept me. Not that he could send me much, but it was enough to keep a roof over my head and the wolf from the door. But then he died; this would have been about two years after I first arrived. My mother tried to keep sending me money, but it was difficult for her and I felt guilty taking it when I knew how little she had to live on herself. I nearly returned to Russia but she warned me against it, said it wouldn't be safe. Those six months I spent in prison nearly killed her, and she was terrified that I'd be re-arrested the minute I stepped back onto Russian soil. So I decided to stay, and tried to make the best I could of my exile. Make the best of the worst I suppose. You can adjust to anything.'

'Can you really?' asked Yury.

'If you set your mind to it.'

'What about homesickness? Weren't you homesick?'

'Of course. Every minute of every day in the beginning. But it's like anything else – the feeling fades after a while, grows into something else. I remember reading in a novel a couple of years ago that it's not what experiences a man has in his life that are important, but what he makes of those experiences.'

That's the thing,' Yury was reflecting. 'That's the thing. How do you learn to live amongst strangers? How do you manage to hang on to your own language and traditions – your own identity?'

'It's not easy.'

'Damn right it's not easy…' Yury had raised his voice.

'Not at all easy…' said Stanislav quietly.

'But not completely impossible?' asked Tamara Mikailovna.

'There are very few things in life that are completely impossible,' answered Stanislav with a smile.

Over the next days and weeks the young couple interrogated him about his experiences in Paris, usually sitting in a squalid little café on Sofiyskaya Street over sweet, muddy cups of Turkish coffee. Although he had only been back in Russia some months, already Paris seemed very far away, and his life there had a dreamlike quality. There was something childlike in his new friends' demands for more stories.

'What else? Tell us more.'

Stanislav remembered how the fresh air of spring scoured the city clean, and the green of the young leaves on the trees along the Seine. Every memory was tinged with nostalgia. He painted them an affectionate picture of the city, full of magic and a tender romance, so much so that he filled them with a desperate desire to go there the minute the fighting let up enough to allow them to leave.

He told them about his favourite café, the Café de la Paix.

'Where else did you like to go?'

'Maxim's or La Coupole sometimes, if I had enough money in my pocket.'

They were insatiable for every last detail. He had to name all his favourite bistros, and he felt he must have described every last inch of the Boulevard Saint-Germain. He spoke at length of the steep delights of Montmartre, the narrow streets that became ever narrower as they ascended the hill, at the top of which stood the Sacré Coeur. The fine houses of Passy. He told them of the grey-roofed buildings, uniform and proud, the lofty crests of the Romanesque and Gothic churches, the ancient bridges, the memorial gates, and how, in high summer, the city shimmered and swayed, like a field of barley on a gentle breeze; he tried to evoke the unique smell of a day at dusk. And then the nights, the darkness punctuated by strong pools of light, throwing out blue shadows through the gloom…

Late one night, after one of these descriptions, Stanislav said, 'I've managed to make myself feel hopelessly homesick.'

He missed Paris more than ever, it was true, but he reminded himself that, in spite of his romantic evocations, his exile there had not been without its difficulties. He remembered the decrepit room he'd occupied for some time in Créteil on the outskirts of the city, in a damp old building which had once been an abbey. And when the money from home had dried up he'd had to live from hand to mouth, taking whatever work he could, with poverty like a dog forever snapping at his heels.

Katya had been forever telling him about his lifeline, and though to begin with he had scoffed at the notion that a line on the palm of your hand could tell you anything about how your life would turn out, he came to accept it was just another way of describing what amounted to fate.

Katya had told him seriously that it was a good idea to learn how to recognise your lifeline, but he just laughed and said, 'Learn how to know myself you mean? I can see the value in that I suppose.'

'As much as such a thing is possible.'

That was the problem, mused Stanislav. Everybody suffers from such doubt. Self-doubt. Doubts about the people around us, even the ones we're meant to love. Doubts about what we should be doing with our lives from day to day, from year to year. Doubts always threaten to overwhelm us.

That's what makes a person's lifeline twist and turn all the time.

How does anyone come to full self-knowledge? How can we ever truly know something inside us for exactly what it is? Isn't every experience mediated by our interpretation of it? What am I? How can I even know that? And if I can't even make sense of myself, how am I to make sense of anything else?

When Stanislav told Tamara about the lifeline she asked him to read her palm. This gave him the excuse he'd been waiting for to touch her. She had long slender fingers, and the fingernails had been bitten to the quick. Although she was a little bony, she had beautiful shoulders, beautiful arms too, and those lively eyes in that intelligent face, and her clear voice.

Gazing at her, he realized she had charmed him, and he wanted to possess her. He desired her more than anything. She'd said something but he didn't really take much notice of her reply.

'I love you,' he told her.

'What?'

'I love you.'

'You hardly know me.'

'I love you,' he told her for the third time.

Tamara did something between a laugh and a snort, wrinkling her nose in a way he found delightful. She looked at him and became serious.

'Don't say that again.'

'It's true.'

She lifted her hand and pointed to her engagement ring.

'And you love me too, I can tell.'

'You have some nerve, Stanislav Markovich! Who do you think you are?'

Stanislav moved closer and they kissed.

17

Every time the Red Army marched past, they'd sing the *Internationale*, but if the Reds were in retreat and the Whites appeared, the song then was 'God Save the Tzar' or '*Bozhe Tzaria Khrani*'. Mishka, Masha and Boris' natural sympathies lay with the Communists. Alyosha noticed that early on, though the soldiers' voices all sounded the same to him. Apart from the Whites and the Reds there were other soldiers – like Nestor Makhno's anarchists – growing like dock leaves in the grass, as well as bands of vagabonds and murderers claiming to be armies for this or that cause.

Alyosha's favourite time of day was when they made camp for the evening, and shared whatever meagre supplies they had found, foraged or stolen that day. Masha would sometimes comb the lice out of his and her brothers' hair and it was during these brief hours of rest, snatched from the hardships of their days, that she told him their story.

They came from a small village on the outskirts of Tzaritsyn on the Volga. Their childhood was an unhappy one of abject, grinding poverty. Their father was a brutal drunkard, though the children loved their mother. Their father had worked the land when he was younger, but he gave that up to be a cabman, after buying an old nag that looked more like a camel. He made very little money, and most of it was spent on drink. So that her children would not starve, their mother took in washing, and when things were really tight she would chop wood for some of the neighbours.

When their father staggered back from the tavern late at night, he'd quite often attack his wife, sometimes with his razor, and terrorise the children, who soon learned to hide from him when he was in a rage. When he was sober he'd be tormented with remorse and self-pity and would beg their forgiveness.

When war broke out between Germany and Russia in 1914 and their father disappeared into the army, his family didn't feel the slightest regret, half-hoping he'd never come home alive.

To their great disappointment, home he came. But the biggest surprise for his family was to see how he had changed. He had transformed himself from his head to his toes. He sat at the head of the kitchen table and began to talk to them clearly and with great conviction. He was full of slogans and was all for land redistribution and encouraging the factory workers of Tzaritsyn to strike for their rights. It was necessary, he said; everybody had to act together to smash the old order. They should create a society where all the good things were shared out equally.

He was soon flung into jail, but not for long, for there was change on the wind and the revolution was raising its head. Their father, once he was released, became ever more energetic and committed: his spell in prison had hardened his convictions and sharpened his vision. He cut quite a figure as he strode through the village, a proud member of the proletariat. He took to wearing a leather jacket, aping the lads of the Cheka. One dark night, he drove a gang in a motor-lorry over to the local landowner's manor-house and threatened to burn it to the ground. Before long, such persecution succeeded in ridding the district of all its old aristocratic families.

A soviet was elected to distribute the land, another to run the factories, and a third entrusted with doling out houses and flats to the poor. Their father was given the job of station master at the local railway station; no mean responsibility at a time when, due to the civil war, the railroads were of vital importance to the

Bolshevik war machine. He proved himself a good leader and was soon promoted and sent on propaganda work to neighbouring towns. The family saw less and less of him until, one day, he didn't come home.

They never did find out their father's fate. There was a rumour he had gone to live with a woman in some village further up the line, another that he had been sent to Chita, a city to the east of Baikal Lake in Siberia, to work against the Whites in the underground. Yet another rumour had it that he had joined Trotskii's train on its way to the front in the north, somewhere around Arkhangelsk.

They faced hard times again, and their mother went to the local soviet to ask for help. Some young Commissar in a leather jacket, who liked to sit sideways by the piano pressing the keys with the finger of one hand for hours at a time, offered her work delivering messages for the Communists. She was even given a bicycle, though the front wheel wobbled alarmingly. The pay was still insufficient for their needs, so they all had to do their bit – even Boris sat on the pavement outside the station offering to clean travellers' shoes, but there wasn't much call for his services.

One evening, Mishka came home covered in blood. He'd been trying to sell firewood on another gang's patch and they hadn't taken kindly to it. Mishka hadn't been wise enough to protect himself by joining a gang, and was punished for it. His nose and jaw were broken, and he looked like hell. After the doctor examined him, he told his mother it was likely he'd lose his left eye.

Several weeks later, Mishka left the house late one night with his father's cut-throat razor hidden in his sleeve. When he returned his shirt was dripping with blood and he held four warm ears in his hands. The family knew it would only be a matter of time before the gang came back with worse reprisals. Their mother decided they must leave the village at once and make for Kursk, where her brother lived. But at dawn the Whites attacked.

Anisya Nazorov, their neighbour, was the first to realise what was happening. She had just risen to milk her cow as usual, when she heard a faint crack from the darkness. She stood at the door of the cowshed to listen. Her cow lowed but then she heard the gunfire again, a little closer this time, from somewhere in the direction of the duck-pond, out on the steppe. She put her bucket down and ran to the gate, where she saw men's shadows running down the village's only street. They came in ones or twos so begin with, then in tens, then in their hundreds. A horse and cart appeared, chased by frightened men trying to beg a lift, but it was so laden already, they were hurled off without ceremony. Soldiers rushed around, yelling orders at each other, some throwing down their arms. More horses and carts cantered by, and the firing grew in volume as it drew ever nearer to the village.

Anisya banged on her neighbour's door, but it was Mishka's disfigured face she saw first, then his mother's, who understood the situation at once. She told her son to wake his sister and brother, and Anisya ran back to her own house to raise her own two, Petrusha and Anyuta. Anyuta, confused and sleepy, began to cry, but her mother calmed her and told her to dress. They left the house at the same time as their neighbours. The two mothers had long since prepared a hiding-place. Behind their cottages there was an old barn, against the wall of which the children would collect cowpats to burn in the winter. There was already a fat stack some two yards high, and a place had carefully been hollowed out in the middle of it by the mothers in which to hide.

'Hurry up, hurry up!'

The children crept into their cave of dung.

'Not a peep out of any of you, mind.'

'Masha, look after Anyuta.'

The children were left in the darkness, but through a small hole they took turns to see what was happening. They could all hear the soldiers arrive, the air filling with the sound of rough voices, horses' hooves, and the engines of the motor-lorries.

'Open up! Open up!'

Banging on doors. Dogs barking.

'Where's your husband? Where are your children?'

Anisya answered, 'He's working away.'

A slap.

'Lying bitch.'

'We'll beat the truth from you if we have to…'

Mishka watched them drag Anisya away by her hair.

'Was that mother screaming?' asked Masha. 'Was it?'

'Be quiet,' hissed Mishka.

'Tell me then! Can you see her? Can you see our mother?'

'No. Now, shut your mouth.'

They'd already corralled some of the villagers in front of the church. Back and forth the Cossacks galloped on their great horses, hemming the people in, thwacking the heads of those who failed to move quickly enough with the handles of their heavy whips. In no time there were some fifty or so prisoners huddled together, some weeping, others mute.

The day wore on as they were, each in their turn, brought before two White officers who sat behind a makeshift table, referring to a list of names in front of them.

They were all subjected to the same string of questions: name, age and occupation, had they voted for the Communists, had they supported the Communists, had they spread communist propaganda? The most important question at the end of each interrogation was: 'Where is the Commissar? Where is he hiding?'

Nobody knew.

'You must know! Where is the Commissar hiding?'

They believed nobody. As far as they were concerned, everybody was as guilty as each other and the punishment would be the same, never mind the excuse. They were all thrown to the ground, their trousers pulled to the ankles, and then with one Cossack sitting on the legs and the other with the head between his knees, they would both take it in turns to whip the prisoner without mercy, drowning his screams by shouting at the top of their voices, 'Christ our Lord is resurrected! Speak the truth! Christ our Lord is resurrected! Repeat!'

'Christ our Lord is resurrected!

'I can't hear you!'

'Christ our Lord is resurrected!'

'I want Lenin to hear you in the Kremlin!'

'Christ our Lord is resurrected!'

'Louder!'

'Christ our Lord is resurrected!'

'Louder!'

'Christ our Lord is resurrected!'

Louder and louder, over and over. This went on through the afternoon and evening and late into the night, when it became Anisya Nazarova's turn to be interrogated. She started to scream even before the men threw her to the ground and ripped her skirt.

'I know where the Commissar is hiding!' the words tumbled out wildly through her tears.

'An honest person at last!' The White Officer's voice was hoarse. 'How do you know where he is?'

'I know,' she said hurriedly. 'I know somebody who can tell you. I know that she knows. She delivers messages for the soviet.'

That's how Mishka, Masha and Boris' mother was arrested.

The children had not eaten or drunk anything all day, and the dung cave was like a furnace. Driven almost mad with thirst, the younger children started to beg to be allowed out for some water and that's when some Cossack heard them; Boris was very nearly killed when the soldier sunk the blade of his sword into the dung just above his head. The five of them were dragged from their hiding place by a grey-haired soldier.

Their mother couldn't persuade the White Officers that she knew nothing, however hard she tried.

'Why won't you believe me? I don't know anything.'

She was beaten savagely.

'I can't tell you anything.'

More questions and more beating.

'Tell us where he's hiding, bitch!'

'I don't know.'

'Where is he?'

Over and over again she told them, 'He must have fled by now.'

She was beaten into a pulp.

In the early hours of the morning Mishka, Masha and Boris were brought in to the room where their mother lay wilting. Whimpering in pain, she managed to whisper, 'Why have you brought them here?'

Then, 'I have nothing else to say.'

And after that, 'I've told you everything I know.'

With a rough razor every button was cut off and then her clothes were torn into shreds. A record was put on the gramophone. She was forced, naked, down onto the table by two Bashkir soldiers to the accompaniment of the song, '*Life is short, live life to the fullest!*' Singing in their strong Moldovan accents, four more staggered in, stinking sourly of horse sweat and vodka. As the men raped her, Masha pulled Boris tightly against her so that he couldn't see, as Mishka bellowed and screamed, made mad with rage and helplessness.

18

The front shifted yet again. There was savage fighting and the ravens ate their fill. The Whites retreated, the Reds returned. This didn't give them any respite, however, just more trouble. Some of the companies of soldiers refused to acknowledge the authority of the central committee of the local soviet, after getting a taste for raping, looting and killing, and continued to operate unilaterally. Late every night, one such gang drove around the village in a grey motor-lorry with a clown, two clarinettists and a trumpeter from the Tzarityn circus, terrorising the villagers, hammering on their doors, wrecking their homes and generally running riot.

Eventually, although the villagers had lost any faith they may have had in the Communists' ability to keep order, the local soviet ordered the gang's arrest. The reprisal was swift: every last member of the the central committee of the soviet, including the younger brother of the chairman, who was only ten years old, was shot dead. There was uproar, and an appeal made to the Communists in Tzaritsyn to restore order in the village. Finally, with swift and ruthless efficiency, the gang was rounded up and hanged in front of the village church.

'Who said we Reds were good for nothing?' asked the Commissar, as the clown's big black shoes pedalled the air.

Since she had been released from the Whites' custody the children's mother had not dared leave the house, and her nerves were in tatters. When they heard that the Whites had regrouped and were about to attack she felt they had no choice but to leave.

'Either that, or I kill myself,' she threatened.

Mishka stole a cart, and the three children pulled their mother and few possessions past the duck pond, out of the village, along the path towards the open steppe. It was laborious work, and every now and then their mother would say, 'Have a rest, children, have a rest.'

Their mother's health was ruined. She coughed incessantly as they pulled her along. They could hear the Whites firing behind them. They were not the only ones fleeing: there were hundreds of others like themselves, and in their wake was an army of scarecrows, those poor souls who had contracted typhus, shivering and weak under their blankets, falling dead by the wayside. When exhaustion overcame them, the fear of contracting the disease spurred the children on. Similarly, fear of the Whites kept the sick crawling onwards.

On the horizon, as dawn broke, a country station shimmered in the distance. They pulled the cart towards the train that stood waiting there, and it was only when Masha happened to rearrange the sacks that covered their mother that they realised that she had disappeared. She must have slipped away in the night. When exactly? How many hours ago? More importantly, where had she gone?

She had bemoaned the fact that she was holding them back often enough as they pulled her along, and said they'd be better off without her. Now it seemed she had acted. The children argued over what they should do. Masha wanted to retrace their steps to try and find her, but the typhus scarecrows lay behind them, and the Whites with their swords held high were almost upon them.

Kursk. Kursk. Kursk. Their mother had wanted them to make for Kursk. There they would be safe. The three travelled on the roof of the train, Masha dreaming of seeing America.

19

Stanislav and Tamara found every possible excuse to be alone. It wasn't easy, and required considerable ingenuity, as she lived with Yury in her parents' house, and they worked together every day in the puppet theatre too.

A narrow little bar on Dumskaya Square was their favourite rendezvous. Tamara started comparing her fiancé unfavourably with Stanislav, and her growing love for the one left little room for any compassion for the other. She loved to hear him talk about all his different experiences, loved the whole process of getting to know somebody and seeing him open up to her. She felt proud that it was to her he confided his guilt at leaving his widowed mother behind in Moscow. Through Stanislav, she learned that every life has its own unique flavour and through him she felt she was seeing herself in a new light. He was never irritable with her, as Yuri could be, who would sometimes become ill-tempered on the smallest pretext. Tamara had always assumed the blame lay with her for provoking him, until Stanislav explained that it was because of some guilt or shame from within himself that Yuri turned his anger onto her.

She felt liberated by this, as though a burden had been lifted from her, and it made her feel even more loving and connected to Stanislav. He also had the ability to dispel the bouts of depression that overcame her from time to time. Although she was only eighteen years old, she was already worrying about growing old. When she gazed into a mirror, she told him, she could feel the germ of her annihilation already there, in her flesh.

'The end of my life-line,' she told him sadly.

'Everybody's life-line has to end,' he replied, taking her narrow palm and stroking it.

Whenever she felt sad, Stanislav could always distract her with stories of his time in Paris, and she spent hours listening to him talk about his fellow countrymen who, like him, had fled Russia before the revolution to settle in Montrouge and Gobelins.

When he arrived there as a lad of fifteen, the first room he rented was in the Rue Denfert-Rochereau. His suitcase, his little stove and his kettle were all he had to his name. Having to stand on his own two feet forced him to turn from a boy into a man overnight, though homesickness often overwhelmed him. He remembered lying on his bed, gazing at black shadows gathering against the ceiling and listening to the lonely drumming of rain on the roof.

But there were the good times too. He recounted how he had been to see *La Pisanelle d'Annunzio*, directed by Meyerhold, with a friend from the Ballet Russes. After the performance he was introduced to Ida Rubenstein. She had kissed him on both his cheeks.

'Thank you for coming to see me,' she'd smiled.

'I'm very glad I came. You were astounding.'

'I hope you come again.'

Near the theatre was a café-tabac, with a few tables at the back where they'd gone for a coffee or an *eau-de-vie* after the performance. Meyerhold was there in the company of Guillaume Apollinaire, and Stanislav had ended up reminiscing with Meyerhold about Moscow until the early hours.

He told her that eventually, through Apollinaire, he came to know the Rotonde regulars.

He was quiet for a while.

'What are you thinking of?' Tamara asked.

'I was just remembering the sister of a friend… I hadn't given her a second thought in such a long time… Her name was Elena…'

'You sound so sad… why? What happened to Elena?'

'Like me, before the 1905 revolution she used to work underground for the Bolsheviks in Russia and fled to Paris. But she was a few years older than I was – it was her younger brother I'd known back in Moscow. I think she was kind to me because I reminded her of him, really.'

He'd been a little in love with her, he told Tamara, not that she ever thought of him romantically. He remembered her telling him that all love was contingent. Even a mother's love. Only nature accepts us exactly as we are – in our sadness and weakness, our happiness and strength, healthy or sick. The sound of the wind, the taste of the rain and the crashing of the waves were what allowed you to escape yourself and see yourself more clearly for a brief second.

Elena had tried her utmost to make a life for herself in France. She'd enrolled at the *Haute École des Études Sociales*, where she'd met a student from Bucharest, another communist in exile. They became lovers and within a year or so he asked her to marry him. He was a good-looking and tender man, and they seemed inseparable and deeply in love. But even after their son was born she could never settle to her new life. She always longed to go home. When her husband returned from work one day, she had poisoned herself.

He told Tamara about another Tamara, Tamara Nadolskaya, a thin girl with drooping eyes, a wide mouth and black curly hair which had already begun to go grey in her early twenties. He used to see her in the Rotonde sometimes and they had a brief liaison. He remembered her telling him about her childhood in Gorenki. They talked of many things: Russian literature, music, the meaning of life. She held a deep conviction that it was their duty to try to change the world for better, because, she said, 'All earthly experiences are relative, even the concept of God, and the only absolute thing in life is change.'

Stanislav had agreed with her that life was in constant flux.

'Nobody's life can be static because time doesn't freeze for as much as a second for anybody,' he said.

'I know. That's a great sadness to me,' she'd answered.

'But that's how everyone experiences life.'

'Just because it's the same for everyone, it doesn't make it any less sad. We can't live in the present because the present doesn't exist for more than a second, and I can never claim yesterday back, only recreate it through a tapestry of memories, often as difficult to hold as water in your hands. Something real happened which isn't real anymore. Or I can't prove it was real. That's the paradox. Nothing in my life is certain. That's what lies at the heart of my unhappiness.'

Tamara Nadolskaya looked for originality of thought, and hated people who simply took their ideas and beliefs from books or other people. They were unimaginative, and beneath her notice. She rented an attic room near the Porte d'Italie, and through the little window, spreading before her for miles, she could see the grey roofs of Paris. She never saw her dreams for changing the world come true, never saw the establishment of social justice as an absolute norm.

It was all such a disappointment.

This was what she noted in a short letter, before hurling herself down onto the street.

'Are you trying to frighten me?' Tamara asked him.

'No.'

'Why are you telling me all these awful stories then?'

'Because I want you to understand…'

'Understand what?'

'What it will mean to be an exile.'

20

Their clothes rotted away on their backs. From time to time they'd steal new ones, but it wouldn't be long before they too turned to rags, and with all the walking, they went through their shoes in no time.

They would often have to waste days in hiding in order to avoid being rounded up and arrested, and take long detours around towns where there was fighting. It was always these decisions that led to arguments between Mishka and Alyosha, who almost came to blows sometimes, with Masha trying to keep the peace.

'You want to mount my sister, Pavel?' whispered Mishka in Alyosha's ear one night. He'd got hold of some vodka from somewhere and had drunk the lot.

Somewhere above their heads a bird rustled noisily through the leaves. The fire's meagre flames were reflected in Mishka's good eye.

'I've seen the way you look at her, you cunt…'

He was forever baiting Alyosha, trying to provoke him to start a fight and give him the excuse he was looking for to beat the living daylights out of him.

'You'd better not, Pavel.'

Alyosha's nostrils were full of the smell of burning.

'If you fancy seeing your mother again.'

He opened his father's long razor and slapped it against his heel.

Masha, from the other side of the fire where she was going through her little brother's hair for lice, asked drowsily,

'What are you two whispering about?'

They didn't answer. Mishka pushed his finger under his leather patch and rubbed the edges of his empty socket. He wiped his mouth with the back of his hand. His good eye was nailed onto Alyosha. Their hatred of each other was naked.

Mishka knew instinctively that Alyosha was hiding something from them. He didn't trust him and was constantly trying to catch him out. Alyosha could constantly feel that one eye trained on him, watching him like a hawk.

Alyosha had listened to Leo the tramp's advice and had presented himself out to the three siblings as one of the proletariat.

His mother was a maid called Dunia, he told them, and his name was Pavel Vadimovich (he had noticed the name on a gravestone in some otherwise forgotten graveyard, and it had stayed with him). Masha and Boris hadn't thought for a moment that he might be lying. Boris had asked him innocently, as he chewed on a blade of grass, 'So have you got a father?'

'Everyone has a father.'

He spat out the blade of grass at him playfully.

'I know that, I meant...'

'I *did* have a father, Vadim Mikhailovich...'

'Did he work?'

'Yes... Not all the time, mind...'

'What did he do, Pavel?'

'Before the war he was a servant for some rich people...'

Mishka had listened carefully, without comment or question.

'He was killed years ago, when he was a soldier.'

Masha asked where.

'A place called Tannenburg.'

He could imagine his life below stairs well enough. By claiming to be Dunia's son, he could describe his old house, and Oxana and Roza and the other servants, without having to make it all up. Masha and Boris liked hearing how pint-sized, pink-cheeked Roza would lose her temper with everyone, especially the parrot, and how when Rodion, a sailor from Krondstat, came by looking to fill his belly at their kitchen table, he would sometimes bring out a length of rope and teach him how to tie all the different knots. But it was hard work lying and he had to be careful not to vary the details or contradict himself.

He compared Inessa Vassilyevna and Fyodor Mikhailovich to two fat spiders feeding off the blood of the workers. She was lazy and spoiled, while he was a big-bellied capitalist who owned an armaments factory.

Even Mishka seem to enjoy hearing about Fyodor being arrested by the Cheka. All three of them laughed at his description of the bourgeois pig being forced to draw a cartoon of himself on the kitchen wall. But Alyosha felt more and more like a sort of murderer, forced to keep on killing and killing in order to kill the memory of the previous murder.

'Tell us about it again!'

'I've already told you that story over and over, Boris.'

'Just *once* more. Go on, Pavel, *please…*'

'Oh, all right, but this is the very last time, understand?'

And with a sigh of contentment Boris settled back to listen, his eyes shining.

21

Stanislav was seeing another woman, though Tamara had no inkling. Always short of money, and finding it a constant struggle to pay his rent every month, he had visited several newspaper editors in Kiev in the hope of selling an article or two. The only example of his work was a piece arguing for democracy that had been published in Moscow just before he left. Perhaps it was a little naïve and confused in its analysis, but he hoped it showed he could write.

While he'd been waiting to see the editor of the *Kievlyian*, Stanislav had started to chat with the girl sitting at her typewriter in the outer office. Rozaliya Sergeyev was a sweet-looking girl, with a guileless gaze, a small forehead and soft brown hair brushed back from her face. Stanislav had noticed a volume by Blok on her desk, and soon they were discussing the merits of various poets, Balmont and Bryusov amongst them. They ended up arranging to meet that evening to continue their conversation.

They met by the river Dnieper. Stanislav was in a celebratory mood, as he had been commissioned to write six articles for the *Kievlyian*.

Over the following weeks, Stanislav grew very fond of Rozaliya's company but for all that he couldn't have said he was in love with her. She was twenty-two years old and although he was not her first love, she had never felt like this before. She was in love with him and it felt like falling heavier and deeper into some swamp where she was in danger of losing herself utterly. This was a totally new experience for her and she found it pleasurably frightening.

In the meantime, Tamara was finding that the burden of deceiving Yury was beginning to tell on her, and with Stanislav's encouragement, she decided that being honest would be best. They decided to tell him together.

'We need to tell you something,' she began falteringly one morning.

It was clear from Yury's expression that he feared the worst. He looked from one to the other with rising panic.

'What?'

Tamara couldn't say anything else.

'What is it?' asked Yury urgently.

After Stanislav explained the situation Yury sat quite still for a few moments. Then, with a grey squirrel puppet on one fist and a red squirrel puppet on the other, he started to thump Stanislav as hard as he could across his head and face. Tamara screamed at him to stop, but Yury had lost all control and started to kick Stanislav violently as well.

'Yury! Stop! You're going to kill him! Stop, I beg you.'

He finally pushed Stanislav away and took his anger out on some chairs, kicking them to smithereens until his anger was spent.

Stanislav sat quietly, holding his bloody nose up, as Tamara rounded on Yury for destroying their only way of making a livelihood.

When Rozaliya saw Stanislav's bruises, the mournful look on her face silenced his weak explanations.

'I knew before you said a word,' she told him. 'There's another woman, isn't there?'

Stanislav, unable to hide his surprise, replied, 'But how did you know?'

'It doesn't matter how. I suppose you'd better tell me who she is.'

They were sitting quietly on a bench under a beech tree in the

Zhitomirskaya Gardens. When he had finished telling her about Tamara, and the fight with Yury, he asked her hesitantly, 'Do you hate me?'

'What do you think…?' Her voice hardened. 'No, it's not that simple… it's worse than hate or jealousy… it's something… I don't even know if there's a word to describe how I feel.'

'I can understand that I've disappointed you.'

'You're not the first bastard to do that.'

'I am a bastard.'

'I'm glad to hear you admit that.'

'But in my heart… I can't live without her… and I can't live without you either.'

22

Yury refused to accept that the engagement was over. He became self-pitying, introverted and miserable. How could Tamara have done such a thing? And for an idiot like Stanislav? He begged her to come back to him. She did try for a while, but his constant recriminations were too much to bear. He'd lose his temper, calling her every crude name under the sun.

She'd turn on her heel and walk away from his insults, but the minute she'd shut the door behind her, Yury would run after her and beg her forgiveness, beg her to just come back to him and it would all be alright. When she insisted it was over, he started to threaten to kill himself, which frightened her into going back to him; and for a while he would hold his tongue, before beginning the whole vicious cycle of argument and insults all over again.

In the midst of all this trauma, Tamara decided it was time for Stanislav to meet her parents. The first meeting was awkward, as it was obvious that Tamara's parents thought she was making a mistake.

Although Viktor was a working man, in charge of a workshop which maintained and repaired train engines, he hated the Communists.

'Just look at how we've all been living since 1917. Are we any better off? Thousands upon thousands have died since the revolution, from fighting, starvation, disease. I've no time for the aristocrats, any more than the bourgeoisie, but I'm not too keen on having to kowtow to that lot...'

Stansilav felt the man was doing his best to pick a fight. He was astoundingly ugly, with one sleepy eye, and three large black moles on his cheeks.

'Last time the Whites attacked, the Reds came over to the workshop. Made us all down tools, and then this Commmissar ordered us all to grab a spade each, and we were made to go and dig trenches on the outskirts of Kiev to stop the Whites. Did they feed us? Did they water us? Did we even get as much as a thank you? Did we buggery. "We're doing this for your sake, brothers." That's what that Commissar told us as he stood over us, watching us work. "Not for my sake," I said to myself, "but to save your own skins, you bloody hypocrite." What have you got to say then?'

'I hate to see people die for no reason,' answered Stanislav.

Once he had left, Tamara's mother turned to her and said, 'You've disappointed your father, Tamara. A Jew? Must you?'

'I love him.'

'Love him indeed! How do you know?'

'I just know. Because he's honest, and has a good heart.'

'Does he want to marry you, then?'

How could Tamara tell her parents that there was no need to marry in order to live happily? That what she was experiencing was entirely delightful, this discovering of herself through somebody else.

Her father picked up his cap and walked out.

'Tamara, child…'

'You have no idea how he makes me feel, Mama.'

'Why have you lost your head over someone like him? You deserve better…'

'I'm going to live with him and you and Papa can't stop me.'

'You're only eighteen years old, remember.'

'Quite old enough to live my own life.'

'How old is he?'

'Nearly twenty-nine.'

'He's too old for you,' she told her daughter gently. 'Much too old. If it's really over between you and Yury, then why don't you look for somebody nearer your own age?'

'Because I'm not in love with somebody nearer my own age!'

As autumn approached, the news reached them that the Reds were moving towards the city from the north-west. There were certainly heavy bombardments of artillery fire to be heard on the wind, from the direction of Borispol. Anton Denikin's army found themselves outnumbered and retreated from Kiev to a fallback position to regroup and gather reinforcements, rather than risk being disastrously routed.

Although Yury was still trying to persuade Tamara to come back to him, after all the weeks of shouting he had settled into a quiet melancholy. When he spoke, he barely raised his voice above a whisper so that it could be quite difficult to understand everything he said. One morning at the theatre, he made one final appeal to her.

'Just try to explain why you choose him instead of me? What does he have that I don't?'

'Yury, why bring this up all over again? I've made my choice. There's no turning back.'

'Toma…' he said imploringly.

'There's no kind way of saying something like this. But I don't want to come back to you. It's all over.'

'No, don't say that, because it's not…'

'But it is. Forever. It's all over…'

'Why are you so cruel?'

'I have to be cruel so that you accept what I tell you!'

'We're engaged. We're going to get married. We're going to live in Paris. All our plans, all our hopes of being together…'

Yury still clung onto some dream. Tamara had no choice but to say coldly, 'I've made my decision.'

She kissed her ex-lover lightly on his forehead.

'Don't leave me.'

'We'll always be friends.'

'No, we won't. I don't want to be friends. Not with you. If you've really left me for good, I've no intention of staying in Kiev.'

'That's up to you.'

Yury Kashinin decided that if he had lost Tamara's soul forever, he would at least join the battle for the soul of Russia. He left the city to enlist with the White army.

23

Stanislav and Tamara tried to keep the puppet theatre going, but as the Red Army approached, their audiences dwindled to nothing. There was sporadic fighting on the outskirts of Kiev and occasional artillery fire. During one such attack, the house where Stanislav and Tamara had lodgings was destroyed and the landlord was killed outright, leaving his wife to discover his mutilated remains.

The Red Army finally marched into the city, past the City Hall and the Exchange: Kiev was in the hands of the Communists once more. Stanislav only now admitted to Tamara that, before leaving Moscow, he had published an article criticising the Communists for shutting down the Constituent Assembly, and thus killing off the first shoots of democracy in Russia. On reflection, it had been a brave but foolish thing to have written. Even worse, he had sold the same article to the editor of the *Kievylian*, who had published it on the front page, and it was so warmly received that it had been reproduced in the Kievshaya *Zhizu*. He feared things would not go well for him under the Reds: it would only be a matter of time before the Cheka came to read it. Then they would make their enquiries as to his whereabouts, followed by the inevitable banging on the door in the middle of the night, the arrest, interrogation… and then they would shoot him.

But they had a little time. Marching down the main street did not mean the Reds had secured the city for good. The Whites had regrouped, and for the rest of the winter fighting continued around

Kiev. The tide appeared to turn at the beginning of March, when news reached the city that the Whites had won a battle to the south of Chernigov and the Reds would soon be in retreat again.

When this came to pass, and Denikin's soldiers crossed the Dnieper, the sound of their boots tramping over the Nikolaevski Bridge echoing around the ancient walls of the citadel, nobody greeted them with more enthusiasm than Stanislav and Tamara. They threw flowers, along with many others, which were trampled under the horses' hooves and great wheels of the artillery carts.

From the procession, a smartly-uniformed soldier on horseback gazed down at them unsmilingly. When Stanislav and Tamara realised that it was Yury Kashivin, Stanislav knew at once he would be sure to want revenge for the theft of his fiancée.

Soon the shops were open for business once more, and a gust of fresh air seemed to sweep through Kiev's streets after the fear and uncertainty of the previous months. A thanksgiving service was held in the Church of Saint Sophia. During the months when Kiev had been under the governance of the Reds, Stanislav had not dared look for work with the Bolshevik papers in case somebody recognised him. So when the *Kievshaya Zhizu* went into print again, he was the first to knock on the door and, perhaps because of the lack of material, he was welcomed and commissioned to write a weekly column.

The respite was short-lived. He only had time to write three columns, and only two of those were ever published, because the Reds sent reinforcements down by train from Moscow to Orel and they were about to invade Kiev once again. The Whites intended defending their position this time, so there would be full-blown fighting in the city. It was time to leave. Tamara packed a suitcase each for them, but Stanislav was worried about Rozaliya Sergeyev. He had been seeing as much of her as ever and he was reluctant to leave Kiev without her.

With the sound of the guns coming closer, he confessed to Tamara.

'Why?'

She could barely believe her ears.

'What does that say about me?'

'Nothing. It says more about me.'

'So do you love me at all?'

'I love you very much. I love both of you.'

Tamara collapsed on the bed, weeping. Stanislav tried to put his arms aound her but she shook him off.

'Don't! Don't you dare touch me. Leave me alone.'

'Tamara, we have to leave.'

'You leave. I won't come with you. Not if you're bringing her with you.'

She was inconsolable.

'Why did I ever agree to live with you? You've been making a fool of me all this time, only I was too stupid to see it. My mother warned me enough about you, but I was too stubborn to listen.'

'Rozaliyna Sergeyev is an orphan. She has nobody.'

'But for you,' she said bitterly. 'You've been sleeping with the two of us.'

There was no way of denying it.

'From one bed to the other. Who's the best? Her or me?'

A fireball exploded in the next street. A building crumpled in on itself, great clouds and billows of dust reaching them and making Stanislav cough.

'Tamara, we can't stay here. It's not safe…' He tried to lift her up.

'Do you intend to carry on fucking the two of us? Perhaps we could make it easier for you if we both shared your bed? It would save you having to get up in the night.'

The next explosion was nearer, hurling Stanislav to the floor.

'Now – we have to go. Move!'

When Stanislav and Tamara Mikhailovna staggered up the street, dragging their heavy suitcases, Rozaliya Sergeyevna was already waiting for them. High above the city, two light fighter planes were purring.

In her anguish, Tamara threw herself at the other girl, grabbing her hair and flinging her hat away.

'You can't have him!'

She yanked savagely at her hair, snarling, 'He's mine! He's mine!'

'Tamar! Tamar!'

'Mine and nobody else's!'

'Let go of her!'

'Just leave us alone! Leave us alone!'

'Let go of her, Tamar!'

In Tamara's fist was a long hank of Rozaliya's hair. Rozaliya stood, too shocked at the suddenness and ferocity of the attack to react. She was shaking.

'No more fighting,' said Stanislav. 'We have to go now. Or we'll be killed.'

They had to run the last mile and a half from Khreschatyk Street, with a young girl in a blue dress, leading an angora goat with two white kids at her tail, running alongside them. But when they reached the station there was no train, and no likelihood that one was on the way. There was no way of fleeing.

Then the Communists returned, a ragged army with most of its soldiers barefoot, and the rest with only filthy *portianki* bandaged around their feet. They all wore peaked caps with a red star, so the only way of distinguishing the officers was by their black leather jackets.

In the wake of this bedraggled army, crowds of people dragged their carts and their possessions, or carried their children, back towards the spires of Lavra cathedral, back to the parks and gardens, back over the Dnieper with its small islands and ancient bridges.

Amongst those thousands who walked wearily down Khreschatyk Street were Alyosha, Mishka, Masha and Boris.

24

The Communists set up their headquarters in the Hotel Continental. The guests were evicted and the entire building was requisitioned for the offices of the Council of People's Commissars. Night and day there were comings and goings, and the noise of motor-bikes and motor-cars drawing up to the wide forecourt. The grand old dining room with its six magnificent chandeliers was turned into a canteen.

Mishka decided this was the best place to forage for food. It was impossible to gain access to the building from the main entrance, as you had to show a pass, but he had soon found a back entrance. He showed the other three the way.

Alyosha came to a sudden standstill, a strange bemused look on his face. Masha noticed and asked him, 'What's the matter? What have you seen?'

When he didn't answer she gave him a little shake and said, 'Pasha? What are you looking at?'

A look of great weariness came over his face.

'What's the matter?' she asked again.

The three siblings stood watching him. Alyosha walked over to the motor-car, ran his fingers over the bonnet which was covered in scratches and dents. His father's motor-car was in a dreadful condition, filthy inside and out, with bullet holes along the side, and the leather seats split open, the wool stuffing blackened and bulging out.

Mishka barked irritably, 'Pavel? You going to tell us what the hell is bothering you?'

Alyosha pulled himself together and mumbled something by way of excuse.

They didn't move quickly enough in the kitchens and were discovered. Mishka was caught, but the other three just managed to outrun the soldiers who gave chase.

A couple of days later Mishka was allowed to go free – once he had agreed to join the Red Army. He was given his food coupons, and every day he managed to smuggle out some food to the other three, although it was strictly against the rules. But Masha and Boris saw less and less of their older brother as he couldn't get away that often and spent most of his time with the Cheka inside the Hotel Continental.

Gradually his vocabulary changed. Alyosha noticed that he had picked up all sorts of new ideas. For instance: 'We have to kill every landlord. We have to kill every priest, and every capitalist and every last enemy of Russia, those within and those without.'

'All at once?' asked Alyosha mischievously.

Miskha didn't even notice.

'If we're to live in peace – we have to kill them all, yes.'

He went on to declare that nobody was too young or too old to do their share. There was a new country to be won and a better society to be built out of the rubble of the old one.

'Men may die but an ideal lives on forever.'

Mishka brought his brother Boris one of the red-starred peaked caps, and Boris loved nothing more than putting it on and marching and swaggering in front of them, pretending to be a soldier. He looked very funny, as the cap was too large for his head and came down over his eyes, and even Mishka laughed at his antics.

Mishka told Boris a story about how there was once a beautiful young woman called Pravda. On her forehead shone a red star, which lit up and filled the entire world with truth, justice and harmony. But one night as she lay sleeping, the red star was stolen by Krivda, who wanted to bury the world in lies and darkness. And so it was for many long years, and Krivda's rule was oppressive and cruel indeed. Until one day the lovely Pravda appealed to the ordinary people, who had been suffering so badly under Krivda's tyranny, to help her save her star so that the light of truth could shine once more. Eventually a brave young worker killed Krivda and returned the star to Pravda. And the second that happened, the darkness lifted and the light returned. The sun of truth and justice ruled once again. Life became sweet and the people could live their lives in peace and harmony.

After she heard the story, Masha agreed at once to wear the red star. Her brother gave it to her, with a warning not to lose it.

'You're the one who's careless, not me,' answered Masha.

Then Mishka held out another star under Alyosha's nose and asked, 'Are you with us?'

Alyosha gazed at his dirty thumbnail.

'If you're not with us, there'll be no forgiveness.'

Boris took the star and pinned it onto Alyosha's cap.

'There you are, Pavel. You're a soldier in the Red Army like me now.'

Mishka managed to 'liberate' some bottles of champagne, and that night the four of them got as drunk as lords before falling asleep in a tangled heap in a small storeroom under the summer theatre, in the middle of the gardens of the Merchants' Club.

25

One coupon couldn't feed the four of them, and the kitchen staff had become far more vigilant about locking up the supplies at the end of the day, so stealing extra food became impossible. The answer became obvious and Mishka arranged it all.

Alyosha, Masha and Boris entered the Hotel Continental officially through the front door. They were each given a pass and ushered upstairs by a taciturn middle-aged woman in a green woollen frock. She chewed sunflower seeds, spitting out the husks into her hand and then burying them in her pocket.

She knocked on a door, and there was a moment's silence before the Commissar's voice ordered them to enter. For half a second, he raised his head to glance at them as they shuffled in to stand before him. Alyosha gazed at the toad's mouth and the pendulous lower lip. Ivan Kirilich.

Would he recognise him?

Eventually the Commissar put his pen down and lifted his head. When he smiled at them he exposed a crooked row of small teeth.

Did he recognise him?

His father's ex-chauffeur stood up, pulling his heavy coat tighter across his shoulders. He was stouter than he used to be, and looked in good shape. But he hadn't shaved in some days and his chin was covered in a ruddy stubble.

Why hadn't he recognised him?

The Mauser rattled in its wooden holster. He blew his nose and complained that he couldn't get rid of this cold.

'It's been plaguing me for days.'

Ivan Kirilich wore a wide leather belt around his middle. Alyosha noticed there were clay models of a dog and a lion and a zebra on a shelf behind his desk. The gun clinked again.

A picture of him jumped into Alyosha's head, in his shirtsleeves, swigging from a cold bottle of beer, the fine hairs on the back of his hand glinting in the sun…

Ivan Kirilich leaned his thighs against the side of the desk and crossed his arms.

He remembered the chauffeur telling him that his Uncle Kozma and Mademoiselle Babin were lovers, and how unwilling he'd been to believe it…

With his reddened, watery eyes he scrutinised them one by one but he didn't linger any longer on Alyosha's face than Masha's or Boris'.

He started to speak.

'You're young people, but not too young to understand the situation here. Russia today is in mortal danger.'

He told them of the need for courage and resolve, but more than anything, he emphasised the need for discipline.

'We mustn't let our revolution go the same way as the Commune. Do you know about the Commune? In 1871? No? When they hunted the proletariat of Paris and shot them like rabbits on the streets of Montmartre? That cannot be allowed to happen to us. That's why it's so important to keep an iron discipline. That's how we will ensure victory over Denikin and his like. That's how the Red Army will sweep the thieves and murderers from Russia's land. And that's how peace will prevail.'

26

Masha and Boris were put to work in the kitchen of the Hotel Continental. Mishka was promoted to work for the Cheka, while Alyosha was placed with a younger gang, in charge of the prisoners. So many had been arrested during the night-time sweeps, they had to be kept in makeshift prisons the length and breadth of the city – monasteries in the main – but Alyosha was sent to guard some old stables behind a girls' school on the Bolshaya Vladimirskaya.

There were no bars on the windows or even any locks on the big stable doors. It was a very crude sort of prison, and the only things that kept the prisoners in their place were the three guards, and their machine-guns, who did four-hour shifts on a twenty-four hour rota.

The stables had been full to bursting point following the return of the Communists to Kiev, but eventually things settled down somewhat and many had been released. The number of prisoners there at any one time varied considerably however: sometimes Alyosha found himself guarding just one or two, but at other times, when there had been many arrests made during the small hours of the morning for one reason and another, he would come to work to find the place overflowing.

There was then no knowing how long it would take before they were questioned. Eventually, however, a squad of soldiers would arrive and call out a name. Some wan-faced creature would emerge, blinking from his corner in the straw and stagger over the cumbent bodies to the door. Alyosha never saw any angry or challenging behaviour from the prisoners. It was as if they had already accepted the inevitable. It was a different matter shooting the women. To avoid a scene, they were marched off between two tall Kalmyk soldiers, straight from being interrogated, to a little orchard a couple of fields away.

27

Late one evening, four Chekists arrived at the stables with ten prisoners, a couple of them with bloody noses, and all with the marks of a beating on them. Mishka swaggered with all his new-found authority, the leather of his jacket still shiny and new, and smelling of the scent of some girl. He ordered Alyosha to take one of the prisoners over to Commissar Kirilich.

When the gun was given to him he had to hold it with both hands to steady it. The heaviness of the stock felt strange.

'Guard him with your life, Pavel,' Mishka ordered him, his good eye as dark as his black eye-patch.

He mimed pulling a trigger.

'Any funny business – '

Without saying a word, the prisoner walked in front of him across the yard. When they reached one of the classrooms, Alyosha ordered him to sit. It was a small wooden chair. The man shrunk into a child.

In a while, Commissar Kirilich came in, took off his jacket, which he hung on the back of the door, strode over to the teacher's desk and placed his papers carefully down on it, all without looking once at Alyosha or his prisoner.

Without any apparent urgency, he started asking questions quietly, methodically and courteously. After some four hours, when the candle was burning low, he ordered Alyosha to take the prisoner back to the stables.

After all that he had heard, Alyosha couldn't help himself – although he had been warned never to talk with the prisoners –

and told the prisoner that he had a relative in Paris. When the prisoner heard the name, he stopped and asked in wonderment, 'You're related to him? Are you? How?'

Alyosha explained the connection under his breath.

'His nephew?'

Stanislav's expression lit up and he said, 'I know Artyom too.'

He smiled broadly and Alyosha felt a surge of warmth towards him.

'I know him quite well. I used to see him in Montparnasse from time to time, and we had a few friends in common. Women mostly…'

Did you know Picasso?'

'Yes, very well. Why, where did you hear about him?'

Alyosha glanced around hurriedly to check they were not being observed.

'My uncle bought one of his pictures and gave it to my father for a Christmas present.'

From the stable door one of the soldiers barked at Alyosha to stop loitering.

28

He banged on the door, then banged again, more urgently and for longer this time. A face still crumpled with sleep peered out at him from a crack in the door.

'What the hell are you doing here so early…?' Mishka asked him irritably in a hoarse voice.

'I want a word with you.'

His nose looked red and meaty and his leather eye-patch was damp. He was in a foul mood for being woken.

'D'you know when I got to bed last night, Pavel?'

'This is a serious matter.'

'What are you on about?'

After all the trouble he'd had finding Mishka (the only thing he'd had to go on was that he was shacked up with a blonde clerk who worked for the Cheka, and that she lived somewhere on the Bibikorskii), he wasn't going to leave without being heard. He told Mishka about Stanislav and that a mistake had been made in his case.

'A bad mistake. You have to believe me or an innocent man will die.'

Mishka looked over his shoulder at the supine body asleep in the bed.

'Under the old regime he was imprisoned in the Butyrki for distributing leaflets supporting the striking workers back in '05. He was only fifteen at the time. That's why he went to Paris in the first place – he had to get out of Russia before they arrested him again.'

Mishka yawned.

'When he was there, he met Lenin himself. Lenin, imagine. Had supper with him and everything. He's been a supporter of Bolshevism from early on. Don't shut the door! Justice for the workers. That's what he wanted. That's what he told me last night. You have to speak to him yourself and…'

'What's he doing writing for some reactionary rag like *Zhizu* then?'

'There's a reason for that too – '

'You can tell me another time – '

'No, no, listen to me – '

He sighed and said, 'Get on with it then – '

'He wanted to leave for Paris but he was short of money…'

'Short of money?' he repeated mockingly. 'Well, poor little thing, I say. How did you and me and thousands like us live? We didn't sell ourselves to Soviet Russia's enemies because we were short of money.'

Alyosha had no ready answer to this.

'I really don't think he's a supporter of Denikin.'

'So you say.'

'What about giving him the benefit of the doubt?'

'Move your foot, you little cunt.'

The door banged shut.

Talking to Masha later, he realised Stanislav's fate was inevitable and there was nothing he could do to save him. As she handed the cup she'd just washed to Boris to dry she mused, 'As far as I can see, they'll shoot anybody and everybody. There's no point trying to reason with them. Mishka's just as blind as the rest. I've never seen anybody change so much so quickly.'

29

That evening, Alyosha was ordered to take Stanislav over to the school, where Commissar Ivan Kirilich went over the previous night's answers to his questions with a fine toothcomb.

Did Stanislav know what the Whites' strategy was? Had he met this officer or that? What rumours had he heard? However much he pressed the prisoner, he was less than helpful, claiming ignorance on most points. It was clear to Alyosha that the Commissar was after some specific knowledge that he seemed to think Stanislav was party to, and was determined to winkle it out of him; but it seemed equally clear, to him at least, that Stanislav knew nothing.

The hours dragged interminably on, and Alyosha, tense as he was, occasionally found himself nodding off, before jerking himself back to attention. Meanwhile, Ivan Kirilich was becoming increasingly frustrated, rattling the Mauser in its wooden holster more often and cursing.

He told Stanislav that he clearly knew more than he was willing to admit, and he intended interrogating him until he told him what he knew.

'I can't help you.'

'Can't or won't?'

'Can't.'

With no warning, Ivan Kirilich slapped him across his cheek. Stanislav, reeling, repeated, 'I can't help you.'

A second blow came his way.

'I still can't help you,' Stanislav muttered again.

There was an irascible look in Ivan Kirilich's eye, and his voice, usually so calm and measured, was raised in anger.

'Don't play the innocent with me.'

'I've told you, I can't help you.'

With the butt of his revolver, Ivan Kirilich dealt a savage blow to Stanislav's head. He slumped forward in his chair, blood spurting over his forehead and nose.

'I'm a man who always gets to the bottom of everything sooner or later.'

Alyosha felt a shiver run through him. Ivan used to say exactly the same thing back home in Petrograd. Memories flooded back. He remembered how the chauffeur had found Lika's loot under her bed. He remembered how faithful Ivan had been to his father…

'Let's start all over again, shall we?'

When Alyosha eventually half-dragged Stanislav out of the school it was a clear, cloudless night. As they followed the uneven path through the little orchard, thousands and thousands of pinpricks of light studded the sky. He smelled the night. He smelled the earth and the moss. Old primitive smells, heavier and stronger than ever.

Ivan Kirilich started to whistle and Alyosha was transported back to Yalta, an eternity ago. Back to the beach. To the sea. To the haze of high summer. Back to the garden and the dull thud of Oxana beating the dust out of his hammock…

The three came to a stop by an open grave, next to another which had been filled with fresh earth.

'Not there… Put him there.'

Alyosha tried to manoeuvre Stanislav according to the Commissar's instructions, but he was a dead weight.

'Put him to kneel there.'

Stanislav slumped over him; he could feel his hot breath on his hand.

'Now shoot him.'

Stanislav made an effort to frame a word.

'Artyom…' Through a mouth thick with blood he muttered, 'Artyom… meet me in Paris…'

Barely audibly he whispered: 'Artyom, help me.'

Ivan hurled Alyosha out of the way.

'What did you say?'

He grabbed the prisoner by his chin and yanked his face up to look at him.

'Artyom? The petit Parisien?'

With a snarl of triumph he asked, 'Is that who you mean?'

Ivan had his chin in such a vice-like grip that Stanislav couldn't answer.

Alyosha stepped forward.

'Ivan Kirilich…'

Hearing the young guard's voice for the first time had an immediate effect on the Commissar. He seemed to freeze momentarily and then his face flamed.

Alyosha took another step forward. His mouth open, Ivan straightened up, as though about to say something, but in his astonishment, stumbled back – and disappeared. As he struggled to his feet, Stanislav grabbed on to Alyosha's arm for support.

Ivan yelled from the grave, 'Alexei Fyodorovitch! Shoot him! Shoot him!'

It was only when he heard the shot that Alyosha realised what had happened.

30

Less than a week after fleeing Kiev, Alyosha began to feel such pain in his head that his ears were filled with a noise like a fire cracking with burning twigs and branches. From ramshackle fences, on trees and walls, posters of Denikin, Kolchak, Kutepov and Shkuro stared down at him. They began to speak to him of loyalty, of honour and swearing an oath of allegiance to the Tzar. Even in his sleep they came to him, haranguing him to do his bit for Russia.

He resolutely kept on walking, doing his best to ignore the splitting pain in his head, which nevertheless seemed to get worse with every mile. He remembered suffering from bad headaches when he was a boy, sometimes lasting days; hermicrania the doctor had called it, but this constant pounding in his skull was far worse. He felt like vomiting though he had eaten nothing that day – and very little the previous day, come to that. Then he could walk no more and lay down on the earth floor of an old hovel, his whole body covered in cold sweat. He was starving and his ribs ached. As the hours went by he felt all his strength leave him, so that he was as weak as a newborn.

Dragging himself up again, he wrapped himself in his old grey coat, hacked off a branch to make a rough walking stick, and started to walk, a solitary figure under the vast expanse of a cloudless sky. His legs wouldn't carry him for long though, and he was forced to lie down again, his heart racing and the pain in his head so excruciating he felt that his skull was about to split open like a rotten peach…

31

The clouds opened up, but the sky behind them was green – a sort of light green like Aisha's eyes. It seemed frighteningly close as well, as though it had stumbled and fallen headlong towards him.

He reached up and tried to push his fingers into the clouds, but the sky pulled away back from his grasp. That's when he noticed his sleeve – it was white, a bright, dazzling white – a kind of white he hadn't seen in a long, long time…

It was remarkable that he was in the land of the living at all. When the old man who found him at the side of the road heaved him onto the back of his cart, his heart had very nearly given up.

Later, in the hospital, they told him he'd kept the other patients awake for hours, shouting in his delirium about seeing Byzantium, until quite a few of them hoped he wouldn't see the morning.

When the fever passed the nightmares stayed with him because they had seemed so vividly real.

He'd been walking with his Uncle Kozma, looking for his father. They'd found him sitting behind the bars of a hay manger, about to be taken before the Commissar. His father was a schoolboy standing in front of his desk, and Ivan Kirilich was interrogating him; but although Alyosha kept trying to warn him, it didn't matter how loudly he shouted, his father just stood there as if he were deaf. A firing squad appeared, and Mishka put a gun in his hand. Under the trees in the little orchard, his father begged for mercy from the open grave…

Winter's harshness slowly yielded to spring. The earth

softened. The trees came into leaf, buds opened into blossoms. He began to recover from the typhus. His appetite returned with a vengeance and he wolfed down every last morsel that came his way, gradually regaining his strength. He learned from the nurses that the civil war was pretty much at an end. Denikin had lost the day, and the only one left flying the flag of the Whites was a Baron Pyotr Wrangel, down in the Crimea. The rest of Russia was in the hands of the Communists, every last acre.

Once he was well enough to leave his bed and sit in a chair, he asked for pen and paper and wrote a letter. As he put the four sheets in the envelope, he had a sudden feeling of remorse, and he took the first sheet out and changed the salutation to include his father as well. But even as he addressed the letter to both his parents, he couldn't help feeling in his heart that his father was dead. Trying to convince himself otherwise was futile. For the first time in years he wept quietly.

One of the doctors promised to post it for him – the doctor who always had a bit more time for his patients, in all their frailty, than the others. He even paid for the stamps out of his own pocket, though Alyosha assured him he would pay him back the minute his family sent him some money, as he had requested in the letter.

No reply came. He had no way of knowing if the letter had even arrived at its destination. He felt forlorn and for the first time as if he were truly an orphan. He struggled daily with an enormous feeling of emptiness, and his longing to see his family overwhelmed all other emotions. Before he fell asleep every night he'd imagine himself walking through the house, starting at the bottom and moving unhurriedly from room to room until he reached the servants' quarters at the very top.

One cold and cloudy morning, when his feeling of loss almost felled him, he made himself a promise: as soon as he was strong enough, he would do everything in his power to get himself back to Petrograd.

32

Stanislav made a mistake. Instead of making directly for Bessarabia and the border with Romania when he fled Kiev, he took Roxaliya's advice and headed south. And the only reason Roxaliya had for going south was that Tamara had suggested otherwise. Things were no better between the women; they could barely look at each other, never mind speak.

As they sat waiting for a train in yet another unremarkable station in the middle of nowhere, some loutish Cossack, swigging vodka from an earthenware flagon, tried to pick a fight with Stanislav. The soldier had decided he had a Jewish look about him.

'You're the servant of the Antichrist.'

Stanislav ignored him.

'You're the servant of the Antichrist. Don't you deny it. I can smell it on you.'

'I'm not the servant of the Antichrist.'

'I'm not asking you – I'm telling you.'

'Leave me alone.'

'If you're not the servant of the Antichrist, prove it.'

The Cossack dared him to drop his trousers. The three of them tried their best to ignore him but there was no getting rid of him. He kept insisting on examining Stanislav's penis and was becoming more and more aggressive.

'You're the Antichrist's servant! I can see it in your fucking eyes, boy!'

He unbuttoned the collar of his tunic and unsheathed his sword.

'Oh, sweet Lord Jesus,' he petitioned the heavens. 'Give me your eternal strength!'

He started to swing the blade dangerously close to their faces.

'Go away!' pleaded Tamara. 'Go away and leave us alone. We're not doing anybody any harm.'

Rozaliya was in tears.

'What the hell is going on here?'

Another Cossack had made his way calmly towards them. He deftly removed the sword from the drunken soldier, then took him to one side to say something firmly but quietly in his ear, which seemed to tame his anger as suddenly as turbulent river water deflected into a calm canal. Stanislav thanked him and asked him his name.

'Muvadov.'

'I won't forget your kindness.'

Muvadov saluted them and they watched him walk down the platform towards the wooden stairs, and then cross the tracks until he disappeared from sight behind a little hut. They were left in peace then, apart from the usual palpable tension between Tamara and Rozaliya.

It was late that afternoon when they approached Sevastopol. Long before they reached the station they could see signs of conflict and confusion everywhere. When they left the train they joined hordes of people making for the centre, by foot or by cart, according to their means. Trying to keep some sort of order on this mêlée were the White soldiers with blue bands around their arms, urging people on if they loitered, shouting out orders and generally trying to keep everybody moving.

Sevastopol was in total chaos, far worse than they had ever seen in Kiev. Stanislav, Tamara and Rozaliya became part of an immense ants' nest of fleeing souls. There were people everywhere. Every hotel, house, hovel and hut was full to bursting. All day, and all night, people tramped the pavements in search of shelter, food, safety. The shops were all doing a roaring trade, and so were the cafés, taverns and restaurants, which stayed open late into the night.

No sooner had the three of them sat down gratefully at the last free table in a café, than a genteel looking woman approached them, her face lined with worry. She had a basket of dusty Parma violets on her arm and held out two little posies to Stanislav imploringly. He refused to buy them as courteously as he could, but after being importuned several more times, by various individuals, he became rather more curt and just snapped, 'No money, no money,' and waved them on their way.

They were even approached by a general trying to sell a sword.

'This sword is holy. Do you know why? Because the Tzar himself held it once. Feel the hilt. This is a once in a lifetime opportunity.'

'No money, no money,' Stanislav repeated to everybody.

After trudging the streets for many weary hours, they were eventually directed to a villa some way above the city. It belonged to a family who had packed up and left for Malta two months previously. They had been landowners with vast estates in Sampsonievski, and this dacha had been in their family since it was built in the middle of the previous century. Their ghosts seemed to inhabit the place, along with their smell, which lingered in the folds of the odd garment, left forgotten in a drawer here and there. On the walls where the paintings had hung there were just white squares. They reasoned they would be safer above the city than anywhere else, especially as they were told there was a lot of sickness and disease.

Food was the first and most important priority. If you had money, it was easy enough to buy supplies. There was no shortage of sugar, butter, meat – if you could afford the price. There were the usual hordes of orphans everywhere of course, with their promises to steal whatever you needed. There was also a thriving black market, where you could buy almost anything.

Over the next few days, all three of them tried to find work, but only Rozaliya succeeded. She was given a few shifts in a dirty and chaotic café. The owner was a pale Azerbaijani, a brittle man with a thin face and mournful eyes whose wife had run off to Sukhami with a circus juggler from Poti (it was more than your life was worth to speak a word of it). He was short-tempered and quick to find fault. The first thing he said to Rozaliya was that if he caught her stealing the food, she'd be out on her ear.

'Not even a crust, understand?'

'I understand.'

'You'd better.'

He was painfully close to her, and she shrank against the counter to try to create a little more space between them. In his sallow face one eye was crossed and his breath stank as though he kept a dead cat in his gullet.

'Because the last one said she understood as well, and look what happened to her.'

Rozaliya Sergeyov decided she'd rather not know what her predecessor's fate had been.

Renting a room above the café was a lady from Moscow. She had lost her reason, and lay on her bed most of the day wearing her husband's military coat and feather hat, crying and begging someone to save her darling Pyotr. Her husband had been working for the *Osvag* – the Whites' propaganda department. Nobody knew for sure what had happened to him, but there was a rumour that he'd been captured by the Bolsheviks, who had tied him between two unbroken horses until he was pulled to bits.

Next to the café was a barber's shop where Stanislav went for a haircut and shave. He'd seen his reflection in the mirror and opened the door on an impulse, though he could ill afford it.

The barber gave him a half-smile that gave up before reaching his eyes, and told him, 'You're my first customer of the day…'

Stanislav stepped into a stuffy, low-ceilinged room. The barber was a short, greasy-looking man with a dirty apron tied across his belly. Stanislav noticed that his hands were shining as he sharpened the blade of his razor on the long leather strop. Like barbers the world over he talked non-stop as he lathered up his cheeks.

When Stanislav told him what he did for a living he said, 'Well if you can turn your hand to plays and such, why don't you call by the Bee-Bah-Bo?'

Stanislav asked him for directions and he and Tamara went to find it later that day. It was a long room with boarded-up windows and a crude stage rigged up at one end from boxes, no more than eighteen inches from the floor. The curtains and lighting were equally primitive. A troupe of actors from Moscow was running the place. Stanislav thought a couple of them looked vaguely familiar from the Café Bom. He introduced himself and Tamara but the welcome was lukewarm at best, as so many came knocking on the door looking for work. However, they did invite them both to come and watch the performance that evening.

When they returned there wasn't an empty chair and they had to stand at the back of the room. The show consisted of a series of sketches and songs, apart from one slot where the well-known Moscow comic Don Liminado spat out scathing and scurrilous jokes about Lenin and Trotskii. The content was no more than propaganda of the crudest sort, but somehow it all came straight from the heart. The cabaret seemed a genuine attempt to try to raise the spirits of people who had lost everything at the hands of the communist thieves.

After the performance, Stanislav agreed to write a couple of sketches and some jokes.

'Good comic material is always scarce,' smiled Don Liminado, his eyebrows still full of greasepaint.

They had nothing to offer Tamara.

33

Autumn arrived and the first cold blasts of winter could be felt upon the air. Stanislav's greatest worry was Tamara. Although she had searched high and low, she hadn't even had a sniff of a job. Disheartened, she had given up even looking – but this left her feeling very guilty and worthless. Rozaliya made it perfectly clear that she resented every penny of her meagre wages that went on supporting Tamara.

Stanislav, in the absence of anything else coming his way, was still writing sketches for the Bee-Bah-Bo. They weren't always deemed to be anti-communist enough and so the actors tended to improvise. Stanislav hated himself for resorting to writing such crude material, but it was that or starve. He had no choice.

With Rozaliya and Stanislav at work, it was Tamara's job to prepare supper and clean the villa. She had never learned to cook, and domestic work did not come naturally to her, so she spent as little time as possible on her tasks. Rozaliya, on the other hand, had always been brought up to help around the house and hated dirt and disorder, which made working in the squalid little café such purgatory.

One afternoon Tamara complained of a bad stomach.

'She's only pretending, to get out of making the supper,' said Rozaliya, completely unsympathetic.

The next day however, Tamara felt worse. She was running a high temperature and took to her bed, where she became delirious. That night, her whimpering and fitful sleep kept the other two awake: so the next day, with no money to summon a doctor, Stanislav sent Rozaliya out to look for camphor, which could be bought easily enough on the black market. A syringe was harder to come by. Stanislav went down to the docks to try to find one, and was eventually given the name of someone who could usually be found on the terrace of the Novo-Moskovskyaya restaurant. He made his way there and sat amongst sailors from Marseille, lawyers from Moscow, aristocratic ladies from Petrograd, and the usual out-of-work actors and tutors. On the wall was a poster with the slogan '*Onwards to Moscow!*' with the hooves of wild-eyed white horses galloping over the bodies of devilish-looking Jews.

With the syringe safely in his pocket he was on his way back to the villa, but he found himself loitering outside the Cathedral to watch a wedding. The young couple stood on the steps with their families, as a man with his head under a brown cloth took their picture with a camera on a tripod. Somewhere out of sight, a choir was still singing.

When he reached the villa, the place was quiet as the grave, and dark and gloomy as ever. He lit the small tin lamp and, shielding the flame with his hand, went into the bedroom where Tamara lay, eyes closed and mouth slightly open. When he rolled up her sleeve she stirred, saw him and whispered, 'I'm dying…'

'Don't be silly. This will make you feel so much better…'

He took her hand and squeezed it gently.

'I'm dying… Stanislav, I *know* I am…'

34

Somewhere to the south of Smolensk, Alyosha broke into a house. In the gloom, he rummaged though the cupboards and although there was nothing to eat he found a twenty-kopeck note hidden under the paper lining of a drawer. He was consumed with hunger.

He heard a noise and froze. Somewhere outside a nightingale was singing. He listened but couldn't hear anything apart from birdsong. He crept through the shadows as quietly as a panther, by now practised at moving softly and silently, though the floor creaked a little when he stepped on a loose board.

From nowhere he came face to face with a bearded man. He grabbed wildly at the nearest thing to hand – a long poker – but the bearded man did exactly the same and it was only when the mirror shattered into long shards around his feet that he realised he had attacked himself.

North of Smolensk, he'd almost been arrested and was beaten twice, once by a policeman and the other time by a crew of ruffians, so mercilessly on that occasion that he lost two front teeth and cracked his jaw. He looked uglier and more dangerous than ever.

A few weeks later, somewhere between Gomel and Roslavi, he joined up with a gang of children who slept in a cave in the rocks about the station depot. The oldest, a girl called Natalie – whom Alyosha had mistaken for a boy to begin with, with her scalp as bald as an egg and hands like spades – had managed to run an electricity supply from the signal box, rolling out the wire and slinging it along branches all the way to the cave every night, and returning it undiscovered in the early morning.

One day though, she didn't return to the cave, and that was the end of their light. The younger children were disconsolate because Natalie had been the nearest thing they had to a mother. Aloysha soon grew tired of their crying and moved on; he never stayed anywhere for any length of time, in any case. With one eye always on the North Star, he trudged wearily onward.

When he reached the town of Safonovo he managed to steal some money from the pocket of a man whose head was deep in a copy of *Pravda*. He went straight over to the station. There was no train to Petrograd, but one was about to leave for Moscow. At the second bell the train slowly chugged away from the platform, and soon the the houses disappeared, and the river, until there was nothing to be seen but poplars and lilac trees.

The movement of the train soon lulled Alyosha to sleep, only to dream fractiously of walking with his Uncle Kozma in search of his father, and finding him behind the bars of a hay manger. Then his father was a child in front of the teacher's desk, and Ivan Kirilich was interrogating him, and Alyosha was trying to warn him, but his father couldn't hear him no matter how loudly he shouted. A firing squad appeared and Mishka gave Alyosha a gun under the trees of the little orchard and his father begged for mercy from the gaping mouth of the grave…

35

Tamara's condition deteriorated and Stanislav began to fear the worst. He sat by her bedside for hours, reading to her, holding her thin wrist between his finger and thumb. She seemed to be listening sometimes, though her eyes were usually shut. When she fell into a troubled sleep, Stanislav would put pen to paper and churn out some sketches or jokes for the anti-communist cabaret, but his heart wasn't in it. Extolling the virtues of the White Armies turned his stomach, as he had seen too much of their anti-semitism, apart from anything else.

He tried to make some sense of his conflicting emotions by recording all that had happened to him since he returned to Russia, but it was such a muddle. How could he begin to try to understand the civil war? How could he persuade himself that there was some higher purpose to it all? Amongst all the hatred and courage and fear, were there some important lessons to be winkled out? Or was it all just a senseless sacrifice?

He saw how people strove to carry on with their lives, even under the most difficult of circumstances. That's why village and town bowed in turn to the Whites today and the Reds tomorrow, for the simple reason that they wanted to save their skins and be allowed to get on with their lives. He knew of many who kept a picture of Marx on one side and the Tzar on the other, ready to turn the frame in a heartbeat depending on who came knocking on the door.

When Rozaliya came home late at night from the café, she and Stanislav would stay up late together, talking, hugging and kissing each other, and sometimes making love.

'I've managed to save enough money… One more month should do it and then we can go.' Rozaliya kissed his chin. 'Paris. We can live in Paris…

'I can't pay for all of us,' she added hesitantly, fearing his reaction.

Her secret hope was to leave Tamara behind in a Russian grave.

Winter was upon them now, with a vengeance. Overnight, it seemed, there was frost on the grass and a low mist shrouded the city roofs. Tamara was fading away a little more each day, reduced to skin and bones.

One night Rozaliya returned from the café full of news. The Azerbaijani's wife had walked into the café that day, after the juggler from Poti had kicked her out of his house and out of his life.

'Everybody in the café fell perfectly silent,' Rozaliya told him as she took off her shoes with a sigh of contentment. 'She's quite a young woman, not much older than me. She was wearing a coat which looked as though it was made out of curtains, all yellow and heavy. And she had a silver chain around her ankle. She's very handsome, with black hair in great ringlets around her shoulders, lovely grey eyes, pretty little hands and this great big slightly lopsided smile. We all just stopped what we were doing and stared at her, none more so than the Azerbaijani. She took our breath away. And you'll never guess what happened next… Stanislav?'

She faltered, for he was gazing intently at her, clearly not having listened to a word.

'What is it?'

'I have to tell you something.'

With a contemptuous flick of her head towards the bedroom where Tamara lay, Rozaliya asked curtly, 'Is she expecting your child?'

'No.'

Relief flickered across her face.

'What, then?'

'Come and sit here by me.'

'Just tell me what's on your mind.'

'You must have realised, Tamara's not going to see the spring.'

Rozaliya plaited and unplaited her thin fingers. She looked away.

'Could you bear it?' he asked.

Silence.

'Roza?'

'If you've already made up your mind why are you asking me what I think?'

'Because I want you to realise it won't make any difference to the two of us.'

Stanislav and Tamara were married at her bedside the very next week. From that day onwards she began to rally and gradually regained her strength and her beauty. Though still weak, she was out of danger.

Rozaliya was very bitter. She found an unexpected ally in the wife of the Azerbaijani, who was now working alongside her in the café, since her husband took her back.

'Why on earth are you willing to put up with it?' she asked, after Rozaliya had confided in her.

'Why do I?' she asked herself, and looked for the answer in vain.

All her hopes were fixed on reaching Paris, and when next she brought the subject up, to her surprise Stanislav said at once, 'You're right, we have no choice. The Whites are going to lose. Once the Reds have the Crimea they'll register us all like they did in Kiev. But this time they'll be even more vicious. They'll shoot us by the thousand. With my record I won't last a day. We have to get out on the first boat that will take us.'

Rozaliya was very quiet, as that 'we' meant different things to each of them.

'You can't forgive me for marrying her, I know.'

'I can't forgive her for tricking you into it.'

'She thought she was going to die.'

'It was all a trick.'

'I still love you.'

'But you're married to her.'

'That means nothing. You must believe me.'

The next morning, Stanislav went down to the beach in the hope of finding some driftwood for the fire. Too many others had already been there before him so the pickings were slim, and the fire he lit for Tamara when he returned to the villa was a meagre affair. As Tamara sat in front of it, a blanket over her knees, she told him she was too weak to travel very far, and it would be impossible for her to leave Russia. She must have heard them talking the previous night.

'But that's why we're here! That's why we risked our lives to leave Kiev! To reach Paris! Don't you remember?'

'Please don't raise your voice – it goes through me.'

Events overtook them. The Crimea fell sooner than they thought. Baron Wrangel's army couldn't withstand the might of the Red Army and it was driven inexorably back, towards the sea, until the order came to evacuate the town. Blind panic hurtled through the streets, screaming at the top of its voice. Thousands upon thousands streamed towards the port. Towards the ships at anchor, the men and the women and the children fled…

Rozaliya had gone off to the café, determined to collect the wages that were owed to her, but when she didn't return Stanislav went to look for her, leaving Tamara on her own. She was still adamant that she wasn't strong enough to face a long sea-voyage and having to make a new home in a foreign city.

'I'm too weak.'

'I'll be there to look after you.'

'Why won't you listen to me? Leave me here, I'll be fine. Go with Rozaliya…'

'Not without you. We can't stay here and wait for the Communists, Toma, you know that. They would have shot me in Kiev if they'd had their way. And what have I been doing since I came here? Writing jokes about Lenin, making a mockery of Trotskii. They'll kill me and will probably throw you in prison just for being my wife. Or worse. I beg you, be ready to leave when I come back with Rozaliya.'

The streets of Sevastopol were dense with people on their way to the quays and it was with difficulty that Stanislav struggled through the crowds, the animals, the carts, and the bikes. When he finally reached the café the Azerbaijani's wife told him that Rozaliya had already gone, but that she'd left a letter for him. Stanislav tore open the envelope the minute he was outside the door and read her brief farewell through a blur of tears:

'Stanislav, I know if I come with you to Paris I'll end my days deserted and alone, on the streets of a foreign city where I know no one… You made your choice because in your heart you *wanted* to marry her. You should try and be honest with yourself about that. Saying you had to marry her because she was dying was just an excuse. You could have said no. You had a choice. As I have now. I choose to stay in Russia.

Goodbye my love.'

36

In Moscow everything was so grubby and dirty and untidy. Even the droika horses had a dejected air about them. The city that Alyosha had visited once with his parents bore no resemblance to this sad, broken place.

The family had stayed that time in the Hotel Metropole and perhaps because he felt so out of place and alone, he found himself making his way there this time too. He walked along the cobbled streets towards the centre, passing shops that were either shuttered up or had smashed windows, repaired with whatever material had come to hand, yellowing newspaper or old rags stuffed into the holes. The people looked grey and poor, and the streets had a sombre air, as if the whole city was in mourning.

Alyosha kept well clear of the young soldiers who patrolled the squares and main junctions. Often they would be sitting around on wooden boxes or barrels, playing cards, their guns wigwammed nearby. He walked under huge banners suspended across the streets, with slogans you could read from afar – '*Religion is the Opium of the People*', proclaimed one. He looked at a poster of a smiling girl who reminded him of Mademoiselle Babin. He hadn't thought of her in a long while and wondered if she might be in Moscow, but thought it unlikely if she was still with her prince.

By the time he reached the Kremlin with its round towers and drooping red banners it was beginning to get dark, and when he eventually found the Hotel Metropole he was almost beside himself with hunger. He was tormented by memories of his last visit there: the meals he had shared with his parents, his first glass of champagne, the big soft bed; how his head had sunk into the feather pillow, and waking to the smell of the roses that the maid had just placed on the table before she opened the curtains. He was overcome suddenly by the realisation that a great chunk of his life had already run its course, and no power on earth could summon it back, or give him the chance to relive one precious second of it, ever.

The name had disappeared from the front of the building, though he could still see the outline. There was plenty of coming and going though, and as he approached he could see that the Metropole was now the Communist Ministry of Foreign Affairs. He decided to keep well clear.

He asked directions to the Arbat area, trying to remember the name of the street where his father's cousin lived, though he had no idea whether she would still be there. He wondered whether Mishka, Masha and Boris were safe. Did they ever reach their uncle's farm? He doubted it somehow. It was properly dark now and he was frozen, the hunger pains in his stomach worse than ever.

Through the dark and silent city streets he went until he came upon a little knot of people huddled together on a corner, selling a mishmash of objects. Among them were three ladies who looked as though they were impoverished aristocrats (so no doubt would be at the end of the queue for food rations under the new order). A few passers-by were rifling through what they had on offer but nobody seemed to be buying. One old man had a great stack of books, badges, and, bizarrely, spectacle frames on offer.

Alyosha was about to move on when he heard one of the women say, 'My fingers are frozen to the bone.'

Something about that voice rang a bell. He turned around and, pretending to examine the box of teaspoons and china at her feet, took a sideways look at her. Hesitantly, he said, 'Zinaida Ernestovna?'

Fear flashed into her eyes and she shrank back into the shadows.

'Who are you?' she asked suspiciously.

Forgetting how much he had changed he simply answered, 'It's me.'

'I don't know you.'

When he told her his name she looked at him for a long time, as if struggling to find the lost boy in this ugly young tramp. Finally a smile broke across her face and she hugged him to her. Alyosha was anxious to find out what she knew of his parents, but she couldn't shed much light on their fate. She was more than ready to discuss her own situation: she had suffered very much, she told him, and was beset by her own pressing problems.

'You can't believe the troubles I have.'

Alyosha was almost dead with hunger and asked if she had anything to eat, but she said no, not unless there was something waiting for her when she went back to her lodgings. It was possible, but she wouldn't want to raise his hopes.

37

On the way to her lodgings, Zinaida told him of all the difficulties she'd had leaving Petrograd. She had done everything she could to procure a visa for Berlin, and even though Orlov had done his best for her, for some reason she had been refused. The scandal of Zinaida's leaving her husband to live with Orlov came back to Alyosha when she mentioned his name, and he marvelled that people ever had the leisure to be concerned with such things.

The room was in darkness apart from one guttering candle. When Alyosha followed Zinaida in, a man turned towards them and seeing him, half-rose, asking, 'Who's that on your tail?'

As Zinaida took off her coat and scarf, though she kept her gloves on, she asked,

'You don't remember him? Alexei Fyodorovich? Inessa and Fyodor Mikhailovich Alexandrov's son?'

Her *crepe-de-chine* dress hung loosely on her, he noticed. The man wore a dirty tunic, unbuttoned to show a chest as white and hairless as a baby's. He ignored Alyosha.

'Did you bring any food back?'

'I didn't sell anything.'

'You're useless,' he told her savagely.

'You do no better.'

'It's easier for a woman to sell than a man.'

'Do you know how many hours I spent out in the cold today?'

'I'm starving.'

'Oh do shut up. All you do is moan.'

After carrying on like this for a while, Zinaida seemed to

remember her manners and introduced her companion to Alyosha as Kukushkin. He remembered that he had met him with Peraskii and Lazareva Petrovna. Kukushkin poured them all some tea from the samovar, and Zinaida managed to excavate a scraping of hard, grey sugar from the bottom of a bowl.

'Better than nothing,'

Kukushkin, fortified by the tea, wanted to know all about Alyosha, and how and why he came to be in Moscow and from where he'd come. Alyosha told them he had heard nothing of his parents and didn't even know if they were alive.

'I did see your mother before I left Petrograd,' Zinaida told him.

'But not my father?'

'No.'

'You might as well hear the truth,' grunted Kukushkin, pouring some vodka into his tea. He didn't offer any to the other two.

'Spare his feelings,' Zinaida warned him.

'How am I meant to do that? The truth is the truth.'

'Is he dead?' asked Alyosha.

It was their silence that confirmed it.

'How?'

'The Petrograd Cheka. They shot him.'

He considered the six words.

The Petrograd Cheka. They shot him.

He said to himself,

'*My father was shot by the Petrograd Cheka.*'

He wondered if their methods were the same as the Kiev Cheka. Did they take him to an open grave in a small orchard? No, more likely it was in a cellar somewhere.

He heard himself say, 'But...'

'But what?' asked Zinaida.

'My uncle Kozma said he'd do everything he could to have my father released.'

'Well, he obviously didn't succeed,' said Kukushkin, hawking phlegm up noisily.

Alyosha said no more, and Kukushkin, perhaps contrite at how harsh he had sounded, started to tell him what a good man his father had been. As he spoke the words, Aloysha stared at the shape his heart-shaped mouth made and how his square little moustache moved a little in tandem. '... principled man... good and fair employer... courageous...'

Alyosha observed him, this short little man, with his unpleasant face, his soft body and his small head with big jug ears and he suddenly found his voice.

'Shut up! Just shut up talking about my father as though you knew him! You didn't! So what right have you got to speak about him?'

'I spoke to him on the telephone once.'

'That's not the same as knowing someone!'

Zinaida was very quiet, as though she might have dozed off.

'I'm sorry,' apologised Kukushkin. 'You're quite right of course, I didn't really know him. I was only trying to make you feel better... I meant no harm by it.'

'What about my mother?' asked Alyosha.

'As far as I know – but don't take my word for it, of course – she's still in Petrograd.'

Zinaida stirred herself at this and mumbled drowsily that she might have crossed the border to Riga.

'She's living in Riga all of a sudden?' asked Kukushkin mockingly.

'Well, that's the rumour I heard.'

He poured the dregs of the vodka into his cup and snapped, 'Don't give out false hope when you know what you just said is just third-hand tittle-tattle, not worth a damn. God knows what's happened to Inessa, especially if she was stupid enough to stay in Petrograd after what they did to her husband.'

And he added spitefully, 'Look what they did to your precious Orlov.'

Alyosha spent an uncomfortable night trying to sleep in a rickety chair, with hunger pangs gnawing at his stomach. The next morning Zinaida went off to try and barter some items again, this time to Sukharevka market where she told Alyosha she hoped she'd have better luck, as Kukushkin had managed to sell his Paul Bourget novels there the previous week for a large chunk of cheese.

Kukushkin moved around the cramped apartment like a lizard, his steps small but swift. For the moment at least, he seemed to have accepted Alyosha's presence there without demur, and seemed quite talkative.

'So did Zinaida tell you what Orlov did?'

'No.'

'The man was a fool. He refused to give up his house to the Communists when they decreed that it was no longer legal to own private property. They'd told him his house would be put into the hands of a Tenants' Committee, but they'd allow him to stay in one room – and he could even choose which room he wanted – as long as he submitted to their decree. But do you know what he did?'

'What?'

'Dug his heels in. Refused to budge. Well, it was only a matter of time... sure enough, one afternoon Zinaida comes over in tears to tell me that Orlov had been arrested.'

He shook his head sheepishly.

'What the hell did she expect me to do? I was a civil servant under the old regime, I was hardly well placed. I was furious with Orlov, I admit that. Why make life so difficult for himself? It's not as though we hadn't warned him, Perarskii and I, that he'd have to give in to their demands, painful though it would be. We might as well have saved our breath. Well, I don't suppose one man should stand in judgement over another… Perhaps if I'd been lucky enough to own a fine house instead of renting an apartment I might have been equally stubborn. It's hard to say isn't it? He decided to make a stand, to face up to the bastards, and I suppose I have a certain amount of respect for him for doing that, in a way. I don't think it would have been my way, that's all. To conform to whoever is in power and work to the best of my abilities. That's what I was taught.'

It was still only mid-morning, but Kukushkin produced another bottle of vodka from somewhere and poured a hefty slug into his tea, before continuing, 'He left me a letter, you know.'

'What did it say?' asked Aloysha.

'That I should look after Zinaida.'

He took another swig.

'That's why I brought her to Moscow. The plan was to get out through the south, but we'd left it too late and there's not a chance of making it through the Crimea now.'

'Aren't there any other ways of getting out of Russia?'

'It's a dangerous business trying to get across the border. Unless you *want* a bullet in your back. In fact, I'd say it was damn near impossible.'

38

That afternoon, Kukushkin suggested he could arrange for him to sleep with Zinaida, for a price.

'How about it? She's still a handsome woman. You could do a lot worse… and you don't know what you'll catch from the ones on the streets. How about it, lad? You're nearly a man now. It's time you were initiated, and she knows her stuff. How old are you anyway? Eighteen?'

'Almost.'

'Seventeen, eh? That's a good age. I remember being seventeen… That's when I became friends with your uncle Artyom.' He smiled. 'Lord, the things we got up to. You wouldn't believe half of them, even if I told you.'

He swigged his vodka.

'What was I talking about, eh? Alyosha?'

'What?'

'What were we discussing just now?'

'Selling Ziniaida Ersternova to me.'

'I can arrange that easily. How about it? Do you fancy it?'

The price was vodka or food. Money was useless. As Alyosha had neither vodka, food nor money, it was academic.

Zinaida returned triumphantly a little later, with some potatoes and a cabbage, and asked Alyosha what his plans were. When he told her he intended making his way back to Petrograd to try to find whoever was left of his family, she admitted that the only reason she had agreed to come to Moscow with Kukushkin was because she was so afraid of what the Cheka might do to her.

'And as it was my fiancé's last wish that I should leave Russia, I was determined to try and honour that wish.'

'With him?'

Alyosha nodded towards Kukushkin, who was by now in a drunken stupor on the bed, muttering something under his breath.

'I want to be rid of him,' she said in a low voice.

The next day it was snowing heavily and the world looked sad and grey. Alyosha was gathering his few things together to leave when Zinaida announced she'd rather return to Petrograd with him than spend her days in this freezing hovel with a hopeless drunk.

Kukushkin narrowed his yellowing eyes and spat out, 'After Orlov said…'

Zinaida interrupted him, 'Orlov is dead, and so will I be if I stay here much longer.'

She had begun to throw some clothes into a battered suitcase.

'I promised him I'd look after you and that I'd make sure you'd get safely out of Russia… so you're not to leave, do you hear me? You just need to be patient… Together, we'll see Paris.'

'You're too much of a drunkard to see further than the bottom of the next bottle.'

'We'll see Paris, I tell you!'

He tried to reach for her but stumbled, and would have fallen if Alyosha hadn't steadied him. He shook him off angrily and tried to grab the suitcase.

'Keep away from me you drunkard,' screamed Zinaida, snatching the suitcase away from him and slamming it shut. 'I loathe you. Loathe the way you think vodka makes you the wittiest man alive. Loathe the way you mock originality or anything that challenges your stale old ideas of what society should be about. Why do you think the Communists have won? Because of fools like you, so smug in your comfortable little world that you couldn't see that change was in the wind until it was too late to do anything about it. Well perhaps they were right all along; perhaps this society needs to be shaken out of its deep sleep and forced to confront reality…'

She buttoned up her coat swiftly.

'By stealing property?' roared Kukushkin. 'By taking people's homes away from them, and the money from their banks? Is that your idea of reality? Look how we're living! For God's sake, woman! Is it easier to be poor because everybody else is poor? Is it easier to be hungry because everybody else is hungry?'

Zinaida snatched her suitcase from the bed.

'After all that I've done for you, this is how you thank me? Where would you be without me? Eh?'

His face was brick-red with fury.

'You unfeeling, ruthless bitch… Well the joke's on you… The love of your life… Orlov… he never wanted you.'

'Of course he did.'

'He was absolutely appalled when you left your husband and turned up on his doorstep. Appalled. That was the last thing he wanted. God, how we laughed.'

'Alexei, come…'

'Yes – go, you bitch! But you'll never see Paris!'

A man begging for more punishment and suffering was the last image Alyosha had as he shut the door on Moscow.

39

In Petrograd's Nicholevski Station a huge mural had been painted. It consisted of four heroic individuals bestriding the lands of the Russian empire: a soldier of the Red Army, a sailor, a Cossack and a peasant. They were all united in hurling a grotesquely fat green toad (tied to a rope), whose protuberant greedy eyes seemed to survey all that lay beneath him, over the border.

Underneath the mural was a slogan:

'*Bourgeoisie, you oppressed us with your fat stomachs.*'

As the train pulled into the station it was the first thing Alyosha saw. He tried to remember the day he had left with Mademoiselle Babin. He could hardly remember his parents' faces, or his uncle Kozma's. His cousins hadn't been allowed to come to the station; they had made their farewells the day before.

As Alyosha and Zinaida walked through the station, they passed several posters calling on the proletariat to support the Third International, with a stern warning on the bottom of each in red, '*Anyone who tears down or covers up this poster is committing a counter-revolutionary act.*'

Outside, Alyosha breathed in the city of his childhood. The buildings seemed smaller than he remembered them, and the February snow looked very grey. They began to make their way to Zinaida Fyodorovna's sister's house, which wasn't very far.

Crunching through the snow, Alyosha could hear the sound of his own breathing, which was slightly laboured since he was carrying Zinaida's suitcase as well as his own small sack. He caught sight of his reflection and hardly recognised himself. During the journey, Zinaida had insisted on cutting his hair short, so now he thought he looked like a hedgehog. She had also insisted on him shaving, so the beard was gone, exposing his hollowed cheeks, and his eyes dark and wide above them.

He looked for familiar faces, but saw not one. He stared at the buildings he would have passed without a second glance when he was last here; he saw the broken windows, the peeling paint of the railings, the exposed iron underneath, red with rust, and the dirt, the stink and the poverty all around.

He had a bottle of cognac in his pocket that he had stolen on the train, and every now and again he took a sip to try and warm himself. It wasn't long before Zinaida had started to complain.

'I'm exhausted. I hardly slept a wink last night. I was too afraid somebody would go through my things. Did you sleep?'

'Not much.'

A motor-car went slowly by – and for one second Alyosha imagined his father had sent the chauffeur to collect them – but at the wheel was a young girl in the uniform of a Red Army private. There was nobody in the back, and the noise of the engine faded as it disappeared around a corner. As they passed the Imperial Yacht Club, Alyosha glanced up and noticed the rather tattered red banners that now adorned the building. Between the banners were large portraits of Lenin, Trotskii and Sverdlov. A young soldier stood guard at the entrance, taking surreptitious drags of a cigarette which he then held behind his back. He looked exactly like Boris.

Could it be Boris?

Alyosha stared at the young soldier, who caught him looking and stared belligerently back, his hard, square young face as though carved from wood.

Zinaida sighed impatiently at his loitering and he hurried on, his arms on fire by now. A woman wearing *pince-nez,* a heavy woollen coat, which was filthy and in tatters at the hem, a ripped blue skirt, and a pair of galoshes on her feet, came towards them. She was muttering under her breath and had a wild, demented look about her as she played obsessively with the purple fringe of her scarf. As she passed them, Alyosha could smell the alchohol on her breath.

On the corner of the street a small crowd of people were selling the usual assortment of bric-a-brac and rubbish: women who looked as though they once been rich, their hands enclosed in fur muffs; school girls, snub noses red with cold, stamping their feet to try and keep warm; and a few ex-officers in their uniforms and medals. Alyosha swept their faces in the hope of seeing his Uncle Kozma or Aunt Ella or Margarita or Larissa but he didn't recognise anyone.

40

Alyosha was invited to stay the night, but he wanted to be on his way. Zinaida's sister warned him to be careful and not to wander the streets after dark as you never knew what madmen were about. They'd steal the shirt off your back without a second thought. Zinaida kissed him on either cheek.

'Thank you for bringing me home and remember, there'll always be a welcome for you here.'

'I'll keep that in mind.'

'Please do. And good luck to you.'

Alyosha crunched through the snow. He was getting closer to home. He took a sip of the cognac. He was getting closer to home. He took another sip and realised he had drunk the bottle dry. With every step he was getting closer to home. A sudden gust of wind sent a sheet whirling through the darkness, and an old manifesto fluttered against his face before vanishing into the darkness.

As he approached the house he started to walk faster. He was frightened. He broke into a run. When he turned the corner into his street he ran even faster, his heart full of hope and his head full of hopelessness. He saw a light on in his father's study. He stopped, taking in great gasps of air, his chest heaving and burning.

When he went to knock on the door it opened against his fist. He stepped over the threshold and was welcomed by a strange and unfamiliar smell; but then he heard the tinkling of the piano, and smiled to himself as he thought of his mother sitting there. He ran through the hall to the salon, flung the door open and rushed in.

The room was nothing like how it used to be. It was a strange mixture of luxury and squalor. Alyosha recognised various bits of furniture from before; the plush velvet chairs, the red sofa with its chintz cover, the sideboard. But the great mirror was now split in half by a partition that had been erected across the room. Another partition had been erected widthways, so he now stood in a room a quarter of the size of the original.

When she saw him standing there, the little girl who had been picking out a few notes at the piano jumped off the stool and ran across to her mother and buried her head in her lap.

'Mama, Mama! Who's that man, I don't like him! He's going to steal my music!'

Alyosha and the woman stared at each other. The house was humming with the noise of humanity, from above, below and to each side of them.

'Alyosha.'

'Aisha.'

They were equally stunned to see each other. A bald dwarf appeared and Alyosha recognised Rodion, the sailor who used to come to the house with Oleg, looking to be fed.

Rodion told Alyosha that he was the Chairman of the Tenants' Committee.

'So what are you doing here?' Rodion asked him.

'This was my home for fifteen years.'

Alyosha felt so overwhelmed that he had to sit down on the piano stool before his legs gave way.

'What are you *doing* here is what I asked you.'

Rodion came to stand squarely in front of him, his legs wide, as though willing himself to appear taller than he was.

'Have you been officially registered yet? Well? Because if you don't have your papers in order, you don't have the right to stay in Petrograd.'

'I've come to look for my family.'

'Well you won't find them here,' Aisha told him.

'What of my father?'

'As an enemy of the people, we heard he was shot.'

'And my mother?'

'Dunno. She managed to escape but I don't know where she went.'

Alyosha couldn't keep his eyes from wandering to his father's empty bookshelves. One of the occasional tables had been broken up for firewood. The fine Turkish rug was stained and frayed.

Alyosha felt his head spin and the room started to dance before his eyes. He had to bend his head between his knees to stop himself from passing out. He could hear an accordion playing somewhere, and as if from far away, Rodion's voice.

'Show me your papers.'

And then Aisha's voice, suddenly fierce.

'Give it a rest for fuck's sake. Can't you see he's on his last legs?'

The darkness passed and he sat up cautiously. Aisha's face had aged terribly, with all that quick young energy that had been such an attractive part of her quite gone.

Rodion persisted, 'Have you filled out the questionnaire? Have you registered to live in Petrograd?'

Although he seemed angry, there also lurked something more like fear behind his words. He pondered for a moment, then put on his coat and muttered, 'I won't be long.'

Alyosha noticed that he had a bad hobble. The minute the door closed behind him, Aisha told Alyosha he should leave immediately.

'This minute, go on, get out!'

Alyosha didn't have the strength to move.

'Look, if you don't get a move on, Rodya'll be back with the Cheka and I promise you, you don't want to be here when they arrive.'

'I have nowhere to go.'

'What about your grandparents?'

'I've no idea what's happened to them. Do you? Are they still in Petrograd?'

'I don't know but you really need to leave – now.'

'What about Oxana's brother? Oleg? Are you still with him?'

Aisha glared at him.

'Rodion is my husband now.'

She said this in a flat, deliberate little voice, smoothing her daughter's hair as she spoke.

'Rodion? Why, what happened to Oleg?'

Aisha gave an exasperated sigh.

'Sweet Jesus, you're annoying. Look it's a long story, all right? Let's just say he changed his mind about the Communists.'

'But I thought he was one of their most loyal supporters.'

'He was – to start with. But after a few years, when Lenin still wasn't prepared to allow free elections and freedom of the press, he became frustrated. There were plenty of his Kronstadt fellow sailors who thought the same. He and Rodion could argue about it for hours. Rodion thought it would be just playing into the hands of the Whites and the foreign imperialists because it would give them a foothold back in Russia.'

'So what happened?'

'Oh you know what men are like: they couldn't just agree to disagree and leave it at that. No, it split the sailors down the middle and of course Oleg and Rodion found themselves on different sides. They ended up hating each other's guts. Well, I was living with Oleg in Kronstadt at the time, and expecting this one. But Rodion came to warn me that I should get off the island because he'd heard that Trotskii was going to send his soldiers across the ice and snow to fight the sailors. Lenin had decided that the Kronstadt sailors were enemies of the revolution. "Enemies of the revolution!" Can you believe it? They won the fucking revolution for Lenin in the first place.'

'So what happened?'

'Rodion told me to try and knock some sense into Oleg's head.'

She fell silent, biting her lip.

'And did you?'

'I tried. Told him I wouldn't leave unless he did and that if we stayed we'd probably be killed, him, me and the baby in my belly. But of course he wouldn't listen. "I didn't risk my life in 1917 for this," he says, all noble and proud. He was going to stay and fight if that's what it took. 'Course I left. Well what else could I do in my condition? And that's the last time I saw Oleg alive. The Red Army went in and killed those poor boys in their thousands. And since then Rodion's been looking after us, me and her.'

She got up, hurriedly scribbled something on a piece of paper and gave it to him.

'Here, take this. It's Dunia's address.'

'Who taught you to write?

'For fuck's sakes, does it matter? I don't know if she's still there, mind. I haven't seen her for ages and there's so much coming and going these days. Now you have to leave.'

Practically dragging him to his feet, and propelling him out of the room she added, 'And don't ever try coming back here.'

Alyosha lifted the collar of his coat and stepped out into the night.

41

In the weak morning sunshine he stood on the Nevskii, his breath condensing in grey clouds. He trudged across the snow, so compacted in places it had frozen hard – he would have been better off wearing skates. Compared with how busy it used to be the place was practically deserted: no crowds, no shoppers, no students, no ladies in their coaches and motor-cars, dressed in their finery. How he, Margarita and Larissa had enjoyed their outings with Mademoiselle Babin all that time ago.

A beggar had already installed himself in a doorway, dressed as a general of the old order. He had the military bearing of an old soldier, an officer probably, as he stood there in his fur cap, carefully cleaning his spectacles with a pocket handkerchief. A short peasant passed by in a heavy overcoat, scooping up a bowl of kasha with a crust of bread.

A middle-aged man with yellow teeth and a spiky beard was haranguing his companion – a young worker by the look of him – as they rushed past.

'Your lot have shot all the best people and now look at the monkeys left in charge.'

'You can talk, as though you didn't whip, imprison and murder for three hundred years.'

Alyosha had spent the previous night with Dunia. The welcome she gave him had been lukewarm to say the least, perhaps because she was tired: she had remarried, had a small son, and was already pregnant again. Then again, perhaps she didn't want to be reminded of the past, or feared she could find herself in trouble for harbouring someone who didn't have the proper papers to stay in the city.

A long, long time ago he remembered feeling her breasts and being astonished at how hard they were.

Her husband had seemed very suspicious of him too, and had looked like thunder when Dunia shared some of their meagre rations with him. Alyosha had gobbled the food down gratefully, and then asked if she knew anything of his mother, but Dunia only knew that she had gone abroad. She did give him the address where she knew his grandparents had been living, the last time she heard of them.

42

He climbed the chilly stairwell of the tomb-like apartment block, up through the stinking gloom to the fifth floor. He knocked three times on the door and eventually heard somebody rattling the chain on the other side.

From behind the chain he saw a pair of eyes peering nervously out at him.

'Who are you? What do you want?'

'It's me, your grandson.'

'Alyosha? Alyosha? Is that really you?'

The door was shut in order to unfasten the chain and then opened again.

'You've come back? You did, you came back!'

Anna Timurovna repeated this several times, her lower lip trembling as she ushered Alyosha in. She was wearing a blouse buttoned up to a high neck, the colour of fishbone, and a gold watch hung from a ribbon on her breast. She had coloured her hair so that the white was streaked with yellow.

'Come back from the dead to us! It's a miracle. Vasillii! Come and see! Vasillii!'

Their apartment consisted of two tiny rooms, but it was as if they had attempted to stuff the contents of a palace into a pigsty. There wasn't room to turn round. Two sideboards were stacked one on the other, and there were at least three too many chairs crammed around the big table, which took up most of the floor space. Every inch of wall was covered in framed pictures. His feet sank into the softness of several layers of Astrakhan carpets, and on top of those were several polar bear pelts, their heads knocking against each other.

The hours disappeared, the day disappeared and the old lamp was lit, which stank. Alyosha had spent the time listening to his grandmother and grandfather tell him all that had befallen them since they last met, in one great river of words, the one cutting across the other to take up the tale, sometimes becoming confused, or arguing about the sequence of events, or disagreeing totally on some points.

They told him how his uncle Artyom had arranged visas for the whole family to leave Russia by crossing the border to Estonia. This had all been arranged on the basis that somehow or other his father would be released by the Cheka. But then he was moved to Niegegorodskaya prison so they knew the Cheka meant to shoot him. The family were desperate to save him and spent many hours discussing what they could do. Anna Timurovna was all for appealing to Maxim Gorkii to ask Lenin for a pardon. Ella was always advising caution, terrified of bringing yet more trouble on their heads. In the end, Anna and Inessa went to see Gorkii without telling Ella, but although he listened to what they had to say politely enough, they left without any assurance that he would help, and they didn't feel he had any sympathy with them.

Then they decided to petition Lenin directly, as every day that went by brought them a day closer to Fyodor's execution. But this was no simple matter, and it proved impossible to gain access to him. Finally Kozma heard that the Red Army were desperate for experienced officers, and though it went against everything he believed in, he decided that he was willing to offer his services to the Communists in exchange for his brother's freedom.

Ella was furious that he could even suggest such a thing, and said some very harsh things to Inessa.

Then they heard that all Kerenskii's ex-ministers were to be moved from the Niegegorodskaya prison to the Cheka headquarters in Petrograd, on Gorokhavaya Street. Worse still, a wild rumour went around that every last one of them would be executed immediately in reprisal for a woman shooting Lenin in an assassination attempt. It really seemed as though time was running out, and Inessa begged Kozma to offer himself to the Red Army. Ella was convinced that if he did this he would be walking into a trap, and not one, but both brothers would end up being shot. It was a terrible time, with the women screaming and cursing each other and poor Kozma in the middle. Ella showed her mettle, when she told them all that it was quite impossible to allow him to sacrifice himself for his brother: he had his own family to think about. His wife and daughters must come first. Fyodor had chosen to serve in Kerenskii's Government of his own free will, and he must now bear the consequences of that decision.

Inessa went down on her knees before Kozma, and through her tears appealed to him to save her husband. Vasillii and Anna also thought that this was the only chance.

Kozma made his decision.

'What was it?'

Kozma went to the Cheka and two days later Fyodor walked out blinking into the daylight. He wasn't at perfect liberty though. He was to report to the Cheka every day and he and his family were not to leave Russia, on pain of shooting Kozma.

'So my father is alive? Where is he? In Petrograd?'

'Helsingfors.'

'And is my mother with him?'

'Of course, and Georgik too.'

It was too much for Alyosha to digest all at once and he was silent for a while, before asking, 'And what about Aunt Ella and the girls?'

'They're in Berlin. The three of them have been there for over a year now.'

His grandparents had that smell of old people in frail health about them.

There was another silence, longer this time, which was finally broken by Vasillii.

'You haven't asked about your uncle Kozma.'

Alyosha hadn't done so because he was afraid to hear the answer.

43

Vasillii was a broken man. When the revolution destroyed his way of life, it destroyed his faith as well. Every last thing he had held sacred and dear throughout his life had been smashed to smitheerens. He had become eccentric in the extreme, so much so that Alyosha wondered if he was quite of sound mind. He wore three of everything – three pairs of socks, three pairs of trousers, three shirts: he would have worn three pairs of shoes if that had been possible. The one pair that he did wear was made of a motor-car tyre.

'At least the Communists won't steal these. Not good enough for them.' He added sadly, 'The devils have taken everything else away from me.'

He would ask the same questions endlessly, such as, 'Why don't people like us have a soviet? Every other rascal has one.'

His wife would answer patiently each time, 'Because we're not Communists. People like us don't want a soviet.'

Vasillii thought the root of the problem was that most people were far more afraid of the Cheka than of their own consciences.

'Otherwise, Mother Russia wouldn't be in this awful mess. That's the tragedy of it.'

He had seen through the trickery of the Communists from the very beginning. What was their foul Marxism but a way of satisfying their desire for faith without betraying their reason? And another thing he loathed about them was their hypocrisy in claiming that men were equal. That was a piece of arrant nonsense that went against every shred of historical, biological and anthropological evidence – and they knew it. When they attempted to force equality among men, they were destroying the thing that made everybody unique.

What the Communists were really terrified of were good, sound, honest words like 'race', 'religion', 'nation', and 'social hierarchy'. In other words, reality. It was just a lie to try to impose some false uniformity on everybody, without distinction. That didn't mean you couldn't call neighbours brothers; and people should respect each other on the basis of equal rights – as long as human differences were acknowledged.

'What's wrong with that, Alyosha?'

'Nothing, Grandfather.'

'Exactly. Otherwise the Communist religion is waging war on the human condition itself, and this is a truly horrific undertaking.'

It was only when her husband shuffled out to try to find some tea that his grandmother opened her heart to Alyosha.

'I so wanted to leave Russia with Inessa and Fyodor, but your grandfather put his foot down and insisted that no power on earth would ever compel him to leave. Back then it was much easier to cross over the border, especially with the visas Artyom had supplied us with.' She dried her tears. 'Your grandfather burned ours before my eyes.'

Vasillii and Anna lost their house when it was given over to a Tenants' Committee and divided up to be shared among half a dozen families and two or three childless couples. There must be some fifty souls living there now, never mind the rabbits and the tortoises, the goats and hens, and cats and dogs. They stayed on for a few weeks in one of the attic rooms but the noise was too much for them, quite apart from the torment of seeing their beautiful home go to rack and ruin, and they asked to be re-housed.

Aloysha saw the deterioration in his grandfather for himself over the next days. For hours every day he simply lay on his bed, with just the tips of his fingers stroking his forehead visible above the blanket. He smoked incessantly when he had the tobacco, and was forever asking Alyosha to roll his cigarettes for him.

'What hope is there for the old values – truth, freedom, morality, individuality, dignity and honour – in a society like this one? How can we save these words from becoming forgotten things? The trouble is, men have always been inclined to create an illusion of the world to suit their own ends. The challenge for wise men, Alyosha, is to come to terms with the world as it is, to acknowledge honestly the truth about our frail and sinful selves.'

Vasillii was adamant there was no future, and no present either. His only pleasure was in discussing the past. He'd go over the same ground time and again, revisiting each small detail of every argument, which his long-suffering wife had already heard a hundred times, so that by now she just turned a deaf ear most of the time.

Russia.

Russia.

Russia.

He was in mourning, and was trying desperately to understand how the passing of all he loved had come to be.

44

A funeral procession slowly crossed Mikailoskaya Square. Vasillii Karlovich took off his fur cap and motioned to Alyosha to do the same. Coming across a dead man in his coffin was meant to bring you luck, he told his grandson. They both stood respectfully as the cortege passed, but from the far side of the square a motor-bike roared towards them. The driver wore grey goggles, a cap and a black leather jacket. The procession blocked his way and he was forced to stop. He hooted his horn a few times, and revved loudly, but the procession continued on its sedate way without taking any notice.

This clearly infuriated the driver of the motor-bike, who revved violently once more, spinning the wheels and sending a stream of slushy snow over Vasillii and Alyosha. He then took a Mauser out of his jacket and fired it into the air a couple of times, once dangerously close. This had the desired effect – the mourners ran for cover, leaving a gap big enough for the motorcyclist to shoot through, splattering the hearse with more muddy slush. Vasillii shook his fist at the biker's back, and told his grandson angrily that the Communists wouldn't even leave you in peace when you were dead.

The incident had thoroughly upset the old man, and all the way to the Peter and Paul Cathedral he talked non-stop, jumping wildly from one subject to another. One of his theories was that Lenin was an imposter. The real Lenin had been murdered by the Germans when he was on his way back to Russia in April 1917, but they had been canny enough to replace him with an imposter without anybody noticing the switch, so that they could bring the war to an end, and make it possible for the the Kaiser's armies to cross over to France to fight the French and the English. That train that brought 'Lenin' to Russia turned out to be a veritable Pandora's Box.

'I do find that a bit hard to believe, Grandfather.'

'I'm telling you, it's the gospel truth! I won't hear anyone saying otherwise.'

Under the portico of the Cathedral quite a few people had gathered to shelter from the fine rain that had started to fall quietly above their heads. Vasillii and Alyosha went in and made their way to the altar at the far end, kneeling near the tombs of the Tzars. Vasillii knelt right down until his forehead was touching the cold floor. He recited a long prayer, begging for forgiveness for his compatriots.

As they left the gloom of the interior, they came face to face with Zinaida Esternova and her sister. When Zinaida heard that Alyosha's family had escaped to Berlin she congratulated him and said she envied them more than she could say. She and her sister were quite desperate to leave Russia but didn't know the best way of going about it.

Vasillii told them that it was impossible for anybody to leave the country legally without making an application to the Foreign Department of the Provisional Soviet District Committee, which involved filling in form after form. It was a tortuously bureaucratic process and the final stamp of approval giving permission to leave was as rare as hen's teeth. If anybody hoped to leave Russia in a hurry, the only option was to try to slip across the border illegally.

45

Alyosha threw in his lot with Zinaida Esternova and her sister. The three of them began to plan their escape from Russia. Zinaida had heard that – for a price – there were scouts who could show them the best place to make the crossing, where the border patrols were scarce. There was a reliable system for communicating with these people. Of course, they asked a great deal of money, but Zinaida's sister had enough for the three of them, and would happily pay for Alyosha as they would feel much safer with a male escort.

The problem was how were they to reach Shuralovo, the last train station on the Russian side of the border, in the first place? Internal travel was impossible without the necessary papers – they would be arrested before they were ten miles out of Petrograd.

In the end it was Vasillii who came to their aid. He had kept up his membership of the Karelian and Petrograd Hunters' Union and was able to procure a pass for the three of them to travel to Shuralovo.

Alyosha tried his best to persuade his grandparents to accompany them. He hated to think of them alone in Petrograd, with nobody to protect them. But his grandfather wouldn't budge.

'For better or worse this is my home,' he declared. 'I'm too old to start again in a new country, and at least here I have my memories.'

Anna packed her grandson's little sack for him with the greatest tenderness, placing each laundered item carefully in its place. His grandfather insisted that Alyosha take his best fur coat, beautifully cut though showing its age a little, and his trusty hunting hat, inside the lining of which Anna had hidden two diamonds and her engagement and wedding rings, to be given to his mother when he arrived in Berlin.

Alyosha's last night in Petrograd was a melancholy affair. The paraffin lamp burned brightly, turning the wick a scorched yellow-black and filling the room with the stink of naphtha and salt. Once they had eaten, Anna suggested doing without it, so they sat in the moonlight; three blue-grey shadows.

'Will you promise me one thing, Alyosha?'

His grandmother went on to tell him she had learned all manner of silly old wives' tales and superstitions when she was a little girl, but in amongst them she had also learned some ancient truths that it would be unwise to ignore. So if a woman came towards him on the morrow carrying an empty pail, he could expect nothing but trouble and sorrow, and should turn back at once.

'Now do you promise me?'

'I promise.'

'On your life.'

'On my life, Grandmother.'

The next day the scout came to collect him as arranged. She was a blonde, blue-eyed girl with limited Russian, as Finnish was her mother tongue. She didn't say much, only that they should go at once to collect his friends, because they didn't want to miss their train. Anna, weeping softly, held his cheeks in her cold hands and kissed him on the lips. He kissed his grandfather, who was making a heroic effort not to show his feelings, and though he didn't really believe it, told them both not to lose hope, and that he felt sure the family would all be reunited one day.

Then he lifted his sack onto his shoulder and followed the girl out of the apartment.

46

The moment Zinaida opened the door, Alyosha knew something was wrong. Her sister stayed with the girl while she gestured Alyosha to follow her to the kitchen. There she told him urgently that they must abort the plan.

'But why?'

'It's a trap.'

'What do you mean?'

'Sshh, keep your voice down, she'll hear you. Look, there's no time to go into it but they're not to be trusted. The minute they've got your money, they kill you. They found the body of a White officer on the banks of the river Sestra with his throat cut. At the exact point where you ford the river to reach Finland. We can't go. We'd be mad to risk it.'

'But you don't know that's what happened; there could be some other explanation. Who told you this, anyway?'

'It was a reliable source. We're not going, and that's that.'

Lowering her voice even more, Zinaida said her source thought the Finnish couriers must be in league with the Red Army border patrols. It was well known that nearly every fleeing Russian was a little private bank on two legs, stuffed with money or jewellery, and the guards and the scouts must be sharing out the spoils between them.

Her eyes wide, Zinaida whispered earnestly, 'If we go with her today, that's how we'll end up. At best captured, at worst, dead.'

Alyosha reflected on what she had said.

'I can't stop you going, but I beg you to reconsider.'

He felt the pass in his breast pocket. It was only good for two days. He knew how much trouble it had been for his grandfather to obtain it in the first place, and how in the end he had been forced to bribe an official to stamp it. How long would it take to procure another, if that was even possible?

'Don't risk it. Think of your poor mother.'

He had no choice.

47

He and the blonde girl had walked every step of the way to Finland Station through the streets of Petrotrad, and now there was no heating on the train and Alyosha's feet were already very cold. When he thought of the journey's end he started to worry that he might freeze to death. More and more passengers arrived, and the seats soon filled up. They were mainly office workers on their way home, but there were a few soldiers and sailors, and some countrywomen with empty baskets and pails, who had come into the city to sell their milk and cheese. The faces around him were pale and weary and they all sat there mostly in silence.

Alyosha couldn't remember ever wanting so desperately for a train to start its journey, but there was a long delay, over an hour, before it finally pulled out of the station. The city yielded to the country soon enough, and then to forest, until out of the window there was nothing to see but trees and the shadows of trees as the train roared through the great forests of the north.

The compartment filled with tobacco smoke and the windows clouded over with condensation. Although more than once Alyosha was tempted to strike up a conversation with the blonde girl, in the end he didn't exchange a single word with her.

As the train stopped at various stations along the line, the carriage gradually emptied, and by the time they reached Shuralovo, he and the blonde girl were the only ones left. When he stepped onto the country platform the sun was low in the branches of the trees, throwing long shadows across the snow.

Alyosha gulped in the air after the muggy compartment,

though its frozen purity burned his nose. He began to walk but then he noticed an old woman walking towards him. The blonde girl turned round to check that he was following her and saw that he had stopped. He saw her blue eyes gazing at him, and there was something a little impatient in the way she stood there, as if suggesting it might be better not to loiter.

The old woman came towards him. He peeped into her pail. She passed by. He gazed down the line. The universe pressed down on his head, crushing him. He had to decide. Her pail had been empty. *He had to decide*. With his back to Russia he made his way down the white lane between the black trees and followed in the blonde girl's footsteps.

48

A raven cawed loudly, beating its wings against the branches. They came to a wooden house in a clearing in the forest, with a candle burning in one window, though the curtains were shut.

Alyosha followed the blonde girl in through the back door. Standing waiting for them was a stout middle-aged woman who, in better Russian than the blonde girl's, invited Alyosha to sit at the table and have something to eat. The girl (Alyosha assumed they must be mother and daughter) went through to the other room to sleep without eating.

An hour or two passed. The woman spoke quietly about this and that, the weather mainly. They had to wait until just before dawn, she explained, before making for the border, as this was the safest time. The blonde girl didn't re-appear from her room, and she didn't make a sound either. In spite of the calmness of the woman, Alyosha began to feel something was not quite right.

On an instinct, he got up suddenly and strode over to the other room, but the woman was faster than him and blocked his way. He shoved her to one side and flung the door open. There was nobody in the bed. The room was empty. He crossed over to the window and saw that it was unlatched. When he flung it open wide and looked out he could see footsteps in the snow, leading away from the house. He peered at the trees. Could he see a needle of light over there?

Moving now like lightning, he grabbed the breadknife from the table and ordered the woman to put her coat on. He shoved her out of the door and motioned for her to strap on the skiis that were propped against the wall of the house, as he did the same. He urged her on through the forest, hitting her across her back if she slowed down, until she begged him not to hurt her, for she was going as quickly as she could.

He heard a noise, and over his shoulder saw the light of a lantern somewhere behind him. The woman gasped that she couldn't go on anymore, her chest was so tight she felt she was going to suffocate. He told her if she didn't take him to the border he would kill her. Her face beetroot red by now she pointed and spluttered, 'It's that way… it's not far.'

He took hold of her by the scruff of her neck and shook her like a terrier shakes a rat.

'Which way?'

He brought his face right up to hers and shouted, 'Which way?'

She answered, 'No… it's that way.'

He left her crying in a heap in the snow.

By now he could see the soldiers on skiis following him, the blonde girl shouting instructions to them. A few words of Russian carried on the night air.

Alyosha floundered on but it became impossible to ski and he ripped the skiis off and started running.

He ran for his life.

He stumbled.

He heaved himself back onto his feet.

He tripped.

Then crawled on all fours.

He scrambled his way up a high bank.

Beneath him, a river, frozen solid.

He half-crawled, half-slid down through the powdery snow. He staggered to his feet but he was winded, and his head was spinning so much he could barely keep his balance.

He heard the soldiers shouting at each other in the trees.

Alyosha put one foot onto the ice and then another, and step by precarious step, crossed the river and reached the far bank. From somewhere within him he found the strength to claw his way up the river bank, then he slid and rolled down on the other side.

He could hear men's voices coming nearer.

He didn't dare look behind him, but put all his efforts into escaping from their sight.

The first bullet sank into the snow by his leg.

He grabbed onto the base of a branch and hauled himself to his feet.

Another bullet whistled past his shoulder.

Once he reached flatter ground, he crawled over to some bushes under the trees, as bullets continued to whizz above his head.

When he reached the relative safety of a tree, he cautiously stood up. He leaned against the great trunk and pressed his cheek against the cold bark.

Alyosha gazed back at Russia for the last time in his life.

1921-1924

1

From a very young age, Larissa had always hated dogs, and she saw no reason to change her opinion as she grew older. If anything, her prejudice against them had grown, and her fear of them was the same, no matter what their size or shape. Small dogs were just as capable of biting as large dogs as far as she was concerned. If one came towards her she would cross the road rather than have to walk past it.

Frau Dorn's dog was rather elderly, but it acted like a young puppy when it found a hand to sniff, or fingers to lick. No sooner was Larissa in through the door than it pattered up the hall on its filthy paws, tail wagging, black shiny nose upturned in anticipation (with that revolting red wart, which turned her stomach) and stuffed its muzzle against her thigh. Larissa, shuddering, squeezed her way past and rushed up the stairs. They rented two rooms in Frau Dorn's boarding house, a five-storey building in a poor neighbourhood of Berlin.

'You're back then, safe and sound?'

She shut the door of their apartment behind her.

'As you see.'

She hung her damp coat, which smelled of petrol from all the motor-cars and omnibuses, on the hook on the back of the door.

'It's good to have you home safe.'

'I come home safe every day.'

'We should count our blessings for that.'

'I'm perfectly capable of looking after myself.'

'Did you get wet?'

'It was only just starting to drizzle as I reached the top of our street.'

'Here, let me feel your arm.'

'Mama, I'm dry as a bone, really.'

After a few more enquiries about her daughter's day, Ella rose to lay the table, carefully and ceremoniously. They had a cup of tea, waiting as they did each day for Margaret to return before eating.

'You'd better make a start on your homework, child, before it gets dark.'

Ella was always very parsimonious with the paraffin, and resented lighting the lamp unless it was absolutely necessary.

'In a minute. I'm tired.'

'You're always tired.'

Larissa didn't reply.

'Lala dear, why are you always tired?'

'Because I am.'

'Are you sleeping properly?'

'Yes, Mama.'

'What's the matter than? There's something the matter, but you won't tell me what it is. You're making me worry now…'

'There's no need for you to worry about *me*.'

'How can I not? I'm your mother. Are you unwell? Should we take you to the doctor?'

'Mama, really I'm fine. And we've no money for a doctor in any case.'

Ella was forever fussing and worrying about her daughters. Larissa often felt every bit as low in spirits as her mother, but she was at pains not to show it, as Margarita was always warning her they had to be cheerful and support their mother as much as they could, so that they wouldn't add to her burdens. It was hard sometimes, though. Larissa hated her school with a passion: hated the pupils, hated the teachers, hated the lessons. Coming home to this cramped little apartment didn't help either, where it was impossible to escape for even five minutes to be alone. She longed to be older.

'What are you thinking about?' asked her mother, who had also been brooding.

'Nothing. When will Margarita be home?'

'She won't be long, I'm sure.'

Larissa was hungry. Her lunch had been frugal. Her mother knew this perfectly well although nothing was said, but the understanding was that the three of them should eat together. The evening meal had turned into a kind of ceremony and for Ella, these little everyday rituals had taken on a great importance.

'Come now, make a start on your homework.'

'I don't have any homework tonight.'

'But you just said that you did.'

'Hardly anything.'

'All the more reason to do it now and have done with it before your sister comes home.'

With a sigh, Larissa went to fetch the German/Russian dictionary from the bookshelf – the only bookshelf. She fetched her exercise book from her bag and started to read, though she wasn't really concentrating.

The day was slowly fading. Ella closed her eyes, plaited her fingers together in her lap and sat, still as a millpond. The windowpane quivered as a train rushed past and, little by little, the windows of Neukölln's apartment blocks yellowed the gloom.

Eventually they heard Margarita's voice and her friend Klara's guttural laugh. Larissa was horribly jealous of Klara, the young woman who lived in an apartment on the floor above theirs, on account of her very good, full-breasted figure, and the fact that she had plenty of clothes to show it off to its best effect, as well as three pairs of good shoes. She had also managed to acquire the best washstand in the block, a mirror without a single crack, a sideboard and a wardrobe to keep all those pretty dresses of hers.

Margarita let herself in and Klara's light footsteps faded as she continued up the stairs. Larissa was always happy to see her sister return.

'You've come back safely then?'

'I come back safely every day, Mama.'

The two sisters exchanged a swift glance as Margarita took off her hat and her beret, damp from the rain.

'It's good that you're home safe and sound.'

'And look what I have!' said Margarita and produced three little cakes with a flourish, a little battered but they would taste none the worse for that. Larissa knew these would have been purloined, not paid for, but of course their mother would never have imagined such a thing.

'What a treat,' said Ella, 'and supper's ready so let's eat. How was your day?'

'Fine.'

Margarita had managed to find work in a local cake and biscuit factory, thanks to Klara. She'd been seeing one of the foremen for a while, before his wife came to hear about it and stormed over one afternoon to create the most almighty scene, throwing her wedding ring in her husband's face, calling Klara a whore, and spitting on the cakes. Klara was very nearly given her marching orders on the spot, but one of the accountants had always had a soft spot for her and managed to have her kept on.

The wages were poor, but Margarita was only too glad to have any kind of work until something better came along, and was realistic about the fact that it might take some time for that to happen. Her days were long: she left the apartment at a quarter past seven every morning and wasn't home until six at the earliest, sometimes later. The work was boring and monotonous too, but at least the girls sat together as they packed up the cakes and biscuits, in their boxes with pictures of the lakes and mountains of Bavaria; and as long as the foreman wasn't sniffing around, they had plenty of opportunity to chat and joke. Margarita thanked Herr Professor K. K. for her fluency in German, augmented by now with plenty of slang and swear words learned on the factory floor.

As they left the factory every evening at the end of their shift, half a dozen women patted them down and checked their bags to make sure they weren't stealing the goods. Margarita would never have dared bring out as much as a crumb with her, but Klara had devised many ingenious ways of smuggling and soon instructed Margarita in her methods. She told her it was a matter of principle, that in this small way they took their revenge on the greedy capitalist who exploited them with such low wages and long hours and Margarita was happy to agree, if it meant her family had a few treats to enliven their dull and frugal diet.

'You'll never guess who I saw at lunchtime,' said Margarita, as they ate their stew.

'Who?' asked Larissa.

'Yevgeny Kedrin.'

Her mother looked up at this.

'What, he came to the factory?'

'No, no, I saw him on the street, just by chance.'

'Really? Did he recognise you?'

'No, Mama, of course not, but I gathered up my courage and approached him. I recognised him at once, from when he came to the house to see Papa. Before the troubles of 1917. Don't you remember? When they would go to the Freemasons' Lodge together?'

'Yes, you're quite right, fancy you remembering that.'

'Well, I asked him if he knew anything of Papa, but he said he didn't.'

The windowpane rattled as a train rushed past.

'But he couldn't have been kinder, and said he'd certainly make enquiries. He still has contacts in Russia. And he wrote our address down in his diary. He was very sympathetic.'

'Sympathy won't bring Papa back,' Larissa said sadly.

'We must keep on praying, girls, and never lose hope,' said Ella.

Margarita hesitated, with a sidelong look at her sister, before saying, 'Yevgeny Kedrin had seen Uncle Fyodor and Aunt Inessa in a dinner at the Imperial Russian Exiles Club too. They've been in Berlin for a while. They're staying in the Hotel Adlon.'

'I know,' Ella replied, 'I received a letter from Fyodor. Heaven knows how he found out where we were living.'

Her daughters looked at her in astonishment.

'You *knew*? For how long?'

'Oh some months now, I forget exactly. Five or six perhaps.'

'Mama! Why didn't you tell us!'

'Yes, why ever not? Can we see them?'

'We most certainly cannot. Understand this: I will never, ever take as much as a kopeck from that man as long as I live. And I absolutely forbid you from having anything to do with him. I'd rather we all starved to death. He betrayed your father.'

2

Alyosha had found a cowshed to sleep in, but was roused from an uneasy slumber by a vicious kick in the ribs.

'Get up and put your hands in the air!'

He opened his eyes to see two soldiers with their guns trained on him.

'We haven't got all day. On your feet. Come on. Get up. So where have you come from, then?'

'Petrograd,' he mumbled, struggling to his feet.

'Name?'

'Alexei Fyodorovitch Alexandrov. My father is Fyodor Mikhailovitch Alexandrov.'

'If I want to know who your father is, I'll ask you.'

By now, they had searched through his belongings and found the two-day pass his grandfather had procured for him – with a different name on it.

'He's a Red. Come to join your scummy Communist friends in Finland, have you? Think you're going to help them fuck up our country like you've already done in yours, do you?'

'Shoot him.'

'It would save us the bother of taking him in.'

'I'm not a Red! The Reds would shoot me if I went back. I'm an exile. You have to believe me.'

'Exile, my arse. That's what they all say.'

'Stick a bullet in his head.'

'Right, get out.'

He obeyed.

'Up against that tree.'

He walked towards the forest. In a panorama of trees and snow, and the vast sky above him as still as ever, he was going to die. After all that he'd been through, after managing to escape Russia, he was going to be murdered here on Finnish soil.

'So shoot me.'

He was tired of begging. That's what they wanted him to do, humiliate himself by pleading for mercy. He'd seen enough of soldiers and armies to understand their nature.

'Cocky little bastard!'

Alyosha glared at the soldier.

'Just look me in the eye and then shoot me, you ugly cunt.'

The soldier strode over to him, his fist raised, but for some reason his companion said warningly, 'Heikki, don't!'

'The little fucker's asking for it.'

'Leave it. I've changed my mind. We'll take him in.'

They tied his hands behind his back and had him walk between them. They trudged through the snow, sometimes a layer of light icing, sometimes in deep drifts. The wind whipped up and then fell again. They moved through a kind of pure silence, their path overshadowed by the tall trees that seemed to bear down on them. They crossed a river using stepping stones, bounding from one to the other and then scrambling up the bank on the other side.

Eventually the path they were following widened into a rough track and they reached the camp, which had been constructed among the pines and cedars. It consisted of several wooden huts and larger buildings, with woodsmoke curling out of most of the chimneys. He heard a horse whinny and a motor-truck's engine refusing to fire. He was marched past several soldiers who were standing around smoking, but nobody seemed to take much notice of him.

Nudging him with the butt of his rifle through the door of one of the long, rectangular long, huts, Heikki said, 'In you get.'

The hut was a prison block, divided into cells, though only one was occupied. He was locked in another, as far away from the other prisoner as possible, and when he tried to start a conversation with him an unseen guard ordered him in a thunderous voice to be quiet.

He felt around his cell, fingered the heavy wooden door and felt the strangeness of the walls. He felt the stillness of the bars, grabbed them in both hands and pulled himself up for as long as he could, testing his own strength. He began to feel as if he was drowning; he had trouble catching his breath. He rolled back and forth on the floor. He had never been locked up in a cell before. Nobody brought him food. He couldn't sleep. His greatest fear was that he would be sent back to Russia. He decided then and there that he would kill himself first.

The night dragged interminably towards the dawn. When it finally broke, Alyosha looked through the bars across the small window and saw a thick, milky fog sliding through the trees towards the camp like some silent enemy. He banged on the door and then kicked the bottom.

'I want food!'

Eventually, they brought him some. He gulped it down, but was still famished when he'd finished the last mouthful. Around midday, two soldiers unlocked his cell and escorted him across the camp to an office furnished with a table, chair and telephone. An hour or so went past, during which time the telephone rang a few times, but was left unanswered by his guards.

It must have been mid-afternoon when a tall, grey-haired officer walked in, smelling of lavender water. He placed a black thermos flask on the table in front of him.

'Do you want to tell me the truth?'

Throughout the ensuing interrogation, the officer kept unscrewing the top of his thermos flask, pouring himself some coffee and then screwing the flask shut again, before slowly sipping the drink. The smell drove Alyosha wild, but he wasn't offered any. Every word he said was transcribed. The hours ticked slowly by.

'Is that all you have to say, then?'

The officer stood up. He had given no indication whether he believed Alyosha or not. As he was about to leave the room, Alyosha asked him, 'What's going to happen to me?'

The officer turned by the door to look at him and said, with a thoughtful look on his face, 'You'll find out tomorrow.'

'You're not going to send me back to Russia, are you?'

'Tomorrow.'

The next day, he was woken very early and put in the back of a motor-lorry with seven soldiers while it was still dark. They drove all day, through hours of forest, fording rivers, and then eventually through meadowland on straighter, smoother roads. One of the soldiers took pity on him and shared his water but not his food. It had grown dark again, the silhouettes of the telegraph poles conjoined with their shadows on the snow, by the time the lorry finally drove through the gates of a prison to the east of Helsingfors.

He was kept there for the next three weeks, waiting for his father to arrive from Berlin to vouch for him.

'Or not,' as the warden suggested one morning at roll-call, towards the end of the three weeks, 'In which case, you'll get a secret trial. Every other Russian spy has been shot so far.'

'I'm not a Russian spy.'

'That's what they all claim. But we have a good man here in Finland for beating the Reds. General Karl Gustave von Manerheim. Every bit as good as Napoleon was in his day.'

A few days later, his name was called during the exercise period in the yard. He followed a warden down several long corridors and doors, to a part of the prison where he had not been before. The warden knocked on a door and told him to go in. He walked into a warm office. A slightly stooped man in a dark coat sat with his back to him. Alyosha hesitated, and the man stood up to face him.

He came face to face with his father.

Two strangers.

Then: 'So here you are at last.'

Fyodor bared his teeth.

'You've changed.'

The father squeezed the son awkwardly, somewhere in the region of his elbow, and then squeezed him again, a little harder.

'You've lost your two front teeth?'

'Ages ago.'

'How?'

'Saving my skin.'

His father bared his teeth again: it was not a loving smile. It never was, thought Alyosha to himself.

'You've been through some terrible times?'

'Yes.'

'Haven't we all?'

Half an hour later Alyosha was on his way to Berlin.

3

Ella rarely stayed up late. After kissing her daughters goodnight she'd retire to her room – dark apart from the flame of a little candle which lit the icon at the foot of her bed, and Margarita and Larissa would hear her offering up a prayer for their father. They had heard nothing of his fate for months. Was he even alive? They could only guess, guess and hope, and in Ella's case, pray.

A train roared past. Grey goblins cowered on the walls. Ella lay down on the bed and tried to fall asleep. She longed for somebody to take her hand and ask, 'Little one, are you all right? Pour all your worries into my lap.' At these times, she could hear her mother's voice. She felt that her own ability to sympathise with people had been emptied out of her, and that her heart had been filled with bitterness.

Larissa and Margarita took it in turns to sleep on the sofa and the floor. They would whisper softly together, aware that their mother lay awake for hours, and would listen to their conversation. Larissa always loved to hear the latest about Lev Ganin. He was a Russian exile like them, and lived in their building, on the same floor as Klara, who had set her cap at him. He was a quiet, reserved young man but he had a sweetheart, a girl called Lyudmila, who was a year younger than Klara, and shared rooms on the Königsallee with two other girls. According to Klara, he was desperate to finish with her, but could never quite pluck up the courage to do so. Klara was equally desperate to see them finish, so that she could take her chance, and even suggested to Lyudmila, in her own inimitable way, that Lev Ganin was not the man for her, and she would do far better with someone else. Even Klara had a moment's trepidation, thinking perhaps she had made it rather too obvious what she was trying to do; but far from taking offence, Lyudmila remained as friendly as ever, and suggested that Klara should come with Lev and her to the pictures one evening, to see the new Charlie Chaplin film.

Larissa secretly admired Lev Ganin as well, so she was always trying to bring the subject round to him, but Margarita didn't really have much interest in Klara's romantic entanglements. Larissa felt that her sister had changed since leaving Russia. She was far more serious – and she had never been one for mischief and fun in the first place. But now there was no place at all for frivolity or gossip. The experiences of the past few years had taken their toll on her, and she seemed burdened with responsibilities and worries.

Larissa had managed to keep her zest for life, even though she didn't have many opportunities for fun anymore. She lived in hope, though, that if Lev and Lyudmila finished, perhaps Lev would prove immune to Klara's charms, and might, one day, notice hers…

4

On the long journey from Finland through Sweden to Berlin, his father had explained to him how the family had arrived in Germany back in 1918. Like Alyosha, they had crossed the border to Finland to begin with, but after a while decided to move to Berlin to join the thousands of other Russian exiles already there. He had booked a suite of rooms for them at the Adlon Hotel – Inessa expected and deserved the best after all the privations she had suffered in Russia – and they had been there ever since. He told Alyosha that when they first arrived, Baroness Kleimichael herself had been there to greet them, and had arranged for five hundred red roses to be delivered to their suite. Inessa had soon made herself at home in her second home, and enjoyed driving around the city in the auto-Daimler that Fyodor had provided for her, shopping and visiting friends.

A full four years after they had been separated, Alyosha was reunited was his mother in her suite of rooms at the Adlon. Inessa walked towards him dressed in a lemon silk kimono splashed with vivid red poppies, her hair tied up in a loose twist, blue spectacles perched on her nose. Georgik was at her side, his baby brother transformed into a sturdy little five-year old.

Fyodor said, 'Gosha, here's your big brother Alyosha. Are you going to say, "We welcome you to Berlin" to him?'

Georgik gazed up at his brother with wary curiosity.

'Gosha? What have you been practising to say to your brother? Hmmm? Say hello at least.'

The little boy shook his head and started to suck his thumb.

Alyosha couldn't say anything.

'Gosha has been looking forward so much to seeing you again after all this time. He doesn't really remember you, of course. We've shown him pictures of you when you were a boy, and we've told him so much about you. Haven't we Inessa?'

Everything was so awkward and strange.

'Hello Gosha,' smiled Alyosha at last.

His little brother was overcome by shyness and hid himself in the folds of his mother's kimono.

'There's no need to be afraid,' chided his mother tenderly. 'It's only Alexei.'

'The way I look is enough to frighten anybody,' said Alyosha. 'Especially with this big gap in my teeth.'

'That's the first thing we need to do. I certainly don't want a son of mine walking round Berlin looking such a sight. We'll arrange for you to see a dentist tomorrow.'

Time stood still.

'Did you bring me anything from Russia?' asked his mother.

'Yes.'

'Let me see.'

He placed his hunting cap in her hands.

'Inessa,' Fyodor spoke softly, 'can't this wait?'

A young maid called Grete was summoned and instructed to unpick the seams with a small scissors.

'What of my parents?' asked his mother. 'How were they?'

'Alive.'

'I told them over and again how it would be living in Russia under the yoke of criminals and murderers, but they wouldn't listen to me.'

She didn't ask anything more for fear of distressing herself.

'Let me see,' she said to the maid impatiently.

Grete brought the rings and gems over to her.

Inessa closed her fist over them and kissed it.

5

Alyosha felt as though he didn't belong. He felt as though he was trespassing on lives that had been carrying on contentedly for years without him. That evening at dinner, Alyosha saw that his mother was wearing his grandmother's wedding ring. He listened to snippets of conversation from the adjoining tables, but couldn't make head or tail of them. They were Russians, but were these people really speaking the same language as him? Try as he might, he couldn't stop himself from shovelling his food down as quickly as he could, much to his mother's embarrassment, as the Grand Duke Kyril Vladimirovich was dining next to them with his family.

'He's still growing,' his father said by way of an excuse, but Inessa hissed at him to at least put his fork down between mouthfuls, adding, 'Alexei, I cannot believe I have to tell a nineteen-year-old young man how to observe the niceties.'

'You have no idea what it's like to feel starved all the time.'

'That is not a suitable topic for conversation.'

'I want more food.'

'Good heavens. Well if you really need to eat more, we can arrange for something to be sent up to your room.'

Alyosha tried to keep his appetite under control, but the second a waiter placed a basket of bread on the table, he instinctively took one roll to eat, and slipped a second into his pocket for later.

His father had given Alyosha his own room, but Georgik, after his initial shyness, asked to sleep with his big brother. Alyosha wouldn't have minded, but he was afraid of frightening the little boy, as he often woke in a cold sweat from a nightmare, screaming for his life, so he'd refused.

He was relieved when he could finally escape from his family, and take off the stiff white collar and silk tie that had felt so constricting all through dinner. He realised it was going to be difficult to readjust to this new life, even though it was what he had longed for.

6

Grete, from Brünn originally, had moved to Berlin the previous year when she was sixteen, to look for work. She was one of nine children, and had followed the example of some of her older siblings who were working variously in Grossglockner, Salzburg and Zell am See.

She was the maid who cleaned Alyosha's room every day and she was the first person in Berlin he felt comfortable with. He loved the way she moved. There was something very sensual about her. Although she was generously built, there was a feline quality to the light-footed way she padded around the room. She had very white skin, lion-yellow hair, grey eyes and generous lips that hid a mouthful of crooked teeth. She was very aware of them, and every time she laughed, which she did often, she lifted her hand to hide her mouth.

She recognised Alyosha's hungry desire at once, and was happy to meet it. He could never have his fill of her. He loved to strip her, to stare at her nakedness. He'd turn her, this way and that, as she lay spread on his bed. He'd lift her leg, stare at her belly and groin, flip her over to admire her back and bottom or tell her to lift her arms above her head so that he could watch her breasts rise.

'Now kneel. Lift your bottom up. Like that, yes. On all fours.'

Then he'd stroke her and lick her. Or he'd tell her to climb on top of him like a leopard so that she could swing her breasts above his nose. She would smile and do as he asked.

'D'you like fucking me?'

'I adore fucking you.'

'You can fuck me forever.'

'Grete, stand over me on the bed again!'

'You never stop do you?'

'Bend over on the bed.'

Then he'd stand at the foot of the bed, spread her legs, caress her all over, kiss her slowly before burying himself in her.

After they'd finished, Grete would hold his little finger between her finger and thumb between her breasts. She told him there was an old superstition where she came from, some bit of folklore, that this was a way of restoring a man's sexual strength so that he would be ready to love again… His pleasure was her pleasure and her pleasure was his. They desired each other constantly.

Their mornings of lovemaking came to a peremptory end.

'I've been let go.'

'What?'

'I'm meant to leave the premises now, this minute. No reference, no nothing. And they've told me if I as much as set foot in the Adlon ever again, they'll have the police after me.'

'Who did this?'

'How am I going to live? What will I do? If I go home my father will beat me black and blue.'

'You won't have to leave. Don't worry. Who should I talk to?'

The Hotel Adlon's chief of staff was Albrecht Tänzer. He wore a black suit and white gloves, and his dark hair was always slicked back with pomade. He never raised his voice but rather whispered his commands as quietly as a monk.

'Can I help you, sir?'

Alyosha explained that he wanted Grete reinstated at once.

'It wasn't I who got rid of her.'

'Who, then?'

'I'm afraid I'm not at liberty to disclose that, sir.'

'If you don't tell me this instant, I'm going to piss all over your shiny shoes.'

Albrecht Tänzer smiled thinly. In his day, he had witnessed all sorts of nonsense from guests of all ages and stations, and he was not so easily rattled. However, when Alyosha unbuttoned his flies and yanked out his penis he began to take the bizarre threat seriously.

'Your mother,' he whispered, turning scarlet with mortification.

7

Inessa was lying on her stomach being massaged when he went to her room.

'What are you doing here? Why are you looking at me like that?'

'Grete stays.'

The masseur poured more oil onto her back.

'Must we talk about this now?'

'What has she ever done to you?'

'I was thinking about your welfare.'

She shut her eyes.

'Well, there's no need. In case you hadn't noticed, I've been looking after my own welfare without you for years.'

'That's only too true, and nobody regrets it more than I. But now that you're back with us, with your family, you simply cannot live like you used to. I know that everything that happened to you on your wandering through Russia was not your fault. It was highly unfortunate…'

'Unfortunate for me, yes it was…'

'Yes, but there it is, we can't turn back the clock, can we? Nevertheless, I hate to think of how you lived then, really, more like an animal than a man. And now that you're back in civilised society, you must see that standards need to be upheld, Alyosha.'

'I don't want to quarrel with you, Mama, but I think the world of Grete.'

'This is just what I mean. However can you 'think the world' of some little strumpet of a maid? It's just not appropriate.'

'It's not fair that she suffers because of me.'

'Please don't be so naïve. You're not a child; you're practically a grown man, and it's about time you started to think seriously about your future. This is what your father and I were discussing last night. Forget Grete, you have far more important things to think about from now on. Now I don't want to hear another word about it.'

'I shan't forgive you.'

'Don't be ridiculous,' she said crisply, wrapping the towel around her and sitting up.

'You're just concerned with what people think of me.'

'That's true enough,' she said calmly, taking the turban off her head and shaking out her hair.

'Well I should warn you, I have no such concern. I'm not a bit ashamed of what I am.'

8

After the girls left, Ella spent most of the day in the flat on her own, with only her memories for company, her heart full of pain and worry. She hated Neukölln, with its narrow, dark streets and rows of grey, six-storey tenements, oppressive in their melancholy uniformity. Like some unending grim barracks, they went on for miles and miles, as far as the eye could see. It was a miserable spectacle, especially under a thick curtain of dark, low cloud which threatened to open and drop its load of rain at any moment.

Every time Ella turned in to the courtyard the stench from the stinking open bags of rubbish that lay everywhere, ripped to shreds by stray cats, assailed her nostrils, and she'd be struck anew by the squalor of the scene. Against the walls were heaps of horse dung, filthy little urchins playing about in them, or kicking a ball. Above her head, dozens of washing lines were slung from window to window, from which a pitiful array of ragged clothes hung drying in the dank air.

Their apartment offered no comfort either. Ella had tried to become accustomed to living in such cramped conditions, but she hated stepping directly through the door into the kitchen-bathroom, with its coal stove, sink and tub shoehorned into a tiny space. Three paces and you were standing in the middle of the living room, full of tatty second-hand furniture and with an air of neglect and poverty about it that no amount of cleaning or polishing could eradicate.

Outside the only window was a high embankment, overgrown

with weeds and brambles. (Frau Dorn would be out there in the autumn, collecting blackberries in a white bowl for jam.) Running across the top of this embankment throughout the day and late into the night were the trains of the Stadtbahn.

A door led from the living room to the apartment's only bedroom – a dark and dingy space, with barely room for a bed and wardrobe. When Larissa looked in through the door for the first time, she mistook the room for a large cupboard, but they had been so relieved to find somewhere to live, they didn't mind too much that there was no entrance, nor even a proper bathroom. With so many exiles from Russia arriving in the city, landlords like Frau Dorn could afford to raise their rents, even for hovels.

The thought of that woman never failed to incense Ella. She had hated her from the first. She was a cantankerous old widow, rapacious and petty, who loathed having to pay out for anything, especially for her tenants, whom she despised, the foreign ones most of all. She had been at great pains to emphasise to Ella and her daughters that if anything cracked or broke, it would be their responsibility to have it mended or replaced.

The only person who ever knocked on Ella's door during the day was the old poet Podtyagin, who lived in the flat directly below hers. His health was poor: he had a weak heart and struggled for breath, and his thin, dry hands were white as a soldier's leaving hospital: he was so poor that he often said the only thing he had left to sell was his shadow.

When he first introduced himself to Ella, he made a point of saying he was only in Berlin temporarily. She claimed exactly the same, as this was the belief of every Russian exile in the city. Sooner or later, the Communists were sure to make a mess of things, and a wiser government would replace them. Then there would be a warm welcome awaiting the thousands and thousands of exiles on their return home.

In the meantime, Podtyagin told Ella, he had plans to move to Paris, as his only sister lived there. He had recently lost his son to consumption so there was nothing to keep him in Berlin any longer. He had been waiting for his visa for months now, and spent days at a time being sent from office to office to present various bored officials with various bits of paper in support of his application.

'At one time my life was a rainbow of activity: I wrote poems, I gave readings, I had my work published. And just look at the life I lead now. It's not really a life at all…'

To Ella, the old poet was a precious remnant of a bygone age and represented the conservatism of the old Russia at its best. In spite of his poverty there was something about his old-fashioned manner which soothed her: the way his hair was always carefully combed, the beautifully folded handkerchief in his breast pocket, the way he enunciated his words with such precision and how he invariably greeted her with a bow and a kiss of her hand; along with all his other little courtesies, which bordered on the sentimental, and as far as Margarita and Larissa were concerned, the comic. It would be impossible for Podtyagin to live in the new Russia. As he said himself, how could a man like him cut his cloth in a shop which had been claimed by tailors eager to follow the fashion of revolution?

His loss of faith in the future of Russia made Ella sadder than ever, though, and she found herself avoiding spending too much time in his company. Worse still, he was forever lamenting the Russia of his childhood, and broke her heart by reminding her of the streets of Petrograd, the squares and churches, the food, the weather – even the smell of the snow; all that she missed and longed for: her husband, her relatives, her home and her friends.

9

A black Panhard-Levassor cut through Berlin's traffic under the Brandenburger Tor and drew up outside the Hotel Adlon. The one-armed doorkeeper looked contemptuously at the small French flag fluttering on the front of the bonnet. The driver jumped out and tossed the key at him, then as he walked past, mischievously pulled the doorkeeper's empty sleeve out of its pocket and threw a fistful of loose change into it. The doorkeeper smiled when the driver chuckled at his own wit, as he didn't have the option of punching him in the face as he would have liked.

Nobody was happier to see her brother than Inessa.

'Let me look at you.'

She held his hands in hers, and then stretched out his arms as though to examine every inch of him.

'Aren't you the dandy!'

They laughed and hugged each other tightly, delighted to be reunited.

'It's so wonderful to see you again.'

'It's been far too long.'

He had already made a dinner reservation for them at the Kemplinski, but Inessa told him it would just be the two of them as Fyodor and Alexei were away. Artyom was disappointed not to see his nephew especially, as he had been looking forward to hearing all about his escape from Russia, but was quite happy to have his sister to himself.

That evening, sitting on a red velvet banquette under one of the huge mirrors, sipping champagne, Inessa told him that Fyodor seemed even busier than he had been in Petrograd.

'He travels the length and breadth of Europe, I never know where he's going next. Mind you, wherever he goes, the first thing he does when he arrives is telephone me. He did so from the Gare du Sud the minute he and Alexei arrived in Brussels, the day before yesterday. He's decided the boy must start to take his place in the world, so he's taking him with him wherever possible.'

'Good idea. High time Alyosha learnt to be a businessman.'

'He'll be twenty next year.'

'I was eighteen when I started in Paris. You really learn everything between eighteen and twenty-five. So what are they doing in Brussels?'

'The consortium is meeting.'

'Which consortium is this?'

'The Russian banks.'

Inessa caught the eye of an acquaintance on the opposite table and smiled a greeting. After a pause she added, 'The three most important banks.'

The three most important banks were the Russio-Asiatic Bank, represented by Putilov, the Azov-Don Merchant Bank represented by Boris A Kamenka, Duke Kokovtzov, Efim Moisevitch Epstein and Andrei Petrovich Vengerov, and the Nobel brothers' Volga-Kama Bank. This cabal had once been at the helm of the imperial economy but now their wealth in Russia was just a row of figures on a piece of paper.

'So what are they hoping to achieve in Brussels?'

'Darling, I haven't the faintest idea. I do love your suntan, Tomya. Where have you been?'

'Morocco, actually.'

'Goodness, that sounds exotic. Isn't that in Africa?'

'North Africa. Very hot.'

'What on earth took you there?'

'Business.'

Their waiter, in his black jacket and white apron, served them their first course of oysters and caviar, accompanied by rye bread, and the sommelier opened the Moselle and poured some for Artyom to taste.

All was warm comfort and luxury, and the two thoroughly enjoyed their food and the conversation. Artyom told Inessa all about his wife Jeanette, and showed her a picture of their son Dimitriy, lying naked on his stomach on a pelt.

'Oh, but he's a darling, Tomya! He has a look of Gosha about him, don't you think?'

'He's a fine little fellow. Matrimony was rather a high price to have to pay though…'

'Tomya! Shame on you! What are you trying to say? That Jeanette trapped you?' asked his sister with a playful smile.

'Well… the trouble is…' he started uneasily but then stopped.

'The trouble is…?' prompted his sister.

'Nothing.'

'Well it must be something or you wouldn't have said it.'

'Doesn't matter.'

'Don't be annoying. This is me, remember? Now tell.'

'It's just… well, the trouble is with this marriage business, you don't tie yourself just to the woman, but to the mother as well.'

Inessa burst out laughing – a light, melodious laugh – and then, sobering a little, ran her nail around the rim of her glass before asking,

'Do you love Jeanette?'

It was Artyom's turn to laugh.

'Let's say I love her the most when I'm with her, and Alondra the most when I'm with her.'

'You rascal. Alondra's the one from Barcelona? I remember you telling me about her that last time you visited Petrograd. So you're still with her?'

'I still see her now and again. A little goes a long way with Alondra. She has a hell of a temper. One minute she's sweet as honey and the next… well I try not to cross her, let's put it like that. But I like a bit of temperament. Can't be doing with those quiet little things who simper and smile at you but who are dull as ditchwater. No, the fiery ones take you to very strange lands sometimes, but that's the way I like it.'

He didn't mention the fact that he was also involved with another woman called Zepherine, by whom he'd had another son.

'Oh you men, it's so easy for you. As long as you're discreet, you can do as you like. Marriage isn't the prison it is for us women.'

The wine had loosened Inessa's tongue and she poured out all her troubles. She was grateful to Fyodor, of course she was, for getting them out of Russia safely; and for being astute enough to have taken most of their money out in good time so that they could live very comfortably. But she had never forgotten Mita Golitzin, and she still grieved for him.

'Just imagine, Tomya, just the other month, in some dull reception, I met one of his fellow officers who had managed to escape through Constantinople, and then on to Trieste. He told me the truth about his death.'

Artyom threw a quick glance at himself in the mirror on the wall opposite.

'I thought his own soldiers had shot him?'

Inessa shook her head and her shoulders slumped a little.

'I suppose that's what Fyodor told you?'

'I believe he did. So what happened then?'

She waited for their plates to be cleared and then said tearfully,

'He was stripped and hanged from a tree by the Bolsheviks. But they did it slowly, so that he died in agony.'

This revelation dampened their light-hearted mood, and later over brandy and cigarettes, Inessa told her brother how she and Fyodor had tried their best to persuade Vasillii and Anna to cross the border to Finland with them.

'Fyodor told them it would only be for a while, that we would all soon be back in Russia. I think he believed that himself for a while, which is why he didn't want to leave Finland. Perhaps our father knew better. At any rate he was adamant that he would never leave Russia.'

The eighteen months they had lived in Finland had been torture.

'Leaving our parents, not even knowing what had become of Alyosha, whether he was even alive... it was a terrible time, terrible.'

'I know. Every letter you sent me then broke my heart.'

'When we first left Russia, Fyodor was lost. Life in that hotel didn't help. We were all packed in there like sardines, and everybody wanting to know your business. I loathed it. Of course Fyodor soon found his feet. Well you know how he is, he has to make himself useful.'

He had joined forces with other Russian businessmen to reinstate the Moscow stock market in Helsingfors. They would assemble every morning and as the bell sounded, would start buying and selling. The whole thing was a fantasy, but Fyodor more than anybody thought it was important to keep a semblance of the free market going. Lenin's infernal order was sure to fall, and when they were all safely back in Russia, he had no doubt that their contracts and transactions would all be honoured.

So just as in Petrograd, Fyodor went about his business every day, leaving Inessa to her own devices. She enjoyed a brief flirtation with a cousin of the Grand Duke Kyril Vladimirovich, but it didn't last long as he was sent away on some secret diplomatic mission to Sofia and Salonica. Although Fyodor didn't hear of it until it was long since at an end, it seemed to throw him. He insisted that the family leave Helsingfors and spend the summer in a villa, on the shores of a lake set among a pine forest.

Fyodor had never been much of a talker, but Inessa noticed that he was quieter than ever, as though he was trying to keep his distress under lock and key. Eventually he told her that he was increasingly convinced that Alyosha must have perished in Russia, and although she tried to tell him he had no way of knowing that, he maintained that he felt it in his bones.

They soon grew weary of the bucolic life, and of each other's company. The country air did nothing to improve Fyodor's spirits or health and Inessa tried to persuade him to go to a sanatorium – she had heard there was a good one in Huevinki. He didn't trust her out of his sight and refused to go. He spent his days lying on the divan rereading Karamisin's history of Russia, or his favourite poet, Catallus; or sometimes he would just listen to Georgik playing outside, or being taught by his governess, Duchess Lydia Herkulanovna Vors, an exile from Moscow fallen on hard enough times to be grateful for the comfort and security such a post afforded.

In the end, Inessa insisted on calling a doctor out to examine him. He pronounced that Fyodor was suffering from a nervous crisis and prescribed morphia. The appearance of the medicine suggested its smell: heavy, thick and dark brown. Fyodor admitted that his exile had affected him profoundly. The doctor suggested some steps he should take towards regaining his health.

'Rather than see your exile as a misfortune, why don't you view it as a challenge to be overcome?'

Fyodor was lost in a maelstrom of emotions, blowing him this way and that. He was not a religious man, but he felt as though his soul needed solace and he told the doctor he wasn't sure he had the necessary strength to do as he suggested.

'I live every day in the hope that some good news will reach me from Russia. I hope, against every instinct, that my son Alyosha is still alive. I hope the Whites will prevail. Your own country is an inspiration – Marshall Gustav von Mannerheim beat the Reds here, as did Miklós Horthy in Hungary. So why haven't Kolack and Wrangel buried the Reds alive as in Siófok Orgovány? Why is the situation in Russia so much more precarious and unpredictable?'

Every disappointment was worse than the previous one and every setback harder to bear. As the doctor was about to leave, Fyodor said he wished he could be more like Anaxagoras, who when someone asked him if he missed seeing his mother country, simply pointed at the sky and said that he didn't.

'That's a very good answer,' said the doctor, 'but perhaps if you can't emulate him, it might be better if you actually put more, not less distance between yourself and Russia, and live in another country where you won't be reminded so often of your motherland.'

'And that's how we came to Berlin,' said Inessa.

10

Alyosha often felt he wasn't in Germany, but in Russia, so many families from Moscow and Petrograd had made their home there. Georgik had so many playmates amongst the children of other Russian exiles, he had barely learned a word of German since he'd arrived.

Alyosha still hadn't fully adjusted to being back in civilised society. He found it hard to sleep in a proper bed and still woke at the slightest sound, alert to any danger, though more often than not it was something as innocuous as children chasing each other down a hotel corridor, or a telephone ringing somewhere. Inessa was always trying to persuade him to have a massage, to take some of his tension away. She was a great believer in massages and saw Felix Kersten, her masseur, even more frequently than she saw her hairdresser. He was a tall, well-muscled young man, with wide shoulders and strong arms, unusually swarthy and dark-haired for a German, but with very blue eyes. He talked softly and effortlessly, in a level tone. He liked to sing at his work, Italian arias in the main. At the beginning of every summer he migrated south to manipulate the flesh of wealthy American women at the Hotel Excelsior on the Lido. He was a great favourite with all and was often taken by motor–boat, by one or another of his clients, to Saint Mark's Square, for ices outside Quadri's or Florian's. He had received at least two proposals of marriage. Alyosha sometimes wondered if there might be more between Felix and his mother than simply massages, but he tried to suppress such an unpleasant thought.

Fyodor would often eat out twice a day, meeting various people, and tried to insist that Alyosha accompany him, though Alyosha would far rather go to the pictures.

'Must I tonight?'

'I insist.'

'I'd really rather not.'

'I don't ask much of you. Go and dress. You'll be grateful to me one day. Making connections is all-important. And it's high time you started to learn how this world really works. You're not a boy any more, after all.'

11

Alyosha travelled with his father to Copenhagen for the inaugural meeting of a company he had set up, ICHC. Sir Henry Deterding from Royal Dutch Shell had agreed to come in with him, and said he was looking forward to meeting the other directors. During the journey Fyodor tried to explain to Alyosha what they wanted to achieve.

'The company is just a front for the *Banque Transatlantique*. That bank in its turn is financed by a bigger bank, the *Banque Commerciale de la Méditerranée*. And the man behind *that* is an old friend of mine, Basil Zaharoff. The Midland Bank is sheltering behind it too, under the guise of 'special advisors'. Now, the main objective of the Copenhagen meeting is to try and re-establish trading connections with Soviet Russia in the hope that in due course we'll be able to attract some practical support from the French Government through another front company, the *Société Commerciale, Industrielle et Fiancière pour la Russie.* Are you with me so far?'

Alyosha was not, but thought it easier to claim that he was.

'You know, I often think of my factory in Petrograd. I hope it's been looked after. I hate to think it might have been allowed to go to rack and ruin.'

'When did the Communists need so many bullets? I'm sure it's being worked round the clock.'

'I don't doubt that you're right.'

He became agitated.

'It's still *my* factory. Somehow or another I must have it back one day. That's why we must have Europe behind us, establish one central European body to try and win back some of our losses in Russia. I've been trying to push for it in various circles for months now. We must vanquish Communism, Alyosha; we must bury the very idea of it forever.'

He felt sorry for his father and for all that he had worked so hard to achieve and then lost, but he really couldn't pretend to be very interested in the unending plotting and discussion that took place around various mahogany tables in various European cities.

As he sat there pretending to attend, sipping water from a crystal glass, more often than not his mind was on Grete.

12

The Copenhagen meeting went well and establishing the ICHC seemed to give Fyodor a new zest for life. He decided to open an office on Französischestrasse, in the business district of Gendarmenmarkt in Berlin. Alyosha was put to work in the room next to his father's, much to his disgust.

His only solace was slipping away to meet Grete. After she lost her place at the Adlon she managed to find work in the Grand Hotel, but her wages were lower and the working conditions were worse. However without a reference, she'd been lucky to find a job at all.

'I hate sitting in that office,' he complained to her one evening, after another interminable day, 'and I loathe having to wear a shirt and tie every day.'

'Why do you put up with it then?'

'I've no idea. I don't want to. I hate going.'

'Why moan to me? Just say you don't want to go.'

'You're right.'

'Don't be such a baby. Catch me going to work if I had any say in the matter.'

'I'll talk to my father. I'll have to. Tell him how I feel.'

All sorts of businessmen came into the office: the Dutch, the Italians, the French, the Americans, the Greeks, and a few Scandinavians. They all walked with a spring in their step and a glint in their eye, ready to make some money, because German property prices were low, and the dollar, the franc and the pound opened doors wide open. Fyodor too had been able to make some very astute property deals, thanks to his foresight in taking his wealth out of the Russian banks in good time, all those years ago.

One night, Alyosha accompanied his father to a building on the corner of Markgrafenstrasse. They were ushered up the oak stairs by a doleful butler and shown into a room with a long table stretching the length of it, where they were introduced by the Chairman, Herr Bleichröder, to the assembled members of the consortium, the *Verband für Handel und Industrie.*

After dinner, over brandy and cigars, it was agreed that money would be channelled monthly from the account of the consortium; in the first instance through a bank in Zurich, and thence across Europe through the Anglo-Magyar Bank in Budapest to the Union Bank in Warsaw and finally through the Deutsche Bank in Frankfurt to the account of the ICHC in Paris, in order to buy arms from the Krupp family, who were more than willing to furnish them, to supply the Russian underground in their fight against the Communists.

'A most successful evening,' said his father on the way back to the Adlon.

'If you say so.'

'Why, what was your opinion, Alyosha?'

'I understood next to nothing.'

'Perhaps you chose not to understand.'

His father was clearly irritated.

'How can you not have an opinion? You must learn to listen, to understand these people's language, and what they mean.'

His breathing became a little laboured.

'Every manual worker knows how to go out and make money from his labours. There's no craft to that. The craft comes in knowing how to use the money you have to make yourself more money.'

'I'm not sure that's a craft I'll ever be able to master.'

'Of course you will. How could you not, a son of mine?'

Fyodor coughed and said earnestly, 'Time passes. We must all face up to the truth. Once I've gone... who'll look after your mother and Gosha then?'

'Must you speak like this tonight?'

'None of us lives forever.'

Some days later, father and son travelled to Rome to meet Sergei Dimitrievich Botkin, formerly the Russian Ambassador to Italy, to invite him to join the board of ICHC. Baron Agro von Maltzan joined them for lunch and they recounted ruefully to Fyodor their efforts in 1920 to buy seventy million bullets for twenty thousand marks through the Schilde Consortium. But by the time the consignment reached the Crimea the Communists had already taken Sevastopol and Wrangel and his armies had fled to Constantinople and Gallipoli. The whole enterprise had been a disaster. Nevertheless, they assured him, they were still eager to do anything that they could to bring about a change of government in Russia.

Fyodor was busier than he had ever been, which meant too much work for Alyosha too. The pile of correspondence that needed his attention seemed never-ending. His father's insistence on meeting everybody face to face, where often a telephone conversation would have done, also added to his burdens as he was expected to accompany him. His life became even more complicated when he was elected onto The All Union Russian Council in Exile.

'I've insisted that they elect you as well.'

'Papa, I have no interest in the business world.'

'How can you say that? We've been working so well together. Don't you agree? I've seen you make real progress in your understanding over these last weeks.'

'But I have no interest in it. I'm truly sorry. I don't think I can bear it much longer.'

'But what will you do instead? You'll have to do something. You can't just laze around all day.'

'I don't know yet.'

'Well, when do you think you might know? How can you be so directionless? Everybody needs an objective in life, Alexei, some ambition or other, or life becomes pointless. What about journalism then? Do you think you could run your own newspaper one day?'

Fyodor made this suggestion in the knowledge that the Council had already begun discussing the possibility of establishing an anti-communist newspaper in Berlin, to be distributed back in Russia. It had been passed in principle and agreed that Fyodor was the man to try and get the enterprise on its feet. This was in addition to his duties with ICHC but he went at it with enthusiasm.

The next thing he knew, Alyosha was being taken to lunch with Eduard Stadtler.

'Who?'

'A Catholic journalist from Düsseldorf,' Fyodor told his son. 'He was a prisoner of war in Russia. He's very keen to establish this paper.'

Eduard Stadtler's first suggestion to them was,

'Why not a daily paper?'

'It's a matter of finance.'

'Not a matter of will?'

'I think you'll find the Council members have plenty of that.'

Later on in the discussion Fyodor made a suggestion of his own.

'My son Alexei here has seen at first hand many of the horrors of the revolution and the civil war in Russia. He has plenty of stories to tell of the cruel and barbaric acts perpetrated by the Communists. I'm hoping you might want to use his experiences.'

'Why not?' smiled Eduard Stadtler. 'But regardless of who does the writing, I think it's important we always bear in mind that two out of three of the country's population are completely illiterate. And is it true that in some villages they still burn witches?'

'Of course they don't,' answered Alyosha. 'Whoever told you such nonsense?'

He had taken against the man and disliked his false bonhomie. He sensed that he had nothing but contempt for Russia and its people.

'Well, perhaps I read some Communist propaganda about the old order,' said Stadtler smoothly, quite unabashed. 'I might have been misled. Which just goes to prove, we mustn't underestimate our enemy. There are plenty of intelligent and shrewd men amongst the Communists. Their simple and dishonest slogans about equality, fraternity, social justice and the worldwide peace their classless utopia will bring about, conceal their real agenda: to overthrow Christian civilization and replace it with the rule of the Antichrist. The revolution was the Mongols' and Jews' attempt to take their revenge on Europe. This battle will be a monumental one between two very different world views, and make no mistake, my friends, there can only be one victor.'

They found another ally in Heinrich von Gleichen, who had been the head of Germany's propaganda agency during the 1914-18 War. Fyodor told Alyosha before they went to meet him, that he was a man worth cultivating, as he had valuable experience that they could draw upon.

Von Gleichen was waiting for them in the bar of the Adlon. He was a white-haired, grey-eyed man, with a long, equine face, furrowed forehead and a patrician air. Staring at them belligerently, he asked without preamble, 'Who killed our dear Saviour, the Lord Jesus Christ?'

His thesis, simple enough, was that behind every evil in the world there was a Jew. The abiding ambition of worldwide Jewry was to govern the world through a consortium, an arrangement not unlike the British Empire. The Jews orchestrated the 1917 revolution. The Jews were responsible for Germany losing the war by betraying the army in the field. The Jews were controlling the Weimar Republic in order to defend their own selfish interests.

'There's no end to their malevolence, and in order to trick nations they can hold themselves out as Communists today, or capitalists tomorrow,' he said. 'Communism is a Jewish disease, and in order to make Europe healthy once more, morally and spiritually strong, it's important for Germany and Russia's best people to unite under one flag, to stop this poison from polluting the world.'

There seemed no end to the man's proselytising and Alyosha was very relieved when the meeting finally came to an end. However, a few days later he was taken to meet Siegfried Dorschlag, the journalist they had appointed as editor.

'I'm a man who loathes deviousness and dishonesty,' Dorschlag told them in his thin voice as they shook hands, 'and nothing gives me more pleasure than exposing hypocrisy.'

He already had someone in mind for chief columnist.

'Heinz Fenner, formerly from the *St Peterburger Zeitung*, is our man,' he told Fyodor. 'His knowledge of Russia is second to none, and he loathes Lenin and all his works.'

'Alyosha, Herr Dorschlag has very kindly agreed to take you on as his deputy editor,' Fyodor told his son, 'so I hope you don't give him any reason to regret his decision.'

'You're welcome here, Alexei Fyodorovich,' said the editor. 'There's important work to be done and I'm glad to have you on my team. I've heard a lot about you already.'

So Alyosha was put to work. Ernst Jenny from the *Deutsche Tageszeitung* had been commissioned to write a series of articles: 'In the Red Asylum', 'Asia in Europe', 'The Imperialism of the Communists', and 'Christ and Nationalism'. He was an old hand and knew exactly how to play on Prussia's fears of the Red Peril.

Alyosha's contribution was to furnish him with a first-hand account of how it had been to live in Russia during such a turbulent period, based on his varied experiences during his wanderings.

As the articles appeared in print, one after the other, Alyosha felt a mounting sense of outrage at the way in which what he had recounted in good faith to the journalist had been manipulated. He had been at pains to point out that, as far as he had been concerned, the Whites were every bit as bad as the Reds in terms of violence and brutality. He thought it was important to recount this honestly. The final straw came when the attack on Mishka, Masha and Boris' village by the Whites was written up faithfully in every respect – except it was attributed to the Communists, wreaking their revenge on the innocent villagers.

Outraged, Alyosha refused to cooperate further.

'Why do you insist on always making life difficult for yourself?' his mother asked him angrily. 'Whose side are you on? Ours or theirs?'

'I'm on the side of the truth.'

'Don't you think it's high time you started to grow up?'

She was on her way out. While his father beavered away night and day, Inessa had been keeping company with the First Secretary she had met at a dance at the French Embassy three months earlier. His name was Albert Dupont; he was around her age, married with three children, a sharp-nosed man, but tall and broad, cutting a fine figure in his official white dress. Inessa spent her evenings in his company, mingling with the officials and diplomats of various countries, dining and dancing until the small hours.

13

Grete and Alyosha often went to the pictures together, usually to the Kosmos on the corner of Kronenstrasse, opposite the Reichshallen Theater. They both loved Harry Piel's films, and Alyosha enjoyed Charlie Chaplin, while Grete's favourite actor was Tom Mix. She loved all his cowboy films and would see them any amount of times without ever tiring of them.

One evening Alyosha took Grete to a new picture house off Unter den Linden, halfway down Mittelstrasse. The film was about a gang of highwaymen in Corsica, who had kidnapped a beautiful young woman called Maria and kept her captive in a cave high in the mountains. Her parents and sisters were almost mad with worry and grief, begging and praying for somebody to save her. Finally their prayers were answered in the shape of young man named Ghjuvan, who came to see the family and offered to save their daughter.

This proved easier said than done, as Maria was closely guarded by her captors. Ghjuvan decided his only chance of success would be to join the gang. Before they would accept him, he had to prove himself in a series of challenges, which had been the death of many a brave man before him. He accepted the challenges, wrestling, fighting and knife-throwing against all comers. Some of these scenes were so thrillingly frightening that Grete had to hide her eyes behind her hands. After Ghjuvan had finally been accepted as a member of the gang, he was betrayed by a thief he had trusted like a brother, and was thrown over a precipice to his death, but he managed to save himself and climb back up the mountain. There then ensued a thrilling chase, with the chief of the gang making off with Maria on the back of his horse, Ghjuvan hot on his heels. After one final fight, Ghjuvan at last emerged victorious, a dead highwayman at his feet and a swooning Maria in his arms.

'Would you?' asked Grete as they emerged blinking onto the street.

'Would I what?'

'Would you be willing to do that for me?'

'Of course I would,' said Alyosha, kissing her passionately, 'and more.'

Her eyes filled.

'But would you do that for me, that's the question?' teased Alyosha.

Grete laughed.

'I'd be too tired to fight anybody for long.'

He gave her a playful nudge.

'Don't.'

Then he grabbed her and tickled her until she was begging for mercy.

'Stop it! Stop it!''

'Tell me what you'd do for me then, and I'll stop.'

'To set you free? I'd sleep with the chief.'

Alyosha stopped his tickling, but Grete could see he wasn't very pleased with her suggestion.

'It would just be a fuck. Nothing more.'

'But how would I know that?'

'To set you free it would be a price worth paying. I wouldn't be ashamed.'

'So would you be willing to fuck anyone?'

'To set you free, to have you back safe with me? Yes I would. I'd be willing to fuck anyone. If that was the only choice I had.'

Alyosha looked at her resentfully.

'What? You think that means I'm easy?'

Alyosha didn't answer.

'You don't trust me? Is that what you want to say to me?'

'I don't know what you get up to every day.'

'Work my fingers to the bone skivvying in the Grand Hotel is what I get up to every day. I dust, I clean, I polish, I change beds, I run around clearing up after everyone. And if it comes to that, I don't know what the hell you get up to every day.'

Grete paused and then sighed.

'This is just stupid. Why are we wasting our time talking rubbish?'

He smiled.

'You're right. Why are we talking rubbish?'

They kissed. Later, sitting at a table in the Café Schwedischer, Alyosha explained to her that things had gone from bad to worse between him and his father. Since he had refused to go to the ICHC office in Französische Strasse and refused to contribute any more to Ernst Jenny's articles, Fyodor had read him the riot act.

'He told me he had no intention of just letting me twiddle my thumbs here in Berlin doing nothing. I said to him, "Why don't you just let me be?" So then he says to me, "If you really have no interest in anything else I at least insist that you finish your education."'

'What? He's sending you back to school?' she laughed. 'You're twenty!'

'He wants me to sit the entrance exams for Zurich University.'

'Zurich?'

'That's where he went. He's already employed Lydia Herkulanovna Vors to tutor me. My mother loves her because she's a duchess. Thinks she'll teach me some manners at the same time.'

'I remember her from when I worked at the Adlon.'

'My parents knew her in Finland.'

'Well, she's a right snobby bitch. Treated me like dirt of course.'

Alyosha glowered.

'Did she?'

'Why does that surprise you?'

'I suppose it shouldn't. She's as much of a monarchist as my grandfather. She worships the Tzar and his family.'

'So how old is she?'

'Forty,' Alyosha told her. 'She's a widow. From Armenia originally. Her husband was an officer with the Whites but he was killed by the Reds in the war.'

Alyosha chose not to tell Grete that his governess claimed the Bolsheviks had thrown him into a ship's furnace. He did tell her, however, how she had told him, with great pride, that she had seen some heads of Lenin and Trotskii in a shop window on Friedrichstrasse. She had returned to the shop the next day, bought as many of them as she could afford, and then taken a hammer out of her bag and had smashed them all to pieces on the counter.

'And you're going to be taught by a woman like that? Good luck!'

It was Grete's day off the following day so Alyosha smuggled her back to his bedroom in the Adlon. Giggling, they locked the door behind them.

Alyosha said, 'Perhaps I should become a thief. I know how to break into houses, you know.'

'That's something they don't teach you at school.'

There was a knock on the door and they froze. Albrecht Tänzer announced himself. Grete whispered anxiously that somebody must have seen her slip into the hotel with him and reported her but Alyosha shook his head.

'What is it?' he called out.

'I have a note from your father; he requested that I bring it up at once.'

'Thank you, just slip it under the door and I'll come and fetch it directly.'

'What does he want?' asked Grete as he opened the note and read it.

'It just says he needs to see me immediately.'

'What, now? Why?' she pouted.

'I don't know, it doesn't say.'

'Well, I suppose you'd better go.'

14

The door of his father's room wasn't locked. Alyosha stepped in. He half-expected to see him in his chair at the bureau where the green lamp angled its light over his work.

'Alexei, come here.'

He'd never seen his father in the bath before.

'Come in.'

In the water a tired man rubbed the black shadows under his eyes.

'I'm glad that you've come. I have something important I want you to hear.'

'About me?'

'About me,' answered his father as he squeezed the soap between his hands.

He had only returned from Cannes a few hours previously, where he had been on ICHC business.

'Would you wash my back?'

Alyosha sank the yellow sponge into the water.

'We met to discuss the future of the oil industry in Russia, which is of enormous concern to us all. Of course, unofficial channels have been established between us and the Communists for some time, to try and fathom which way the wind is blowing. The hope was to try and win a monopoly from the Soviets. But it's impossible to do business with these people: the discussions have more or less foundered. So I made a proposal to which Sir Henri Deterding has agreed: that ICHC and Royal Dutch Shell lobby all the other European companies and banks with interests in Russia to boycott the Soviets. We simply refuse to buy or sell until Lenin agrees to compensate everybody fairly for all the property that he nationalised.'

'Is that the important thing you wanted to say to me?'

'No.'

For some reason his father seemed reluctant to get to the point and continued to talk of the boycott.

'In my heart I feel sure nothing will come of this scheme, any more than the others. And do you know why?'

'Why?'

'Because the companies and banks will be too greedy for a profit to keep to the boycott. They'll all be running to do business with the Kremlin behind each other's backs. Shave me with this razor, would you? While we were in Cannes there was a French and English consortium meeting just up the coast, in San Remo, carving up the oilfields of Persia and Mesopotamia between them, with the intention of keeping Standard Oil New Jersey from establishing any kind of foothold in the Middle East. My friend Basil Zaharoff is equally determined to keep the Americans out as well. We have a vision of a new order in the Middle East, which would then spread in due course through the lowlands of Southern Russia, across the Caucasus to the shores of the Caspian Sea and beyond, to keep centuries of oil out of America's greedy grasp.'

'Papa, you're talking too much for me to be able to shave you.'

'The trouble is, of course, that the London and Paris mandarins see Russia simply as a second India. As far as the English are concerned, the point of Russia is to compensate them for losing their markets in the Far East to the Americans. It's no secret that Washington is keen to be the first to set up a trade agreement with Russia, before any European consortium – such as ICHC – makes its move. That's my greatest worry, really: once the first country acknowledges Lenin's illegal government, then all the other countries of the world will follow suit and legitimise Communist Russia. And once that happens, the situation of exiles like ourselves will be a thousand times worse. Pass me that towel, would you?'

Alyosha turned his back as his father stepped naked out of the bath.

'Dry my back.'

He could hear the strains of the orchestra from the ballroom three floors beneath them, where his mother was dancing her way from one officer to another. As if his father had read his mind he said, 'I've always loved her.'

Alyosha patted his back.

'In my own awkward, selfish way I don't doubt. But I have loved her. I was never unfaithful to her…'

Alyosha patted a little more vigorously.

'And she loves me in her own way. I'm sure of that by now.'

He smiled tenderly.

'I won't be there of course, but you'll be able to judge for yourself when she stands at my graveside.'

His son saw things rather differently, but said nothing, finding the conversation rather bizarre in any event. After knotting his dressing gown, Fyodor Alexandrov poured them both a cognac.

'Draw your chair nearer.'

For the first time, Fyodor told his son about his experiences at the hands of the Cheka when he was imprisoned in Petrograd.

'Ssshh!' he said. 'Listen…'

Alyosha listened.

'Sshh! Just listen!' he whispered.

The only thing Alyosha could hear was the orchestra.

'Can't you hear her?'

'Hear who?'

'You're not listening properly. A woman screaming.'

That's what drove his father mad, the belief that the Cheka was torturing his wife in another cell, the thought of Inessa being hit and mistreated. Night after night he heard that noise, that screaming. Night after night, night after night, though the prisoner sharing his cell told him it was only the water gurgling in the pipes. He had been losing his reason, slowly but surely. He knew that if he stayed in Russia he would go mad, without a shadow of a doubt. That's why they had to escape to Finland. For the sake of Inessa. For the sake of Gosha. For his own sake.

His father never mentioned his brother Kozma. Not one word. Alyosha knew that his nervous disorder had been all due to that betrayal.

15

Alyosha refused to be taught by the Duchess Lydia Herkulanovna Vors and he refused to do anything else either. As this made relations with his parents very unpleasant he tended to keep well clear of the Hotel Adlon during the day. Unless Grete had a day off he'd usually end up wandering the streets of Berlin aimlessly on his own.

One afternoon as he was sitting in the Café Adler, he saw a girl walk by in her school uniform. He rapped furiously on the window but she didn't hear him. Flinging some money down on the table he rushed out after her. When she heard her name being called, she looked back and for a moment, not recognising him, but seeing him run towards her, looked absolutely petrified. Then, although he had changed so much, once she looked at his face properly, Larissa knew him.

'Alyosha!'

They hugged. Larissa danced up and down, squealing with delight.

'Where did you come from? Where have you been? How long have you been in Berlin?' and a hundred other questions.

'Come back with me to the Adlon!'

'Oh, Lyosha, I'd love to, but Mama will be expecting me back. If I'm even a minute late she begins to fret. But why don't you come home with me? You can see Magarita then.'

He went with her happily. On the upper deck of the omnibus to Neukölln, they talked nineteen to the dozen, interrupting each other, laughing for no other reason than their delight at finding each other again. Years of separation were shoehorned into a forty-minute journey. To Alyosha's amusement, his cousin managed to make several references to a certain Lev Ganin – she was obviously very taken with him – who had finished with his girlfriend Luydmilla because his wife Marie was about to join him from Russia. He also heard all about the hateful Frau Dorn and her dog, and Klara who lived in the flat upstairs.

She told him that Margarita had recently started a new job, clerking for a small bank on Schutzenstrasse.

'Before that she was working in a cake factory, which was hateful. But I do miss the cakes she sometimes brought back…'

'Margarita? Working in a cake factory?'

'She had no choice. She took it because that's all that was available. She said anything was preferable to nursing. Mama made us do that back in Petrograd for a while, don't you remember? But she made a really awful nurse – how she hated it! Mind you, I'm sure she's very good as a clerk. You know how organised she is about everything. Not like me…'

Even Ella had managed to find work, as a cleaner in the Berlitz School, which had taken over some old offices, formerly housing an insurance company, above the Gerold department store on the corner of Friedrichstrasse and Leipzigerstrasse. This had come about quite by chance when the three of them had volunteered at the Red Cross centre on Uhlandstrasse. Their mother had become so withdrawn and reclusive that it had taken a while to persuade her to come with them in the first place, but it had done her so much good. She had needed a great deal of encouragement to take the cleaning job she was offered too. Of course the wages were awful, but work was work. The best thing about it was that she was forced out of the flat, where she just sat and moped all day, and it brought her into contact with other people.

When Larissa opened the door and led him into their dark and dismal home, his heart sank. Alyosha stood in the tiny kitchen-cum-bathroom as a train roared by, shaking every window in the place.

'So this is where the three of you live.'

'Oh, I know, it's not much of a place, is it, but you know, we do well enough here.'

Larissa told him she was perfectly used to living in such confined quarters, but she would *never* get used to her hateful school. She'd actually been playing truant that afternoon when he saw her, wandering the city streets.

The door opened without warning. Ella turned at once to take off her raincoat and hang it up. She held a string bag with half a dozen onions in it. She became aware of Alyosha sitting there just as Larissa said, 'Mama, look who I found.'

But she didn't hear her daughter, as her eyes were nailed onto her nephew. In her mind, it was not Alyosha before her but his father, Fyodor Mikhailovich, whom he resembled so much more now, than when she had last seen him.

'He's invited the three of us to have a celebratory dinner with him at the Adlon tonight.'

'What is there to celebrate?' she asked bitterly.

'Well, that the family is reunited again.'

'Are we indeed?'

'We found each other in a foreign city. That's a reason to celebrate surely?'

'And your father? What about him? Or have you forgotten about him?'

'No, Mama, of course I haven't but…'

'Will Kozma be at this celebration tonight? What would be the point of it without him there?'

Her daughter's high spirits were completely demolished: shattered into dust, so that Larissa felt like spearing a fork through her wrist. Her mother had always had the ability to make Larissa hate herself, and this feeling of utter worthlessness was so much worse since they had become exiles.

Alyosha felt he should try to fill the excruciating silence.

'There's no need for you to come tonight, Aunt Ella; it was just a thought. Another time, perhaps. I'll have a word with my father.'

'And that will make everything all right, will it? After he broke his solemn word to my husband? After Kozma joined the Reds in order to free your father from the Cheka? The condition was that your father should remain in Petrograd. And what did he do? Save his own skin with never a thought for his brother.'

'I can't answer for my father.'

'Don't blame Alyosha, Mama, it was nothing to do with him.'

'There's no knowing whether Kozma is alive or dead. That's the worst thing. I hope against hope that he might be alive, but in my heart...'

She could feel the tears coming and she didn't want to cry in front of him.

'Would you leave, please?'

Ella's implacable fury made meeting his cousins problematic, but they were determined to see each other. The girls managed to visit him at the Adlon, and he and Margarita had an emotional reunion. The girls were thrilled with his room, with its high ceilings and Murano chandelier, the enormous, soft bed, the highly polished ebony furniture, the thick, floor length curtains, the central heating and the sumptuous carpets. They were even more thrilled to see their little cousin Gosha when he returned from his swimming lesson.

'Haven't you grown?'

'You're such a big boy now, you were just a baby when we saw you last.'

'And so handsome! I'm sure all the girls are after you! Do you have a sweetheart, Gosha?'

'Lala,' Margarita scolded. 'Behave.'

Larissa started to play a game of catch with a soft ball that Georgik had brought with him.

'Catch it! Oh, well done! Aren't you a clever boy!'

They had so much news to exchange, and so much reminiscing to do. The girls asked Alyosha about Mademoiselle Babin.

'The last time I saw her,' he told them, 'she was on horseback trotting down the lane from the dacha with Prince Yakov Sergeevich Peshkov riding at her side.'

'Were they in love?' asked Larissa.

'I think they were.'

'What do you mean, you think?'

'I don't really remember properly,' he bluffed, knowing his cousins had no idea that anything had occurred between their governess and father. 'So much has happened since then.'

Larissa tried to imagine where she might be now.

'Married and living happily with her handsome prince somewhere I hope. Harbin, perhaps, or Shanghai or San Francisco.'

'And whatever happened to Valeriya Markovna?' wondered Margarita. 'D'you remember her?'

'Of course we do.'

'How could we not?'

'I wonder if she pines for the Herr Professor K. K. as she plays her piano of an evening? Do you remember when she used that chamomile dye and her hair went that awful streaky blonde colour?'

'What happened to *him,* anyway?'

'Actually, I can answer that,' said Alyosha. 'He wrote to Papa. He's teaching in a boy's school in some town on the Schwarza River in Thuringia.'

'And is he still a bachelor?' asked Larissa.

'I expect so.'

'Still writing the history of the Russian Orthodox Church in his spare time?' asked Margarita.

'What do we care? Come along, let's go down to the restaurant, I'm starving.'

Over lunch Margarita told them about her job at the bank.

'I don't hate it, although it's boring sometimes. All I do all day is add up rows and rows of columns with another girl, in a room at the back.'

'It sounds awful.'

'Well, I hope they put me on the counter soon. They've half-promised.'

'Or you could look for something else altogether,' suggested Larissa. 'Something that suits you better.'

'There's not that much choice for someone like me...'

She had been to several interviews for various jobs, one with Alexander Kerenskii himself, though she hadn't dared tell her mother who was convinced he had been instrumental in betraying Russia to the Communists. He had his own newspaper in Berlin and had been looking for a girl to clerk. In order to reach his inner sanctum, she had to pass through four different doors, each one opening only when you said a certain password. He told her he had to take these precautions because so many people were after his blood.

'It seems he really is in danger of being assassinated. It's not surprising really. I was quite determined to take the opportunity myself to tell him exactly what I thought of him for letting the Communists steal Russia from us.'

'How did he treat you?' asked Alyosha.

'He was polite enough. I suppose when you have as few friends as he does in the world you'd rather not make any more enemies than you can help. He asked me about my life here in Berlin, how we lived and so on, and about my life back in Petrograd. "How would you solve Russia's present situation?" That's what he asked me, imagine!'

'Well, how did you reply?'

'I told him we needed to reinstate the unity of the Tzar, the Church and the people. There's no future for Russia otherwise.'

'What did he say to that?'

'He smiled – like this. And then he asked me, "What exactly does uniting the Tzar and the people mean?" And I told him "I want to see Russia as it was before 1917." And then he asked me again, what exactly did uniting Tzar and people mean? I tried to remember what Papa used to say on the subject... that a spiritual unity was founded on devotion and tradition... and how political maturity and social wisdom had to come out of the teachings of our Lord Jesus Christ.'

'I'm sure that shut him up,' crowed Larissa, delighted at her sister's cleverness, though not at all sure she understood her.

'"Unfortunately we live in the twentieth century." That was his reply. And he didn't give me the job of course.'

Glowing from her sauna, Inessa entered the restaurant and joined them at their table. Kissing the girls warmly enough, she said,

'What a lovely surprise! Now, you must tell me all your news.'

She listened politely enough, even asking a few questions, but her son could tell she wasn't really interested in their lives. She soon started to tell them all the lovely things she had been doing in Berlin, and what a wonderful city it was, especially after the tedium of Finland. She described her world of dining out, and dancing and visiting the theatres and the shops.

'I've even taken up tennis again.'

She told them she had hired a coach, a tall, thin young man, prematurely balding, poor thing. His name was exactly the same as his father's, Vladimir Nabokov, the editor of the *Rul*. And did the girls like her hair, she'd found the best hairdresser in Berlin, she'd give them his name if they wanted, only they should be sure and mention her name otherwise they didn't stand an earthly of getting an appointment...

Alyosha, knowing how his cousins lived, was deeply ashamed of his mother's frivolity. Margarita and Larissa listened in silence but after a while Margarita said, 'Thank you for lunch Alyosha, but I think we'd better go or Mama will begin to worry.'

'Now that we've found you, be sure to come and see us again,' smiled Inessa. 'Here we'll be until we can go home to Russia. Before long, I hope.'

On the way out of the hotel, they came face to face with their uncle. Fyodor Mikhailovich had come from another ICHC meeting and was with Rittmeister Paul von Rosenberg and Major Willisen.

He introduced them.

'My son Alexei you've met of course, and this is my brother Kozma's older daughter, Margarita Kozmyevna Alexandrov.'

A curtsey.

'And his younger daughter, Larissa Kozmyevna Alexandrov.'

A curtsey.

Alyosha was transported back to that morning, an aeon ago, when the three of them were introduced to Mademoiselle Babin in his father's study. Fyodor told his colleagues he would join them in a moment and they walked on.

'How is your mother?' Fyodor was asking. 'How is poor Ella?'

'She's at work.'

'Doing what exactly?'

'She cleans offices.'

Fyodor exposed his teeth but he didn't smile.

'And what about you two?'

Unlike his wife, he was genuinely interested in their welfare.

'Margarita works in a bank,' said Larissa brightly, as though hoping that would compensate a little for his evident embarrassment and shame over what Ella did for a living.

'Do you enjoy it?' he asked her.

'Not really.'

'Well, I suppose at least you're getting experience.'

When he asked her what they paid her, and heard how pitiful her salary was, he tried to hide his guilt and discomfiture, but told her, 'I'd be more than happy to give you that myself. I'd much rather you be allowed to finish your education.'

Margarita, regretfully, knew her mother would never let her accept her uncle's offer so made up some excuse about not having enough Latin to be accepted at a gymnasium. He tried his best to persuade her, telling her any deficiencies could easily be made up with a little extra tuition, but she held her ground. Larissa took the opportunity to tell her uncle how much she loathed her school and he said he would be delighted to arrange for the Duchess Lydia Herkulanovna Vors to tutor her instead. Of course Ella would have to be told; there was no way of keeping it from her. But surely she would allow it, for the sake of her daughter's education. It was a problem that they lived so far away – the journey would take Larissa forever every morning.

Alyosha had none of his father's or Margarita's scruples about deceiving Ella. When he saw his father alone later that day he told him that if he genuinely wanted to help his cousins, then he could rent them a better apartment nearer to the Adlon so that Larissa could have her lessons with the Duchess. Once his father had agreed to this, he enlisted Larissa's help to persuade Margarita to claim she could pay the rent from her salary.

16

Klara was sorry to see her friends leave Neukölln, but she didn't blame them one bit, not when they'd been offered a three-bedroomed apartment in Leibnizstrasse, off the Kurfürstendamm, at such a ridiculously low rent. She would have jumped at the chance herself. Margarita told her mother she had heard of the place through one of her colleagues at the bank and it was such a bargain, she could afford to pay it, even on her salary. Ella was unworldly enough to believe her daughter, and in her heart was only too glad to be able to leave their hovel. Margarita and Larissa had even managed to convince her that an *émigré* had set up a small school near the new apartment, where Larissa could enrol.

Before they left Ella went downstairs to knock on the old poet Podtyagin's door.

'Leaving?' he repeated, looking bemused. 'Leaving for where? Russia?'

'If only,' she thought to herself, but answered, 'For another apartment.'

'I'm still waiting for my visa to France. I've heard nothing…'

She hurriedly told him she had to go, or she would be late for work, but had come to invite him to a little leaving party that her daughter's friend Klara had arranged for them.

17

On their last evening, the few tenants they had made friends with during their time at Neukölln gathered to raise a glass and eat some of the cake that Klara had filched from the factory. Podtyagin arrived clutching a bottle of vodka, and everybody seemed in good spirits until he started to question Lev about Marie.

'Where is your wife? Why hasn't she reached Berlin yet? Shouldn't she be here by now?'

'She'll be here soon.'

'Didn't you tell me she'd got as far as Warsaw?'

'No, I don't know if she's left Russia.'

'So when are you expecting her in Berlin then? Do you have a date?'

By now everybody else had grown quiet and was listening too.

'I just don't understand why she's such a long time coming, Lev.'

'She'll come.'

'But what's the matter? Is there some obstacle?'

'No.'

'Do you have a picture of her?'

Suddenly, Klara stood up, put down her glass and walked out of the flat. Margarita went after her.

'What's the matter?' asked Podtyagin, 'have I said something I shouldn't have?'

By the time Klara and Margarita rejoined the party, Podtyagin was properly drunk.

'To Ella and her daughters!' he raised his glass in a toast.

'Ella and her daughters!'

'Good luck to us all!'

Klara sat down without looking at Lev, and neither of them said another word all evening.

18

Moving apartment seemed to have given Ella a new lease of life. She went off every morning to the Berlitz School with a spring in her step, and she took a little more trouble with her appearance too. Although she complained that they were far too expensive and she couldn't possibly afford them, she even bought herself a pair of new shoes. One evening she even ventured over to the University to listen to Karl Stählin give a lecture on Russia.

She enjoyed her work much more since she had been made receptionist. It meant she had more to do with the teachers and pupils and on discovering that she had done a little teaching prior to her marriage, she was asked if she would like to teach the occasional class, to cover for sickness. She turned down the offer, though one of the older teachers tried to encourage her. Margarita and Larissa were all for her accepting as well, but Ella was too shy and unconfident.

Then several tutors fell ill with influenza, and the head of the school himself approached Ella and said he was depending on her to help them out, otherwise he would be forced to cancel some of the classes. So she began teaching the elementary class and found the work very much to her liking. She was offered a permanent teaching post in no time and moved from the front office to a classroom. Better yet, her wages were increased. Although naturally frugal, she decided to splash out on one thing.

When Margarita returned from the bank one evening, the first thing she saw when she stepped into the living room was Larissa sitting on a stool with her back to her, her mother at her side turning the pages. She nearly burst into tears of happiness; one of the things she had missed the most in Berlin was a piano as, even if they had been able to afford one, there would have been no room at their old flat. Ella turned and smiled at her and Larissa rose and beckoned her sister to take her place. Margarita started to play and soon the three of them were singing. For the first time in ages the three of them felt something close to happiness.

Larissa was flourishing under the tutelage of the Duchess. Not only did she enjoy the lessons, she had also found someone she could confide in, as she had done with Mademoiselle Babin, to whom she could tell all her worries and hopes. Although the Duchess insisted on always being addressed by her full title (she loathed the fact that she had lost all her wealth and much of her social standing), she proved nevertheless to be a sympathetic listener. Larissa told her all about Lev Ganin, and how disappointed she had been to discover that he was married. The Duchess in turn was more than happy to talk about her short marriage. She had been very much in love with her husband. The best thing about marriage, in her opinion, was that it sheltered her from the burden of choice. Once the ring had been placed upon her finger, she knew everything had been decided for her. She could never see herself remarrying because it had been such an act of faith to do it the first time: to summon up the moral stamina to make the decision, to make the promise she would be required to keep for ever. On the morning of her wedding the realisation came to her that she had chosen this one future at the expense of any other, and that she was about to declare her choice to the world.

Larissa ventured timidly, 'But that was the right choice of course?'

'For me, yes it was.'

'When the time comes, I hope I make as good a choice as you did.'

19

In the afternoon, while Ella was at work, Alyosha arranged to visit Larissa in the new flat on Leibnizstrasse. The lobby smelled of flowers, rather than the aroma of boiled cabbage and dog that had permeated their old building, as the caretaker was a conscientious woman who kept the public areas sparkling, though she was every bit as ill-tempered as Frau Dorn, and made it clear she didn't think much of the new Russian tenants on the third floor. It was a small price to pay for the benefits of their new home, which was so much larger and brighter than the Neukölln flat, and in a much more affluent area. The place was nicely furnished too, Alyosha noted, with a Biedermeister table and chairs, a comfortable sofa, and soft carpets underfoot. Better yet, their conversation wasn't constantly interrupted by the noise of a train roaring past the window.

'Thank Uncle Fyodor again for us, won't you?' asked Larissa as she poured her cousin a cup of coffee. 'It's so much nicer here. And I never have to go that hateful school again.'

'Though I don't know why you think the Duchess is such an improvement – you should see the way she looks down her nose at me. Still, I'm glad you like her. How's Margarita?'

Larissa giggled. 'Oh Margarita is *very* well, thank you for asking.'

'What do you mean by that? Come on, spill the beans.'

'She's found herself a sweetheart.'

'Really? Did she tell you this?'

'As if Margarita would admit to such a thing. But she doesn't need to, I've worked it out.'

'Have you indeed? How?'

'She's wearing perfume for the first time ever,' said Larissa triumphantly.

Alyosha laughed, 'Oh well, proof positive then. So who is it, somebody from the bank?'

'I don't think so.'

'A Russian?'

'I'm not sure. She won't tell me, no matter how much I pester her. You know how she is.'

'What has she got to hide?'

'I've no idea. When I told the Duchess about it, she said perhaps Margarita is ashamed of him. But I said, knowing Margarita, it's more likely she's ashamed of me and our mother.'

'Don't be silly, of course she's not. She's just… secretive.'

'I don't really care. Time will tell, and she'll have to introduce us to him eventually. Anyway, what about you? Isn't it high time you found yourself a wife? I'm sure Uncle Fyodor and Aunt Inessa think so.'

'Don't be ridiculous, I'm far too young.'

'Well, what about a sweetheart then?'

Alyosha gave some light-hearted answer but he too had his secrets. He didn't tell his cousin that he already had a sweetheart and he was worried sick about her.

He had already asked about her at the Grand Hotel. Her friend, one of the other maids called Valborga, had told him that Grete had simply left one morning and not come back.

'For another hotel?'

'I don't think so. She'd have told me. And anyway, she'd have had to work out her notice if she'd wanted a reference but she just went.'

Alyosha had asked if the hotel had her parents' address in Brünn, but they only had her Berlin address on record. He'd also asked Grete's landlord if she'd left a forwarding address but he told him she'd just disappeared, without even giving him any notice.

He'd gone back to the Grand Hotel a couple of days later but Valborga had nothing new to tell him. Disconsolate, he'd ordered a rheinbecker and started up a conversation with the bartender.

'Staff? They come and go. You'd be surprised.' He was drying glasses unhurriedly, then placing them in neat rows back on the shelf. 'They pay badly here. Nobody stays long.'

'How long have you been here?'

'Since the beginning of the year. Why? Are you looking for work?'

'No. I expect it's hard to remember everybody. If there's so much coming and going.'

'I've got the memory of an elephant.'

'So do you remember a girl called Grete working here?'

'I do indeed.'

'But she doesn't work here anymore?'

'No, she had more sense than to hang around.'

'Why do you say that?'

'Just that she didn't work here for long. I remember her leaving.'

'Do you?'

'I remember the exact morning. It was about eleven o'clock and I was just coming in for my shift. Grete was standing there, in her coat, her bag in her hand. A motor-car pulls up. Black. Mercedes? Rolls Royce maybe. Anyway, when Grete sees it, she just opens the door calm as anything and gets in.'

A vivid picture grew in Alyosha's mind, of lonely Maria in her cave in the mountains of Corsica.

'So if you don't mind my asking, why all these questions about Grete?'

'I haven't seen her for a while.'

'Neither have I. My bet is one of the guests took a fancy to her and offered her a cushy little deal. It happens you know. Not that often these days, but it does happen.'

Grete seemed to have vanished off the face of the earth.

20

Fyodor was lunching with the Grand Duke Kyril Vladimirovich at the Imperial Russian Exiles Club, discussing ICHC business, when he had to excuse himself to get some air. A touch of indigestion, he murmured; he'd be back directly.

Half an hour later a servant was sent to look for him. He found him kneeling at the side of one of the marble benches at the bottom of the garden, his head lying on it at an angle, his eyes open but unseeing, spittle collected at the sides of his mouth. On the bench beside him was his open wallet and in his hand was an unfinished letter which his wife later discovered was addressed to Lenin, appealing for information about his brother Kozma.

The Duke instructed his driver to take Fyodor at full speed to a clinic on Weichelstrasse. Three doctors tried their utmost to save him, one of them a specialist from Potsdam hospital, but he was already dead by the time Inessa, Alyosha and Gosha arrived at the clinic. They gathered around his bed. Death had already pulled at the corners of his mouth, made two deep hollows of his eyes, and had sucked the last bit of warmth from his hands which lay folded neatly on his breast. It reminded Alyosha of Leo the tramp, as in death his father looked so similar. The room smelled strongly of camphor. Inessa kissed her husband on his forehead. Alyosha did the same but Gosha refused. He couldn't understand why his father wouldn't wake up.

The post-mortem showed that Fyodor Miklhailovich Alexandrov died from a brain haemorrhage. He was fifty-three. His sudden death was reported in the evening edition of the

Berliner Tageblatt, and the next day in the *Vossische Zeitung*; after that, various obituaries appeared in the European press. Many of them gave glowing accounts of his life and spoke of his invaluable contribution to Russia's last Provisional Government.

His death gave some Monarchists the chance to give a good bludgeoning to Alexander Kerenskii, and several articles appeared in the *émigrés'* newspapers in Berlin and Paris that were deeply critical of him. These in their turn gave rise to a spate of letters agreeing or disagreeing with the editorials, many of them savage and occasionally intemperate in tone. There were a few sane voices here and there, who asked why it was that a defeated people always argued among themselves, one correspondent suggesting it was because there was no one central power for them to rally around. There also appeared several letters noting how kind and generous Fyodor Mikhailovich had been to his exiled compatriots in Berlin, always offering assistance when anybody came to him asking for some help to keep body and soul together until they could all return home.

In the days leading up to the funeral, Alyosha was haunted by the smell of camphor. Even in his room in the Adlon, when he was lying on his bed, he could smell it. It reminded him of the hospital in Russia. And every time he closed his eyes he could see his father's still, dead mouth.

There was much coming and going at the Adlon, with people calling to pay their respects, and the funeral to be arranged. Alyosha tried to support his mother, speaking to the mourners in their sober black suits when she was too tired to see them, and answering the telephone in her room which seemed to ring incessantly, when she was having a rest. He listened as patiently as he could as sober men praised his father and listed his virtues.

Watching his mother one afternoon as she sat with some visitors, straight-backed and slender in her chair, he thought that black suited her.

Ella had been one of the first to arrive, with Margarita and Larissa, to pay their respects, but his mother was lost in her own private world and Alyosha had to tell his aunt she was resting. Ella told him they'd call again and left.

The Grand Duke Kyril Vladimirovish came to see them and said that if they didn't object, he would be honoured to take over the funeral arrangements. He emphasised to Inessa the importance of giving Fyodor his due and a funeral of some splendour was to be the order of the day. But shortly after, a deputation of Russian businessmen asked to speak to Inessa. They were dismayed that the Monarchists were claiming her late husband as their own. Then a deputation from the Kadet party arrived saying that Fyodor was their man: a member of the liberal bourgeoisie through and through.

Inessa had no idea which of these factions most truly represented her husband's views but she didn't want to offend any of them, or create any bad feeling. She had very little interest in politics: when one of Fyodor's colleagues tried to explain to her that the Kadet party was riven with internal wrangling and was losing members daily, to the Monarchists on the right and the Social Revolutionaries on the left, her eyes glazed over with boredom.

In the end the way forward was to establish a multi-party funeral committee. Alyosha was elected a member and after the first meeting he told his cousins he had never seen so much hate amongst men. The funeral arrangements were ostensibly the only item on the agenda but in fact the future of their country was what was under discussion. First there were the recriminations: they all blamed each other for the fall of Russia. As far as deciding anything went, they couldn't even agree on a chairman. They decided to reconvene the next day, in order to give everybody a chance to reflect and come back with some constructive ideas. But the second committee was no better than the first, and the third ended in a storm of abuse, accusation and counter-accusation, insults and threats of violence, ending in so many members storming out that they had to call the meeting to a halt as it was not even quorate.

The Imperial Russian Exiles' Club commissioned a sculptor to work on a marble tree, split in two, as a poignant but relevant symbol of Fyodor Mikhailovich's life and his contribution to the glory of Russia. When Alexander Kerenskii's former ministers heard of this they decided to plant a poplar tree themselves, as a symbol of eternal life and as a symbol of hope of seeing democracy restored in Russia. Others insisted a plaque was the correct memorial, and a wealthy individual said he intended commissioning a biography. Several poets wrote long eulogies.

Two days before the funeral there was still furious disagreement about the Order of Service, and eventually, with things in danger of getting out of hand, Inessa was forced to arbitrate. After all, it was important to present a united and dignified front. Exiles were arriving from Munich, Hamburg, Paris, Nice, Prague, Sofia: from wherever Russians had settled in any number, it seemed, one or two representatives came, determined to pay their respects. The sympathy cards that flooded in had postmarks from all over Europe: Baden-Baden, Brussels, Stockholm, Königsberg, Breslau, Lyon, Frankfurt, Dresden, Leipzig, Stuttgart, Halle, Heidelberg, Götingen, and many smaller towns they had never even heard of.

Fyodor Mikhailovich was buried in the Friedhofskirche cemetery of Saint Konstantin's church on a boiling July afternoon, in front of a crowd of over three-and-a-half thousand mourners, sweating profusely in their heavy dark clothes. Metropolitan Evlogy and two other priests from the Russian Church on Unter den Linden officiated, the wide, colourful sleeves of their cassocks the only colour among the sea of black.

Artyom came from Paris to stand next to his sister at the

graveside. Inessa wore a slim-fitting black coat and a chic little hat with a veil covering her face. Alyosha stood on her other side with Gosha between him and the Duchess Lydia Herkulanovna Vors, who held the little boy's hand throughout. On the other side of the coffin stood a row of men, all wearing black armbands over their sober suits. Alyosha recognised Prince Lvov, and Alexander Kerenskii, who had brought four personal bodyguards with him, all wearing identical green-shaded sunglasses.

The Grand Duke Kyril Vladimirovich and the remains of the Tzar's court stood together. Men of commerce formed another group – the chairmen of all the Berlin banks; the Deutsche, the Disconto-Gesellschaft, the Dresdner, the Darmstädter, and all the most important companies had sent representatives as well, Waldstein, Delbrück Schickler and Bleichröder amongst them. Everybody was in the prison of their faction, and they all studiously ignored each other by nailing their eyes on the coffin.

At the moment when Fyodor Alexandrov was lowered into the grave, Inessa sank to her knees and begged for his forgiveness for having been so uncaring of him. Alyosha heard a buzzing noise, like the hiss of bees. For one second he remembered his father's voice when he described his mother's screams in the pipes of the Cheka. The hissing went from bad to worse, until the crowd resembled a nest of serpents. The air started to rain earth. Two of the bodyguards lifted umbrellas above Alexander Kerenskii and ushered him away.

'Traitor!'

'Coward!'

First the odd voice was raised, and then others joined in, accusing him of giving Russia to the Communists.

'Yes, go! Nobody wanted you here!'

He was the focus of all their frustrations. A small stone hit him on the back of his neck. He stopped and turned to face his accusers and said in a clear voice, 'You're at liberty to put the blame on me. But I make a public promise here today that Fyodor Mikhailovich Alexandrov's body, along with that of every other exile who has died in foreign lands, will be buried in Russian soil in the near future.'

He was abused even more but blustered, 'Our exile will be a short one, I promise you.'

As Alyosha ushered his mother towards the Auto-Daimler, Ella and her daughters approached them. Ella placed her hand on Inessa's arm and squeezed it tenderly. Then, as he was helping his mother into the motor-car, he was tapped on the shoulder. Turning, Alyosha came face-to-face with a man he had not seen for a long time.

The man shook his hand, and squeezed his shoulder.

'I'm very sorry for your loss.'

There was no time to respond, as Alyosha's mother and brother were waiting for him. He got into the motor-car and as it drove slowly off, Alyosha gazed at Stanislav Markovich's face once more. He was standing with his back to the high cemetery wall, one hand in his pocket, sucking on his pipe as he talked with Margarita. Something about the way they stood there together made Alyosha think that he must be her secret sweetheart.

21

For a barely decent period Inessa wore her widow's weeds, and there was plenty of huffing and tutting when she put them aside. The news soon spread that the beautiful and still youthful widow of Fyodor Miklailovich Alexandrov was lying alone in a very wealthy bed. Like bluebottles around a pot of honey, she attracted all sorts of specimens to the Hotel Adlon.

One of the first to introduce himself was a wine merchant from Arras – a big-bellied man with a furtive smile and large feet. An ever increasing number of invitation cards appeared on the mantelpiece, and flowers arrived daily. She was entertained and dined by several officers and diplomats. A wealthy landowner, whose family were well known for breeding bears in Zarla, called to invite her to the opera. A military attaché from the Argentinian embassy wanted to teach her the tango. The Hungarian chargé d'affaires took her on a picnic to the shores of the Wansee, and sailing on the Havel. He promised her the best sunsets in the world if she accompanied him to his family's vineyards around Lake Balaton. She was offered Ranhenegg castle as a token of eternal love by some aristocrat, and a wealthy French businessman was all for stealing her away to spend a month with him in Le Pouldu. Then there was the Jewish newspaper proprietor, and a few dim-witted, ridiculous Englishmen with names like Dickie or Johnny, from one college or another in Oxford or Cambridge, bored witless over the summer, and prepared to try their luck. And there were the professional gigolos, a plague of those. Snake-hipped, with slicked-back hair, the Kukis and the Sigis and the Fufus were experienced fraudsters, though one or two of them were the bisexual sons of ancient aristocratic Swabian families.

Alyosha saw his mother's *joie de vivre* return. She had a spring in her step and a sparkle in her eye once more. She adored all the attention and it seemed she was having the best time of her life. She took up smoking and was given a black holder decorated with a little circle of diamonds by the brother of Ahmed Zog, the future King of Albania. She was out almost every night. There was always some cause or excuse for celebration although, as far as Alyosha was concerned, his mother's friends spent their whole time celebrating themselves.

He, meanwhile, had troubles of his own. He had never been able to find Grete. She had disappeared from his life as quietly as mist from a stream. Had she left Berlin? Had she gone home to Brünn? Had she been kidnapped like Maria in Corsica and kept in a cave? Was she even alive?

His other preoccupation was Stanislav. He kept thinking about the stable in Kiev. The classroom. The wide sky and the small orchard. The grave. The gun... He tried to ask Larissa about him without admitting that he already knew him.

'So where did he and Margarita meet each other?'

'Why are you so interested all of a sudden?'

'I just want to know who he is, that's all.'

'In the Kaiser Friedrich museum. She said she happened to go there during her lunch hour because it was raining, and he struck up a conversation with her. And then they went for a coffee to that American bar opposite. Do you know the one I mean?'

'Where you can sit and watch the boats come and go on the canal?'

'That's the one. Well, of course they started to talk about Petrograd, and Moscow and home – you know how it is when two Russians meet. She said that's what brought them together really. I don't know why she was so secretive about it for so long, though. But that's Margarita – she always keeps her cards close to her chest. And I suppose she thought Mama mightn't like it.'

'So when did you meet him?'

'Stanislav had invited her to a party but Mama said it wasn't right for her to go there on her own, so Margarita dragged me along as escort – wasn't that lucky? It was in an apartment near the Nollendorfplatz. You could hear the music from two storeys down. They had a gramophone and lots of jazz records. Anyway, when we went in, Margarita couldn't even see if Stanislav had arrived because, apart from some candles they'd stuck in saucers, the place was dark, and filled with cigarette smoke too.'

'So was he there?'

'Oh, and I forgot to say, another funny thing, everybody was dancing barefoot. And the men all looked like women and the women like men. I asked Margarita if we should take our shoes off as well but she just said, not unless I wanted to.'

'Stanislav?'

'Yes, yes we found him. He was wearing a yellow shirt, open at the neck. Margarita could hardly open her mouth, she was so shy. It was so funny, Alyosha, you know how bossy she is with me. Anyway he was very friendly and offered to fetch us some drinks. I wasn't going to stand around being a gooseberry all evening so I started talking to some boy and he asked me to dance.'

'Did he indeed? So both my cousins have sweethearts now do they?'

'Don't be silly, it was only a dance. But I kept my eye on my sister and guess what?'

'What?'

'Well, they just sort of stood there, staring at each other, not saying anything. But then… oh you should have seen them, Alyosha. Margarita of all people. He just leaned in and kissed her. In front of everybody. And she let him.'

She started laughing.

'You know how prim and proper she is. She must really like him, don't you think?'

Alyosha was more concerned to know what Stanislav had said to Margarita about him. Had he told her he'd been working for the Cheka in Kiev? He knew that his cousins would find that hard to forgive. And if it became common knowledge, it would make life very difficult for him in the *émigré* community in Berlin – very difficult indeed.

22

Inessa found that she enjoyed gambling, and she spent many of her evenings playing baccarat, poker and roulette in the Imperial Russian Exiles' Club, where losing pile after pile of wooden chips became as easy as breathing. By now she had become an honorary member of the inner sanctum of men who were still intent on bringing down the Communists in Russia. As the widow of one of their most prominent and respected members, she automatically had their trust and although she had never been very interested in politics, she was flattered to be included in their discussions and to be asked for her opinion. And she found it thrilling to be at the centre of so much intrigue. Furthermore she thought it a very fitting tribute to her husband to be a part of the continuing crusade against Communism in his name.

Boris Savinkov, one of Alexander Kerenkii's former ministers, had become a dear friend, and it was he who introduced her over cocktails one evening to a thin man by the name of Sidney Reilly, and his wife, Pepita Bobadilla. Over dinner, Savinkov and Reilly outlined their plan to win Russia back through a *coup d'état*. They explained that there already existed in Russia a network of activists who would be more than ready, if they were given the word, to rise up as one and attack the Kremlin. It was only a matter of time, and, more than anything, money, before they would be able to return to their mother country.

'I'm absolutely convinced of it,' said Savinkov, blowing cigar smoke over his lower lip.

'So am I,' agreed Reilly. 'And even if it's a gamble, surely it's a gamble worth taking when European civilisation is at stake.'

Inessa was only half-listening because the man who had just walked in had claimed her attention. She felt her insides melt.

At the roulette table later that night, her cheeks blazed and she felt almost feverish. She wanted to take all her clothes off and lie there on her back, quite naked. She felt the dampness between her legs. Finally, she caught his eye. He smiled at her and she smiled back. They had never exchanged a word, although they had come within a hair's breadth of doing so many years previously. She wondered if he would remember.

When she saw her chance, she took it.

'Inessa Vasilievna,' she introduced herself.

'I know.'

He kissed the back of her hand and smiled his famous smile.

She felt her heart beating furiously, faster and faster; she was overcome by a burning thirst as if she'd swallowed hot coals. He asked whether she'd like champagne. This gave them an excuse to move to one of the tables in a private corner. Inessa felt dizzy; she felt herself walking along a precipice.

'I'm sorry for your loss.'

Alexei Dashkov hadn't changed a bit. He still had that ineffable quality of stillness which had always made him so madly attractive.

They talked of this and that, until she blurted out,

'What about the Pavilion on the beach in Yalta? Do you remember it?'

'I've been there once or twice…'

'That's where we met before,' said Inessa hoping he remembered, 'a long time ago.'

'Of course. The Pavilion in Yalta…' he said, doing his best to pretend he remembered. He didn't. He didn't remember her at all. But when Inessa reminded him that Nina Charodeyeva had been there, he could at least talk about her.

'Dreadful woman…'

'I heard that she passed away.'

'Forgive me for saying so, but thank heavens. Malice was her middle name. She had such an enormous estimation of her own talent, but she couldn't find a good word to say about anybody else.'

'I still have the autograph you gave me in Yalta.'

'I'm surprised you could read my scrawl. I think my handwriting has improved a little since then.'

He brushed the nape of her neck with his fingers. Inessa thought she was already head over heels in love. Hadn't she always been? Hadn't she named her firstborn after this man?

They compared notes on leaving Russia.

'After the 1917 revolution, I left at once for Vienna. That's where I've been ever since, working in the theatre.'

'So what brings you to Berlin?'

'To be honest, I don't think I'll be here for long. I think that Hollywood may be beckoning. We'll see.'

Meeting Inessa, Alexei Dashkov thought he might be a step closer to his destination.

23

Alyosha decided he needed to speak to Stanislav. He couldn't go on like this, and it would be better to know one way or the other whether he had said anything about Kiev to Margarita. There was so much hatred towards the Communists amongst Berlin's *émigrés* he would surely be run out of the city, especially if they thought he was spying for the Cheka. Surely Stanislav would realise that?

One afternoon, Larissa met him after her lessons with the Duchess, full of excitement.

'Is it true that your mother is going to marry Alexei Dashkov?'

'I believe so,' he said with a show of indifference.

'Alexei Dashkov! Just imagine! Isn't it romantic?'

Aloysha grunted.

'But it's happened so quickly. The Duchess told me that they only met a fortnight ago. They must be so much in love.'

'I think it's far too soon after burying my father.'

'Well yes, it is quite soon but I suppose life goes on, Alyosha.'

'Well you know what they say: marry in haste, repent at leisure.'

'Why are you being so mean? I think it's lovely.'

'I don't trust the man. He's two-faced.'

Alyosha had been suspicious of Alexei Dashkov from the second his mother had introduced them.

Larissa added, 'And another thing, the Duchess told me they were going to make a film together. Is that true?'

'They're talking about it,' said Alyosha, before adding sourly, 'with my mother's money.'

'It will mean work for lots of Russians though, won't it?' asked Larissa.

'I hope so, at least some good will come of it then,' said Alyosha, 'but I think Dashkov is more interested in getting noticed by Hollywood than helping out his fellow countrymen. I bet you that's why he wants to make the film.'

'Do you think we'll be invited to the wedding?'

'I'm sure you will.'

'Perhaps they'll have to invite Stanislav as well by then. He and Margarita are getting very serious. She's even introduced him to Mama.'

'That *is* serious. What does he do, anyway?'

'I'm not sure.'

'Do you know where he lives?'

'Yes.'

Once he had the address, Alyosha went to find him at the earliest opportunity.

24

He crossed the Nollendorfplatz, with its concrete eagles, and strode quickly through a web of smaller, winding streets, but soon lost his bearings and had to ask the way. He was directed along Tauentzienstrasse and across the Wittembergplatz, where the streets became meaner and poorer with every step he took. The address took him to a drab tenement building even more squalid than the one where his cousins used to live. The street beneath was littered with dog dirt and rubbish and the people he passed looked dirty and badly nourished, the children invariably barefoot.

He knocked on the door, thinking things could not be going well for Stanislav if he had to live in this slum. The curtains were shut and there was no noise from within, so he was about to turn on his heel and leave when he heard the door being unbolted. The two men stared at each other without speaking. Alyosha was surprised he had not noticed previously how much Stanislav resembled an orang-utan.

'I thought you'd find me eventually.'

He opened the door wide and invited Alyosha in. The yellowing wallpaper was decorated with faded blue roses. The curtains were yellow as well and years of tobacco smoke seemed to have permeated every nook and cranny with a stale, sour smell. The furniture was shabby and sparse.

'I haven't dressed – you'll have to forgive me,' said Stanislav, tying the belt of his dressing gown tighter. 'I've only just got up. What time is it anyway?'

'Almost three.'

'Sit. Not there, that chair isn't safe.'

Alyosha remained standing.

'So you're seeing my cousin?'

Stanislav said calmly that he was.

'Why? Do you feel protective?'

'As it happens, I do.'

'Fair enough.'

He took his pipe from the shelf and sat down.

'So is that why you came out all this way to see me?'

'No.'

Alyosha felt he'd been shut into a dark room with a snake.

'I didn't think so. You might as well sit.'

'How did you leave Russia? Did you find it difficult?'

'It wasn't easy. I buried my wife in the Black Sea. And you? How did you leave Russia? Did you find it difficult?'

There was an edge to their conversation.

'Through Finland,' answered Alyosha.

'I was aiming for Paris. Well, we both were. Tamara and I. We met in Kiev. After she died I couldn't face going to Paris without her. I'd promised to take her there so many times. So I came to Berlin instead.'

'I'm sorry.'

There was a pause as Stanislav filled his pipe with tobacco. Then he asked, 'You're anxious about something?'

'I think you know why.'

'Do I?'

Stanislav held a match to the tobacco and sucked on the pipe.

'Yes, I think you do.'

He sucked again.

'Are you going to say anything to Margarita about what happened in Kiev?'

Stanislav didn't answer.

'I can't stop you from telling her, I know that. But I'd appreciate it if you didn't.'

Stanislav folded his arms across his chest.

'Why would you appreciate it if I didn't?'

'Look, I saved your life in Kiev. Without me, you wouldn't be here now.'

Without saying a word, Stanislav gazed at him through the smoke.

'So...?' asked Alyosha.

'So...?'

'I feel there's something that isn't being said here.'

'There's always something that isn't being said. Each one of us has something or other we want to hide. You're not the only one. Look.'

He took the pipe out of his mouth, stood up and leant his head towards Alyosha, parting his hair.

'Do you see it? Hard not to, isn't it?'

He sat back down.

'Do you remember how I was given that scar? I can't help you. I'll say it one more time. I can't help you. Where were you when that was happening? Standing by, watching. What did you do? Nothing. You didn't say a word. Nor did you lift a finger to try and stop that animal of a Commissar from beating me. What did you do then? Dragged me along that path towards the grave. I was covered in blood, and could barely speak. If the Commissar hadn't fallen into the grave, you would have shot me.'

'That's how you see it?'

'What other way is there of seeing it?'

'I did my best to help you...'

'You did nothing to help me... what happened was an accident.'

'No, I tried to save you before then. There are people in Russia who could tell you. Masha. Mishka. If you could speak to them.'

Stansilav smoked silently.

'I swear, I did my best to save you…'

'You did nothing. After you shot that Commissar? What happened then? All you did was save your own skin.'

'The same as you. We had no choice. We both had to get out of Kiev.'

Stanislav's pipe was like a gun in his fist.

'You think I'm still working for the Cheka?'

'Between every man and his conscience I say.'

'I'm not working for the Cheka.'

'You worked for them once. Or are you denying that as well?'

25

There was an open-air café-concert in the Tiergarten.

'Alexei Fyodorovitch,' Margarita introduced them, 'this is Stanislav Markovich.'

'But you can call him Alyosha as we do,' added Larissa brightly.

They shook hands.

'I'm happy to meet you at last,' said Stanislav.

'Likewise.'

'I've told Stanislav all about you already, Alyosha,' said Margarita, squeezing her sweetheart's arm.

It was a mild evening. They ordered Dunkel beer as the band began to play.

'So what's the latest about Alexei Dashkov's film?' Larissa asked her cousin.

'I've no idea; you'd better ask Mama.'

'Do you think they'd let me be an extra in it? How I'd love to be a film actress!'

'I thought you wanted to be a nurse?' teased her sister.

'I'm allowed to change my mind, aren't I?'

'Of course you are,' said Stanislav. 'We all change.'

'I think I'll ask Aunt Inessa if she can put in a word for me. It would be so exciting.'

Stanislav and Alyosha gave no indication that they had met before. As was always the case when Russian exiles gathered together, the talk turned to their mother country.

'I remember the voyage from the Crimea across the Black Sea,' said Stanislav, knocking his pipe against the wooden bench. 'The ship came to a stop in the middle of it, because they'd run out of coal, even though we'd all paid handsomely for our passage. We were sure the Bolsheviks would attack us and we'd all drown. We were sitting ducks after all, stranded there; we could be seen for miles. A schoolteacher from Bryansk had the idea that saved the day.

'He told the men to take the grain supply down to the engine-room, down in the bowels. We carried tons of the stuff down there, an armful at a time, and it was only by burning the lot that we managed to reach the coast of Turkey in one piece. Even then, we were lucky to be given permission to land. If they'd even imagined there might be any disease on the ship they'd have made us sail on, without a destination. By then we'd run out of fresh water as well, so we were desperate with thirst. And these brusque Turks in their little boats coming up alongside and demanding a lira for a bucket of water. Talk about profiteering: bear in mind that a lira was worth God only knows how many rubles. No wonder so many of us took against the Turks. Then, when we finally got onto dry land, our living conditions were foul and primitive – wherever you went, you couldn't escape the stink from the open sewers. I spent my first nights sheltering in a cave.'

Margarita took his hand and squeezed it.

'I'm not looking for pity. I know other people suffered far worse than I did.'

Stanislav held Alyosha's gaze.

'What sort of a place is Constantinople?' asked Larissa.

'Very beautiful, and the city is full of wonders. The minaret of the Blue Mosque. The towers of the Top-Kapi Palace. The Rumeli Fortress. And you would have loved the Grand Bazaar, Larissa. Anyway, I found my feet after a while. They took me on as a barman in a club called la Rose Noire. '*Après le Ciné, faites un tour de fox-trot à la Rose Noire*,' the touts would shout. I remember standing one Sunday morning in front of the Orient Express terminus, feeling that Europe was so near and yet so far away.'

As darkness fell, the strings of coloured lights suspended among the trees were switched on, and couples began to dance. Stanislav offered his hand to Larissa and she leapt up, beaming. They made their way through the tables towards the band.

'Are you happy?'

'Yes, I think I am,' answered Margarita. 'Can I ask what you think of him? Do you think we're suited?'

'What does your mother say?'

'She thinks he's rather too old for me.'

'How old is he?'

'He'll be thirty-two in September. I'm twenty-one this year. Do you think that's too much of a gap?'

'No, that's not too bad.'

'Oh good, I'm glad you don't think so. I wish Papa could have met him.'

'Perhaps he will one day. You never know.'

'I doubt it. I know Mama and Lala still hope, but I really don't think we'll see Papa again. I'm certain he's dead.'

'There's no saying.'

'Why torture myself by holding on to some forlorn hope?'

Her cousin couldn't come up with a reason.

'Alyosha? Can I ask a favour? Rather a large one I'm afraid.'

'What?'

'You heard Stanislav talk about that awful voyage out of Russia and after in Turkey. He's a man who's suffered a great deal. But what he didn't tell you, because he didn't want to upset Lala… His wife died on that ship. He had to bury her at sea.'

Alyosha had to pretend this was the first time he'd heard of it.

'Can you imagine how awful that must have been for him? And if you could see where he lives Alyosha, his room makes our old place in Neukölln seem like a palace. A hovel seems too kind a word for it. But he has a talent. He's a writer, a dramatist, but he can write film scripts as well. If only he was given the chance to show his worth.'

She didn't have to say more: he knew what she was asking.

'I know it's asking a lot… but would you put in a word?'

A flushed and breathless Larissa plonked herself back down on the bench next to her cousin, nearly tipping a glass of beer. Stanilsav slipped in beside Margarita and kissed her, saying he was too old to keep up with her sister.

'What were you two being so serious about, anyway?' Larissa asked them.

'Nothing important,' answered her sister.

At the end of the evening, as they were making their goodbyes, Stanislav came over to Alyosha where he stood on the cobbled pavement.

'Which way are you going?'

'Not the same way as you.'

It was quite dark now. Motor-cars passed by, their headlamps illuminating them for a few brief seconds in a streak of light.

'It was an enjoyable evening.'

'Yes, it was.'

Alyosha swayed slightly on his feet. He'd been drinking heavily.

'Margarita tells me she had a word with you about…'

'Yes, she did.'

'And?'

'And?' imitated Alyosha.

'Will you put in a word with Alexei Dashkov for me?'

'I doubt it. The last thing I want is to have to ask favours of a man like my stepfather.'

'And the last thing I want is to stay poor. It's killing me slowly.'

'I can't promise you anything.'

'Any more than I can promise not to mention your connection with the Kiev Cheka.'

26

Much to Larissa's disappointment, even Inessa didn't quite have the nerve to arrange the lavish wedding she would have loved so soon after losing her first husband, so her marriage to Alexei Dashkov was a small and discreet affair; she consoled herself with the thought that there would be plenty of opportunities to celebrate in the future. Alexei Dashkov had been more than happy to move in with his wife to the Hotel Adlon. It suited him very well: he drank champagne for breakfast, champagne for lunch and champagne for supper.

Alyosha didn't have the stomach to approach him directly. He went to his mother instead.

'Why this sudden interest in scriptwriters?'

'He's talented and he deserves a chance.'

'But how on earth would you be the judge of that? You don't have the slightest experience… No, no, leave such matters to the people in the business. Men like your stepfather. You really don't know anything about it.'

'Look, I'm not asking him to employ Stanislav Markovich.'

'Well, what are you asking then?'

'Simply for him to see him. I know how busy he is, but I'm sure he can make time for one meeting. Really, that's all I'm asking.'

His mother asked suspiciously, 'Do you owe this man money?'

'No, Mama, of course I don't.'

'Really, Alexei, I'd prefer you to be honest.'

'I don't owe him a single pfennig!'

'Then why are you pleading his cause with such enthusiasm? It's not as though you've ever shown an interest in helping anybody before.'

'Well if you must know, he and Margarita are seeing each other and she asked me to put in a word for him.'

'Oh, darling, you should have said that to begin with. Of course I'll ask Alexei to see him.'

Stanislav was duly summoned to meet with Alexei Dashkov and although the meeting was short, to his great surprise he was offered a commission, and put on a six-month contract. Although the salary was not as much as he'd hoped, he was very pleased. The next time they met, Margarita hugged her cousin warmly.

'Thank you so much, Alyosha,' she said.

Stanislav shook his hand and held it tight for a moment, saying,

'I won't forget this kindness.'

'I hope you won't,' answered Alyosha.

Even before the filming started, the production was over budget.

'I'm a perfectionist in my craft,' Alexei Dashkov announced to the cast and crew on the studio floor. 'I insist on every last detail being just right.'

As the sets started to go up in the studio on the outskirts of Berlin – once a hangar that had housed Zeppelins – as the actors started to learn their lines, and the first day of filming fast approached, this attention to detail manifested itself in all sorts of ways. From the beginning, he wasn't satisfied with the colour of the Constantinople sky. It wasn't blue enough. Though he had never actually visited the city, he *knew* the sky was bluer than that. Stanislav tried to assure him that the shade was just as he remembered it but the colour of the sky was the least of *his* worries. Alexei Dashkov was forever asking for rewrites on the script, and although Stanislav had been eager to please his employer to begin with, he was growing increasingly frustrated.

Margarita felt she hardly saw him, he was so busy, and when she did, he was usually preoccupied and sometimes ill-tempered.

27

She arranged to meet him one afternoon after she'd finished work at the bank, at the Café Leon on the Nollendorfplatz. Up on the second floor there were always Russians to be found, so deep in conversation they could make a single cup of coffee last for hours. She sat by the window and waited, watching a blind old soldier outside, tapping the pavement with his white stick, a cardboard box at his feet for change. She waited three quarters of an hour before deciding Stanislav wasn't coming and returned to the apartment. She didn't say anything to Larissa, who was full of excitement as Alyosha had promised to take her to the studio for the first day's filming. Suddenly Ella cut across Larissa's babbling.

'Have you both forgotten what day it is today?'

The harm had been done. For the rest of the evening the three of them were subdued and silent, remembering the day their father had left, the day he didn't return.

28

When Alexei Dashkov arrived at the studio for the first day's filming, he was in such a foul mood he stormed off to his dressing room, slammed the door and refused to come out. Various people were sent to cajole, persuade and remonstrate with him but there was no budging him. The entire studio was in uproar as, without the leading man, a whole day's filming would be lost: but the other actors, the extras, the technicians, including the two cameramen who had been brought all the way from Hollywood at great expense, would still require paying, just to stand around doing nothing.

The chauffeur eventually explained the reason for the tantrum: on the way to the studio from the Adlon, the Mercedes had suffered no less than four punctures.

'What? All at once?'

'More or less.'

As he turned into Friedrichstrasse, the chauffeur had noticed some out-of-work layabouts smoking and kicking their heels. He thought no more about it until they flung some glass under the wheels and then ran off, shouting obscenities as they went. The wheels exploded two by two. The heavy motor sank into the tarmac and although the chauffeur gave chase, it was futile as they'd long since disappeared.

It became obvious there would be no filming that day. Larissa was horribly disappointed. She had been so looking forward to seeing the film studio at work. Without any studio lights the cavernous space was rather gloomy and so chilly that she was shivering. She pulled her thin cardigan around her shoulders but it didn't help much. She suddenly felt as though she was being watched and, glancing over her shoulder, saw that a smart-looking young man was gazing at her appreciatively. He was standing on his own in the shadow of the mosque. He wore a pair of rather fine cream leather gloves, spotless in spite of their delicate colour and his blond hair was cut so short that he almost looked bald. He had a monocle corked into his left eye, attached to his collar by a thin leather cord.

He came up to her and introduced himself. He lifted her hand to his lips, pausing for a split second to look at her before kissing it. Larissa wondered if he was an actor and imagined him kissing her on the nape of her neck. 'Stop it, that tickles,' she heard herself scolding him playfully.

Their romance started that evening and it was as happy and light-hearted as Larissa could have wished for.

29

As the rumour had reached her from more than one source, Inessa took to visiting the set at some point every day, always beautifully dressed and her make-up and hair immaculate.

Inessa had insisted on being involved in the casting and had been most put out when her husband overruled her and offered the female lead to the ravishing Yulia Gosovska, rather than the older actress Inessa had favoured. Her jealousy and hatred of the young actress knew no bounds; and when the rumour reached her that one of the carpenters had come across Alexei Dashkov pawing Yulia by the back door of Maxim's nightclub on one of Constantinople's back streets, under an artificial moonlight, all her worst fears were confirmed.

Inessa continued signing the cheques, the filming carried on, and every day people would gather at the studio doors hoping to be taken on as extras or casual labour, even though they were all turned away. They would still return the next day, and many of them offered to work for nothing, as long as they were fed.

As the chauffeur slowed the Mercedes, Inessa and Alexei Dashkov did their best to avoid the mournful eyes that tried to catch theirs every morning. It was difficult, because the voices begging for work were, more often than not, speaking Russian in the various accents of Petrograd, Rovno, Vinnitsa, Poltava and Odessa. Although the chauffeur avoided the front gates and drove to the back of the lot, there were still people there. Some poor brute leaned forward to speak to them through the window but, because he banged the glass with the palm of his hand at the same time, Inessa didn't catch what he was saying. However, once she was safely inside the studio fence she told the chauffeur to go outside and offer a day's work and three square meals to her late husband's former banker.

It turned out Andrei Petrovich wasn't looking for work for himself, but for his daughter Galina. She had always longed to be in a film, ever since she had seen Vera Voronina acting on the screen.

Inessa didn't disappoint her. Galina was taken on as an extra in one of the late-night scenes, sitting at a table in the smoky Rose Noir nightclub. That's where Alyosha noticed her. He didn't recognise her immediately, partly because they had dressed her like an exiled princess from the Tzar's Court but also because she had changed so much. An image of her leaped into his head, dawdling along the quay in Yalta all those years ago, a great solid lump of a girl, gazing at him from under her white parasol as her father said something to her. How she'd changed. She had grown quite tall and graceful and something about her reminded him of Masha – where was she by now he wondered?

Galina wasn't required to do much acting, just to take a sip from the glass in front of her occasionally and watch couples dance the foxtrot. The scene dragged on, the set became increasingly hot and stuffy, and one of the make-up girls fainted. It became an interminably long day because Alexei Dashkov was not happy. He insisted on reshooting scenes until he considered them perfect.

'Again! Again!' he would yell, standing on a chair in his white cap.

Finally he was satisfied and a collective sigh of relief went around the set. Alyosha went over to talk to Galina. She had lost all traces of her former shyness and awkwardness.

'So are you allowed to sit with me?' she asked.

'I can do as I please.'

He pulled up a chair at her table in the Rose Noir.

'I would have known you, for all that you've changed,' she said examining his face.

'Being a princess suits you very well.'

'A very poor princess.'

Her family was having a hard time of it. Her father's bank had gone to the wall, with various court cases pending in Paris, and although he had been searching for employment in the banking world, not only in Berlin but in Hamburg too, he was competing with dozens of others like him. At the moment he was working as a waiter in a club called the Bürger-Casino. Her mother was in low spirits, and her father's sister had been for some time in a private clinic on the outskirts of Potsdam. She told him she would be visiting her this Sunday, and Alyosha found himself offering to accompany her.

30

He arranged to meet her outside the French Church on the Gendarmenmarkt.

'Why don't we go to the Café Kranzler? Have a schnapps before we board the train?'

Sitting opposite her on the train he found it difficult not to stare at her legs, which were rather attractively encased in black silk stockings. Sharing their compartment were two old peasants in traditional Sunday outfits. Galina and Alyosha spoke Russian together and made a few sly little jokes about them.

From the station it was only half a mile to the clinic, along a country lane. They arrived at the iron gates, and Galina rang the bell. A man in a green felt hat and a grey suit asked for their names, and who they were visiting, before opening the gates for them. The clinic was housed in a substantial mansion, set in pretty grounds, though an eight-foot wall surrounded the place.

They found Lazarevna Petrovna reclining under a blanket on a lounger on the patio at the back of the mansion. She stirred when Galina called her name, and lifted her sunglasses to look at them. She stood up and moved over to sit on one of the wooden benches on the lawn. They came to join her, and she spread her blanket over the knees of her niece and her friend. It was late September and the autumn sun might be giving a creditable impression of a summer's day, but the coolness of the air belied it.

Galina kept the conversation going, telling her aunt all about her recent experiences as an extra. Lazarevna was particularly interested in hearing all about Yulia Gosovska, and her niece racked her brain for as many details as she could, doing her best to entertain her. Throughout, Lazarevna Petrovna held Galina's fingers in one hand and Alyosha's in the other. Alyosha sensed she must be a very lonely woman.

By and by, she took them inside to her room, where she consented to remove her sunglasses and blanket. She wore not a scrap of make-up, and her dark, bag-ridden eyes gazed out at the world from a ghostly white face. Her hair though, was fashionably and expertly shingled, and her clothes were of a good cut and quality. Alyosha sat in an armchair and Galina lolled on her aunt's bed, flicking through a magazine she picked up from the bedside table.

Now it was Alyosha's turn to be interrogated, and Lazarevna had soon established that they had met before, many years earlier in Petrograd. Alyosha had a vague memory of standing between her and Zinaida Ernestovna in a fashion show. To his young eyes at the time she had seemed achingly sophisticated. He felt very sorry for her, reduced to this.

She told him she thought the world of his mother and sympathised with him for his recent loss.

'If I hadn't been so ill, I would have made the effort to attend the funeral.'

The lunch bell rang. It was time to bid farewell. Galina pulled on her satin coat trimmed with monkey fur, and picked up her gloves. Her aunt walked them to the reception and kissed her niece, then Alyosha. As her lips touched his cheek, he felt her fingers in his pocket. Back in Berlin, after seeing Galina onto her tram, he stood outside Friedrichstrasse station, took the envelope out of his pocket and opened it. He read her scrawled letter. On the way back to the Adlon he wondered what he should do next.

31

It was to the famous Hocher restaurant that Herman Schwartz took Larissa Kozmyevna. There was a bottle of champagne chilling in a silver bucket at their table. She had never smoked before, but when he offered her a cigarette from his engraved cigarette case she took one. Herman snapped the case shut, slipped it back in his pocket, tapped his cigarette on his nail and put it to his lips, then held his lighter out, and Larissa leaned towards the flame.

In his company Larissa was very aware of her Russian accent, and felt embarrassed, as his German was so correct. He asked her many questions about herself, but she was uncharacteristically shy and didn't like to show her own curiosity. From his waistcoat pocket he took a chain, and at the end of the chain was the smallest watch she had seen in her life. Down his nose Herman squinted at it, as he held it flat on the palm of his hand.

Larissa had been worried about what to wear, as her wardrobe was very sparse and she was terrified she wouldn't pass muster, but a friend of Margarita's at the bank lent her a dress, which was only a little too large. Her sister helped with her hair, and lent her lipstick. Staring in the mirror, Larissa had felt she looked older than her age, and when she thought of the evening ahead, she felt like pinching herself.

Larissa, gazing around her at the gentlemen in their tight black jackets and the ladies in their expensive dresses, listening to their conversation and their laughter against the soft music of the band, felt out of place. Herman looked at her through his monocle and smiled. She smiled back but she still felt uneasy.

'Do you know something?'

'What?'

'You're the most beautiful woman in the room.'

She was quite overcome.

'Nothing would give me more pleasure than seeing you in a dress that would show off your naked shoulders.'

He wanted her to buy such a dress.

'Don't worry about the cost. I'll pay.'

She felt once more as though she were in a dream, that she would wake up any moment. It felt like something out of a fairy tale. What had somebody like Herman Schwartz seen in her? He was from one of Berlin's richest families.

Herman shaved twice a day, once on waking and once before going to bed, no matter how late the hour. He shaved every bristle meticulously so that his face was perfectly smooth; and he shaved so closely sometimes that his skin was quite blue, as if he'd just been out for a very long walk on a very cold winter's morning. She later learned that this habit explained the ugly scar on his cheek, when he had tried to shave himself after rolling home drunk after celebrating a friend's birthday at the Kemplinksi.

What soured the evening rather was that she spent too long talking with the waitress rather than with him. She didn't have much choice: when she and Klara saw each other, they nearly screamed out loud. Herman could hardly bear it when they started to 'catch up' on 'what everybody was up to'.

He half-listened to Klara telling Larissa that she had been sacked from her job at the factory for stealing some biscuits or other, and Larissa telling Klara that Margarita was seeing a Russian called Stanislav, and that Ella was regarded very highly at the Berlitz School and was teaching in the evenings now.

Herman's patience wore very thin when Klara loitered at their table after serving them with their main course, to talk some more, and was in danger of losing his temper, especially as Klara hadn't even recognised him and had barely acknowledged him at all.

When Klara brought them their coffee, and a cognac for Herman, she was still talking about various tenants from Neukölln, an area Herman had only ever driven through at speed on the way to somewhere rather more pleasant. Smoking his cigar, he leaned back in his chair as they discussed some man in whom he had absolutely no interest: they thought he had been waiting all this time for his wife Marie to arrive from Warsaw. It turned out that Lev Ganin didn't even have a wife.

'Really? She doesn't exist? Are you sure?' asked Larissa, stunned.

'Positive,' said Klara.

'But why would Lev claim to have a wife in Russia in the first place? What for? I don't understand why he would do such a thing.'

'Your guess is as good as mine. I did wonder if he didn't know how to turn me down, you know, when I was after him, and so he created this imaginary woman, as an excuse. But that would make him a complete idiot wouldn't it?'

Klara realised she had stayed at their table far too long, and that Herman was put out. But she couldn't help herself when there was so much news to catch up on after all this time. She also noticed him staring at her breasts, but then a lot of men did that. In the end the maître d' called her away and gave her a dressing-down in the kitchen.

The meal cost Herman over nine million marks.

Larissa felt Herman's fingers play gently on the nape of her neck. He took a little strand of hair that had come unpinned and curled it round his finger, round and round until it pulled at the root; it was painful but pleasurably so. Larissa longed to go on to a nightclub, to dance until the small hours, but she had promised her mother she wouldn't be home too late.

The chauffeur opened her door but before she stepped out, Herman held her wrist and asked her to wait a moment. He took a little box out of his pocket and told her to open it later. He kissed her tenderly on her lips and wished her good night.

It was a beautiful and expensive bracelet.

32

Alyosha was ushered down the yellow corridor to her room.

'Did you have any difficulties finding it?' was the first thing she asked him, before even greeting him. For some reason he had imagined himself embracing Lazarevna.

'I didn't try.'

Her face fell.

'You're here to get better from the morphia…'

'I don't need a sermon, thank you very much.'

From somewhere out in the garden a cry turned into an anguished scream.

'You've disappointed me, Alyosha.'

This time her face wasn't quite as ashen. She had put some powder on her skin. Her lips were red and matched her nails.

'If you don't bring me some, I'm going to die here…'

That loneliness again.

'Alyosha?'

He felt himself weaken.

'I can't promise…'

'Just for me? Hmmm?' She was gazing at him. 'Why else did you come here? All this way?'

She took his hands and placed them on her thighs; he could feel the heat of her; and how bony she was. Her hair was jet black, her eyes almost as dark, a little watery. Her mouth was slightly open, showing her surprisingly white teeth…

She rubbed her knee slowly against his leg. He stumbled, took a step back. Her expression was perplexed and agitated.

'I was at fault…'

He made to leave.

'Don't, please, I beg you…'

'I won't come again.'

'Don't you leave me too…'

She wanted him to stay, but Lazarevna didn't push herself onto him again.

'Let's be friends.'

She showed Alyosha a glimpse of the fragile nature of her soul. There was something tender about her. He felt he was walking a dark path through a forest where he could easily lose himself. The challenge was to fight against the temptation. He felt for her, he truly felt for her – and wanted to help her escape the awful loneliness that imprisoned her.

She had never married, but had had several unhappy relationships and secret affairs – some fleeting, some lasting a little longer, and one which groaned on for several years before ending in recrimination and bitterness. She found scandal like a moth finds a flame, and was responsible for ending more than one marriage, so that in some circles her name was unmentionable.

In Berlin she had been practically excommunicated after a woman killed herself because of her. Another of her lovers had fled to China to avoid the debts he had racked up on her account. Whatever the story, Lazarevna always got the blame. Her circle of friends diminished and she was pushed out to the margins. Even her own brother refused to have anything to do with her, though Andrei Petrovich had somehow raised the money for her to stay in the clinic. The consensus was that she had wantonly thrown everything away, and that she was her own worst enemy. But Alyosha thought she was still astoundingly attractive, in spite of her slightly ravaged appearance, and there was some mischievous quality about her that he found appealing. He'd been dreaming about her, and one morning he'd woken with the feeling that he was the one to save her. He was sure he could help her. He was playing with fire, he realised that, but still there was something about her that drew him in, in spite of himself…

33

When Herman insisted she go to Wertheim's, Larissa hardly bought anything, accustomed as she was to being frugal. After admiring the dresses, the underwear and the little boxes of perfume and toiletries, she came away with two men's handkerchiefs that she had wrapped and gave to him as a present. He laughed so much his monocle fell out and Larissa was quite put out that he found her so comical. He told her to spend, and to spend as much as she needed to: only he wanted all his friends to admire her when they were out together.

His friends consisted of a crew of young men who drove at great speed around Berlin with willowy young girls with short hair sitting in the back. On fine summer evenings they raced through the Grünewald, out of Berlin towards Potsdam, or sometimes they went north through the lovely area of Sachenhausen, north of the city.

With the wind in her hair and the road stretching before her in its limitless possibility, Larissa felt her life was all honey. She gave Herman a sidelong glance, driving the open-topped Mercedes with only his little finger resting on the steering wheel. The other motor-cars darted across each other's paths, the boys sounding their horns energetically and the girls squealing with laughter as champagne spray spurted over their heads.

After the excitement of the drive, the tranquillity of the lake would be all the sweeter. A white sailing boat skittering across the Wansee and a cloud of midges, were the only things that disturbed the quiet enjoyment of the evening.

They usually drew up near one of the bars, lit up by rows of little Japanese lanterns. They'd sit on benches at wooden tables to drink and sing and smoke. Larissa was the only Russian but everybody was perfectly friendly with her. There were two or three sons of generals of the Kaiser's old army, and the rest were all children of wealthy families.

They dressed well, though one or two were rather bohemian, as if they wanted to flout their conservative upbringing. Larissa, in her new clothes, was thankful that she didn't feel out of place in their company. She felt that she and Herman, in his white flannel suit, were the smartest couple there. Herman was in excellent spirits, and had caught the sun on his nose and forehead, which were slightly pink. Somebody started to sing, '*Was ist des Deutschen Vaterland*' and first their table joined in, and then the others, their voices united amongst the branches.

Larissa was sitting next to a quiet girl, slightly older than herself, and noticed that she was looking at the bracelet she was wearing.

'A present from Herman,' she explained.

She remembered the warm feeling that filled her, after their evening in the Hocher, when she'd opened the box back in the quietness of her bedroom.

'Very pretty.'

The girl half-smiled and pulled on her cigarette.

'It suits you.'

Thanking her for the compliment, Larissa felt suddenly like a little girl.

By now everybody was on their feet, singing with all their might, beer glasses held high. The girl rose and Larissa followed suit but she felt out of place as she didn't know the words, although she tried to join in the fun. She noticed that Herman had his arms around his companions and that his face had turned brick-red.

She felt the girl lean on her; the flesh of her arm was hot against her own, and she thought she heard her say something. Larissa turned to look at her and the girl smiled, sipped her beer and licked her lips, and said something again, but the only word that Larissa understood was 'spite'.

34

Lazarevna realised it was not going to be quite as easy as she'd anticipated to get her way with Alyosha. Though she was confined in every way, she was willing to wait. So she spoke amusingly and laughed gaily during his next three visits, but when Alyosha came for the fourth time he found her lying on her bed in her pyjamas with the blinds closed.

'I'll have no choice but to tell them what you've been doing to me.'

Alyosha thought he must have misheard.

'What I've been doing?'

'Don't come any nearer. Stay where you are. The staff have seen you coming and going, spending time here with me in my room. You've already lied to them, saying we're related...'

'You said it was the only way they'd let me visit you...'

'So that you can help me,' she said with heavy sarcasm. 'You know how you can truly help me – but you refuse. Well, you'll have to now.'

Alyosha was overwhelmed by sadness, which he tried to ignore. He said quietly, 'Blackmail won't work with me.'

'It doesn't have to come to that.'

She had a distant, longing expression. He felt empty. She softened, sitting up.

'Sit next to me here – come.'

Alyosha remained standing.

'I was only pulling your leg.'

She smiled, lit a cigarette and changed the subject.

'Have you ever smoked hashish?'

'Several times.'

'When?'

'Back in Russia, With Mishka, Masha and Boris.'

Laza scrutinised him for a moment, picking a speck of tobacco off her tongue.

'The first time I ever tried it was in Tehran, shortly after the 1917 revolution. I was lucky enough to get out of Russia through Baku, on a ship that was transporting goats down the Caspian to Enzeli. Goats are smelly creatures. Pretty revolting actually, and Enzeli is a hellhole. I was cheated the minute I arrived, when I tried to exchange ten thousand rubles – all that I had – for Persian currency. I was none the wiser until I went to buy food and drink and saw how little I had left.'

She told him how she had crossed the two hundred miles to Tehran by camel, in a long caravan taking people like her to their exile; parched Russians, wailing wordlessly and shrivelling under the blistering sun. She was lucky to survive, as dozens were buried along the way in the sand dunes. Smoking hashish dulled the pain, dulled the homesickness too. She'd had no wish to loiter in Tehran and set off as soon as possible, making for Tabriz, a seven-day journey across another desert, from where it took her another three weeks to reach Baghdad, the filthiest and most disagreeable city she had ever seen.

The next step was somehow to reach Constantinople. She was advised to visit the Turkish Council. She was warmly welcomed and taken out to dinner that night, to a club for English and French businessmen mainly, with great fans turning lazily overhead, and brisk waiters in white mess jackets darting between the tables, carrying silver trays on the tips of their fingers. Laza paid for her supper, and her room at the Darush Grand Hotel, by sleeping with the Deputy Chairman of the Anglo-Persian Business Council, who was also generous enough to pay for her first-class ticket on the Baghdad-Constantinople Express.

Listening as she recounted her adventures, Alyosha thought the blackmail threat must just have been a bad joke.

'Will you bring me the morphia?'

He felt that the room had darkened.

'Honestly, I can't.'

'Only you can help me.'

She stroked the back of his hand. A sort of powerful silence filled the place, some kind of still oppressive stillness, the lull before the storm.

'I really can't.'

'Alyosha, don't force me to force you.' This was said in a piteous voice.

He hardened his heart against her and decided to call her bluff. He walked out of her room, down the corridor and out of the main entrance under a cloudy sky. He could still taste the rain on the air. The earlier showers had left little puddles on the path. As he reached the iron gates he saw the man in the green hat and grey suit step out of his hut.

As Alyosha put more distance between himself and the clinic, his spirits rose and he decided he would never again visit Lazarevna Petrovna. On the train back to Berlin, she faded altogether from his mind, and his thoughts turned to Grete and the continuing mystery of her disappearance. He still missed her.

Lazarevna telephoned Alyosha late that night.

'If you don't bring me some tomorrow, Galina will tell your mother what you've been doing to me. I've told her everything.'

The next morning, Alyosha went directly to see Galina to assure her of his innocence. She could barely look him in the eye, and clearly didn't believe him, but eventually agreed not to go to his mother.

A few nights later he was woken from his sleep to hear a

distant and weak voice on the telephone talking of reporting him.

'Unless…' and even then she sounded mournful rather than resolved.

After a restless night spent worrying, nothing happened the next day and Alyosha relaxed a little. Calling her bluff had paid off.

But the next day on Galatia Bridge he was arrested in front of the cast and crew.

35

She only caught the tram if she was utterly exhausted, or if she left the Berlitz School very late. During the summer months, when it stayed light for so long, she walked every step of the way back to the flat, walked until her feet were throbbing. Sometimes, she would even feel faint and then she would have to rest for a while. When she had a free afternoon like today, Ella might break the journey home with a visit to Vikentiy Lvovich Weinstock's bookshop. She rarely bought anything, but loved browsing through the volumes. She much preferred old Weinstock to his assistant Smurov, though he was from Petrograd, because he made his disapproval at her never buying anything very obvious.

'This is a shop, not a library,' he once said to her curtly.

The young man didn't know the half of it. Ella's frugality meant she spent as little as possible on food as well. When the other teachers assembled at lunchtime and opened their lunch packets, she would make some excuse not to join them. She spent her lunch hour wandering aimlessly up and down Friedrichstrasse, or sometimes sitting on a bench on Unter den Linden watching the world go by.

In the early days, when she returned to school, somebody was sure to tease her about where she went on her lunch hour; but Ella was not somebody who reacted well to having her leg pulled, and she was soon left in peace.

Sometimes she walked by the Russian Embassy, and on one occasion stood outside for a while to see who went in. A great wave of homesickness swept over her and she very nearly walked in to ask for the right to go back to Russia. She realised it was just a foolish whim, for she could never leave Margarita and Larissa on their own in Berlin. But Berlin could never be her home; she would never put down roots here. In her case, it was too late. Nothing brought her any peace; there was no comfort in sleep even. As she lay in her bed every night, the same old memories would creep in over her shoulder to lie with her, reproaching her with every decision she had ever made.

Yet even if she were to return to Russia, to whom would she be returning? She had no idea if Kozma was still alive, and although every day she continued to hope and pray that he was, after more than four years of utter silence it was hard not to give in to despair. Her only comfort was in knowing that her situation was hardly unique, and that many had suffered far more than she had. She remembered a morning when she had gone with her daughters and the old poet Podtyagin to volunteer at the Red Cross Centre, which was in an old school behind the station in Uhlandstrasse. She found herself in the company of other Russians and they all had their tales of sadness and confusion. That was the day she came to understand and sympathise with old Podtyagin as she heard him talk of his sister, who had succeeded in leaving Moscow and reaching Paris after all sorts of difficulties.

Ella felt she was living in some strange limbo, neither wife nor widow, but swinging from one to another on the pendulum of her emotions. Would she ever know deliverance?

36

Inessa arranged the lawyer for her son. There was no choice. He managed to prevent Alyosha from being incarcerated in Moabit prison, but it was a close shave as the accusation was such a serious one. There was no choice either but to pay the hefty bail, and even then Alyosha had to sign in at the police station every day.

'When it comes to court, it will be her word against yours,' his mother told him. 'You do realise that don't you?'

'Do I look like a fool?'

'Well you've certainly acted like one. If your poor father was alive… perhaps it's just as well he's in the ground. He would have been so ashamed…'

'He would have believed me.'

'Look at the trouble you've brought on yourself.'

'I've been wronged.'

In her statement Lazarevna claimed that Alyosha had promised to bring her morphia on condition that she slept with him. One time, when he didn't have the morphia and she refused to sleep with him, he raped her.

'I didn't.'

'You're telling the truth?'

'Yes.'

'Are you? Look into my eyes…'

'I'm telling the truth.'

Inessa was, as usual, on her way out, this time to supper with Katharina Schratt, the former mistress of the Emperor Franz

Joseph, and the Duke of Almássy, who had just returned from his travels in East Africa. It was clear his mother thought he was guilty, and blamed the barbarousness of his life in Russia, before he managed to escape, for the destruction of his morality.

'Do you know the difference between good and evil? I doubt very much that you do.'

How could Alyosha explain to her that he had seen the longing for love in Lazarevna? The desperation to be free from the loneliness that had driven her to the clinic in the first place? Or had he only managed to fool himself that he and he alone could save her?

'Why did you go there, Alexei? Why visit her on your own? A woman like her? Hmmm?'

'Addicts,' spat Alexei Dashkov, already on his second bottle of champagne. 'Why would you fraternise with addicts?'

The next day, Inessa asked Andrei Petrovich to meet her at the studio office to discuss the matter.

'This scandal won't be good for anybody. It will bring every Russian in Berlin into disrepute. Things are quite difficult enough for us as it is. Don't you agree?'

'Yes, I do agree.'

'I'd like to think there is some way we can keep this from coming to court. We've known each other a long time. You know as well as I do, I hope, what a high opinion my late husband had of you, Andrei Petrovich.'

'That was entirely mutual.'

'Is there no way, for his memory's sake, that this can be resolved?'

'Where my sister's concerned, I'm just not sure it's that simple.'

'What good will a thing like this do any of us?'

The ex-banker looked through the window.

'Can't we come to some understanding?'

'I understand what you're suggesting…'

'It just seems to me…'

'But I can't answer for my sister.'

'But you could talk to her?'

He nodded.

'I'm very grateful.'

'I can't promise anything, Inessa Vassilievna.'

'I'm sure you'll do your best for us.'

A substantial financial settlement was indeed reached. Inessa wrote a cheque that would buy Lazarevna half a factory and she withdrew the charges. Andrei Petrovich was happy to have kept his old friend's son out of the courts, but his daughter was absolutely furious that Alyosha seemed to have got off scot-free. She confronted him at the earliest possible opportunity.

'I did nothing wrong, Galina. Your aunt took her revenge because I wouldn't bring her morphia.'

'She would never do that. You took advantage of a defenceless woman. I hate you.'

'She took advantage of me.'

'How can you say such a thing? What you did was unforgiveable.'

Alyosha sighed.

'Maybe you can buy my father, but you'll never buy me. I'll see you and your mother pay for this one way or another.'

She began to tell everybody who would listen at the studio what a despicable person Alyosha was, until Inessa heard of it and summoned her.

'This is how you thank me? I didn't have to employ you, but I took pity on you and my kindness is what puts food in your stomach and money in your pocket. And this is how you choose to pay me back.'

'Your son raped my aunt.'

'As to that, your aunt has been very happy to receive a large sum of money from me.'

'Your son is still a rapist.'

'If you say that once more…'

'I'll say it to anyone who's willing to listen.'

She was sacked on the spot and escorted off the lot by one of the security guards.

Her anger consumed her, and her hatred of Alyosha and Inessa took over her life. She made it her mission to make life difficult for them. She let it be known that Inessa had paid her and some of her favourites in dollars, which created much bad feeling, as inflation meant the papiermark was worth less and less every day. The talk at the studio was of nothing else. A meeting of all the extras and crew was called and it was decided that they would go on strike, the extras taking their costumes home with them to prevent the studio from simply rehiring. Then Yulia Gosovska heard from the wardrobe mistress that Varvara Lvovna, who played the ingénue (and was having an affair with one of the two American cameramen, who no doubt had advised her), had a contract that stipulated she be paid in dollars.

'Why is she being treated better than me?'

The extras and crew could not afford to strike for long and were soon back at work, though still disgruntled. But Yulia Gosovska was made of sterner stuff and dug her heels in. For the scene on Galatia Bridge by moonlight, when she was meant to sing a song of longing for Russia, she refused.

'I shan't be treated with so little respect,' she proclaimed in a dramatic voice, standing on the Bridge so that everybody could hear and see her. 'I deserve better. I've worked with the very finest of Moscow's Imperial Theatre.'

This was the emotional climax of the movie and Alexei Dashkov was beside himself.

'What am I going to do? That idiotic woman is going to ruin my picture!'

He tried to reason with her, to cajole, to flatter, and to beg, but in vain. In any event, Inessa was adamant they would not pander to her.

'We'll have to get rid of her.'

'That would be insanity now that we've shot so much already.'

While they argued about how to proceed, the filming was yet again at a stop. There were still bills to be paid however, and Inessa was to be found signing cheques at her oak desk in a bright pool of light under her Jupiter lamp. By the end of the first week of filming she had spent three billion marks. Employing crew and cast between six in the morning and nine at night cost five million marks a day, on top of all the other production costs. If she carried on like this, she would have spent the fortune her ex-husband had so carefully accumulated in no time.

From the beginning, Alexei Dashkov made constant changes to the script in order to make his own role more important. He invariably had the most lines in any scene and he had fiddled so much with the plot that it made very little sense. When he had worked in Russia there had always been a producer, keeping the project on time and within budget; but here he had perfect freedom to do as he wanted and it had gone to his head.

Alyosha looked on in alarm but it was difficult to speak to his mother, as his stepfather always seemed to be within earshot. When he did manage to voice his concerns she seemed reluctant to listen to him. She put all her faith in her husband, who had explained to her that money was of the smallest importance compared with creating a major artistic masterpiece, which would cement his reputation. Celluloid would be the most important artistic medium of the twentieth century, he assured her, and this film, about the pain of Russian exiles in Constantinople, would open the world's eyes to their suffering. It would also, he hoped, open the door to Hollywood.

Alyosha knew from bitter experience about hardship. He knew how it felt to be poor. He knew what being starving felt like, and how itchy lice were, and how you stank when you hadn't washed for a month. His mother hadn't experienced any real privation in her entire life, not really – though Inessa thought that having to leave her home and her country made her an expert on suffering – and he knew that she would never cope without money. He took his opportunity to speak to his mother while she was being treated by Doctor Ko, an ancient llama-doctor from a high monastery in Tibet, a knotty nut of a man with a little white goatee. He was industriously mapping her four pulses when Alyosha entered. His mother was furious for the interruption and insisted that he leave the room and come back later.

In the presence of his little brother Georgik, Alyosha confronted his mother. He begged her to stop her insane spending.

'Do you want to leave us with nothing?'

'Oh, really, not this again. Do be quiet.'

'I can't be quiet. You must think of the consequences. What would you do without money?'

'You're giving me a headache.'

'What would become of Gosha?'

'How can you reproach me about my spending? Do you know how much I had to pay that woman to keep you from prison?'

Before Alyosha could respond, Alexei Dashkov marched in, dressed as Baron Wrangel, with Stanislav on his heels. They were discussing rewriting some scene. He took no notice of Alyosha but said to Inessa, 'I've let Yulia Gosovska go.'

'Not a moment too soon.'

'I had no choice.'

He could take no more of her histrionics; it was taking its toll on him emotionally, sucking all his energy and leaving him drained, when he should be putting all his efforts into his artistic vision. That's why he had called Stanislav in to rewrite her part.

'Don't write another word,' begged Alyosha.

More new scenes would mean more spending. Alexei Dashkov poured himself a glass of champagne and said loftily that you couldn't put a price on artistic integrity. Inessa nodded adoringly.

Alyosha walked out of the room, barely concealing his disgust.

37

By the time Ella arrived back at the flat she was starving and her throat was parched. She poured herself a glass of water and unpacked her few purchases. She had bought some coarse liver sausage and a pot of cheap jam, which, along with the margarine she now spread on her morning crust, was a very poor substitute for the creamy butter and comb honey she used to enjoy.

Margarita and Larissa had been out every night that week. It surprised Ella that Larissa had suddenly taken such a lively interest in music after all those years of complaining over piano practice. Well, things had changed, and that was good. She was now happy to queue for tickets to the opera or a concert for her and her sister – in the gallery of course. Margarita, who had always been musical, liked to follow the score, which she would borrow from the lending library.

They had both grown up. They were no longer girls but young women. Had she brought them up well? What would Kozma have said? Was she giving Larissa too much freedom perhaps? Did she go out too much? She had protested to begin with, but her will had weakened. She often felt so listless, and it sometimes seemed like too much of an effort even to cook for herself. But she reached for the cast iron frying pan (which was almost too heavy for her) and placed it on the stove.

She had barely sat down to eat the greasy meat when somebody knocked on the door. She sighed and rose to open it. A tall, bony man stood there. Ella gazed at his dessicated face. There was something utterly unwholesome about him. He looked like an owl. He asked her name and she answered, holding the door only half-open, she was so suspicious of him.

'I've called once already today,' said the owl.

He held out an envelope under her nose.

'The rent hasn't been paid for over two months now,' he said baldly. 'If you don't settle within the week you're out.'

He was an agent on behalf of the owner. He made it quite clear that his own livelihood depended on collecting all the rents promptly, or he'd lose his bonus at the end of the year.

'That's why I won't put up with any nonsense from you or anybody else, so don't even try and come up with excuses; there's not one I haven't heard by now, and frankly I'm not interested, because as far as I'm concerned you pay up or get out,' he said, without drawing breath. 'Do I make myself clear?'

As he glared down at her with his great dark eyes, Ella tried to tell him that he must have made a mistake, because they paid their rent every month promptly and that her older daughter always took care of it from the bank where she worked.

'I'm not sure exactly of the date she makes the payment, but I can assure you she never fails to pay it.'

Ella added that she was sure if there had been any misunderstanding, her daughter would rectify it at once. The owl obviously didn't believe a word of it and became very unpleasant, accusing her and every other Russian, Pole and Bulgarian, and all the other foreigners he had to deal with of dishonesty.

'It's no wonder things are as bad as they are in Berlin, and every other city the length and breadth of this country, with parasites like you trying your luck. If you're not willing to pay your way, you can get out and go back where you came from.'

She was about to protest but he carried on.

'You lot, you're all the bloody same, you're just a heap of trouble. I never get this sort of rubbish from my own people, just you lot!'

By now he had whipped himself into such a frenzy, she had to listen to him rail against the French, and losing the Ruhr and the Saar, and the unemployment. He was shouting by now, and was frightening Ella, so she was very glad when he eventually stomped off, after telling her he'd be back to get what was owing. Ella sat back down by the table, where her supper had long since grown cold.

38

When Margarita walked into Stanislav's flat the first person she saw was Asia Turgenev, red-faced and sweating, her blouse stretched tight across her breasts. Sitting nearby, gazing at her longingly, was André Beli. There were at least ten or eleven other people squashed into the tiny room, and the air was thick with tobacco smoke though Stanislav had just opened the window. She went to stand by the poet Boris Pilnyak and listened quietly to the discussion. As usual things had become very heated. They were discussing Russia of course, and the poet from Moscow, who was visiting Berlin, had succeeded in ruffling a few feathers amongst the exiles. Pilnyak himself seemed far from sober.

'The days of child's play are long over… it's high time everybody came home to shoulder the burden of getting Russia back on her feet. Especially people like you…'

Stanislav winked at Margarita and mouthed something she didn't understand.

'… the thousands that turned their back on her in the hour of her need…'

Hardly anybody agreed with him. Many were of the opinion that they should do nothing that might bring succour or support to the Communists who had violated Mother Russia.

'… you intellectuals…'

Pilnyak raised his voice to make sure everyone heard him.

'You always want to challenge… always want to oppose… you're never willing to bend to the will of the people because you're too proud and pleased with yourselves. Don't ever forget that it was the will of the people which created the revolution, the will of the people which fought and spilt blood, and the will of the people which won the civil war against the combined might of Denikin, Kolach, Wrangel, Japan, America, France and England… And what do you do? Sit here finding fault, squabbling, still claiming that the government of Russia today is undemocratic and unlawful. What was our last government? The one you supported so loyally? What was that? What were three centuries of the Tzar's so-called benevolent government?'

André Beli passed the bottle to the next man. It was Lev Ganin.

'Yes, there was a revolution,' answered Asia forcefully. 'The popular spring revolution which showed us clearly what the people thought, that they were sick and tired of the war. But that was a bourgeois revolution. And it was a government of that colour that grew out of it…'

'What happened next was nothing like it. As autumn turned to winter the Bolsheviks took the opportunity…'

'– to turn things –'

'– can I say?'

'– to turn things –'

'– they tried that July –'

'– to their own advantage –'

'– do you remember?'

'And saved Russia!'

Asia raised her voice.

'And keep her whole, so that she didn't split into a thousand fragments. Would any government other than Lenin's have been able to accomplish such a feat? I doubt it! Instead of all this bluster, why don't you at least acknowledge that fair and square? But no, what do you do? You sit and judge from a pretty graveyard like Europe. It's the Communists who have stopped Russia from turning to ashes. I have faith in the new Russia which has risen from the revolution. Europe today can't keep on playing the fool, and it's high time she realised that the salvation of communist Russia will be her salvation too. That is the only future. For us here today, there are only two options: to turn our backs forever on Russia and set our sights on the west, that is, to sink deeper into the depths of exile and end our lives in some gutter of a city like Berlin or Paris, or acknowledge our responsibilities, pack our bags tonight and leave tomorrow morning for Moscow.'

'To a house destroyed by a storm.'

Lev Ganin said this quietly with his eyes on the tip of his cigarette.

'Which is not necessarily a bad thing.'

Like all self-righteous people Boris Pilnyak was never without a ready answer.

'Sometimes we need a tempest to show us where the house is weak. Once it's blown over, we can see where we need to strengthen the foundations, and where to cut out all the rotten timber which made the roof so dangerous.'

Asia turned to Margarita.

'You're soberer than any of us… it's easier for you to think clearly… what's your view?'

With his pipe in the corner of his mouth, Stanislav gazed over at her.

'Would you consider going back to live under the order of Lenin and his crew?' Asia asked then.

André Beli started to hiccup and the young woman sitting next to him slapped him vigorously on his back.

Margarita answered crisply, 'It wasn't a revolution that brought the Communists to power but a *coup d'état*. All Communists are thieves and murderers, devoid of conscience. And I hate to think of Russia today wincing under their heel. They were responsible for driving my family into exile. While I live I will never forgive the Communists. I'll do everything within my power to bring them down.'

The depth of her anger was evident in her face, but the poet from Moscow was unconcerned, as if he had heard tens if not hundreds of other people expressing exactly the same sentiments.

'*Coup d'état*? Even though they had the support of the working class?'

Somebody in the corner laughed.

'The working class indeed!'

'Yes, yes; it's easy enough for you to mock and laugh. But what other government can protect Russia's interests today with the world as it is?'

'By stealing people's property?'

'By giving property back to the people. That's what Jesus would have done.'

'Share out your own property was what Jesus advocated, not steal other people's.'

Boris Pilnyak laughed.

'Is that what all this bitterness is about? Because they've taken your house from you, and given it to the homeless?'

He stared belligerently at Margarita. She felt an icy column of hate rise inside her and answered, 'I couldn't care less about bricks and mortar. But I do care about my father.'

She had to go back to work.

'Slava?'

She wanted a word. Stanislav walked out with her.

'Aunt Inessa hasn't answered any of my messages. I've left several: at the Adlon of course, but at the Russian Club and the studios too. I think she must be deliberately avoiding me.'

'You don't know that…'

'But she's stopped paying the rent on the apartment. Why didn't she at least give us some warning? Instead of letting that dreadful man come, knocking on the door and scaring my poor mother half to death. What do you think I should do now?'

'Shall I try and get hold of her for you?'

'Would you?'

'I have to meet Alexei Dashkov in the Adlon tonight in any event to discuss the script.'

'More rewrites?'

'No doubt. If I see Inessa Vasilievna I'll tell her you need to see her urgently, shall I?'

'I just hope she'll be willing. Mama is worrying horribly.'

'I'll do my best.'

Margarita thanked him and gave him a kiss before rushing off back to work. As she strode quickly along the pavements, she passed men who had lost their arms or legs, begging. There wasn't much to choose between the beggars of Berlin and those of Petrograd, she thought. Perhaps they were a little better dressed here in Berlin, their hands white and soft and their nails clean.

She went through the doors of the bank. There was quite a crowd in the foyer, a ragbag of agitated people, and one young woman in a chair with a baby wailing indescribably loudly. Margarita squeezed past them to the counters, where the staff were standing in little knots, conferring anxiously with each other. She saw that a few of them were smoking, which was forbidden, and a couple of the young cashiers were crying. With a mounting feeling of alarm, she made her way to her office in the back. The manager was slumped in his chair, his assistant rushing around ineffectually, now fanning his face, now bringing him a glass of water.

'What's happening? What's the matter?'

The bank had gone bust.

39

Larissa was lying naked on silk sheets, enjoying a sense of freedom that made her feel as light as a bird. Herman's bedroom was as big as their entire apartment. She loved nothing more than walking around in it, imagining that it was hers.

Was that the lift coming up? The ping of the doors opening? She waited for the click of the spindly key turning in the lock, but the door didn't open. She shifted lazily onto her side. She'd been expecting Herman for the last hour and it wasn't like him to be late. Punctuality was very important to him. Keeping time was a point of honour, as important as keeping his word. The one time she had kept him waiting, though only by a few minutes, Herman had sulked and refused to speak to her until they stepped onto the deck of the yacht. It was only when he raised the anchor that he finally managed to raise a smile.

On the round bedside table there was a picture. She sat up and picked it up, marvelling at the heaviness of the silver frame – much heavier than it looked. She held the picture between her knees, plaited her hands behind her head and studied it minutely. Herman looked so young – almost like a schoolboy – even with his monocle. She was eighteen, almost nineteen, to his twenty-five. But she felt much older than her age. She was so glad that she and Herman had gone to bed together. She had been just as eager as him – not that he'd said much after the deed was done. But perhaps lovers weren't meant to talk after making love. Perhaps she was being unsophisticated. She lay there, her flesh suffused by a sweet warmth.

She remembered how she had stepped out of the lift and walked out of the building. She remembered how the doorman had lifted his cap to her. She had blushed to think he might know what she had just been doing. Might he guess? Did she look different? She smiled as she remembered…

She put the picture back and walked across the deep carpet, down the three steps and into the living room. She started to dance. Herman had suggested more than once that she move in with him, and nothing would have pleased her more, but she knew it would have killed her mother. Herman was inclined to sulk when he didn't get his way, and she had to be extra loving and tender for a while until he came to himself again.

As he had no need of a job, Herman liked to sleep late, and rise later. A bath, a shave, a careful choice of clothes, and then he'd generally drive over to the Kemplinski for lunch. He'd call for Larissa once she'd finished her morning lessons and then they'd visit friends or go back to his flat to make love. Sometimes they'd take a bath together afterwards. Every evening there'd be somewhere to go. Larissa could never stay all night at Herman's, for her mother expected her back. Ella knew about Herman, and although she hadn't yet been introduced to him, Margarita had assured her mother that he was a very respectable young man from a good family, and this was enough to quell her anxieties.

One afternoon, without warning her beforehand, Herman had driven Larissa through some high and ornate cast-iron gates, crowned with two eagles, wings spread, along a long straight drive to a little palace, surrounded by meticulously kept grounds.

'Come on! No need to be shy!'

A parlour maid in a blue uniform opened the door for them and Larissa found herself face to face with a woman in early middle age, a pack of yapping corgis at her heels. She wore a wide-brimmed bonnet, and a large flower-filled trug on the floor suggested she had just come in from the garden. She offered her cheek for Herman to kiss, who then introduced Larissa to his mother.

They lunched out on the terrace, surrounded by great pots of flowers. The table was covered in white linen, the cutlery was of heavy silver and they drank from crystal glasses. They were waited on by a butler and two maids, and served with consommé, followed by lobster in aspic and finally a Nesselrode pudding. The conversation was a little strained but, as the coffee was brought, Herman suddenly announced that he had something to say.

'Larissa?' he turned to her. 'Will you marry me?'

She almost fainted.

'Will you?'

She blushed to the tips of her ears.

'Herman!'

'Must I ask three times?'

He pushed a little red box across the table to her with his finger.

'Open it.'

Larissa looked at his mother.

'Open it now.'

As Larissa lifted the engagement ring, her fingers shook.

'Herman?' she pleaded in a whisper.

'Give me your finger.'

She felt a circle of gold squeeze around her flesh.

'Do I get a kiss?'

His father unhooked himself from the edge of the table and rolled his wheelchair away. His mother was still smiling quietly. Herman smiled as well.

'Everybody happy?' he said, raising his coffee cup to his lips.

A moment later the butler appeared, and whispered something in his ear.

'Excuse me,' said Herman, rising from the table. 'Telephone.'

He disappeared through the French doors into the house.

Larissa was left alone with her prospective mother-in-law and desperately tried to think of something to say. She felt very uncomfortable until his mother's good breeding showed itself and she started a conversation, though nothing more was said about the engagement, or about Larissa's relationship with her son. She didn't even ask how long they had known each other. Larissa might not be particularly worldly but she knew already that she would never be truly accepted in this family.

As they drove back to Berlin, Herman didn't utter a word; he just smiled to himself every now and again. He never laughed, Larissa had noticed. She had thought it odd to begin with but had grown used to it by now.

'Are you serious?' Larissa asked him at last, holding her finger up.

He took out his monocle, blew on it, polished it on his waistcoat and then recorked it, wedging his thigh against the steering wheel as he did so. He smiled.

'Herman!' She punched him lightly. 'In front of your mother and father… that was a truly appalling thing to do, I nearly fainted with embarrassment… how could you…?' she faltered. 'Why were you called to the telephone anyway?'

'I wasn't called to the telephone. I was called to my father. Didn't you guess?'

'I wondered. Was he displeased?'

'Uh-huh,' he said in an American accent.

Silence.

'What did he say exactly then?'

'Does it matter?'

His voice was filled with nonchalant contempt. As they drove, dusk turned to night, and Larissa felt the darkness gather around her. She knew she should be feeling happy. She was, but Herman hadn't noticed how angry she was; she was furious, while at the same time excited, and proud. Of all the girls in the world he had chosen her to be his wife. She of all people! Herman touched the nape of her neck and a thrill went through her. When he kissed her shoulder she felt a strong impulse to make love then and there.

40

Earlier in the day low clouds had gathered over the forest, promising rain. Alexei Dashkov approved, as he thought it lent a sinister atmosphere for the outdoor filming sequence. In fact he was far happier with the weather than he was with the script. As usual, he had been rewriting it himself, adding lines here, cutting there, but there was something still not right, though he couldn't put his finger on exactly where the fault lay.

He showed his wife the script but she had very little interest in reading it. Inessa was still bad-tempered and irritable after Alyosha and Margarita had pretty much ambushed her at the Adlon the previous evening, while she was being massaged by Felix Kersten, asking her to honour her late husband's promise to pay the rent on behalf of Ella and the girls. Margarita had told her that although she had hoped to be able to meet the rent herself, now that the bank had gone bust she was out of work. She hadn't much hope of new employment either, though of course she was searching.

'So you think it's easier for me to keep the three of you? Is that what you're suggesting?'

'Not indefinitely, it's just…'

Alyosha appealed to her.

'Mama, please.'

'It's all very well for people to come running to me all the time asking for handouts.'

Inessa went on in this vein for quite some time, making it clear to Margarita just quite how much financing her husband's film was costing her, and how the strike had been a major blow, on top of which recasting Yulia Gosovska had meant digging deep for extra finance to reshoot. By now she had very little in reserve. It meant she had to curb her former generosity and make savings where she could. They would all have to make sacrifices. And having delivered her sermon, she gathered her things and went to her room.

'You wait here,' Alyosha told his cousin. 'I'll go and speak to her, see if I can't make her be more reasonable.'

Margarita thanked him.

Inessa was sitting at the oval mirror preparing to go out.

'Alyosha, well, don't just stand there, make yourself useful and fasten my necklace would you?'

She was on her way to the casino for an evening's gambling.

'Thank you.'

His fingers touched the nape of his mother's neck and a strange thrill went through him. Inessa admired her reflection, turning her face this way and that to consider her earrings. Alyosha took a deep breath, and started to appeal to his mother to reconsider. He put up a spirited argument but his mother was implacable and he returned to Margarita with bad news.

'I tried my best… I'm so sorry.'

'You've nothing to apologise for… you did all that you could.'

Margarita returned to the apartment with a very heavy heart.

41

Larissa heard the lift at last, and, as the only thing she had on was her engagement ring, she skipped back to the bedroom, in case Herman had brought somebody home with him, as he sometimes did. She half-closed the door and peeped out. When she saw Herman with his back to her, kneeling by the desk, looking for something in the bottom drawer, she slipped noiselessly over to him, pressed herself against his back, threw her arms around him and nibbled his ear.

'Don't.'

Without even looking at her he crossed over to the kitchen. What on earth was the matter with him? He skulked there for a while and Larissa suddenly felt self-conscious about her nudity, and shivered a little.

Herman reappeared from the kitchen. Still not looking at her he said, 'Collect your things.'

Had she heard him properly?

'Don't come back.'

What was wrong with him? Was he ill?'

He returned to the desk.

'Quickly please. Leave.'

His voice had risen. She fled to the bedroom and, shedding hot tears, flung on her clothes, hoping that any second Herman would burst in apologising or explaining it was a joke. But he didn't. When she returned to the living room he was sitting at the bureau, his hands on the arms of the chair, his eyes fixed on the desk in front of him.

'The ring.'

He clicked his fingers. Larissa stared at him in horror. He shouted, 'Give it to me.'

'I have a right to know why.'

He didn't reply.

'Herman?'

She had mustered some courage from somewhere.

'What have I done?'

Silence.

'Herman? I must have done something.'

Silence.

'Won't you tell me?'

And a longer silence, deeper and blacker.

'My father has killed himself.'

Because of their engagement? Surely not.

'Why? When?'

She moved towards him, full of love and pity. Poor boy, no wonder he was angry with her. But Herman pushed her angrily away.

'Because the studio has gone bust…'

Until that second, Larissa had no idea that Herman's family even owned Starken.

'Go back to your own people. Go back to your own country, to your rat holes in Russia or wherever…'

As Larissa left the building the young lad was there as ever, to lift his cap and open the door for her. She hoped he couldn't see how much she was shaking: her insides were churning, her head felt as though it would explode, and a fog of pain blurred her vision. Yet the city was carrying on with its day, as always. It was raining and the wheels of the vehicles streamed through the puddles on the streets. Around her, and everyone else, was an invisible enemy. The invisible enemy had just killed Herman Schwartz's father. The invisible enemy had turned her fiancé against her.

Margarita had tried to explain to her about inflation, but she had difficulty imagining it, apart from prices going up. Money was just money surely, but for some reason beyond reason money had lost its head. Money had caught some vile illness, like influenza, and its temperature had shot up so high it was dizzy with fever, and businesses and banks were dying of it.

42

Alexei Dashkov was so unhappy with Stanislav's latest rewrites he instructed his chauffeur to fetch him to the studio for a meeting.

'Tell him he has to come back here with you immediately,' he said, walking back and forth in his Baron Wrangel costume and admiring himself in the mirror, 'and don't take no for an answer. I need to teach him one or two things about scriptwriting, once and for all.'

When Stanislav read the latest shambles the actor had made of his carefully crafted scenes he realised it was not salvageable. But as his final payment had yet to be honoured, he decided he would bite his tongue one more time and try to write whatever would pass muster with Alexei Dashkov. However, when he arrived at the studio he was told to go not to the office where he usually met Alexei, but directly outside onto the set. Two journalists were visiting that morning, to watch the filming and hopefully give them some favourable publicity so Alexei couldn't spare the time for a separate meeting.

To Stanislav's horror, Alexei, in front of the journalists, now proceeded to make some general criticisms of Stanislav's work, picking scenes seemingly at random from the script, and finding fault with the structure, or the dialogue, or both.

'Perhaps it all makes perfect sense to you but I have to admit I find it all rather unclear and clumsy, not to say confusing at times. The scenes don't seem to follow each other in a natural way and, worst of all, the plot doesn't fit with the Constantinople scenes that we've already filmed.'

As the young actress who played the part of Anastasia, the Tzar's daughter, refilled his glass with wine, he turned to a page of the script and asked, 'What exactly are you trying to say here, for instance?'

Stanislav was furious at the way he was being made to take the blame for the deficiencies of the script, and at being publicly humiliated. He defended his work staunchly, but the last straw was when Alexei declared that he had no choice as producer but to rewrite the entire script because it lacked any theme.

'Theme?' asked Stanislav in astonishment. 'Since when has the theme been important to you? The most important thing seemed to be how many lines I gave you.'

'All pictures need a theme.'

The actor then went on to claim that Stanislav's original script had been far more sympathetic to the Reds than to the Whites. Not having anticipated an attack on these grounds, Stanislav listened in growing amazement.

'Why have you emphasised what brave fighters they are? Why have you failed to show their truly dark side? And their barbarousness? And why are you so ambivalent about the White generals?' he asked in his big bass voice. 'What do you have to say for yourself?'

For the first time Alexei Dashkov had put his finger on something. Stanislav didn't think he had been particularly partisan towards the Communists – but neither had he utterly condemned them. He had tried to make his script nuanced in its portrait of the two sides. Something had happened to him, he realised: a change had crept over him, quite gradually, over weeks, as if something was forcing him to decide to which side he belonged. Russia? Or Europe?

He agreed to the rewrites and sat in his usual corner, typing away industriously, though he was still smarting from such a dressing-down. It was mid-afternoon when he saw two men, briefcases in hand, approach Inessa. His curiosity was piqued when he caught snatches of their conversation.

'... and the other account?'

'... I'm afraid so.'

'... credit on the American Express?'

'... that as well, Madam.'

The film was killed that very afternoon.

43

As Larissa walked up the street, she saw an old woman, exhausted, sitting on her haunches with her chin on her breast. People rushed by as though she didn't exist. Larissa shook her hair out of her eyes, wiped the drizzle away from her eyelashes, and as she approached, saw that it was her mother.

'What's happened? What are you doing here?'

She was light enough to lift easily.

'Mama? What's the matter?'

Ella leaned against the railings, frail and weary. At her feet was a battered empty biscuit tin.

'Come on – let's go home.'

Larissa picked up the tin and wedged it under her arm as she led her mother slowly towards their flat. Once home, she sat her down. Ella remained still and silent. In her brown cardigan, her face ashen and her eyes dull, she made a mournful sight. By the time Margarita came home after another afternoon spent tramping the streets looking for work, Larissa had managed to unearth what had happened.

With the rent unpaid, the owl had called several times, each time more threatening and offensive than the last. Ella had decided it was time to use all the money she had so carefully saved from her wages. With a biscuit tin full of marks she had gone to the Travel Bureau on Unter den Linden during her lunch hour; one of the teachers, whose sister worked there, had told her they charged less commission than the banks on the exchange of marks for sterling, dollars or francs.

Ella couldn't remember making her way back to the apartment, or why she was sitting in the street when Larissa saw her. She hadn't even realised that it had begun to rain. When Larissa got her inside, her breathing was laborious and she complained that her chest was tight and that she felt dizzy.

That night, Margarita and Larissa watched helplessly as their mother wept for the first time in front of them. Not for Kozma this time, but because everything was spinning out of control here in Berlin, exactly as it had in Petrograd.

'Soon we won't be able to pay for food. There won't even be any food. Why should the farmers send their produce to Berlin for paper pretending to be money? We'll be queuing for a bowl of gruel, begging for a crust, an apple, a potato, an onion. Everybody starving, some out on the streets protesting, some out on the streets selling themselves.'

The Communists were sure to stage a *coup d'état* here in Berlin, just as they had done in Petrograd, and the three of them would be stranded, without any way of fleeing for shelter to another country. They must act now before it was too late! They needed visas for France.

'We'll be shot if we stay here! Listen to me!'

'We are listening to you, Mama.'

'We must make our way to Paris.'

How were they to do that when her entire savings had been worth less than a dollar?

When they had finally persuaded her to go to bed, the two girls sat up talking. Margarita asked whether it would be possible for Larissa to ask her fiancé for a loan, to pay the rent at least. Larissa told her everything. Margarita was horrified and hugged her little sister tenderly.

'I'm sure when he's had time to get over the shock he'll see none of it is your fault. You just need to give him some time, Lala.'

'That's what I thought to begin with. But I've been thinking... Do you remember me telling you what that girl said to me? Back at the beginning of the summer, when Herman took me sailing on the Wansee?'

Larissa remembered the hot touch of his flesh on hers, and how a little charge had made all the hairs on her arm stand up.

'Something about spite?'

'Yes, that was it. I didn't understand at the time, but I think I do now. That's why he was with me. He chose me, a poor Russian girl, on purpose, just to spite his mother and father, because he knew how they would hate it. They wanted him to marry into his own kind.'

Margarita wouldn't believe Herman could be that cynical and tried to comfort her.

'No, no, that can't be it; it's just grief that's making him behave in this way... give him time, and he'll come back to you, I'm sure.'

'No. He won't marry me now. The reason for doing it has gone...'

That night, Larissa pressed her face tightly against the pillow to muffle the sound of her sobs. In her bed, Margarita lay awake for hours, knowing they would have to pack up and leave before they were thrown out on the street; but wondering how they would ever find the rent to live in even the cheapest of lodgings.

44

Having invested so much in the film Alexei Dashkov and Inessa were determined to have it edited and shown to the public. Undeterred by several scenes remaining unfilmed, Inessa borrowed enough money to have it edited. It was finally screened at the Kosmos, Berlin's biggest picture palace. Within twenty minutes, people started to laugh in places where they were not meant to laugh, sometimes until the tears ran down their faces.

Alexei Dashkov, enraged, stood to his feet and started to harangue the audience. He was booed and heckled until he stormed out.

Only a few members of the audience stayed until the end, Alyosha among them. As he came out blinking, into the Berlin evening, he was tapped on the shoulder by someone. He turned to face the journalist Ernst Jenny, who greeted him like an old friend.

'So what are you doing these days? Were you anything to do with that?' with a nod to the poster advertising the film.

'I did have a small part as an extra, but I'd be surprised if you spotted me. So what did you think?'

Ernst Jenny cupped his hand against the wind in order to light his cigarette. He inhaled deeply and grinned.

'Like everybody else you'll find out tomorrow morning when you read my review in the *Deutsche Zeitung.*'

'I look forward to it. So how long have you been working for them?'

'Since your father's paper went to the wall. It was a crying shame that happened. But without his financial and moral backing, it was inevitable.'

He hailed a passing taxi, which drew up beside them.

'Why don't you join me for a drink?'

Alyosha hesitated, as he had never taken to the man.

'The club's not far.'

It was probably the rain that persuaded Alyosha to jump into the taxi. They drove through the ever-changing streets, now flooded in orange pools from the lamps, now blue-grey and shadowy, and arrived at the club somewhere south of Spittelmarkt, near the Spree. Ernst paid the taxi driver and flicked his cigarette butt into the dark river.

The Bürger-Casino greeted them with thick blue cigarette smoke and energetic piano playing. The place was enormous and filled to bursting but Ernst pushed his way through to a second room, darker and emptier, the tables lit by red lamps. On the walls were portraits of various men. A young dark-skinned man rose when he saw them and came over. He and Ernst kissed.

'This is Alyosha. Alyosha this is Bartos.'

They sat. On the dance floor couples were dancing, cheek to cheek and chest to chest: older men with much younger male partners, dressed up as schoolboys.

'Champagne I think.' He turned to Bartos. 'Is Mina here?'

'She was earlier,' he answered in a thick accent.

'Let me tell you a secret, Alyosha.' Ernst leant confidentially towards him and lifted his hand to cover his mouth in mock conspiratorial fashion. 'Bartos here is a little Red. Aren't you, Bartos dear?'

This was obviously a well-worn cause of mirth between them.

'Imagine, Alyosha. A man like me sleeping with the enemy.' He patted his chest in mock fear. 'Whatever would people say if they knew?'

Bartos smiled at Alyosha.

'Here she is. Hey, Mina, over here!'

Alyosha had his back to the man but when he heard his voice he recognised it at once. He turned to see Andrei Petrovich, in a waiter's uniform. His father's former banker looked surprised to see Alyosha.

'Some champagne, Mina. Better make it a magnum,' ordered Ernst.

'Anything else? Something to eat?'

'Later perhaps.'

He went to fetch their drinks, without saying a word to Alyosha.

'Why do you call him Mina?' he asked.

'All the waiters here have a girl's name.'

'It's a tradition,' added Bartos.

'So they decided on Martina for him,' Ernst said, lighting a cigarette. 'Sometimes they call him Tina but we call him Mina.'

Ernst insisted on telling Alyosha all about Bartos. He was from Hungary, and had left school when he was ten to work in a shop. He was sixteen when Béla Kun established the Hungarian Soviet Republic in Budapest in 1919, and he joined the Reds. They were soon defeated by Miklós Horthy's troops and there were brutal reprisals against those who did not manage to escape. Bartos fled to Romania, but he found there was no welcome for Communists. He had to move on to Slovakia, hoping he could sit it out and return to Budapest at some point, though there was no knowing if that would ever be possible. Eventually, Bartos had enough of Bratislava, and decided to try his luck in Berlin.

Andrei Petrovich brought a large silver ice bucket and glasses to the table and proceeded to open and pour the champagne.

'I didn't want to stay here in Berlin to begin with, either,' said Bartos.

'Why not?' asked Alyosha.

'Too big, not friendly.'

There was something horribly sad in Bartos' voice.

'I wanted to go to Hamburg. I'd heard they always needed men on the ships.'

'You'd have made a lovely little cabin boy,' quipped Ernst. 'Thanks, Mina.'

Andrei Petrovich moved away but he had caught Alyosha's eye.

'Tell him why you couldn't go to sea, Bartos,' prompted Ernst.

'No papers.'

They clinked glasses.

'Tell Alyosha where I found you. You've forgotten to say that. You always forget to say that.'

'In a lodging house on the corner of Grenadierstrasse and Hirtenstrasse.'

'Worst flop-house in Berlin,' Ernst declared.

Bartos didn't disagree but he looked a little sulky.

'Heaving with Jews from the East: Poland, Hungary. Galicia too, come to that. Crawling with lice, the lot of them. Who saved you from the gutter, Bartos?' Ernst tapped the back of his hand with his finger. 'Don't you forget it, now.'

When Ernst and Bartos went off to dance, Andrei Petrovich came back over to the table.

'I don't know what to say,' he said to Alyosha. 'I'm so ashamed.'

'There are worse occupations, I'm sure.'

'Not for a man like me.'

'What about your sister?' asked Alyosha.

'What about her?'

'Well, couldn't she have offered to help? My mother certainly paid her enough money. And didn't you pay her bills at the clinic?'

'Yes I did, but your mother's money all went to Lazarevana, Alexei Fyodorovitch.'

'She didn't give you any?'

'Even if she'd offered I would have refused it. When she was so ready to take the money, it didn't take me long to realise that you were innocent. But she's a good actress and she took me in for a while.'

Andrei stared down fixedly at the table, unable to meet Alyosha's gaze. He was in pain.

'My wife is dying. I don't know what will become of Galina. Not a day goes by where we don't fight like cat and dog. She used to be such a gentle girl. I try my best. But I don't think it's enough. That's why I hate myself.'

He began to weep quietly.

'I had a life once. But it's as if all that I had is so irrelevant now, it leaves me feeling utterly worthless. I wake sometimes and it's as if I've forgotten everything. Did Russia even exist?'

With eyes full of tears he smiled and asked, 'What future do I have? I can't put down roots. I can't plan anything.'

Alyosha was at a loss to comfort a man so defeated.

45

The reviews of the film were so appalling that only two cinemas would screen it, and it closed at both after just four nights. The only exception had been Ernst Jenny, who praised the underlying vision, beauty and tragic grandeur of the heroic efforts of the White Army to reconquer Russia. Alyosha had never opened the pages of the *Deutsche Zeitung* before then. It was an anti-Semitic paper, full of stories of avaricious Jews and forever calling for the repatriation of the various refugees from eastern Europe that were 'swamping' Germany.

'What do they know anyway? Philistines!' Alexei Dashkov said, fuming.

'Exactly,' agreed Inessa. 'What do they know about art? Nothing.'

This was especially galling after he had arranged a grand party until the small hours, for all the critics. They had been quite willing to partake of his generous hospitality, to swill his champagne and smile, before running back to write their poisonous little reviews.

'How can they be such hypocrites?'

Hadn't he and Inessa gone out of their way to be charming? She so vivacious and chic, he with his witty repartee. Yet all their efforts had been wasted. The picture was a flop.

Their finances were in dire straits, and the Adlon was pressing Inessa to settle her account. A wiser couple would have settled up, packed, and left such an expensive hotel for more reasonable accommodation. Alexei Dashkov started to plan his next project. Inessa heard herself, for a second, sound exactly like her mother.

'You can't possibly be serious?'

When Alyosha heard he was equally incredulous, but his mother merely said, 'He's not a man for idle talk.'

'You'd be insane to agree to such madness. He's an idiot, and if he hasn't proven that to you already I don't know what it will take.'

'How many times have I told you, I won't have you speak of your stepfather with such disrespect!'

'I'd rather not speak of him at all, but please tell me you're not going to struggle to borrow money to finance another film?'

'If that's what he wants.'

'You would never have been this accommodating to Papa.'

Inessa knew this was true, but ignored it.

'What about us? Why don't you ever think of us, of Gosha and me?'

Only two diamonds remained around his mother's throat, as the other had been sold. When Alyosha heard that Alexei Dashkov had been seen walking arm-in-arm with Varvara Lvovna one evening on the shores of Wansee, he made sure to tell his mother, and everybody else while he was about it. His mother chose not to believe him. Alyosha begged her to leave the actor, leave Berlin, make a fresh start in Paris. Life there would be easier. Uncle Artyom would be sure to help them with visas. Inessa flatly refused to countenance such a plan.

46

When the landlord opened the door, Ella's shoulders sagged. Against the wall on the right was one flimsy wardrobe, the centre mirror cracked. Opposite was a double bed and, on the far side, a small round table and two chairs. A once grand but now shabby red sofa had been shoehorned in against the other wall. Behind the door stood an old-fashioned washstand, but water had to be carried up from the kitchen on the floor below, which they shared with the other tenants; and the room only had one window.

The landlord turned the key between his fingers. Ella went to gaze out of the window. Larissa didn't look the landlord in the eye, any more than Margarita, but with a slight nod of her head she indicated that they would take it. But he seemed reluctant, telling them he'd had trouble in the past with foreigners, and started to interrogate them, so Margarita had to assure him that they didn't suffer from typhus, cholera or syphilis. Neither did they intend bringing strange men back late at night, nor did they have head lice, or suffer from any contagious diseases. Finally, as if he was granting them a great favour, he agreed to let the room to them.

Margarita placed all her money on the table. She had been forced to sell the piano, and her father's watch and medals. Ella would be spending all her days here, because the pupils of the Berlitz School had disappeared almost overnight as the fees became an unaffordable luxury. The only glimmer of comfort was that Larissa had been accepted on a nursing course and, better yet, would be able to stay and have her meals in the hospital for nothing. This was a huge relief to Margarita, who was still out of work.

At some point every day, usually late afternoon, Margarita would meet Stanislav at the Langrafa Café on the Kurfürstendamm. They would make their small cups of coffee last them an hour, sometimes two. He had not been able to find work either, so had agreed to write several articles for the periodical *Smena Vekh.* He gave them to Margarita to read, and she took him to task for how much he seemed to have softened in his attitude towards Russia. She was as uncompromising as ever.

She also wanted to ask his advice. In her daily scouring of the newspapers for work, she had come across a small notice asking for young women to join a dance troupe to perform in a dance-café. There would be three nightly shows, at seven, nine and midnight. Should she apply?

Stanislav sucked on his pipe.

'They'll be more interested in you showing your legs than anything else.'

She tapped the advertisement.

'I think it's respectable. "No fraternising with the customers." That's what it says here – look.'

'That's what they all say, just to keep the police off their backs.'

With the next month's rent looming, Margarita decided to go for the audition and was sent into a largely empty room, apart from some seats. There were eight or nine other girls there already, and every one of them was taking off her knickers. A girl with wide shoulders and a wider mouth saw the look of horror on her face and said, not unsympathetically, 'Your first time?'

Margarita nodded.

'It's a matter of how desperate you are then, isn't it?'

Margarita lifted her skirt, took off her knickers and stuffed them into her bag. One by one, the girls were called through. When it was her turn, she found herself in a smaller room, thick with cigarette smoke. After a cursory chat about her previous experience, which she invented, she was asked to stand back and lift her skirt nice and slowly.

A hundred thoughts flashed through her head.

'When you're ready.'

She tried her hardest to expunge the image of her father…

'And higher…'

She complied.

And her mother praying…

'And again…'

And Larissa after Herman broke her heart…

She lifted her hem higher.

And Alyosha goading Herr Professor K. K…

'Higher.'

She saw herself, with her eyes tightly shut.

She was holding her skirt over her head so that the two men and the woman with the spectacles could see properly.

47

When they offered her a contract, worried though she was about leaving her mother alone every night, she felt she had no choice but to take it. Work was work, money was money.

She was to start rehearsing the next day. She also dreaded telling her mother that she would be making her living by kicking up her legs on stage in front of anybody who could pay, but when she finally blurted out the news, explaining that she would be on trial for a month, but if they offered her a permanent place in the chorus her wages would more or less double, Ella seemed entirely unmoved. She simply smiled gently and said, 'There we are then, if that's how things are to be.'

The rehearsals swallowed up all her time. Margarita did not see Stanislav at all for the first week at the dance-café, but when one of the other girls brought in a copy of *Smena Vehk*, she borrowed it during the break and read his latest article. She was both hurt and incensed, as he argued in it that it was high time Russian *émigrés* went home. She could hardly wait to see him to give him a piece of her mind.

48

Alyosha was summoned to his mother's room at the Adlon. His stepfather was also there, standing with his arms folded, looking thunderous.

'Yes?'

'Don't come the innocent with us,' growled Alexei Dashkov. 'You know exactly why we want to see you. You owe your mother an apology.'

Alyosha was genuinely mystified.

'For what?'

'Don't take us for idiots, you shameless little shit. I want to hear you admit you stole her things, and ask her forgiveness.'

It was such a bizarre accusation that Alyosha started to laugh.

'What? Are you serious?'

His mother said in a sad voice, 'Alexei, please don't make things worse by denying it. We know it was you. We have a witness.'

Alexei Dashkov added, 'And on top of that, you had the barefaced cheek to beg some dollars from her last night. What did you do with her silk stockings, give them to some addict friend in exchange for her favours, eh?'

Alyosha saw red.

'Says the man who fucks anything that moves.'

'Alexei! For shame! And in front of your little brother!' gasped his mother, putting her hands over Gosha's ears too late.

'How dare you speak to me like that,' bellowed Alexei Dashkov and, stepping towards him, gave Alyosha an open-handed clout across his head. Without thinking twice, Alyosha kneed him in the groin viciously and watched with grim satisfaction as he cupped his testicles in agony, falling gently to his knees, grimacing in pain.

'You've been asking for that for a long while,' said Alyosha, and followed it up with a punch to his stepfather's temple. Alexei Dashkov keeled over onto his side, hitting his head against an occasional table. A pot of roses and a bottle of perfume toppled onto the floor as Inessa screamed at her son to leave her husband be.

He turned to leave, but heard heavy drumming steps on the carpet. As turned the doorknob he glanced over his shoulder, and came face to face with Alexei Dashkov, purple with rage. With both hands, the actor grabbed his throat, tightened his grip with all his strength, and growled with fury. 'You vicious, evil-minded little bastard.'

'You're choking me! Let me go!'

'I never want to see your miserable face anywhere near Inessa or me.'

'Let me go!'

'If they found you dead in a Berlin gutter tomorrow I wouldn't give a damn.'

'Let me go! Let me go!'

They lurched across the room, smashing the perfume bottle underfoot, drenching the room in the smell of gardenias. Panting for breath and turning puce, Alyosha tried to lift his knee but Alexei Dashkov had learned quickly, and had squeezed his legs protectively together. Alyosha was aware of his mother's voice from somewhere begging them to come to their senses.

'For God's sake, stop it before you kill each other!'

To Alyosha's astonishment, without him doing anything, his stepfather's expression transformed itself from wild aggression to unalloyed agony.

'Aiiiiiiiiiiii….'

A mounting sharp scream emitted from his throat.

‘iiiiiiiiiiiiiiiiiiiiiiiiiiiiiiiiiiiiiiiiiiiiiiiiiiiiiiiiiiiiiiiii…’

Alyosha was released, and Alexei staggered back, crumpling as though his leg was full of pins and needles, and he’d lost all strength and fury.

Now he wailed.

‘Ooooooooooooooooooooooh.’

Gosha’s young teeth were sunk, ferret-deep, in his ankle.

The famous actor howled, ‘Fucking sweet Jesus!’

And screamed again.

‘Aaaaaaaaaaaaaaaaarrrrrrrggggghhhhh!’

The little boy had bitten down to the bone, so that when he finally released his jaws, Alexei Dashkov could do nothing but hop around the room, wailing with pain.

49

Early the next morning, Inessa entered her son's bedroom.

'Yes?'

She stood stock-still, and said her piece.

'I may be your mother…'

There was to be no forgiveness.

'… but I'm his wife.'

'Listen, Mama…' Alyosha began groggily, but she cut across him.

'It's time you listened to me for once.'

She didn't want to choose between the two of them, but she had been forced into that position. She would be writing to an old friend of his father's from his days in Zurich, and asking him to find an appropriate school or college where she could send Alyosha.

'I'm too old for school and no college would take me. Besides, what if I don't want to go?'

'I'm not giving you the choice. Somewhere will take you. I don't much care where.'

Later that day, Alyosha almost barrelled into his stepfather in the foyer, as he walked in with his new scriptwriter. Alexei Dashkov stared at him coldly, and then walked on without a word.

From then on, Alyosha felt as though the hotel staff were staring at him behind his back. Other guests, who had always greeted him courteously enough, now seemed to go out of their way to avoid him. When he complained to his mother that the ridiculous accusation of theft must have got out, she had no sympathy.

'You brought this on yourself, so you have nobody but yourself to blame.'

Alyosha decided to take his fate into his own hands. Packing a few items of clothing, Karamisin's *History of Russia* and a volume of his father's of Catullus, he broke into Alexei Dashkov's room and stole as many dollars as he could find.

'And over there.'

Gosha told him where to look.

'There as well.'

Some were hidden under the carpet.

'And just here, if you want some more.'

Attached to the back of the wardrobe.

'Don't forget over there, as well.'

Behind the painting above the bed.

'You're worth your weight in gold, Gosha.'

His little brother had watched unnoticed as his stepfather squirrelled Inessa's money and presents of jewellery away in all sorts of nooks and crannies. Alyosha stuffed it all into a pouch which he kept down his trousers and hugged the little boy goodbye.

'Where are you going?'

'I don't know yet.'

'Where will you live?'

'I don't know that either.'

'Do you know anything?'

Alyosha smiled and whispered in his ear, 'The Grand Hotel. But don't say a word. Promise?'

He nodded.

'I know I'll see you again before long.'

'When?'

'Soon.'

Alyosha walked out of the Adlon Hotel.

50

Their trainer, a bony woman whose name was Waldshmidt but who insisted on being called Madame, as if she was a proper ballet teacher, was a hard taskmistress. They started work at eight in the morning, and rarely finished before eight in the evening. The performances were draining, and lack of food had weakened the girls' bodies, so they were often drooping with exhaustion by the end of the day.

Margarita was not only more clueless than the rest, as she had no experience or training, she was also the only girl to have kept her hair long; the rest all had fashionable little bobs or shingles. (The main reason she had left it long was that she couldn't afford to have it cut at a salon.) But Madame put her foot down and said she must cut it like the other girls so that she didn't stand out in the chorus. Once she had done this, and started to learn the routines, she felt slightly more confident that Madame wouldn't let her go at the end of her probationary month.

On a precious free Sunday afternoon, she met Stanislav in the Tiergarten. They strolled past two little boys in short trousers trying to fly a kite, but there was not quite enough of a breeze to send it skyward. This didn't seem to spoil their fun, as they ran back and forth, pulling the kite behind them, even though it fell to earth time and again. Margarita noticed that it was made of worthless papiermarks.

The article that Stanislav had published the week before was like an unspoken reproach. Margarita already felt instinctively that a distance had grown between them. Eventually she asked, what exactly had he meant by the title: *The tyranny of capital: can it survive?*

'Nobody can deny any more that a class struggle exists.'

He was slightly patronising, she thought.

'I'd say it was more obvious now than ever before.'

He was of the opinion that the Communists were far more honest than the bourgeoisie, acknowledging and proclaiming the true state of affairs, and fighting to change it, in contrast to the capitalist class which fought the class battle covertly, denying that such a condition existed in the first place.

'Every day of our lives,' he said, stretching his arm towards Brandenburger Tor, 'even doing something as simple as walking down Friedrichstrasse, around us there are invisible but vicious battles going on, behind the windows of banks, and insurance companies, in the offices of political parties and newspapers, even in the cinema and theatre programmes.'

'I never expected I'd live to hear such things come from your lips.'

'This is how I used to think when I was a boy of fifteen.'

'I can understand a boy of fifteen getting caught up in the superficially appealing nonsense of Marxism, but not a grown man with experience of the world – and of the Communists.'

'Marxism makes perfect sense of the history of the world to me.'

'But not to me.'

'Look, the bourgeoisie are playing a very cunning game, denying the existence of the class war, but perpetuating it all the while with every weapon in their armoury: patriotism, nationalism, racism, religion, money, privileges and honours to buy or pacify every objection to their order. An order that dances before our eyes like a masquerade. But what underpins it? Profit at the cost of everybody and everything. And what comes in its wake? Wars. Inflation. Strikes. Unemployment. Suffering. Madness.'

'And all this is the fault of capitalism?'

'The bourgeoisie believe in the harmony of conflicting interests which are totally at odds with each other, until the economic, social and political contradictions inherent in capitalist societies are pushed to the extreme – and then they snap.'

'But conflicts have been part of the fabric of every human society in recorded history,' argued Margarita. 'There's nothing new about it. In fact, it's as old as mankind.'

Stanislav ignored this and continued.

'Moral hypocrisy keeps all capitalist societies going…'

'A hypocrisy you're very keen to expose?'

'Apart from socialist parties and the labour unions, who within capitalism speaks up against unemployment, bad housing, lack of education, poor health? Who truly tries to protect the rights of the workers? Who has hit back and smashed this iniquitous order?'

The billions of papiermarks came crashing down just by them, a couple of yards away.

Margarita remembered reading somewhere, when she had first arrived in Berlin, that French society before the revolution was a much happier place than after it. Was that the case in Russia too? How were things really over there now, she wondered?

'What about democracy?'

'Here?' asked Stanislav, 'or in Russia?'

'Russia.'

'How do you define democracy? One man, one vote? Political equality? That the tramp and the aristocrat are equal before the law?'

'All of those things.'

He tapped the ash out of his pipe against the arm of the bench.

'How does democracy fare side by side with economic inequality? There doesn't seem to be much democracy where it really counts, does there?'

Margarita suddenly realised what he was really telling her.

'You've decided to go back to Russia, haven't you?'

He mused before answering, then said, 'What's there to keep me here in Europe?'

She was silent.

'Will you come with me?'

She remained silent.

'Will you at least think about it?'

She promised she would. They kissed and made their farewells. Larissa was visiting that evening from the hospital and Margarita was worried about her mother.

51

Could Margarita go back to a communist Russia? On the S-bahn she took out a copy of Anton Chekov's short stories. She was soothed by reading of a country doctor called Dmitri Startsev visiting a Mr Turkin, his wife Vera, and their daughter Catherine, who, like herself, enjoyed playing the piano. Chekov described the sounds and smells of their household; the chink of knives and forks, and the savoury odour of onions frying in an old cast-iron skillet escaping out of the window to the yard, making the mouth of any caller water.

The longing for a good square meal, or homesickness for her mother country: Margarita didn't know which left her feeling more hollow. Apart from awakening all sorts of memories, the story itself was sad. Doctor Startsev was introduced to Catherine, who was eighteen, and very like her mother in disposition. She was a vivacious and beautiful girl, with a zest for life. Her piano teacher was Madame Zarkovsky, and although Catherine was not the most gifted player in the world, she had already convinced herself that she was good enough to study at the conservatoire.

Doctor Startsev had fallen head over heels in love with her, and begged her not to torture him further (as he couldn't live a second more without her) but to accept his hand in marriage. But she wouldn't give up her dream of winning a place at the conservatoire. It was plain to everybody else that she wasn't likely to see her dream come true, so they all thought it would be better for her to marry someone like Doctor Startsev, who could offer her a secure and happy future. In a small, undistinguished place like Dyalizh there wasn't much hope for anything else. But Catherine rejected the doctor's proposal, so confident was she that one day she would be a very famous pianist, performing all over the world.

Four years later, when Doctor Startsev next called on the family, he had changed. Catherine had changed too. Although she continued to play the piano she had not won a place at the conservatoire. She was often low in spirits and her mother would take her off on holiday to the Crimea to lift her depression. The loving feelings which Doctor Startsev had felt towards her had long since disappeared. Neither of them ever married.

Margarita mused on how often something of this kind happened in Chekov, in both his stories and his plays. There was always some fateful moment when lovers grew close and discovered some glimmer of happiness, but then for some reason one of them faltered, or took a wrong turning or perhaps simply said or did something they shouldn't have, sometimes something as seemingly unimportant as a moment's discourtesy or a slight slip in manners, and their brief opportunity for happiness – their unique chance in life – was lost for ever.

So much in love turns around sheer chance, she thought, that you should take it when it presents itself, because that might be your only opportunity. Stanislav had decided to return to Russia. That's where he saw his future. But what about her feelings for him? As far as love went – true love – perhaps there was some black hole, some longing that nobody could ever really fulfil, never mind how perfect he was, or how happy the relationship?

If she wanted this relationship to live, could she follow him? Was Stanislav, her first love, her only love, the one for her for the rest of her life? If he was, if he really was the one, then surely her self-examination had been answered, her decision made. But could she leave her mother? Or would her mother come with her? And what about Larissa? But the most important question was this: did Margarita know her heart well enough to commit?

52

One afternoon, Madame was called out of the rehearsal room. It had been a long and gruelling day, and the girls were glad of the rest. Margarita sat down thankfully next to her friend, Lida, who was of Russian-Jewish extraction. There was only a month between them in age, though Lida, who was a confident and plain-speaking girl, always said it made no sense to celebrate a birthday: why would you want to commemorate growing another year older, another year closer to the grave? She was from Moscow originally, where her father had been the head of an insurance company on Lubyanka Square. When the revolution had erupted on the streets of the capital, and ranks of soldiers started to march across Moscow at night, the family packed what they could and made for Kiev. A year later, Lida watched Russian soil disappear from sight, from the deck of a ship bound for Constantinople. From there they found another ship to take them to Malta, and from Malta to Genoa. As her father had business connections in Berlin, he decided that it would be a good place to wait until it was safe to return to Russia. And there they still were…

When Madame returned, she announced that the rehearsals were over. The dance-café would no longer be in need of their services, as the owner had gone bankrupt and had been forced to close. The girls sighed as one, and Margarita, already in pain from a pulled muscle, lacked the energy to do anything but close her eyes in despair.

Lida persuaded her to come for a drink to the Café Dalles on the Neue Schönhauser Strasse.

'They used to call this place the Palace of the Angels. Much better name, don't you think?'

'More poetic.'

'I wonder why they keep changing the names of places all the time? It's so confusing.'

Over coffee, Lina told Margarita she could put in a word for her at Dirk's place. It was no secret that Lina was bisexual. When Margarita first met her, she'd been having an affair with a lesbian called Anna. They often went to the Monbijou where Anna was the *bubi* and wore men's clothes, smoked cigars, and wore a monocle. Lida took on the role of her *garçonne* and wore her hair short, pencilled in her eyebrows, and squeezed her shoes into the highest heels she could find. But Anna had met a rich, middle-aged lesbian and left Lida for her. Lida's heart was broken for all of two days, and then she started to scour the Lonely Hearts columns in the *Blätter für Menschenrecht.*

Through one of these, she ended up with a lover called Selli, who took her to a private club for Jewish lesbians which met every second Tuesday in the Zauberflöte. Selli was also bisexual and had a male lover, Dirk. Soon Lina was sleeping with Dirk as well as Selli, and quite often they made up a threesome. Dirk owned the Rio Rita Bar and had offered Lina work there.

'I can get you in if you want. Interested?'

'What exactly would it involve?'

'Taking your clothes off, obviously. And you'd be expected to do some things… '

'Do some things…?'

'Some entertaining. Look, with things as they are, you're not going to be offered anything else. It pays well. It pays very well. Once you get used to it it's not so bad. And the money makes it worthwhile anyway.'

Margarita wasn't sure.

Everything I was, and everything I am, is in the balance, she thought.

'What else will you do?'

'Let me think it over.'

It didn't take her long. There was a food bill to be paid and no way of settling it.

'When can we go over?' she asked Lida.

'You free tonight?'

'Yes.'

'Say nine? I'll speak to Dirk.'

When Margarita walked into the club with Lida it appeared like any other chic nightclub. There was the usual dance floor in the centre, surrounded by tables and chairs, and a long bar at one end. The décor was tasteful, a little American. Lida told her it was a popular spot with tourists, especially Italians from Turin and Milan, for some reason. Dirk was nowhere to be seen, so Lida introduced her to Blaz, the blind pianist.

'Welcome to the RRB.'

Blaz felt her face with his hands. When he spoke his eyes rolled in his head.

When Dirk eventually appeared, he was nothing like Margarita had imagined. He had a large, square-shaped face, a mop of hair, bad skin, pitted and scarred, and an abrupt and rather charmless manner. He was certainly not one for small talk, not with prospective employees in any case, and he explained how the club worked and what her duties would be without preamble. Then he ushered her down a corridor.

'Our VIP rooms are down here,' he said blandly, opening one of the doors onto a dimly lit, luxuriously furnished room smelling of lemons.

'They pay Gaba, not you, for your time out, and then Gaba settles with you at the end of your shift.'

‘Time out?’

‘Here.’

Dirk gave her an impatient look as if she was being obtuse. When they returned to the bar, Blaz was playing the piano.

‘So, any questions?’

Margarita felt weak. Lida held her hand behind her back, and gave it a squeeze.

‘When can she start?’

‘When does she want to start?’

‘Margarita?’ Lida prompted.

She hesitated for a moment before answering.

‘Tomorrow night.’

‘Fine by me,’ said Dirk. ‘You have something to wear?’

‘Yes.’

‘Nothing under your dress. RRB policy.’

Margarita nodded.

‘Can she stay tonight to watch the girls working?’

‘Sure.’

Blaz had changed into a black suit, and had oiled his hair. The rest of the band: violinist, saxophonist, flautist, accordionist and drummer – were dressed like tennis players, in white short-sleeved shirts and loose white trousers. Every now and again Blaz left his piano stool and stood before the microphone to sing. He had a pure voice and sang with gusto, his eyes rolling with the music.

The girls sat up at the bar or at the tables, chatting and smoking. Nobody seemed to be listening to the band. The Rio Rita didn’t really attract many customers until around eleven o’clock, but by midnight it was full, and all the tables were taken. There was a lively hubbub the length of the bar: a constant ebb and flow of people laughing, smoking and drinking. Blaz had taken his jacket off and loosened his tie, and the band was playing energetically, the young drummer tossing his sticks up in the air and expertly catching them after every riff. The couples spilled over the edges of the dance floor and the air was thick with the smell of lipstick, brandy and tobacco. Margarita was observing it all, but keeping an eye on Gaba. The head waiter moved calmly and unhurriedly among the guests, and every now and again one of the girls, in a diaphanous evening dress exposing her shoulders, would come up to him to have a word. Margarita didn't see any money being exchanged, but in a moment or two the girl would slip away with her partner towards the VIP rooms.

Margarita felt as though her life was shattering into splinters.

'Fancy trying to get those two chumps to buy us champagne?' asked Lida. 'Did Dirk explain?'

'Yes, we get commission on every bottle we persuade them to buy.'

Lida smiled at the men and in a while they came over to where the girls were sitting. Erdmut was the one who put his arm around Lida's shoulders and Fester was the one who sat next to Margarita. They both smoked Turkish cigarettes and Fester smelled strongly of sweat. Erdmut was a stockbroker and Fester was an industrialist from the Ruhr, on a business trip to Berlin. The bottle of champagne was brought to the table and poured. Glasses were chinked.

'Chin-chin!'

Erdmut lit Lida's cigarette. The club lights changed, turning Fester's lips blue and his bald head pink. Accompanied on the accordion, Blaz sang a sentimental ballad, which was greeted by deafening applause at the end. This was followed by a lively dance and Lida rose and led Erdmut by the hand to the dance floor. Margarita felt a hot hand on her thigh and a syrupy voice whispering something in her ear. Fester's sweat stank like old money. He stuffed his nose into her neck and licked her ear; she felt his hand creep up to stroke her breast.

'Don't.'

She could feel his body pressing against hers.

'Shall we go somewhere more private…'

'No.'

She pinched his nose, hard.

'Bitch!'

Fester raised his hand to slap her but his arm froze in mid-air. He turned his head to see the man who had grabbed his wrist standing over him.

'Let go of me.'

'I will. So that you can leave. Now.'

Alyosha opened his jacket to show the hilt of a knife.

'I don't want any trouble.'

'Good. Off you go.'

The industrialist got up, threw Margarita a poisonous glance, and fled.

'I wouldn't have expected to find you in a place like this.'

Alyosha picked up Fester's champagne glass and drained it.

'Neither would I,' she answered sombrely, 'but things are pretty difficult.'

He didn't reply.

'This was my first night. I'm meant to start properly tomorrow. What brought you here?'

Alyosha pointed at a young dark-haired girl two tables away.

'I'm watching out for her.'

'Watching out?'

'As a favour to her aunt.'

'I don't understand,' said Margarita.

I'm staying with the two of them. I have to lie low for a bit.'

'Why?'

'It's a long story.'

'I have plenty of time.'

Alyosha explained about the fight with Alexei Dashkov in the Adlon, and how his stepfather had made his name mud, lying to everybody that he had stolen from his mother. With the other guests all shunning him, it had become impossible for him and he decided to leave. He was perfectly frank with his cousin about stealing as much as he could from his stepfather.

'And thanks to Gosha I came away with quite a haul. He knew exactly where it was all hidden.'

'Why didn't you tell your mother what he was doing to you?'

'She wouldn't have listened.'

The sheer sadness of it all.

'So where did you go then?'

'I went to stay in the Grand Hotel, which isn't a bit grand, on Marchstrasse, by the Knie S-bahn. But I didn't stay there long.'

'Why?'

'A late-night knock on the door. Police. I only just managed to throw some clothes on and escape through the window. If I hadn't made friends with the receptionist they'd have had me, but she phoned up and warned me. Alexei Dashkov must have reported me. He probably put the fear of God into poor little Gosha, because he was the only one who knew where I was.'

'But you got away?'

'Yes, but it was a close shave. The worst of it was I left most of my things and my money in the Grand. I pretty much only had the shirt on my back. I had to steal some new clothes, a coat and a hat. It's not so difficult. Food as well. But I needed money. That's when I decided to break into a house. Charlottenburg, I thought, lots of rich people live there. But it was difficult. Those big houses always have staff, so there was always a gardener around, or delivery men, or a cleaner or a maid. Anyway, late one afternoon I was scouting around Neu-Babelsberg, staking out some villas along the Griebnitz-See, big old houses, with lots of trees and bushes in the gardens, great for cover. There was hardly anyone about, the odd boat on the river, so I picked a house and in I went; they'd even left a window open for me, would you believe it? There I was, rifling through a desk in the study, when

I heard a noise on the stairs. I took a paperknife and went towards the French doors, but the door opened and a young man in golfing clothes stood there, staring at me. To be honest I don't really remember much of what happened next. There was a fracas, a bit of a scuffle: he hit me on the shoulder with a golf club and I just wanted to get out of there but…'

'But what?'

'I stabbed him.'

'Oh God, Alyosha. Where?'

'Here.'

He pointed to his chest. He was daring her to judge him. Margarita asked falteringly, 'Not in his heart?'

'Maybe. I'm not sure.'

She felt her stomach lurch and thought she might be sick.

'Deep?'

'Hmmm?'

'How deep did the blade go in?'

'There was blood all over the furniture… blood everywhere… '

'Was he alive?'

Lida had returned to the table with a red-faced Erdmut at her heels.

'Where did Fester go?' asked the stockbroker, wiping his forehead with a white handkerchief.

'He went for a walk,' answered Alyosha shortly, without looking at the man.

Margarita introduced her cousin to Lina and Erdmut.

'More champagne?' suggested Erdmut. He was enjoying himself.

Another bottle was duly ordered and opened. When the waiter moved away, the dark haired girl with kohl-rimmed eyes came up to their table.

'Apollonia.'

Alyosha gestured for her to sit.

'I can't stay long.'

Margarita could see the girl was curious about her, but the music was too loud for her to hear what they were talking about. She soon stood up and went to the bar.

'That's the one you're keeping an eye on?'

Alyosha nodded.

'What does that involve exactly?'

'I see her home safely every night.'

'Are you here every night then?'

'More or less, yes.'

'And where are you living?'

'I have a room in Apollonia and her aunt's apartment.'

He gave her the address, as Lida threw back her head and laughed while Erdmut tickled her.

'She didn't have the happiest of childhoods,' said Alyosha, nodding in Apollonia's direction. She was sitting on one of the barstools, exposing her long shapely legs for all to see. 'Her father was killed at sea during the Great War. Then she lost her mother when she was still young. That's when she went to live with her aunt, her father's sister. She was educated by the nuns at a convent. And beaten and mistreated while they were about it. One of the punishments was to hit her on the face with wet rags. And they used to tie the girls' hands to the mattress every night. But she has the sweetest nature in the world, I've never met anybody so open-hearted. As for the aunt...'

His voice faded into a bitter note.

'What about her?'

He hesitated before saying, 'We've all got to earn a living, I suppose.'

Lida led Erdmut back to the dance floor.

Margarita's mind wandered back to the boy in the villa in Neu-Babelsberg.

'The stabbing... is the boy alive?'

Alyosha shrugged.

'Don't you care?'

'I haven't told you the most important thing yet.' He helped himself to one of Erdmut's cigarettes and lit it. 'When I was looting Alexei Dashkov's room in the Adlon, I found more than just money.

'When I first arrived in Berlin, after my father came to Finland to fetch me, I fell in love. At the time I'm not sure I realised that's what it was. I thought she just satisfied my desire. You know, I couldn't stop eating to begin with, because I'd gone hungry for so long and it was the same with her – I just wanted her every minute of the day, could never get my fill of her. Her name was Grete, she was from Brünn, but she'd come to Berlin to find work, and they'd taken her on at the Adlon. My mother wasn't happy that I was sleeping with her of course, and she arranged for her to lose her job. That didn't stop us from seeing each other though, far from it. But then around fifteen months ago, no, more like eighteen by now, perhaps, Grete disappeared from the face of the earth. I asked and I searched but nobody knew a thing. And now I think I know what happened. I found a cheque stub made out to Grete. My mother paid her to leave Berlin.'

Blaz was singing again, clicking his fingers to the rhythm.

'I even think that Uncle Artyom was involved as well. It's possible they took her away in his car. The car was black. The barman in the Grand Hotel told me. My uncle has a black Panhard-Levassor.'

'But there are hundreds, if not thousands of black cars in Berlin.'

'Yes, but my gut tells me it was his. He did it for my mother. I'm nearly sure of it.'

'So do you think Grete is in Paris, then?'

'The more I think about it, the more convinced I am that's exactly where she is. And I'm going to do my best to find her. Margarita, I'm determined that I'm going to find her.'

53

Another article by Stanislav was published in *Smenavekh*, proclaiming unambiguously that there could be no future or function for Russian *émigrés* in Europe. Exile in Berlin was only ever meant to be a temporary affair and now their place was home, back home, doing their best to build a new society on firm foundations. Russia was the future, and she was showing the way forward to the rest of the world. There, a new civilisation was in the making: a new way of thinking and living. The people of the new Russia weren't concerned with personal happiness but rather dreamed of the well-being of the proletariat and humanity writ large. This was as different as could be from the selfishness and individualistic pride that were so prevalent under the old regime, calling for a visionary, creative way of thinking; but it required too a certain amount of self-sacrifice. Who was courageous enough to take this path?

The next time he met Margarita he came determined to persuade her to leave with him. He appealed to her on a personal level too.

'What am I doing in Berlin, living a hand-to-mouth existence? What would you have me do? Should I just spend the rest of my life churning out propaganda for the bourgeoisie or wheedling commissions from the likes of Alexei Dashkov – a man who wants to see the old Russia re-established, while he makes a name for himself in America?'

He told her he was ashamed he'd ever become involved with such a film – however much he'd tried to inject some balance into it – and was relieved when it sank without trace.

'All I see for me here now is poverty, suffering and worst of all, no hope for the future.'

Surely Margarita, Larissa and her mother were in exactly the same boat? If anything, their hovel was worse than his, and they had that pig of a landlord who only ever showed them contempt.

'You of all people should be able to identify with the plight of the working class; after all, you know what it is to work on the factory floor where you girls were treated no better than animals, to be searched and patted down at the end of every shift in case you had stolen a few biscuits from your employer.'

He reminded her of the pitiful wages, and no union to protect them or fight for their rights.

'And then when you worked in the bank you weren't much better off. How much respect did you get there? None. They threw you out with no ceremony and no notice, without thinking twice.'

'Like everybody else…'

'But who gave a damn about you? Nobody.'

'The bank went bust. Nobody was to blame.'

'And what are you doing now?'

She hadn't said a word to him about the Rio Rita Bar.

'Looking for work.'

'Like the thousands of others who try to live in hope that there's something around the corner. But in the meantime they live in misery and poverty, and that poverty breeds hopelessness. Margarita, people need hope: when that goes there's nothing left. And Russia gives us that hope. I'm convinced that Communism will make people's dreams for somewhere decent to live, a job they can be proud of, an education for their children, come true. And we can help make it happen.'

Margarita said nothing.

'We Russians are inclined to look at the past through rose-tinted spectacles when we should be learning how to love the future.'

Margarita honoured his passion but remained to be convinced.

'There is nothing for you here: this society is in decline. It will soon wither and die. That's why I'm so happy that my daughter is being brought up in Russia.'

'Daughter?'

Had she heard him right? He had never once mentioned a daughter.

'You have a daughter?'

It was his turn to be silent.

'In Moscow? Petrograd? Where?'

'Petrograd.'

They were both silent until Stanislav added, 'She lives with her mother.'

Margarita's mind was spinning. She had always thought he was a widower, and childless. Stanislav explained to her about the love affair in Paris years ago, when he had fled there to escape the Okrahna, the Tzar's secret police.

'So you never married her?'

'No.'

'And how old is your daughter?'

'Fourteen this year.'

Margarita squeezed her beret and then twisted it with both hands as hard as she could.

'Will you come with me to Russia?'

She smoothed the beret flat again and put it on her head.

'I love you.'

'I love you too.'

She walked away from him, out of the café, and didn't look back. She thought for a minute she would go to the hospital to see Larissa, but decided against it as she would almost certainly be working and not able to talk.

When she opened the door to the flat, her mother was sitting in her usual chair by the table, gazing out of the window. Margarita took off her coat and beret and hung them up. The room was chilly, and she rubbed her fingers. She felt like a hot drink and asked her mother if she would like some tea. Ella didn't answer. When she repeated the question and her mother still didn't answer, she went over to where she sat, squeezed her shoulder and then placed her hand on the back of her mother's neck. It was like ice.

On the table was a sheet of paper but the only words written on it were, 'Dear Kozma,'

Margarita moved around to see her mother's face. She stared into the staring eyes, mute and lifeless.

54

On a bitterly cold January afternoon, the three cousins huddled together in the cemetery of Saint Konstantin's Church. Larissa was shivering in spite of her heavy coat, and her scarf which was wrapped across half her face, and hat pulled down low on her forehead. Even her tears felt cold on her face. Margarita stamped her feet and clapped her hands together as unobtrusively as she could, as the young priest offered a prayer for her mother's soul.

They were quite alone in the cemetery, apart from a crow high in the bald branches of the oak on the far side. So different from his father's funeral, thought Alyosha, on that sultry summer's afternoon when thousands had sweltered above his grave.

They each took a turn to throw a fistful of dirt across the coffin as Ella was laid to rest in the Berlin earth. Then, arm in arm, Margarita and Larissa walked out of the cemetery. Alyosha followed, carefully closing the gate after them. They made their way to the Schloss-Café, where there was a fire lit.

'I'm freezing,' said Larissa, holding out her hands to the flames, 'and I can't feel my feet at all.'

Alyosha ordered coffees.

'Poor Mama,' said Larissa in a moment, the tears gathering, and then they sat in silence, each lost in thought. Eventually Alyosha roused himself and said, 'How's the training going, Lala?'

'I'll be a qualified nurse by the summer.'

'Well done.'

'It's a shame Mama won't be here to see me in my uniform.'

'I don't expect I will either,' said Margarita.

'Why? Where will you be?'

'I've decided to go back to Russia.'

'Since when?'

'I'm not sure. But I've decided.'

'With Stanislav?

'That I haven't decided.'

'And leave me behind here in Berlin?'

'You're perfectly capable of looking after yourself. Or you can come with me. Russia needs nurses too.'

'I don't want to go back to Russia. And I don't understand why you want to either. After everything you've said.'

'I think things will begin to change over there now that Lenin is dead.'

'Thank goodness you'll still be here, Alyosha.'

'Not for too long, Lala.'

Margarita tried to catch his eye but he was looking at Larissa.

'Don't tell me you're going back to Russia as well! What's the matter with everybody? Is there some virus going around that's making you all soft-headed?'

'Not Russia. I'm going to Paris.'

'When?'

'Tomorrow, I think. In the morning if I can. I feel it's high time I started to live my life again.'

'Why are you sounding so dramatic? Can't you live your life here in Berlin?'

'No. Impossible. There are just too many complications. I want to put some things behind me and turn over a new leaf. I hope that Paris can offer me something new.'

'Like what?'

'The chance to reinvent myself...'

The cousins made their farewells, wishing each other luck. He watched as Margarita and Larissa walked arm in arm towards the U-bahn and stood there for a while, as they descended the stairs into the station, until they disappeared from sight.

He felt at once melancholic and hopeful as he turned and walked slowly through the city streets and squares, making his farewells with each. As each step measured the hours before his departure, his heart lifted and he felt a happier and a more contented man.

Paris, Paris, Paris, he repeated to himself.

In spite of all his trials, Alyosha felt deep in his heart that his life was just about to begin.

To Paris, then.